Forgetfulness

Forgetfulness

The Holocaust Orphan Jay's Lost
Dutch-Jewish Family Story

RICHARD REITSMA

RESOURCE *Publications* · Eugene, Oregon

FORGETFULNESS
The Holocaust Orphan Jay's Lost Dutch-Jewish Family Story

Resource Publications
An Imprint of Wipf and Stock Publishers
199 W. 8th Ave., Suite 3
Eugene, OR 97401

www.wipfandstock.com

PAPERBACK ISBN: 979-8-3852-1868-4
HARDCOVER ISBN: 979-8-3852-1869-1
EBOOK ISBN: 979-8-3852-1870-7

VERSION NUMBER 06/24/24

Contents

Harold Runter's Letter to his Dutch-Canadian Cousin Jay Knuffels

TO:
Jay Knuffels
2005 Sleeping Bear Street
Smithers, BC Canada
June 28, 2020

Dear Jay.

THANKS AGAIN, JAY, FOR recently calling me up. I am deeply sorry to hear that neither your father nor your mother, before they passed away, ever told you anything about your birth parents. All they ever said was that they adopted you as a war orphan.

You also told me about the ancestry DNA test that you took recently and that you were surprised to learn that one of your birth parents was a full Jew. To find out more about your Jewish parent, you went to the Netherlands and spoke with an old man from the town of Ter Loo where your parents lived before emigrating to Canada in the late 1940's.

That gentleman, Mr. Klompemaker, told you that you might be able to resolve the riddle of your birth by speaking to a living descendant of the Ruintjer family because he knew, from local sources, that various members of that family had been involved with the effort to rescue Jewish children during the years of the Jewish holocaust.

Klompemaker's suggestion resulted in the long phone conversation that we had a few weeks ago. As I told you, at that time, I do indeed have some answers to the questions that you asked me because our respective

Dutch families were, as it turns out, joined at the hip for well over three decades. I have, as you will see in the following story, for years already, been trying to reconstruct the history of both of our families.

My uncle Zak was secretly married to your birth mother (Korrie) during the war years. During those unsafe times, Korrie as well as your mom, Elske, were very close friends; the two of them helped find safe hiding places for Jewish children that had been secreted from Amsterdam and Apeldoorn. After Korrie was murdered by the Nazis, you were, for all practical purposes, a Jewish orphan. It was Elske and her husband Piet who rescued you by adopting you as their son.

The long letter that follows, Jay, is the result of several years of research into the history of our strangely interwoven families. In the story I hope to answer some of your questions and, in the process, will also reflect on both what pulled our oddly joined families together and what pushed them away from each other.

Now that I am an old man, Jay, I have for many years tried to understand the deep feeling of guilt that I feel towards you personally; like many other Dutch people, I have spent most of my life papering over the most acute pain of the war years which shaped your life. The Jewish Holocaust not only killed your mom and your grandmother, but also 100,000 other Dutch Jews.

The first part of that letter will introduce you to the quiet Zak who was married to your birth mother during the war. In the second part, your kind mother, Elske, plays a central role. The third part is about the dark war years when your Jewish birth mother, Korrie, lived, suffered and, as you will see, also died.

Please bear with me, Jay, as I try to tell the story that has left deep tracks in both of our lives.

Yours sincerely,

Harold Runter (formerly Ruintjers)

"It is, today, simply a fact of life that people become
deeply emotional whenever anything is said about
the Jewish Holocaust. This is especially the case
with non-Jews because they carry a heavy load of
self-recrimination and self-guilt."

—[Dutch historian] Wybenga (1970)

We will just remember the good
And will forget all the bad

—Statement often repeated by Dutch WWII survivors.

PART ONE

Metastasized Silences in Harold
and Jay's Families after 1945

Chapter One

Harold's Fear of Family War Ghosts
(1992)

"[The road to] Hell is paved with good intentions."
—SAMUEL JOHNSON

STEWARD RUNTER, MY AGING dad, had just joined me on the porch of my house in Clearview (Ontario), when he became aware of an old man painstakingly shuffling into our line of vision. We were sitting close together, and that is why I could clearly hear him angrily mutter the words, "that's old Piet Knuffels." For a few critical moments my mind refused to connect the dots, and I did nothing when my dad abruptly stood up and, going to the neighbor's yard, released a powerful German Shepherd from its dog run. The animal, with a few bounding leaps, raced up to the old man and knocked him to the ground.

I was horrified and, racing to the prostrate man, could see that he had been seriously injured. I knelt beside him and told him to remain calm while I went to get help. I was about to enter the house to make a 911 call, when I was stopped in my tracks by my father's angry voice. "Leave him alone, he said. "Just let that German Shepherd finish off that old German!"

It was what he said as well as the hateful way that he uttered the word "German" that turned my feet into lead. Was he, in his own mind, still fighting Hitler's henchmen who had controlled the Netherlands during the five war years?

I was also deeply shaken by the setting of this act of violence. Why was my father now venting his frustration and why was he doing that on my street and in the vicinity of my house? In his outburst I again heard the echoes of the many explosions from the world war that had destroyed so much in his far-away old country. I found it hard to focus my eyes on the quiet street and to really see what kind of help the injured man needed. At that moment it had not yet dawned on me that the man who was lying on the street in front of my house was your father.

The sound of an ambulance brought me back to the present. Someone had beaten me to the phone and had made the 911 call. Your frail dad was swiftly placed on a stretcher and taken to Mount Sinai Hospital.

When our street was finally quiet again, I was still in a daze because of the many memories that had been brought up by the name, "Piet Knuffels." At one point a scene from an old war movie flickered in front of my eyes, and I imagined that I could see the faces of the half-crazy Nazi soldiers laughing hysterically when their savage beasts chased after a screaming Jewish girl in the Amsterdam Dapperbuurt area.

That's one scene in the 1988 movie, *Not Courageous Enough*. I am not sure if you saw that historical portrayal of the Amsterdam general strike of 1941. That movie, in graphic images, portrays the brutal way that the strikers were treated by the Germans. I know that I certainly was not *dapper* or courageous on that day when your dad got hurt. While witnessing my father's angry outburst, I was like one of the many passive Amsterdam onlookers who never stopped peering out from those high row-house windows through which they could clearly see the action on the wide Dapperstraat. As the soldiers were coming down the street, those matrons did not, even for a minute, stop hanging out their clothing on the external drying racks and take the time to call out a word of warning to the strikers or to that little Jewish girl who was innocently playing on the street.

They were passive onlookers who seemed to be unmoved by the terror, screams and brutal noise coming from the street below them. Ruth, with that bright red ribbon in her hair, and with that torn and hopelessly inadequate coat, desperately tried to outrun the dogs, but she was far too slow. Those canine monsters quickly caught up to her, pulled her down, and tore her frail body to pieces.

You probably remember that neither of us spoke about our respective parents later that day when we met each other in the hospital lobby before going in to see your father who was still in shock from the broken hip as well as from a severe concussion. My father accompanied me on that first visit but, after a few minutes of stony silence, he just left the room. He was not even able to muster a few words of sympathy for your dad and he certainly said nothing about the dog which had already been euthanized by the well-meaning owner who blamed himself for your father's injuries. As we sat across from each other in that hospital room, I was never open about the wrong that my father had done to your dad. I also wish that I had been honest with my neighbor so that his poor dog would not have been unnecessarily killed. I was silent because I was a prisoner of my fears.

And this, Jay, brings me to the first reason for making this letter to you so long. I hope that you will read it and eventually also consider forgiving me for not telling you that my father was directly responsible for your dad's fall. How could I just sit there and let that nasty drama play itself out? I certainly should have run after my father and stopped him from carrying out his impulsive dog-assisted attack.

And I should have introduced myself to your father during the ten years when he lived nearby and quietly walked by my house almost every day. But the introduction never happened because of that one disturbing day, in 1957, when our young lives were wrenched apart and sent into very differing directions. I did not see Piet Knuffels because I had, as a young boy, whisked his face out of my mind.

If you are willing to overlook my cowardice in that hospital room, I hope, you will also stay with me as I ruminate about the time when we were both scrawny Dutch Canadian immigrant kids who were like brothers as we adjusted to the turbulent move from Holland to Canada. I use the word "adjust," and that term is now familiar to you as a sociology professor. During those years, as kids, we lived under the illusion that we had put all things Dutch behind us when we stepped off the ship, *De Rijndam*, and took that long train ride from Halifax to southern Ontario. When we were still newly arrived immigrant kids at our school, we were unable to see that everything about us was foreign in the eyes of our classmates. They, of course, noticed our odd carrot-top haircut and would have been made to feel very uncomfortable by our itchy, tight-fitting wool undershirts, but they never poked fun at us. They even listened with grace to our use of Dutch expressions while trying to speak English. I distinctly remember looking at John Johnson's puzzled face when I told him that I liked to run "hard" after school was over. He simply smiled even though he did not understand that I was trying to impress him with my running speed.

Our new countrymen welcomed us with open arms and greeted our eccentricities and strange clothing with warm smiles and open doors. I am thinking of that gracious gentleman who, on the train from Halifax, kindly offered me a bottle of Canada Dry ginger ale after my young unblinking eyes had already bored two holes into his treasure trove of ice-cold drinks. I had never tasted anything like that in the old country and had an instant love for this new prickly beverage. I am also thinking of the Canadian official who, as I waited in the strange Department of Transportation office two weeks after we had come to Canada, offered me a cup of hot chocolate. I saw his gentle face and beaming smile, but could not understand why he shook his head when he handed my father his new Ontario driver's license. I did not realize, at the time, that he was overlooking my father's vague sense of Canadian road rules. He was undoubtedly also in a state of shock and did not want to redo the road test during which my dad had hurled his powerful 1949 Ford down those long, wide, and hilly Canadian roads even when he was unable to comprehend the road signs or understand what the official was saying to him in English about upcoming hazards. The driving test was quickly over after they had raced down a steep hill and my father had not responded to the command "slow down!" until the instructor had screamed out those words as they were approaching a treacherously sharp curve in the road which was hidden behind tall trees.

During those first years, as immigrants, we treasured anything that reminded us of the old country. The basic symbol of something Dutch was, of course, that bulky moving crate into which all our things from old country had been packed. In the weeks leading up to the big move to Canada, our parents worked with professional packers who helped them carefully and lovingly put all the family valuables into that specially built family container or *kist,* which was securely hammered shut and then shipped to the new country. Anything that did not fit into that huge wooden box was left behind, and my parents would often longingly talk about something from the old country that they missed and then wistfully add: "But it didn't fit in the crate and simply had to be left behind." The memories of Hitler's occupation of the Netherlands were deliberately not put into that crate, but, as I discovered after my mother passed away, many of those tattered thoughts tagged along anyway as quiet stowaways hidden inside the things stuffed into that formidable box.

I am not sure what you think of as you reach back into your memory and remember those first years in Canada when we were intimate friends and our parents owned the two different farms adjacent to each other on the same dusty country road near the little town of Taqua, Ontario. Like most Dutch post-war immigrants, they had wanted to get as far as possible away from the bitter war years and their way of doing that was to fall in love with the beautiful Niagara peninsula area. We, as children, knew almost nothing about the war that our parents had lived through. We experienced the war as a vast mountain of silence which had not been put in the moving crate and shipped to Canada. It was, however, always vaguely visible to us, and we knew that it could, like a largely dormant volcano, erupt at any time and spew out quick bursts of red-hot lava and billowing clouds of smoke.

I am sure that you also remember how the allure of war secrets and war violence captivated our imagination as children. My dad, in my mind, was not a dysfunctional and angry old man, but a hero who had been part of "the underground." That was a topic that always came up when there was war talk. Both of us were absorbed by the romantic image of an army that fought a holy war against the evil Nazis, and we were convinced that those battles did really take place under the ground. Our fathers, in our imaginations, were tough soldiers who swiftly moved around like gophers in subterranean tunnels as they got ready to attack the forces of evil that controlled the city streets and country roads above the ground. We dreamed up thousands of different ways that those sacred saints defeated the evil Germans who, with their fierce dogs, hunted terrified Dutch citizens.

I'm sure that you have not forgotten how, as young farm boys, we lived out the experiences of those underground soldiers when we dug deep tunnels into the soft red sand adjacent to the long driveway that led to our farm which was known as the "Runter Farm." That odd name had been my dad's attempt to anglicize our unwieldy Dutch name "Ruintjers." He had painted that name with bright orange letters on the side of the barn facing the dusty country road. You probably remember how much fun you had teasing me for being the runt of the litter, and that I was always a little self-conscious of the fact that my father was, in fact, a very short man. I did not want to be short, so, from the time we came to

Canada, I carefully tracked the process of my growth with lines and dates on the big central post in our barn.

As best friends, we dreamed up thousands of different games. From our cool underground cavern, we would peek out of the portholes that we had created, with home-made weapons, we routinely stopped wave after wave of invading German armies. Sometimes we even imagined that we saw Japanese troops coming at us. We may even have blunted some Russian Communist incursions because those were the McCarthy years, and we were duly awestruck by the nuclear fallout drills. When the annual nuclear alert alarms went off and we marched into the dark basement of our school, we moved swiftly because we knew all about the importance of such underground bunkers. On the farm we were even prepared for winter war because as we helped place the square hay bales inside the barn during the summer months, we created a web of tunnels deep inside the haymow for an imaginary winter war. We expended all that effort because we desperately wanted to normalize the dark war tragedies that our parents had hidden from us.

If the topic of war did come up among our parents and their friends, the discussions would abruptly stop whenever we, as children, came within earshot. Even when we were still quite young, we instinctively knew that no tears were ever really erased by all the stories of heroism. In our lives, the war was, in fact, like an ever-simmering Mount St. Helens which could, at any moment, send out bursts of noxious and poisonous fumes into the atmosphere. The hot lava of anger or the smoke of hate seemed to always be near the surface of the mountain we associated with the word "war."

My stoic and mercurially quiet mother never breathed a word about the war years. When pressed for information about the German occupation, she would not answer the questions, but mysteriously recite something that sounded like a Frisian memory verse: *It goede ûnthâlde wy, en it rare ferjitte wy.* She was as determined to remember the good as she was to forget the bad. To forget was, for her, an act of will. A thick wall of silence often surrounded her and caused questions about the past to evaporate into the mist. She never even told me about her younger sister Tammeke, who, I later found out, had first been sexually abused by her German captors and then went through a second indignity after the liberation of the Netherlands. Her head was shaved by her irate countrymen because they assumed that she had been sexually involved with Heidrich, a German soldier, who was stationed at a nearby garrison. I only met that emotionally scarred woman one time. Because of her agoraphobia, she almost never left her house, and no suitors ever visited that twentieth-century Miss Havisham.

I mention my mother because I am also addicted to a forget-it-all approach to my past. I hate dwelling on my personal past and I certainly do not want to think about the experiences of my parents. Didn't Jesus, in the Bible, say, "let the dead bury the dead?" And what about the edgy Dutch injunction which we both heard so often when we were growing up? "Don't dredge dead cows out of the canal." Who is interested in the ghastly stench of decomposed carcasses?

I fled from my past for most of my life but, during these past few years, I have come to realize that the past is never actually dead. When it looks as if it has died, it is only in hibernation.

I have never had any understanding of what happened during those five years of Nazi occupation of the Netherlands because I was terrified by the ghosts that my parents had seen. What I see now is that that fear and amnesia have caused me to bleach away some elements of my own identity. But it is not easy to rediscover the past once it has been lost. Reconstructing the inner fabric of my character is not helped by just re-membering those moments when the malevolent rumbles of that distant war rolled into the life of our family and stirred up a spirit of controversy and anger. Those dark memories, if not placed in the calm light of the midday sun, are best dropped into the deepest of wells.

My dad was never like the author Brian Castor, who, in his book, *The Long Walk*, reflects on the Iraq war and the impact that it had on his personal and family life. Unlike that warrior, my father belonged to an earlier era. He, like many of his fellow immigrants, was convinced that the move to Canada would make all war memories go away. The cheerful Canadian soldiers who had liberated the Netherlands were, to him, symbols of the kind of freedom that he was looking for. He wanted only to be able, as quickly as possible, to walk and talk like them.

But the transatlantic move did not make the grim war memories go away. In my life, I have come to realize that when I am not prepared to voluntarily walk back to my past, then it will forcibly drag me back to its darkest corners, and that is precisely what happened when my father released that dog. Your ailing father fought valiantly for three weeks, but was never able to recover from his hip fracture. Our combined hospital vigils ended when your father died, but that drama dragged me into deep and murky corners of my memory, and I also want to extricate myself from that abyss by putting those memories on paper. I sincerely hope that you will travel with me for a few more miles because our childhood friendship and estrangement is tied into that more ancient memory.

Chapter Two

The Frozen War Anger of Harold's Dad
(1957)

"Almost everyone [in East Germany] was a collaborator [with Communist USSR]. If they weren't working with the Stasi, then they were working with the party, or with the system more generally."

— *(Applebaum)*

You, Jay, probably don't remember the small collection of Dutch and Frisian books that was always on prominent display in the Runter family dining room; they had been placed in a small bookshelf that was attached to the wall. That inner dining room, or *foarkeamer*, had a kind of holy significance for our family. It was only on Sundays after church that we spent time in that room.

One bright summer day, in 1957, my father brusquely summoned me into that dining room during the middle of the week, and I could see from his red face that he was very upset. He did not even notice that I was walking with my dirty outside boots onto the richly embroidered and hermetically clean carpet of that almost sacred room.

As I prepared myself for what I felt was going to be a very severe tongue lashing, I reflected on all the possible crimes that I might have committed. But my mind was blank. I knew that I had done all my chores. I had seen to it that each of the two newborn calves had drunk their full bottle of milk that morning. I had even fed the chickens and collected all their eggs. I had not, as had happened during the previous week, run the tractor into one of our fences. I certainly had not committed the unpardonable sin of taking our family car for a joy ride. Still, the message on my father's face was painfully clear. I was in trouble.

Watching my father closely, I soon became more and more frightened because I saw that he was beginning to act strangely. His normal eruptions of anger never took any violent physical form, but he made up for that limitation by using his loud voice effectively and employing the growling Frisian language as a powerful megaphone. There were, perhaps, no overt profanities in his volatile tirades, but he freely used the words "stupid" or "stupid head." Those unflattering terms either functioned as sentence starters or as codas to the stream of words that would rapidly and loudly issue from him. As those abusive words overwhelmed me, I sometimes had the feeling that I was being slowly stomped into the ground by repetitive stomp, stomp, stomp sounds. I made that connection because the Frisian word for "stupid" is *stom*.

I know that you often witnessed such outbursts and did not like it that I would simply bend my head and meekly apologize for the mistakes that Dad attributed to me. I often didn't defend myself when confronted with his vocal criticisms because I knew full well that, at times, I was clearly in the wrong.

I still remember that one windy October day when, as a first grader, I was sitting in our grand old Ford in the parking lot of the grocery store as I was waiting for my dad; he had stepped out to quickly get some sugar. After he had left me alone in the car I jumped into the driver's seat and, with my hand on the steering wheel, felt that I had become the master of the car.

Then, out of the corner of my eye, I saw an elderly gentleman vainly grasping for his hat that a fresh gust of wind had dislodged from his head. The hat flew into the air and then gently came down again on the ground. But it did not remain on that one spot for long because it swiftly and willfully sailed across the whole length of the parking lot. The old man stumbled after his hat and repeatedly failed to pick it up. It was as if the hat had become possessed by an evil genie, because every time the man's hand almost touched the rim of his hat, it mockingly raced away again.

From the shelter of the car, I was first only amused by the drama playing out on the windy parking lot, but I was soon laughing hysterically as the hat continued to play the catch-me-if-you-can game with its owner. I had not seen my dad come back to the car shortly after the hat was finally re-captured by the distraught owner. My father, on the other hand, had not only seen the evolving drama, but had also heard the last spasms of my gleeful laughter.

I was startled when he abruptly opened the car door and began to berate me for my callousness. Even now I still cringe when I think of what he said that day. "You should have used your strong legs to help that elderly gentleman retrieve his hat instead of staying in the car, and like some wild baboon, laugh at him!"

When my father called me into our fine dining room, the anger that radiated from his whole body was not loud or explosive, but dangerously compressed. He just stared at me, and then, after several seconds of dark silence, his right hand shot up to the bookshelf which contained over twenty untouched Dutch books. I had been aware of them, but viewed them as nothing more than random items that had come from that Dutch crate that had crossed the Atlantic Ocean so many years earlier.

On this memorable day, however, Dad flung open the sliding glass door that protected the books and then he took down the volume with the title, *Friesland: Annis Domini: 1940–1945*. I had a vague memory of having seen it on the shelf but, to my eyes, it had been as invisible as the nondescript decorations on the wallpaper of that room. I had most certainly never taken it into my hands. I had no idea that the subtitle, on the inside title page, explained that the book was about the mysterious underground movement in Friesland during the years of German occupation. The reader is told, in the introduction, that there is a "profound danger that our post-war generation will forget those things that must never be forgotten." During all those years when I grew up in Canada, that blue book had quietly guarded all the subterranean secrets that we had enacted with our war games. That book, like our own past, had never been opened, and its contents had never been made clear to us.

But now I am running ahead of my story again, because my father, with thick, deeply creased fingers, didn't even open the book. He certainly did not mention that, many years earlier, he had written "page 213" inside the front cover of that book. Nor did he explain that, with that note, he was referencing a part of the book where an operation of a Dutch underground execution squad—*knokploeg* or *KP*—is described. Some guys from my dad's hometown of Ter Loo had been part of that squad that killed Vergonet; he had been a German mole who had worked his way into the Dutch underground.

My father did not tell me about any of that. I only got a chance to carefully read that book much later and long after he had passed away. Instead of saying anything about the book, he only partially opened its front cover and took out an old, brown newspaper clipping. In recent months I have repeatedly looked at that small sliver of newsprint from that *Fries Dagraad* of October 1946 and I still find it hard to imagine what motivated the newspaper editors to publish that snapshot of those eight frightened children whose imprisoned parents had been found guilty of having been German collaborators.

But I am again rushing ahead with my story because on that day, I didn't even see the book. I was, instead, thoroughly absorbed as I watched my father's fingers slowly unfold the aged newsprint and carefully pressed out all the creases. He wanted me to clearly see every face and every word that was visible on that sliver of newsprint. After the careful opening ritual, he said only two words. *"Sjochst do?"* I clearly understood what he was saying. He was asking if I could see what was in front of me. He was probably not speaking very loudly, but to me it seemed as if lightning and a direct clap of thunder had just struck our house, though I saw no evidence of a storm. I watched closely as he pointed to a photo of eight boys that had been placed next to the short article. Soon my dad's index finger started to glide from one face to the next one in the picture; when it had reached the image of the sixth boy, it stopped moving.

I tried to look closely at the picture of the frail, frightened young boy, but it was still partially hidden by my father's wrist. It was a blurry image of a small, four-year-old chap whose emaciated body seemed too weak to support the dark brooding head that was placed awkwardly above it. He almost looked like a disheveled and randomly assembled store manikin. I did not understand why my father was pressing harder and harder against that incriminating sliver of paper. What did he see in the face of that frail boy? I couldn't even make out what he meant when he burst out with the words "That's the boy of a traitor." He momentarily lifted his hand as he said those words, and then slapped it down again. I saw the tension in his face, but simply could not understand what he was trying to show me.

I knew that my dad had a love for drama. It had been on display more than once as he read from the Anne Devries children's bible after mealtimes. I still remember the time when he was reading the story of Moses discovering that the Israelites had erected a golden calf for the worship of the pagan god Baal. The patriarch had left the people alone for only a short time in order to meet with God on Mount Horeb. Moses reacted to that betrayal by angrily smashing to pieces the two stones on which the Ten Commandments had been written.

My dad, to portray the drama in that story, picked up the story Bible and slammed it down on the table. "They were all traitors" he thundered. "All those who betray God are listening to the Evil One."

The terrifying thought that all traitors are evil hovered in my mind as I looked more and more closely at that picture of the little guy who was the object of my dad's wrath. It finally dawned on me that the boy in question vaguely resembled you, Jay. He had the same dark eye lashes, prominent forehead, and long nose. In his sad eyes I did not see the spirit of fun that always radiated from your face. But I could see similarities, and that caused me to quietly panic as my eyes went down to the names under the picture. As my dad continued to press down on the chest portion of that child's picture, I quickly saw that the boy in question was identified as "Jacob Knuffels." After seeing that name in black and white, it still took me some minutes before I remembered that "Jacob" had been your Dutch name and that it had been changed it to "Jay" when you came to Canada.

After my dad noticed that I had read the name under the picture and connected it with you, he picked up that toxic piece of paper and carefully folded it up again. Then he quietly slipped it back under the front cover of the same book which, in turn, he then placed back on the shelf. The only sound in the room was a slight click as he shoved the sliding glass door back in place in front of the mute books. My father looked at me closely as he calmly and deliberately told me to sit down. He then went to the other side of the table, pulled out a chair, and sat down.

I tried to avoid facing my dad by looking at the pattern on the thick, carpet-like runner that covered the table. but he ordered me to look directly into his eyes. He kept his eyes fixed on me as he enunciated words that, even today, cause me to tremble.

"Starting today, Harold, you may no longer be Jay's friend. He is the son of a traitor."

For me it felt as if I had been hit in the face by the final judgment of an angry God. Was this like the time when God gave Moses the law and he underscored those commandments with the roar of thunder and the flash of lightning on the top of the mountain? Could it be that your father had been a turncoat in the same way that the people of Israel had been traitors when they abandoned their God and worshipped a golden calf? Was there no forgiveness in this picture? Had the kind of gentle words that Jesus used in the Sermon on the Mount been whisked out of my dad's Bible? How could he have instructed me to be disloyal to you, my lifelong friend?

I listened to that voice of anger and, as you well know, I used a letter to tell you that our friendship was finished. I did not even have the courage to talk with you after receiving those orders from my dad.

O what a tangled web we as humans weave! Is it possible that we can sort this all out in the open and put some balm on an old wound?

I do not know the real answer to that question, but I do know that I very much want, with this story, to ask your forgiveness for my ruthlessness on that day in 1957 when I silently accepted my dad's judgment that you were to be treated as an evil person simply because your father had been accused of wrongdoing during the war years. As I again and again look at that increasingly aged newspaper picture, it is not possible for me to imagine what it must have felt like to have been ostracized from family and from society. Along with thousands of other Dutch kids of people accused of collaboration with the Germans, you were placed in a no man's land during the first months after the war because your parents had been put in prison. You, as a young boy, had had nothing to do with what your parents may or may not have done. My father, however, felt compelled to place a load of guilt on your head, and I walked in my father's muddy footsteps when I abandoned you as a friend.

That dark chapter in my life, as you can probably guess, is the second ugly thorn that I would like to remove from under my skin because it has been building layers of calluses for over fifty years. As I sit here and vainly tug at the deceitful thorns of 1993 and the brambles of disloyalty that go back to 1957, it often feels as if I am involved in an exercise of utter futility. Each one of those briars is fastened to a much larger subterranean root system that is invisible to the human eye. Why spend blood, sweat and tears trying to dislodge nasty roots that lead straight back to the upheaval of that most horrible of wars? It is no longer any fun to grope around among those heaps of ordnance which are ready to explode in deep catacombs where so many bodies are buried among the ashes of unfulfilled hopes. It almost feels repugnant to even think about going back to that cool cave that we, as kids, dug in the ground next to our driveway from where we could be ready for all the different enemies coming down our country road. As children we always knew when hostile troops were coming because we could always see the telltale billowing clouds of dust that trailed anything that went down those country roads. Now, however, it seems as if I can no longer see anything clearly.

Other major changes happened during that summer of 1957. Not only did all the new cars around us begin to sprout increasingly impressive fins, but your dad sold the family farm, bought a home in St. Catherines, and went back to college to obtain a teaching certification. After finishing his training, he taught junior-high math for the rest of his working life. You, in the process, became a town kid.

The changes in the Runter family were more subtle. I knew there had been a heated argument between our fathers, but the cause of the feud was a mystery to me. On the day when my father summoned me into our dining room, I noticed that our whole house was eerily quiet. No doors were being slammed, and all the lights had been turned off. My mother was working in the garden, and she seemed to have inexplicably forgotten her ritual of always having a hot cup of tea ready for me after I stepped off the school bus.

As I reflect on that eventful year, I realize that something deep inside my father must have started to unravel. The outward signs of the injury became increasingly clear as the years passed. As a troubled and self-absorbed teenager, I did not see any of the changes that were happening in my immediate environment. Now, looking back to that year, I can see that it also marks the beginning of the time when there was serious trouble in my relationship with Dad. I turned from being a largely dutiful son into a quiet and aloof rebel. I still did the assigned chores on the farm, but from that point on, I worked with an edgy and hostile silence. If I did have to again face my father's vocal anger, I no longer bent like a willow, but would, instead, walk away from him in a sullen huff and then sulk for hours in one of my secret hiding places.

My favorite place of escape was that dry spot under the wooden bridge adjacent to that quiet ravine which was just up the road from the Runter farm. There, in utter silence, I would mourn our lost friendship. I no longer threw stones into the water because it reminded me too much of all the times when we practiced skipping flat stones across that clear quiet pool. Usually, I wouldn't even hear the loud thud of the tires as the cars and trucks rattled across the wooden crossbeams of that bridge, and I most certainly no longer imagined that the vehicles might be part of an invading German or Japanese army.

Our family farm was also affected by the changes that came after that year of trouble. Until that time, our dairy farm had run smoothly because good management skills had guided all the daily decisions. No costs were spared when it was time to purchase the dairy cattle. Dad purchased only the best animals for the Runter dairy herd. During the successive years, the young calves were carefully weaned and eventually brought to maturity before being added to the slowly growing herd that brought a modest but steady prosperity to the farm operation. Visitors to the farm often complimented us for the fact that our house and barns were always well painted and that the yard area around our farm was tidy even during the busy summer season. Because of the financial health of our farm operation, our machines were well maintained and survived the onslaught of the summer haying season without suffering from undue wear and tear. My quiet mother proudly maintained the lawn, the vegetable garden, and her increasingly expanding flower beds.

But those good years came to an end after that day when our respective lives went in different directions. In my heart I never really believed that your dad had been a collaborator. How could such a quiet, pensive, and studious man have been disloyal to his country? Why had my father always been so aloof towards your dad?

That friendlessness was not reciprocated by your family. Your mother never failed to give me an effusive welcome whenever I came home with you after school. She seemed to always smile as you and I began our hunt for something tasty to eat in the kitchen. She also had the kind of laugh that could lift us up and carry us along with its almost hysterical glee; she was, to me, the personification of joy. She was also very opinionated, and with her clear voice and flashing eyes, was able to forcefully defend her thoughts. I still remember the time when we told her about the nuclear safety drill which we had had at our school and how we had all huddled along the basement wall of our ungainly school building. She laughed lightly as she observed that it would take more than those frail walls to protect anyone from the destruction of a nuclear holocaust. She didn't say it, but she knew that those worthless drills were nothing more than fig leaves that would not protect us if there were to be a real hot nuclear war.

There were also other changes that happened during that watershed year of 1957. My father's zest for farming just vanished and, consequently, he no longer took the time to calculate exactly when to mow the hay and make sure that there would be three or four sunny days before the it was to be baled and brought into the barn as dry, richly smelling feed for the cattle. He no longer took care of the work of routine maintenance. He often forgot to lubricate the hay bailer, and it would, in turn, break down on the day when our fifty-acre hayfield was ready to be baled and a thunderstorm was in the forecast for the next day. After the rains, it would take days for the hay to be dry enough to be safely brought into the barn. Year after year, as the paint continued to peel off our farm buildings, we seemed to end up with more and more inferior fodder in the hayloft of our barn. You and I could never have made tunnels with such dusty, sagging bales, and even if we had tried to carry out such a hopeless plan, we would have suffocated in the dark dungeons.

Then there was the decision that my father made, in 1959, to become a real estate agent. He had always had an entrepreneurial side to his character which, at times, produced real financial benefits. I still remember how, during the first years, when we were on our Canadian farm, he bought a new International Harvester tractor and a high-quality hay bailer. The loan for the purchase stretched the family budget, but he was able to pay it off in one year because he took on custom jobs from many of the neighboring farmers. Despite his imperfect English he was somehow able to convince them that they should make use of his hay bailing services.

My father's real estate venture was ultimately a failure because he lacked the ability to interact with people quietly and gently when he was in protracted sales settings. He did not take the time to listen carefully to potential buyers and discover the hopes and dreams that they had in mind for the property that they hoped to eventually purchase. For ten years, his realty job not only drained capital out of our little farm, but also caused him to not notice when things around him were falling apart.

From the sharp darts that sometimes came from my mother, about "that rotten real estate business," I knew that she always hoped that Dad would become interested in running the farm once again. She had a scrappy tenacity which she had inherited from her own parents; they had eked out a livelihood from a very small farm of 30 acres in Siccum, Friesland.

My paternal grandparents' farm was known as a *heren boerderij or* "lordly farm." Such farms were, by comparison, larger in size, and the owner/operators would usually leave much of the daily work in the hands of their hired helpers. Dad, while in the Netherlands, had wanted to be such a lordly farmer, but his 45-acre farm made him a small farmer in the old country. After arriving in Canada, he was convinced that his newly purchased 255-acre farm made him a kind of lordly farmer. It took more than a decade for the reality to sink in that, in the Canadian setting, he was still the owner/operator of a small farm.

I know, Jay, what you are thinking. Why is Harold crawling through all those dusty tunnels of the past? I ask myself that same question, but am discovering that many of the meandering roads in my life take me back to that fateful summer. A wall of separation had come down between us because of some mysteriously unattended wounds from a war that had happened almost 60 years ago and in a country that is still thousands of miles away from our respective Canadian homes. That mystery has, as it were, been like a vague toothache that periodically flares up with those bursts of sharp pain.

During the 1960's, my dad's ideas became increasingly strange and disconnected from the troubling reality of daily life on the Runter farm. At times, however, he could still be lots of fun to be with. I remember one occasion in the early 1960's when, as a blushing teenager, I had not only begun to notice girls, but was also having my first secret crush. It was on one of those classical moments of father-son road-trip bonding that I received a brief glimpse into a closed chapter of his life. He asked me, that evening, if I wanted to come with him to look at a cottage that a neighbor owned on Point Peele and that he wanted to list with his company, Peninsula Properties Realty. I agreed to come along for the cool evening drive, and my father was in the very best mood after he had inspected the property and we finally set out for home during a long moonlit evening.

While speeding along, he turned to me and asked if I had a girlfriend. In the dark interior of the car, I could not see the expression on his face, but instantly withdrew into my passive-aggressive cocoon. But that reaction, which had become instinctive by then, was quite unnecessary on that balmy summer evening because dad had wanted to embark on his own journey down a romantic memory lane. He started by telling me that he was about my age when he got to know a girl to whom he had been very much attracted. He thought that she also had feelings for him, but in fact, she fell in love with, and married the man who had been his best friend at that time.

I have, for decades, forgotten about that late night conversation, but recently something else came out of our family crate which has made me begin to go back to that almost idyllic moment of bonding with my father, and I vaguely wondered if the unnamed girl that he had begun to like was actually your mother. She and my dad had known each other in the early 1930's before my parents had even met each other. When your mom made some reference to my dad in my presence, she always said the words "your father" with a tone suggesting that she knew him quite well.

My mother never criticized your mom, but whenever I came into her kitchen (after having done some after-school grazing in your home and having spoken about having enjoyed some or other home-made Dutch pastry that your super-cook mom had made), she would invariably find something to do at the stove. At the time I did not make the connection, but did notice that she would frequently serve a discreet number of tasty store-bought almond tarts during the following Sunday's coffee time at our home. Those sweet succulent cakes had come from the Dutch import store, and they gave an especially satisfying edge to the cup of coffee that was ritually served at our home after the morning church service as the words of the preacher were, so to speak, also placed on the coffee table and examined in a spirit that was not always equally gracious. My mother never explained why certain Sundays were set aside for those tasty treats. What I knew was that they always gave an extra zest to the hum of conversation that enveloped her as she quietly kept the of cups coffee filled.

My mom was, by nature, a very reserved person. My dad, on the other hand, was like Pyotr Verkhovensky in Dostoyevsky's *The Demons*. Pyotr, in the words of that great writer, "came into the room talking." That was my father. He loved to talk and fill the room with his insights which were, at times, not based on any facts. But my verbose father and my demure mother formed a tight partnership during those first years in Canada. After meeting each other in the late 1930's, they had, with some haste, married during the first year of the war. Like many others, my father had hoped that a wedding ring would help keep him from being required to work in Germany. Your quiet dad has probably never spoken about the horrific years he spent in Germany during the war, and I am sure that he never spoke about why he was accused of helping the enemy during those troubling years.

In my next letters I hope to peel off a few layers of the ancient scab that not only enveloped the lives of our respective parents, but had also caused our friendship to end so abruptly at the end of the 1950's.

Chapter Three

Harold and Jay Debate about Change and Enduring Values

(1960)

"[the words "good" and "evil"] have become very old-fashioned concepts, yet they are very real and genuine. They are concepts from a sphere which is above us."

—SOLZHENITSYN

IF YOU ARE STILL travelling with me on this increasingly long Odyssey, Jay, I know exactly what you are thinking as you sit in your rustic summer home in Smithers BC and look out at the beautiful mountains that gently envelop your scenic city. You may think that I am dredging all this old garbage out of our past because in some mysterious way, I want to justify myself for something that happened long ago and that has no relationship to your life. You may even be angry with me because I have now even dragged your deceased mother into the picture.

In one sense you are correct. I am a Frisian like you, and, while arguing, we both like to have the last word. The average Dutchman likes to joke that their northern countrymen have heads as hard as rocks. Both of us have a touch of that genetic ailment. We were not only stubborn, but also took pride in our immovable attitudes. As friends, we had farm equipment debates that lasted for as long as we were neighbors. Your father was a green "John Deere" man and always purchased all his farm equipment from the local John Deere dealer, while my dad was a red International Harvester man Neither of us ever vacillated from our convictions about which brand of machine was "good" and which was "bad." It was not a question of better or worse, but the red stuff was either perfect or it was abysmal junk. My short father loved to sit on the bucket seat of his red International Harvester tractor, but as I looked at him, I always knew that your dad's bright green John Deere tractor, with its powerfully thudding engine, was, by far, the superior machine. I routinely brushed those evil suspicions away and remained as loyal to red as I was to the Toronto Maple Leafs hockey team. During all our years of friendship, I never capitulated to the heretical notion that green was better than red. For me, similarly, GM cars and trucks from Oshawa were vastly superior to the junk arriving from the Ford factories in Detroit.

In our absolutism we mirrored the edgy bipolar language of the larger world in which we found ourselves. We wanted to paint the farm implement world with colors that were either clearly red or clearly green. We experienced that same kind of duality every year as the nuclear attack drills were ritually re-enacted and as we again heard about the dangerous USSR. The fear of the red threat that wafted from Washington during the McCarthy years did not really disturb the rustic tranquility in our homes because we didn't have a television or a subscription to a daily newspaper. But, as children, we not only knew that the red communists were our enemies, but also that they wanted to overrun the Netherlands and the rest of Europe in the same way that the Germans had done in the 1940's. My dad often said that he was glad that he had come to Canada and put an ocean between himself and communist USSR.

When I was still a youngster, I often had the feeling that the bipolar language used to describe the physical world around me must, in some ways, be connected to the spiritual-warfare sermons that I heard in our church. As the small teaspoons quietly clinked against the sides of the coffee cups and stirred up the rich cream and the sugar on the Sundays after the worship services, I would often quietly listen to the conversations about that bad King Saul or the notorious traitor Judas. They were not godly people like King David or the Apostle Paul. As those meandering conversations switched to topics that I did not comprehend, my eyes would sometimes drift up to the small bookshelf and my eye would catch the title of two of the black books that seemed to peer out at me. They were both written by Klaas Schilder and one had the title, *Wat is de Hel* and the companion book had the title, *Wat is de Hemel.* I had no idea what was in those books but, from the spine label, I could see that the author's name was "Schilder" which, I knew, meant "painter." Starting with that word I just assumed that the "hel" book was filled with graphic and ghoulishly dark paintings of hell, and that the "hemel" book was filled with luscious and radiantly bright pictures of heaven.

From the daily Bible reading around the family table, and from weekly sermons at church, it was unambiguously clear to me that the world was filled with people who were either on the narrow road that goes to Heaven or on the wide road that goes to Hell. At that time, Dante's *Divine Comedy* or Michelangelo's painting of the *Last Judgment* did not guide me in my understanding of Heaven or Hell, but I did have a vivid image of both from the sermons at church and the Bible readings after mealtimes. Hell, I assumed, was a place filled with crying and teeth grinding as opposed to Heaven which would be a place of joy where there would no longer be any tears. I imagined that Schilder's books contained bright pictures that would, in starkly different colors, paint the black and white differences between the realm of darkness and the realm of light. Those two theological books, like two brooding eyes, always looked down at me as I sat in the corner and listened to the hum of Sunday talk in our formal dining room.

I was always convinced that there could be no ambiguity in the heaven-and-hell painter's palate of colors, and that takes me back to one day, years after the end of our friendship, when we sat across a table as rivals. After 1957, you and I lived in different school districts and we rarely saw each other again except in passing at intramural events, and that is what occurred in 1960 when we both belonged to the debating society of our respective high schools. It was your school's turn to choose the topic of the debate and, as I learned later, you formulated the question that we were to discuss.

The thesis that we had to argue—for or against—was formulated somewhat as follows: "The core value systems on which societies are based and by which personal lives are shaped, are either absolute—not able to be changed—or they are fluid." A "yes" was to mean that root values *do not change* because they supersede societal settings in which they function, and a "no" was to mean that *even root values are flexible and evolving* because they are always being reshaped by the changing society in which they function.

Since your high school had had the privilege of creating that question, our team was given the first opportunity to respond to the thesis question and defend the "yes" position. For us, core societal values were to supersede societal settings. I was, as you may remember, the first one out of the gate, and I immediately launched into some form of jeremiad which still makes me blush today.

I still cringe as I replay the carefully formulated statement that my teacher and debate coach, Mr. Cooperman, quietly shared with me the next day. "Enthusiasm is OK in debates, but it must be properly framed in an orderly thought process."

Somewhere in my stream of words on that day, I must have said something like right is right and wrong is wrong because things in the world are not grey. They are either black or white! Those were the fighting words that you picked up in your calm, measured response. Whereas my mind was bubbling with images of David versus Saul, Daniel versus the lions, and Jesus versus Pilate, you had begun to struggle with the books of authors such as Walter Rauschenbusch and Joseph Fletcher. The term "situation ethics" was coined in the later 1960's, but the concept was already in the air after the death of Stalin because there was a general sense of exhaustion with the idea of a sharply divided bipolar world.

The rest of that debate is a blur in my mind, but I am sure that you played with my blunt black/white argument in the same way that a skilled angler can slowly reel in an especially energetic fish. I imagined that I saw a smug look on your face as you calmly looked around at the audience and told everyone that we do not live in a black-and-white world, but in one that only has shades of grey. I am not sure, but I think that you may have ended by telling us we can no longer mimic Virgil and stupidly think that it is fun to sing about man's love for weapons and war. "Virgil's *Arma virumque cano* from over 2000 years ago, becomes a death cirge if we sing it in our modern Nuclear Age!" What is really etched on my mind is not that the judges unanimously declared that victory, in this war of words, went to your team, but that you personally received a standing ovation for your philippic.

As I sat in the corner of the team bus on the way home, I slipped into a dark mood, and my feelings of loss switched from one frame to another as quickly and abruptly as the pictures from an old carrousel projector. There was no image of a knight in shining armor riding off the battlefield. Instead, at one moment, I felt like a pathetic crybaby because my annoying tears silently reminded me of a long-lost friend whom I had betrayed and who now, it seemed to me, had betrayed the value system that had united us. To me it seemed that you had scorned all those good-versus-evil underground games we had played together. As I thought about what had just happened, I felt as if my head was trapped in a pear-shaped bottle and was ready to explode with a Munch-like scream. During the next dark moment, I was a pathetic soldier who had lost the battle and was flat on the ground and bleeding from all parts of his body. Then my mind would switch to that awkward moment when I just stood there like the wife of Lot who had become a pillar of salt when, with a fixed stare, she saw the horrific destruction of Sodom and Gomorrah. After your presentation, I also opened my mouth, but nothing came out because I was at loss for words; you had skillfully disassembled every part of my jerry-built argument. To me, the vast array of words that came from your armed camp felt like an oppressive swarm of gnats which, by stinging me repeatedly, gave me the urge to scream out for help.

All those fleeting images that came to me after the debate eventually blended and, in my mind, always evoke the feelings of coldness and emptiness that also comes over me when I look out at a country landscape after a fierce winter blizzard has let up and has finally allowed the flotsam and jetsam to come to rest in a vast and seemingly endless desert of whiteness. Today, long after that stormy debate and the old sense of loss gone, I sometimes still feel that I am picking up the pieces from that troubling confrontation. With the wisdom of hindsight, I can see that verbal battlefields may be good places to bring perspectives into focus, but they are wretched places to go to if one wants to recover rare and lost treasures such as friendship, grace, hope, love and faith, and to bring those gifts into the full light of day so that the multicolored nature of life can shine clearly in the sun. As we first squared off in the debate, I had a fleeting hope that you and I could still recover our childhood friendship, but that hope swiftly vanished when the first verbal bullets began to fly. Now our childhood friendship has been dead for over fifty years, and that high school battle-of-words is almost as ancient as the Korean War and the Demilitarization Zone that still divides the sad Korean Peninsula.

I did not drag you along with me on my meandering journey through 1957 to the black-and-white debate of 1960 as well as to the hospital bed of your dad in 1992 because I like to relive pain, but because I may have found a ray of sunlight that can melt some of the ice that has quietly built up in the long-lasting DMZ winter that has so long divided our respective families and ripped our boyhood friendship to shreds.

The beam of light is historic in nature and puts a focus on the time when our respective parents were still young adults. In the process, it also takes us both to the dark years of the 1930's depression and to the frightening time of war when Nazi terrorists ruled the Netherlands.

In parts two and three of this story I hope to filter some of that light through the prism of time in the hope that I can demonstrate that during those dark years there were also times of hope in the lives of our respective families.

Chapter Four

Harold Obtains His Uncle Zak's War Journals

(2008)

Now, as I think about that 1960's school debate, the feelings of loss and self-pity are gone, but something from that day has stayed with me. Was I, in the words of Kant, stirred out of my dogmatic slumbers? That's probably an overstatement, but even as I looked at your calm face and as the words "black," "white," and "shades of grey" seamlessly slid out of your mouth, I vaguely felt that some of the sharp edges of the faith, in which I had been raised, had been blunted by having run into your wall of arguments.

I woke up one morning, after that debate, and had a fleeting feeling of glee because I imagined that I had found the magic glue with which I could quickly and easily repair the damage that had been done to my world. That fix came to me on the day when the word "white" ceaselessly bounced around in my mind like an India rubber ball. The word reminded me of something that I often heard from my uncle.

Uncle Zak was skilled at finding edible mushrooms and he used the word "white" in a curious way. He always said that the brilliant white mushrooms are often the most poisonous ones. That's why he always encouraged me to carefully look for the hidden mushrooms that were not easy to spot in the grass or leaves. Zak also urged me to always examine the areas under a mushroom's cap as well as around the stem in order to make a positive identification and in that way know if it was either edible or poisonous.

I never became a mushroom hunter and have always lacked the courage to eat any that I found. The reason for my caution is simple to explain. I never developed the eye to see which ones must stay on the ground and which ones could safely be included with the evening meal. My fleeting insight, which came too late for the debate, was that there is indeed a moral dividing line in the world, but it is not as clearly visible as the difference between black and white. It is hidden in the same way that the boundary line separating poisonous mushrooms from edible ones is hidden to those who do not have an eye for the differences between mushrooms. For several hours on that day, I felt I had won the argument with you. Hadn't I defended the truth even if I had lost the public debate?

I mention my uncle Zak to you, but your memory of him may be somewhat vague because he was, in some ways, an invisible man. From the time we emigrated from the old country in the late 1940's, he lived with us in that small, mushroom smelling annex that had been added to our house. Like all of us who left the Netherlands in that tidal wave of Dutch immigration, he also received the Dutch government subsidy to help with the relocation costs. What you probably do not know is that 1957 was also a transitional year for him. He went back to the old country during that same fateful summer when our ways parted, and your family sold the farm before moving to the city of St. Catherines.

I never really understood why the departure of Uncle Zak to Friesland in 1957 was so closely connected to the slow and seemingly unstoppable decline of our family farm. But there was never any doubt in my mother's mind that both the success of the farm as well as its eventual demise hinged on the presence or absence of this quiet, unassuming tall man who was the older brother of my father. *Omke* Zak, as this tall uncle was known to me, always acted as a discreet and amenable farmhand on the Runter farm, but he was much more than a farm helper. He was my father's older brother and was also part owner of the operation. Whenever one or other mishap happened, after 1957, I would often hear my mother say to herself in Frisian: "If only your uncle Zak were still here, then everything would be different."

I also never understood why he was utterly unable to speak. I had heard vague stories about some debilitating childhood illness but, at the time, had never heard of children having had seizures that destroyed parts of their brain.

Zak, after his return to the Netherlands, vanished from my life; I never saw him again because he stayed in the old country until he passed away in the late 1960's. Throughout that decade, I often heard rumors about his planned return to Canada but, despite my mother's hopes, it never happened. She was convinced that Zak, with his wide range of skills, would have been able to quickly end the Runter farm's slow slide into bankruptcy.

Zak was only a distant and mysterious glow of light in my life until May 8, 2008, the day my mother called and urged me to pay her a visit. Over the phone she told me that that there was something very important that she wanted to tell me. I did not know what she had in mind, but soon found myself driving down the familiar road that took me to the old Runter farm. By that time Steward had been dead for several years, and all the farmland belonging to the original farm had been sold off. Mom still lived in that same old red brick house that had been part of the farm. My sister and I had never been able to persuade her to go to a rest home. Each day, consequently, she continued to painfully coax her increasingly arthritic body through the familiar rooms of that tall, old drafty farmhouse. During the cold winter days, she simply piled more blankets on top of herself and waved away all talk of moving to a comfortable retirement home. "I'm OK here. If it is a little cold today, it's because the wind is from the north. Tomorrow it will shift to the south, and the house will be warm again."

After coming through the unlocked door, I found my mother sitting comfortably in what had been the old formal dining room. It was now my mother's bedroom and the place where she, in an easy chair, spent most of her time. She loved the sunlight that poured in through the tall east and south facing windows. When asked why she had not eaten a small meal that had been left untouched in front of her, she would often respond by saying that she had soaked up the sun all day and had little need for additional nourishment. She would, in her brusque Frisian way, sometimes add, "I did not, at first, want to follow your dad when he decided to emigrate to Canada, but now, even as a widow, I would never go back to the Netherlands because I have fallen in love with the bright Canadian sun."

The dining room was now the only room in which my mom spent any time, and she was unaware of the clutter created by the many relics from the past. My sister and I were never able to convince her to get rid of any of the original furniture. She wouldn't even allow us to move any of it or take it to the upstairs storage area of the house. The small bookshelf still hung from the wall, now awkwardly up against the large wood-encased grandfather clock. The ancient coffee table had been shoved close to the foot of her bed.

That old relic was not, in any way a regular store-bought coffee table, but was instead an ornate wooden chest close to four feet in length and slightly more than two feet wide. It was almost always covered with a thick, deeply maroon, carpet-like covering which hid the gloss of its deeply varnished surface. The covering also shielded it from sun damage. The only thing that I knew about this peculiar coffee table was that it had been made by that mysterious uncle who had lived with us during our early years in Canada. I also knew that he had constructed it from the pine boards that had made up the crate which had crossed the Atlantic Ocean in the hold of our passenger ship, *De Rijndam*. Often, when I was still at home and as the hum of adult conversation filled the room around me, I would stare at that ornate box and my eyes would be drawn to one of the lower boards where the word "*Rijndam*" was still visible through all the layers of varnish.

Throughout the years, I always wondered what could possibly be in that mystery chest; it was never moved from its assigned spot in our lightly-used dining room. What secrets were our parents keeping from us? As a child I would sometimes try to unobtrusively lift the heavy lid, but it was secured by the two locks that were built into the wood. I am not sure that I ever actually tried to open it, but the idea always hovered in my imagination. The truth is that I was always a little afraid of this family chest because it reminded me of the Ark of the Covenant. Wasn't that ancient box packed with power? From my dad's reading of the family Bible, I knew that Uzzah had been killed for just touching the ark.

The minute I walked into the room, on that quiet day in May 2008, I noticed that my mother was staring at that mystery chest, and then I heard her say, in Frisian: "Today that thing has to be opened!" Her voice was strong and had a tone that resonated with an aura of powerful finality. It was as if she were a judge who was finally passing a death sentence on a criminal whose trial had lasted for many years. Then, wielding her cane like a gavel, my mom hit the guilty chest with a loud thud.

In all the years that I had known my mother, she tended to be very quiet and accommodating. She rarely asserted her will. That demure attitude certainly shaped her relationship with my father during their almost 50 years of marriage. He was, from her perspective, the rightful head of the household. But, at two critical junctures in our family life, that theology of "headship" collided with an immovable rock when my mother's voice, like a judge's gavel, came down with a resounding "no."

The one time occurred in the early 1960's when our farm was slowly sliding into increasingly serious financial trouble and my dad, day after day, suggested to my mother that we sell everything and go back to the Netherlands. One evening, as my dad was again brainstorming about the idea of leaving Canada, my mother abruptly got up, went to the kitchen and, with that voice that echoed with resounding finality, said: "If you go back to Holland, then you will be going alone, because I'm staying in Canada. I will not go with you." The judge's gavel had come down, and the case was closed. My father never again brought up the idea of going back to the old country.

The second time I heard my mother use that resolute voice happened in 1957 after our respective fathers had had that mysterious dispute in which my dad had obviously accused your father of being a traitor. After that initial argument our pastor and one of the members of the church council came to our home for the purpose of ending this feud between two brothers in their church. As a child I felt the excruciating tension in our Sunday dining room as the councilman and our pastor quietly sat across the coffee table from my father and mother. I was familiar with the normal annual visit by members of the church council. They would come once a year to take stock of the spiritual health of our family. Children, like my sister and I, were supposed to stay through the whole *huisbezoek*. Often those visits barely veered away from farm talk to discussions about matters of faith and church life. Such visits always ended with a short reading from the Scriptures and a time of prayer.

On this occasion, however, I was summarily dismissed and specifically told to leave the house after the polite introductions and weather chatter had come to a swift end. As I passed through the kitchen, I noticed that my mother had not even prepared the obligatory pot of coffee, and there were no sweet cakes for the guests who, as a rule, would have been treated as royalty. This time they had just shown up at the door with the hope that they could pacify my volatile and highly provoked father. As I was hovering around outside, I did not hear a word of that conversation, but the angry words "traitor's son," were still ringing in my ears and I sensed that the well-intentioned peacemaking efforts of those church leaders might face some heavy headwinds.

The next day my suspicions were confirmed when my father, during breakfast time, mentioned that he was thinking about looking for another church. In the days that followed, he continued to mention different churches in the area that we could visit. With her stony silence, my mother checkmated all his talk. I noticed, as she placed the bowl of oatmeal in front of me on the table, that it came down like a heavy cement block. It was as if she wanted the furniture to do the talking for her. By the third week my father, in his stream-of-conscience musings, had cycled through his reflections on the United Church, the Episcopalian Church, the Baptist Church and the Lutheran Church.

During the fourth week, on a Saturday evening, my dad abruptly announced: "I just spoke to Mr. Klarken. He is a member of the Canadian Reformed Church. He has invited our family to attend their morning service tomorrow and to come for lunch at his home afterwards. I shook his hand and told him that we would come. So, we will have to get ready for church twenty minutes earlier in the morning because it will take a little longer to drive to that church."

That announcement was made immediately after we had all finished eating our Saturday pea soup and sandwich supper. I still have a vivid image of my mother abruptly standing up from the table and announcing, as she picked up the heavy stainless-steel pot: "I will never, never join a Schilder Church." She took two steps to the nearby kitchen counter and set that pot, still half filled with pea soup, on that hard stone counter with a thud. I had no idea what had just happened, but my mom, with that loud crash, wanted to underscore something. As I looked out of the kitchen window, I imagined that I could see a bright banner with the word "schilder" hanging in the thin air and shimmering in the same way that those heavy three-foot icicles had glistened last winter as they caught the last rays of the bright setting sun. I still did not understand anything about this mysterious painter. All that I knew was that his heaven and hell books, like silent soldiers, always stood on that small shelf in our family's Sunday dining room.

At that time, I did not know that Dr. K. Schilder wasn't a painter at all, but a controversial Dutch Calvinist seminary professor whose writings and ideas helped energize the Dutch underground movement during the war years. In June of 1940, when almost everyone in the Netherlands was still deeply depressed by the quick and ruthless way Germany had conquered most of continental Europe, this fearless author was telling his readers that it was time to 'Come out of our Cellars of Fear and Put on the Uniform of Faith." Schilder's fighting words were spread far and wide through his little church paper, *De Reformatie*, during the first months of the war. Before the summer of 1940 was over, the Germans had stopped that paper's publication and put Dr. Schilder in prison.

I also knew nothing about the church that my dad wanted us to go to. The only thing that I was vaguely aware of at the time, was that the so-called "Schilder Church" was even more conservative than the Calvinist church to which our family belonged. My classmate Paul, whose family belonged to that church, wasn't even allowed to watch television at a friend's house. His family, like ours, didn't own their own TV set.

I am, of course, again drifting away from the topic, but I needed to do that to give you a sense of how amazed I was when my mom announced to me that the chest-like coffee table, which had never been opened during the almost 60 years that it had been standing on that same spot, had to be opened immediately. I had to push aside all childish feelings of awe in the presence of what I had long felt was our family's exact copy of the Ark of the Covenant. Could it hold some fragments of the two stone tablets on which the Ten Commandments had been etched in Biblical times? Moses had, after all, gone all the way back up Mount Horeb and come back down with a new set of stone note pads on which those commands were again etched. Even the tablets that had been placed in the temple of Solomon were copies.

Those were some of the images that flashed through my mind as I walked toward my mom and took the two keys that she had taken from her apron and placed in my hand. They were still somewhat warm from having been in her apron pocket; to me they felt uncomfortably hot and that is why I had the urge to push them into the locks as quickly as possible. Both keys looked alike, but each one had been specifically designed for each of the two locks on the box. It took some fumbling for me to get the right key into its own lock, and when I turned the first key, the lock opened almost effortlessly. It seemed as if it had been oiled recently. As I put my hand on the second key, I turned around and looked at my mother, and she had her finger up in the air and was shaking her head ever so slightly.

When my mother asked me to again wait before opening the chest, there wasn't a trace of the kind of sharpness that had been baked into her voice during her younger years when her life had been overshadowed by the vain hope that our family farm would again become a successful operation. This time there was such a melancholy tone in her "nee," that when she again started to talk about her long life, I felt as if I had to stop breathing for some minutes. She had always been a thoroughly practical person who was not easily deflected by talk of dreams, poetry, and the mysteries of life. She was, in other words, not a storyteller like my father. On this day, however, there was a dreamlike quality in her voice when she began telling me a long story which brought back thousands of memories of my father.

"In spite of your father's character flaws, he was a good man, and that is why I want you to hear me out. Your dad and I did not have a long time for any courtship after we first met. We had to quickly get married because your grandmother, Beppe Katje, was afraid that the Germans would pull him, as an unmarried man, off the farm and ship him off for work in Germany. Because we got married so hastily, it seemed as if we never had any time for quiet conversations. I knew that I loved him because he could make me laugh until I almost cried, but I was not always sure that he loved me. And, of course, we were not as ready to talk about our feelings as you young people are today. We were married in a quiet church service in 1941 when the German occupation had already lasted for over a year, but it was during a time when the Nazis had not yet sunk their claws very deeply into our fatherland."

I listened carefully to her and did not want to break the magic spell by interjecting any of my own words or thoughts. My parents' marriage had indeed been an extremely buttoned-up relationship and that was reflected in the austerity of our home. Money was only to be used for things that were viewed as being necessary. It was not to be used for "unessential" things such as a dozen roses purchased on Valentines Day. That's why it did not surprise me at all that even their wedding date had, for all practical purposes, been set by my patriarch-like maternal grandmother. Feelings were not a topic of conversation at our farm. I never once heard my father say, as he left the house, that he loved my mom and, even today, as I leave her at home in that lonely farmhouse, I must remind myself to say to her that I love her before I give her a quick, obligatory goodbye peck.

My mom took me along as a magic blanket of memories carried her back to her youth. "Before your dad and I were married, I had often wanted to ask him about your uncle Zak; our neighbors in Canada always called him "Zip" because he was unable to talk. He and your father were brothers and also very intimate friends. It was that intimacy which sometimes gave me a vague sense of discomfort. Your dad was very short and the talker, while Zak was the tall, hulking older brother who was utterly speech impaired. Even though he was unable to talk, he was able to carefully listen and clearly understand everything that was said to him. People who didn't know him, sometimes assumed that he was mentally disabled, but the exact opposite was the case; that became very clear when we first came to Canada, and he learned to understand the English language before any of us did. Because of his verbal handicap, he was able to pour all his energy into developing his auditory skills. When your father and his brother worked as a team, they were like two skilled canoe paddlers who, in tandem, could effortlessly and harmoniously ease their craft through smooth as well as rough waters.

"I was not consciously aware of it at the time, but I was vaguely envious of their closeness and wondered if the tight bond between the brothers would ever bring trouble into our marriage. I had never even dared to give expression to those worries, but before the day of our wedding, they had already been lurking in the back of my mind.

"Our honeymoon was a very simple affair because it was wartime and there was no money for anything extravagant. Your dad simply wanted to go somewhere, so he rented a tandem bicycle on which we cycled from Ter Loo to a somewhat far-away lakeshore cottage. I had wanted to stay closer to home and, at most, go to the nearby city of Sebeek. I was afraid of the omnipresent German occupying troops patrolling the highways with their loudly roaring motorcycles and those seemingly omnipresent sidecars. But your dad, with his can-do approach to life, dismissed my worries by saying that the Germans had their hands full with their murderous attack on the vast country of Russia and didn't have the time or manpower to do anything more than perfunctory patrols on Dutch highways.

"We started on that long, lovely bike ride along all those beautiful Frisian roads which were, on either side, lined with serene canals. There was still some light car and truck traffic because during that early part of the war, it was still possible for ordinary citizens to get gas. On the first day of that ride, the wind gently nudged us along from the west. As our pedals rhythmically and easily pushed the bike forward, I felt an almost lightheaded surge of joy at the thought of spending the rest of my life with that strong young man in front of me.

"During the months before our wedding, I had often wanted to ask him what it was that tied him so closely to his tall brother, but I had never been able to find the right words. Now, in the open air, the hidden worry that had been lurking in the back of my mind just burst out in the form of a very natural question. Your uncle's birth name was 'Yske,' but shortly after the Nazi occupiers came in 1940, everyone mysteriously began calling him 'Zak.' I had also noticed that he seemed to almost never leave the premises of the family farm, and I rarely saw him around when I came over for Sunday dinners. He had not even come to our wedding. So I asked your father why everyone in the family had recently started calling Yske by the name, 'Zak.' Was that his middle name?

"On that quiet country road, as the sun was gently shining down on us, there were no prying ears as your father started to freely talk about something that he had never even broached before our wedding day. I had, of course, known that your uncle was not like the rest of us because he had a speech impediment; the source of his illness was a tightly guarded family secret in a day when mental illness was viewed as a kind of leprosy. It was feared, at that time, that if you got too close to someone with mental impairments, you might catch the supposed disease. Now that I was married to your father, I was allowed to have access into the inner recesses of the Runter storeroom of family secrets."

As my mother continued to talk, it was almost as if she was beginning to metamorphose into my father who, in his emotionally intense monologues, often shifted into the most ecstatic moods. I can almost see you roll your eyes as you read this, because, even when we were childhood friends, you were often deeply skeptical whenever I used the argument that something was a fact simply because my dad told me it was true.

The secrets that my mother then poured out to me were, in some way, like those Russian nesting dolls which can be set alongside each other and arranged from largest to smallest. They can also be inserted into each other and become one colorful, oval-shaped icon. I feel, even today, that I am still finding additional small dolls inside the multi layered secret package that my mother started to open for me on that day. As she said the words "secrets," my eye moved swiftly from her almost serene face to that ark-like chest that seemed have come to life as a light breeze came through the large bay windows and caused the semi-transparent sheer curtains to flutter slightly. It was as if undulating sunlight had stirred up a sea of motion in the deep veneer of the coffee table.

The quiet and almost metaphysical peace of the room brought back to my mind a long-lost memory of the utter silence in our church after our pastor, in his thundering voice, had read from the book of Revelations about the seven seals that were to be opened at the end of times.

At the climax of that reading, he abruptly shifted to a much lower voice as he came to the following passage: "When he opened the seventh seal there was silence in heaven for about half an hour." After that reading there had been utter silence in our church; no one was fidgeting on those hard pews, and all the crying babies had momentarily forgotten that they had voices.

My mother caught her breath for a minute after she had used the word "secret" but that break lasted for no longer than a fleeting second because she was immediately back in the middle of her story, and it spilled out in one large jumble of words. I am still trying to put all those words into sentences that somehow create a unified tale. "Your father was short and was physically never very strong, but he had the instincts of a charging stallion and he was determined to storm ahead and tell me all the family secrets immediately so that I would know everything about the family into which, of course, he had brought me when he carried me over the proverbial wedding threshold."

My dad's instinctive impulsiveness was something that always troubled me because I am, like all chronic puzzlers, a person who likes to figure things out before acting. I often felt that he was like that almost proverbial racehorse, Secretariat, who, "in frenzied excitement [ate] . . . up the ground" and was able to win the Triple Crown in 1973. My short father was, however, quite unlike that noble stallion in many other ways. He was neither powerful nor tall. He was, on the other hand, chronically impatient. He simply could not wait for the starter's pistol to sound before dashing off on a new exploit.

"As you know," my mom continued, "your dad liked to be dramatic when he told a story and that is also the way that he was as we biked along those absolutely level Frisian roads. Our eyes would often be attracted by those quiet canals which were starting to turn green with the summer plant growth and jelly-like egg pods which would ultimately evolve into the kinds of frogs that continually jumped into the canals from the sides of the road. Your Dad was a good cyclist and usually kept his eyes on the narrow road that opened up in front of us, so I had the luxury of being able to let my eyes fully take in the absolutely picturesque beauty of the landscape. Friesland is nothing like Ontario which has so many ugly lumps, rocks and crooked roads."

I did not contradict her by saying that I love the hills, cliffs and the many curves in the roads that weave throughout the province of Ontario.

I allowed her instead, to continue taking me along with her on that almost mystical journey into a distant past.

"I still remember, as if it were yesterday, when your dad turned
around and looked at me quickly as he said, in a secretive voice, 'my
brother Yske is dead.'

"The tandem bike swerved when your father said those words. Instinctively I attempted to turn the fixed handle bar so as to put the bike
back on a straight course. 'Watch out!' I screamed in a shocked voice,
and then, in almost the same breath, 'What do you mean? Yske did not
come to our wedding, but I just saw him recently as he was doing the
evening chores.'

"Your dad then explained to me that during the previous summer,
your grandmother had called her four sons into their living room and
told them that she was afraid that Hitler was preparing to round up and
kill anyone who had either physical or mental disabilities. As a very vigilant mother of a child with handicaps, she had no trouble believing the
vague rumors that were circulating about the fact that such a plan was already being set in motion in Germany. She obviously hadn't known about
Hitler's secret operation, code named 4-T, which was not only moving
full speed ahead in 1940, but would, in three short years, lead to the
systematic massacre of 70,273 mentally disabled German citizens. She
also did not know that the 4-T murder machinery would also function as
an onramp to the full-scale massacre of European Jews—the Holocaust.
What she did know was that she would use every fiber in her body to
protect her tall, silent son. She was not going to let the Germans hurt this
young man who had caused her so much suffering and so much joy."

As the word "dead" echoed around the room, my mom momentarily
stopped talking, but she quickly went back to what, it seemed to me, had
been a magical bike ride. "Your dad's eyes were only off the road for a
split second, and soon we were biking straight again. That is when he said
that the family had decided that not only would Yske go into hiding, but
measures would be taken to make it appear as if he had died. Through
reliable local sources, they were able to obtain a fake death certificate and
they had an actual tomb stone placed on the family burial plot. It was also
decided that the name 'Yske' would vanish and be replaced by the new
name 'Zak,' and he would, as much as possible, remain in hiding on the
farm. The new name, 'Zak' was a token of invisibility because it means
'bag' in the Dutch language, and during those days, barns were filled with
bags in which animal fodder was stored.

"I am not sure about how much your father explained about the changes in the life of Yske. Only four of our close neighbors knew the new Zak, because he avoided having any contact with strangers.

"As we continued to rhythmically bike along that quiet Frisian country road, your dad also told me that they had built a special hiding place for his brother. He also told me that his mother specifically told him on the day of that family conference, that it was his job to be Zak's caretaker.

"The minute your dad mentioned to me that he was to be the 'caretaker' of his brother, my previously undefined worry about the close bond between the two siblings took on a precise and, to me, frightening shape. Had I married a man who had to be the babysitter of his older brother?"

My mother had been speaking to me in the Frisian language when she told me about that bicycle ride and the secret family door that her husband was opening for her on that quiet morning ride. As she was talking, I felt that I was being swept along on a magic blanket as the quiet, euphonic tone in her voice took me past all the waves of the Atlantic Ocean and to her old country. There was also a rich unity in the flow of the story, because she did not, as I heard her do so often, randomly switch from Frisian to Dutch and then again attempt to slip into English. This time it was different because through her story, she was taking me with her along straight Frisian roads.

The minute that my mother used the word "babysitter," her tone changed, and her sentences became shorter and more clipped. It was as if a corn popper was breaking up the gentle and almost lilting flow of my white-haired mother's story. But the change in tempo did not last very long, because as she leaned further back in her chair, the spirit of serene calmness slowly came back into her voice.

"When I asked your father what it meant that he had to take care of his tall, quiet brother, he didn't answer the question but, instead, slowed the bicycle down and asked me if I felt like taking a break for some lunch.

"I was not at all hungry, but agreed with the suggestion. Soon we had pulled the bike off the road and leaned it against a road sign. We then found a place to sit in the tall grass beside the road. From that vantage point we could see thousands of small minnows gliding through the murky canal water. Your father said nothing more about food, but in a very low voice, started telling me about the curious symbiotic relationship that he had with his brother. Some of what he said was based on personal memories and other details came from his own mother—your *Beppe* Katje.

"He told me that both he and Zak had never known their father because of World War I and the following influenza epidemic. Between 1914 and 1918 their dad had been called up repeatedly by the Dutch army and placed on guard duty because of the ongoing need to repel all potential incursions into the neutral Netherlands by either the Allied or Axis armies.

"The Great War came to an end in 1918 but, for the family, it was also the year when the Ruintjes home was almost destroyed by two separate calamities. The first disaster was the sudden death of your grandfather. He was one of the over 50 million people who, in 1918, died because of the international influenza pandemic. Your *Beppe*, a mom with six young children, was now thrust into the position of being the owner and operator of the family farm.

"Later, during that same year, she suffered from a second calamity when her four-year son, your uncle Zak. was struck down with a debilitating set of seizures which left him flat on his back and in an almost vegetative state during the first three months after he had become ill.

"During that year of Job-like calamities, the small, tight-knit community of Ter Loo rallied around the family and, for months, helped your grandmother with farm duties. Her immediate neighbors were helpful but puzzled by *Beppe's* fierce loyalty to her sick and almost totally paralyzed son because they knew that her doctor repeatedly told her that there was nothing that he could do to help Zak regain the ability to speak, walk or move his hands in more than small spastic motions.

"But *Beppe* was not deterred by the doctor's pessimism. A few days after the seizures, she noticed that her speech-impaired son completely understood the words spoken to him. She eventually succeeded in getting him to awkwardly walk and take care of himself, but all her efforts to again teach him to speak failed. For that reason, he was always viewed as a mental invalid by the people in the town. He was, in the Dutch lingo of the time, a *stakker* or 'pathetic person.'

"While we were having our simple picnic, your father told me that his older brother had always been his quiet and obedient playmate to whom he could spill out his most fantastic ideas. As I listened to him, I could see that Zak had been an almost physical extension of your dad. And the reverse was also true. Your father's voice had, by default, become Zak's voice in the same way Laurel Engels Wilder became the eyes of her blind sister Mary. The two brothers, during their school years, were an odd duo. The awkward, tall, silent, pliable, and much older Zak was always only a few steps away from his very talkative, short and domineering brother. They learned to read and write as they, in step with each other, went through the first and second grades. For Zak it was a slow, painful, and frustrating process because he so easily forgot the things that he had learned the day before. His long-term memory had, it seems, been injured by his childhood seizures.

"I tried to calm down, as your father told me all about the special bond that he had with his brother, but it was not easy for me to understand what he was saying because sibling love had been absent from my life. I have never been close to my aloof older sister. But your dad did not give me a chance to collect my scattered thoughts and worries because he was swiftly rolling toward the climax of his story, which, he felt, would set me at ease. He told me that Zak's strange forgetfulness never went away, and that was why, as a younger brother, he often spoke up for him and helped him remember things.

"But, during the year when both were in the sixth grade, things began to change gradually. That was the year when your father convinced Zak to write down everything that happened to him each day and to use his written notes as memory prods that he could consult if he needed to go back to something from the past. That was, consequently, the year when Zak started to use his note pad and pencil as his voice."

Because my mother's voice had become increasingly low and soft, I knew that she was now exhausted from the sheer effort needed to both forget the dark war clouds, and to remember that wonderful honeymoon trip. I was at the point of placing my hand on her shoulder and telling her to just take it easy and to remind her of what she had said, so many times whenever unpleasant memories were stirred up in our home: "We must remember the good and forget the bad things that have happened to us."

Those words remained unspoken in my mind because my mother, with considerable effort, pulled herself up in her chair and declared with authority: "Open the chest and look in!"

While listening to her saga, I had slipped into a kind of reverie, but now, with those words, I was fully awake. I promptly pulled open the cover of the ark-like box and I saw that it was empty. I had no time to be disappointed because my mom explained that I was looking at a false bottom which could be removed—by the twisting of a windmill like lever in the bottom of the box. After that barrier had been removed, I found myself staring at several rows of small black booklets. Each volume looked like the small flat Bibles that our pastor always carried in the inner pocket of his suit jacket, except that they were half the size. It looked as if someone had cut the small black booklets in half and placed them in the bottom of the box. There was also a year identification affixed to each volume. In one corner, the first volume had the years 1924–1929 written on it. There was one volume for each of the succeeding years between 1930 and 1939. Several volumes were devoted to each one of the five war years. Two volumes covered the years 1946 to 1957.

I had no idea what I was looking at, so I asked my mother, "What are these strange little booklets and what are they doing in this unusual box?"

She answered with one simple sentence. "You are looking at Zak's memory."

I shook my head in disbelief as she continued to talk. "Zak was almost religious in the way he wrote down everything that happened to him on little note cards and carefully preserved all those paper scraps. Your father had told him to stop his note taking during war time because it simply was too dangerous. One could not take the risk of having written records fall into the hands of the Germans. But Zak dismissed his brother's fears and maintained his journal during the five war years He didn't tell anyone, including your father, what he was doing."

"When he went back to Friesland Zak told me, with a brief note, that the envelope he was giving me contained a key to the living room box and, simultaneously, to his memory. He also said that if he did not come back to Canada, then I could do with it what I wanted. I never told your father about Zak's memoirs because I did not want to think about them. In the last ten years I have sometimes peeked into the box but that is all that I have done; I have never been able to make myself open any of those small volumes. Now they are all yours."

I took the keys that my mother had given me, and after locking the box again, I attached them to my ring of car keys.

My mother passed away less than three months after I heard her story, and as we cleaned up the old farmhouse for the eventual sale, I was the one who inherited the ark-like box and its undisturbed memories. Each time, as I drove my car and looked at the heavy dangling keys, I again wondered if I should open the box, and my thoughts would drift back to the times when my quiet Uncle Zak lived on the Runter farm during our first years in Canada.

I am sure that you probably also remember Zak because he knew more about the farm games that we played than either of our sets of parents. He was tall and quiet in the same way that his younger brother, my dad, was short and verbose. He was much liked in our neighborhood because he was very skilled at solving practical problems. Even though he often appeared to be invisible, he always came quickly when some crisis was brewing on the farm or in the neighborhood.

You probably remember, Jay, that hot summer day when we had escaped into the shelter of our secret cave. At one point I had left you alone because I had gone to our kitchen to see if my mother would let me have some food for our planned underground banquet. As I came back to our hideout, I saw that an avalanche of sand had almost completely closed off the cave entrance, and I could only vaguely hear your muffled call for help. I dropped the cut watermelon slices on the ground and screamed out for help as I desperately clawed away at the sand with my bare hands. My fingers were bloody when I felt a tap of on my shoulder. It was my uncle Zak. He had heard my cry for help.

His very presence was like a cool gust of air on that wretchedly hot day. When I was close to his powerful presence I always felt as if I had passed an invisible border and entered a zone of safe and calm restfulness. It was the same feeling I would have whenever I sat on the lush grass and under the towering Elm trees in our front yard. Those majestic trees, with their high canopy and straight trunks, were wonderfully present, but at the same time invisible in the sense of not blocking one's view.

My uncle showed no panic when he saw my dirty and tear-streaked face. He raised his finger as he strode to the barn. He soon came back with a long rubber hose. Then, with the help of a long stick, he pushed that hose through the tiny part of the tunnel entrance through which we could still hear your muffled calls for help. He had tied his ever-present handkerchief at the end of the hose to make sure it would not fill with sand. You must have heard me explain how to use the hose as a breathing tube because, as I put my ear on the outside of the tube, I immediately heard you draw in deep breaths of fresh air and I knew that the danger of suffocation was over. Over the next three hours, Zak calmly dug a new tunnel to our cave and brought you out to safety. There was no drama, and, as far as I know, he never told either your or my parents about this incident.

He always seemed to enjoy hearing about our games. We also never received any notes from him about the risks associated with our potentially deadly underground hideouts. In his voiceless way, he showed us how to carefully cut planks and then hammer them together and place the solid panels along the sides and under the ceilings of our retreats. He was too tall and gangly to get into our caves but, when we were not there, he was somehow able to peer in and stabilize the jerrybuilt ceilings and walls that we, in our pride, had thought were utterly immovable. He was, in fact, our secret safety inspector and would often take out his pad and sketch out precise details for an ongoing safety plan.

I know exactly what you are thinking at this moment, because now, so many years later, I have the absurd feeling that I can still read your mind in the same way that I was able to in those days when we had so much fun together. "Of course," you are thinking, "your uncle said nothing critical because he was physically unable to make any intelligible sounds!" However, his speech impediment did not seriously hinder him as he went about his daily work because, as you know, he had those two trusty note pads in the two pockets in the front of his overalls. The pad on the right side of his overalls was for the purpose of responding when he was in a face-to-face conversation with someone. It was, in modern lingo, his instant message tool, and for those missives, he would use a pencil because that gave this thrifty Dutchman the option of erasing the completed thoughts and reusing the scraps of paper.

The small note pad in the left pocket of his overalls was, during a typical day, pulled out at least as often as the one on the right. The left pocket notes were for his memory bank. He always used a pen to make entries in that pad, and as he wrote things down, he always had one knee on the ground while the other knee functioned as an improvised desk. He was intensely concentrated in this prayer-like posture as he wrote the little notes which formed, as a collective whole, an ongoing personal journal or diary.

I remember that I often tried to peer over his shoulders to see what he was writing down, but all I could see was what looked like a set of black parallel lines where the tightly packed rows of words were located. If I tried to stare too intensely at the moving pen and at his long ink-stained fingers, he would write a note on the pencil pad, and it would say in Frisian: "With this little book I can remember everything." I would stare at him and at the note pad and have a feeling of awe as I thought about all the stuff that my quiet uncle could remember.

You, Jay, were not the only friend who went out of my life in 1957. Zak also left us during that eventful year and went back to Holland. I never again saw his gentle face and I no longer received those kind notes that he would slide under the door of my bedroom after I had had a particularly bad day.

Once I owned Zak's journals, I had no idea of what to do with them. I most certainly had no plan to write a history of the Dutch underground movement in the region of Friesland where my parents had lived before emigrating to Canada.

During the first six months after my mother's death, the keys to the box continued to tantalize me as they dangled on my car key chain while I drove down the quiet streets of our little town. But I always turned my eyes away from them because I did not want to go back to that noisy, brutal war that had left so many scars in our parents' lives.

My mother only referred to Zak's journals one more time after that special day when she had asked me to open that box for the first time. It happened when she was in hospice and the cancer had already severely weakened her. She encouraged me to really study the memory pellets in Zak's little books. "If you do that," she said, "then you will find out exactly why your uncle had always tried to convince your dad that Piet Knuffels was never a traitor. Piet," she continued in a soft raspy voice, "never capitulated to the Germans during the war years."

By the fall of 2008, I felt that I had taken a giant step when I took the journals out of the box. Earlier I had placed the box in the garage and would stare at it for a few moments whenever I parked our car. But, as the leaves began to pile up under the trees in our yard, it occurred to me that the wet winter weather would probably harm the little booklets in my unheated garage. So I took the volumes to my small study and placed them on a high shelf that I had made for them. There they remained largely undisturbed for a long time. Sometimes I would randomly pull one of the booklets off the shelf and try to make sense of some of those endless series of notes. Every time I opened even one volume of those booklets, I would again be reminded that it would take a lot of time to understand the Frisian words as well as to untangle Zak's idiosyncratic way of writing. On top of that, I saw that he had used numerous abbreviations for a wide variety of words that he had used.

It was not until a year later that I decided to take the time to see if I could penetrate the secrets captured in those little booklets and reconstruct, in some fashion, Zak's memory of the eventful 1930's and 1940's. What made me come to this conclusion was not some heavenly inspiration, but a simple childlike question that my own grandson directed to me after I had read him Maurice Sendak's book *Where the Wild Things Are*. He opened that book to the page where Max no longer wanted to be King of the Wild things. It was the moment when only the right half of

Max's body was still beastly grey because his left hand had become hopefully white and his pensive face was resting on an equally white left knee.

As I was reading that part of the book, my grandson, Stan turned to me and asked, in his halting way, "How, how come that Max could smell far away good things when he was so close to noisy and stinky monsters?" I didn't know how to answer his question, and that's why it bothered me for a very long time. How can we possibly listen to quiet voices from a distant era when, day after day, we are bombarded by incessantly loud clamor? How can we, in other words, listen to quiet underground streams of life when our eyes and ears are drawn to the latest amazing races?

Stan's question continued to torment me as the months passed. Why had I listened to the roaring word "traitor" from my long-deceased father and not paid any attention to any quiet voices that might have mellowed that ancient sentence of judgment? I am not sure that I will be able to find a truly quiet and steady voice in Zak's memory pellets, but I want to give it a try and I hope that you will stay with me as I set out on a long journey that will take us into your and my past.

I assumed, when I first began to read and understand the content of those small booklets, that I would quickly find the facts which would either confirm or refute what my mother had told me about your father. What I discovered, once I was able to read the unusual handwriting and interpret the abbreviations, was that I was increasingly being drawn into what looked like a hopelessly confusing blizzard of war trivia which seemed to be as forgettable as yesterday's weather reports.

But, as I dug ever more deeply into the little booklets, it slowly became clear to me that this was not just a war story that happened yesterday, but was actually a very personal story of anger, revenge and forgiveness that had, mysteriously, become part of my life and also affected your life. Even today it as if I am still blindly walking in circles—in that blizzard—as I continue to walk in the footsteps of my already deceased father. He, like many of his contemporaries, never fully escaped the deadly cesspool of anger created by that epic war.

The only reason I was eventually able to find a few consistent patterns in all those murky details, is that my uncle, in his calm way, had thrown a few seeds on the ground which gave me a path to follow through the deep forest of confusion. I hope that in the second and third part of this letter, I will be able to slowly push back some of the curtains of war noise so that you and I can at least hear some of the quiet sounds of faith, hope, and love that were suppressed but not erased by the tumult of war. This will not be easy because in the echo chamber of a noisy war, it is often very difficult block out the screams of anger and hear the deep and quiet cries of a human heart that have, for some mysterious reason, not yet been poisoned by the fumes of hate.

I hope you will continue reading my summary of the many thoughts that my uncle quietly engraved in his little booklets. The breadcrumbs that he dropped for us are explained in the little volume that starts with 1930. In those early booklets he wrote a kind of introduction to the whole set of volumes; he observed that he had collected and organized all his many notes and carefully bound them because he was not only afraid of forgetting things himself, but also felt that we "seriously risk forgetting those [war memories] which should not be forgotten" as we move forward in the ongoing rush of our daily life. Then, in that same short introduction, he is also pessimistic because as he briefly notes, "These volumes are filled with dark details about many horrors that often kept us awake during the war years and that is why I did not want anyone to look at them until after I have passed away. That is also what I told my sister-in-law who knows that I placed them in the bottom of that chest in the living room of her home."

He ended his brief introduction by quoting from *Friesland during the Year of Our Lord 1940–1945*: "We must not forget what the war martyrs expected of us as war survivors. They want us to live in the same spirit in which they lived as well as to strive for the same ideals that motivated them in their lives as well as in their premature deaths. They were energized by a holy altruism—which meant that they were as prepared to freely give as forgive. They were always ready to make sacrifices and strive for those things that give value to life." Zak had underlined the word "forgive" with a red pen, and throughout his little booklets, he placed many little red stars beside a host of different entries. Those red stars, which wend their way through the many volumes, are the bread crumb trails that I am carefully following as I try to reconstruct Zak's story.

PART TWO

Metastasized Anger:
Jay and Harold's Parents
during the 1930's

Chapter Five

The Skating Competition
(1933)

"The Nazis, with their diabolical perspective, believe that justice is served when the strongest get their way."

—KRONIEK

I AM GOING TO start this letter with an extensive quote from Uncle Zak's journal to take you back to the decade of the 1930's when Steward, my dad, and Piet, your dad, were close friends and, as such, sometimes got into the same kinds of trouble as we did:

> Today our mom called my younger brother Steward and myself into the formal dining room, closed the door and quietly told us to sit down on the chairs by the table. She placed herself on the opposite side of that table and put a poster, a newspaper clipping and a wet music sheet on the table and then, in a quiet but firm voice, she asked us to fit the puzzle pieces together.
>
> "Why," she asked us in her clear voice, "are you boys bringing these three Nazi things into our Christian home? Have you and your friends become members the Dutch Nazi political party?"
>
> She did not wait for an answer from us, but instead, simply outlined some new ground rules for our home. First, we must stop having any interaction with any Nazi organization.

Secondly, we were to cut off all contact with "that Nazi girl."
Thirdly, we were supposed to talk to our pastor Sven and ask
him why we, as Christian believers, should not have anything to
do with the evil Nazi party.

She also told us that if we did not do as she had directed us,
then she would no longer allow Steward to drive the family car;
she even threatened to simply sell it.

She then abruptly got up and left the poster and clipping
on the table. While she was leaving the room, she gave the one-
page sheet of music to me and I clearly saw, from the expression
on her face, she was about to cry.

I had never seen my tiger mom cry because she always exuded strength. But, on that particular day, she was obviously still
in shock from what had happened to me earlier that morning.

I had been walking on the canal side of the Hendrikskade
street in Sebeek, when a small group of Nazis came marching
towards me from the opposite direction. The trouble started
when we were close together on that narrow street. The marchers had probably noticed my ungainly walk because something
provoked them to laugh and, after signaling to each other, they
began to loudly shout out the words of one of their acrimoni-
ous songs.

We are strong, strong, strong.
And know how to deal, deal, deal
with the weak, weak, weak.

As the marchers, including Klees Koorder, sang those brutal words they formed themselves into a V-shaped formation
that, like the blade of a snow plough, pushed me ever closer to
the canal. The last young man, with his elbow and leg, tripped
me and, simultaneously, pushed me into the canal. As he did
that, a sheet of music, from which he had been singing, slipped
from his hand, and fluttered into the canal.

Everyone in the unit pretended that they were unaware of
what had just happened to me because they didn't stop; they just
continued to march down the street.

I fell into the cold black water like a silent rag doll because
I was unable to call out for help. A quick-acting bystander rescued me from the icy water. I was brought to the back of the
Grobbema bakery, and there I was able to warm up and change
into the dry clothing that the gracious baker's wife provided. She
also placed a bandage on the cut that I had received when my
head struck a chunk of ice in the water. As I was being pulled out
of the water that wet sheet of music had stuck to my coat.

Zak, on rereading his journal, must have felt that the above quote had been about an important juncture in his life; he had not only placed many stars next to each paragraph but had also underlined every sentence with a red pencil.

In this part of the letter, Jay, I will try to explain why it was that Zak and Steward had gotten into trouble with their fierce mother who was, of course, my grandmother or *Beppe* Katje. I will, from this point on, just call her "Beppe."

From growing up under the shadow of my father, I knew exactly why he would have been very upset with Beppe and with her threat to get rid of the family car. He was a man who always wanted to go fast, and the different cars that he owned always gave him the means to satisfy that deep passion.

His love for speed made him a kind of misfit in the rural Friesland of the 1930's; the excruciatingly slow pace of social change and the painfully fixed rhythm of farm life was an endless frustration for him. His sense of imprisonment was enhanced by the simple fact that his oldest brother was the heir who would eventually take over the family farm. Steward, my dad, was the young wolf of the pack and, as such, should have left the farm and made his own way in the world.

But my father was trapped on the Ruintjes farm because the Great Depression, like an insidious dry rot, was slowly killing all economic vitality in rural Friesland. The musty smell of rural poverty was slowly creeping into every crevice of farm life. Both Steward and Zak had had to leave school after they had completed the eighth grade in order to help with the farm operation; there was no money to pay for farm helpers or to finance more schooling. Steward was convinced that he was doomed to remain nothing more than an unpaid helper on their slowly dying family farm.

Once per month, however, the young Steward was given the freedom to use the old family car (the Skoda) to take Zak to Leeuwarden for his regular medical checkups. Zak's painstakingly slow recovery from his childhood seizures had, through the years, been monitored by doctors from that city.

It was in late October 1933 when Steward picked up a small brochure that described the rules for the anticipated Eleven-city skating competition, known as the *Elfstedentocht,* that was to take place on the frozen canals in Friesland. He was excited by the idea of that race, and desperately wanted to get involved with the anticipated festivities in some capacity.

It did not take long before the restless young man came up with a plan that even surprised Zak. It was during the morning of a freezing cold day, and Steward had just finished milking the first cow in the herd, when he got up from his one-legged stool and threw it against the wall. Zak heard the crashing sound and also clearly heard the excitement in his brother's voice: "I know who has to enter the skating competition as the representative of our town of Ter Loo. Joost Boosterma will be the perfect man for the job because he is very fast on his skates and he also has the powerful body that is needed for such a grueling race."

Steward's dramatic announcement was in large print in Zak's journal and there was a little side note stating, "Joost is actually a member of the regional chapter of the Communist Party."

Zak was worried about associating with an outspoken atheistic communist; Steward brushed all those concerns aside because he was transfixed by the idea promoting a champion skater. Would it really happen? Would Joost accept the challenge? Would they be able to use the family car? Would he, as the race progressed, be able to provide ongoing support to their champion?

I have never met Joost Boosterma, but from my father's stories and the elliptical references in Zak's journals, I have a vivid impression of the man. He had long blond hair, a broad face as well as powerful shoulders, legs and arms. My short dad probably instinctively admired the stature of this tall, young Goliath. He also loved Joost's loud voice and contagious laughter. When the two of them were together, they would take turns telling the most outrageous stories and then both laugh loudly at their own tall tales.

Joost was a canal dredger who was hired by the local farmers to remove all growth and sludge from the canals located on or adjacent to their properties. It was excruciatingly hard manual labor. All day long he would edge along a canal and toss his long-handled rake, with its extra-long tines, into the middle of the murky water and then pull it, along with all the trapped algae, frogs, mud and fish towards himself. That was the easiest part. The challenge came when he had to drag the slimy green and black gunk up the side of canal and then place it on the top of the embankment. He might have to repeat that action more than once at the same spot before inching forward and repeating the same laborious motion—endlessly lifting more and more heavy wet sludge out of the mud-sated waters of the canal.

Once one side of the canal had been raked clean, the job was only half finished. He still had to go to the other side of that same canal, and there he would endlessly go through the same motions. I remember, as a little boy, sitting beside such a dredger, and for hours, scooting slowly along the ground ahead of him and watching as he pulled up all kinds of flotsam and jetsam from the canal. In my imagination I also hear Joost, as he did his back-breaking work, bellow his communist lyrics out across the quiet Frisian landscape. Momentary pauses would happen when he pulled up a live fish that he would quickly toss into a water-filled bucket. There would be a longer pause if he pulled up a piece of scrap metal—a prize he could later sell to the local scrap dealer.

Farmers would have only the briefest of business conversations with this loud, tall, brash giant; they liked his work, but wanted as little as possible to do with his communist ideas. Joost, in turn, had become quite used to his solitary lifestyle and was surprised when Steward invited him for a beer at the local pub to ask him if he would be willing to be the skater representing their little town of Ter Loo during the upcoming skating competition. Joost liked the challenge, but said it would only happen if he got some financial help. His old skates needed to be repaired and he would also need people on the route who would be able to provide him with the food and assistance that he would need.

The conversation with Joost fired up Steward's imagination; he was delighted with the idea of forming a team of people who would assist his champion. Zak, as Steward's quiet brother, functioned as the team coordinator. The third team member, the freckled Thijs Houtma, was the Van Gogh of the group and, as such, made the outstanding banners to be hung in each of the cities along the skating route. He was a member of the Baptist Church of Sebeek and, along with his father, was a house painter. The elder Houtman contributed many partially used buckets of paint for the team's publicity program.

The fourth team member, Geert Grobbema, was invited to join the team because of his social skills. His role in the group was very important because he knew a lot of people from the region. His father was a baker who would make deliveries in the countryside in a dangerously corroded green truck. At each of the farmhouses on the route, he would stop his truck and carry a heavy wicker basket filled with fresh bread, cakes, and candies into the kitchen. As his dad's helper, Geert would quietly listen as the daily conversations with the customers seamlessly drifted from orders for bread to discussions about local, national and international news.

Geert became the team's chief fund raiser. He used all his social skills as he approached people and asked them to make a small financial contribution to the team. He was always able to join in a conversation, but he did not always use that gift when he was with his friends. Often, he just sat back and listened to the more boisterous members of the team. Zak always enjoyed the company of the gentle Geert who had been an altar boy in the Roman Catholic Church of Sebeek.

The fifth team member, Hobbe Tuinman, always remained a kind of mystery to me. He belonged to the national Calvinist church and was, for all practical purposes, the resident scholar of the group. Steward often had lengthy arguments with him because, as a budding scholar, Hobbe wanted to write down exactly what the group planned to do. Once the war broke out, Steward was adamant that the group should do everything in its power to avoid leaving a paper trail that might fall into the hands of the Germans. Hobbe was not only compulsive about keeping a record for the group, but he also brought books and magazines to their group meetings. Steward, who liked to address Hobbe as "our little professor," repeated the same warning at every group meeting. "We only talk here. Do not write anything down!"

As you can see, Jay, I have abruptly jumped from the year of the skating competition in 1933 to the war years when, as a tight-knit group of friends, Steward's team, became one of the many cells of the Dutch underground movement. I have already listed Steward's other friends but have not yet brought your father into the picture. Piet Knuffels and Steward had been close friends long before the 1930's. It had been Piet who had guessed, based on the weather report in the newspaper, the *Fries Dagraad,* that the magical eleven-city race might become a reality during 1933. He was also the person who had persuaded Steward that they should make a side trip to downtown Leeuwarden to study the route of the skating competition.

And that is exactly what they hoped to do after Zak's November 13, 1933, doctor's appointment. They hoped to spend several hours exploring the downtown area and collect some tips that might help Joost on the first leg of the race. How, for example, should Joost cope with places where the ice was still too weak under the bridges?

After they had parked their car in the downtown area of Leeuwarden, all those carefully prepared plans were forgotten because they were distracted by the sound of marching music that came from a nearby street. After a few minutes, they saw a small group of young men marching towards them and at the same time, trying disparately to stay in step with the music they were playing. To the three men from Ter Loo, it seemed as if the chilled marchers, whose fingers were half frozen, were hopelessly out of step with their music.

Most of their attention, however, was focused on the young girl who was walking along with the band and who was handing out the Nazi posters. They all saw that she was stunningly beautiful and were at the same time drawn in by her crystal-clear voice. She repeatedly reached out to the Ter Loo boys with the words: "Join us by walking along beside us for a few blocks." Each one of the three young men seemed to be in a trance as they took a handful of pamphlets and helped her distribute copies to the stray passersby.

Before long, Steward approached the young woman, introduced himself, and asked her what her name was. She answered clearly and without any hesitation. "I am Elske Scheepema, and Dokkum is my hometown."

Steward had planned to ask her what the march was for, but she did not even give him a chance to ask his question. There was a cheerful tone in her voice as she informed her admirers that those boys were all crazy. "I'm not sure what my dad is doing by carrying the flag of this absurd Nazi movement. I attend these events because my mom wants me to keep an eye on Dad. It also gets me out of the house and that is the only thing I enjoy about these outings."

When the cold marchers finally came to the end of their planned route, they dispersed and, in small groups, returned to their respective homes. Elske's father joined his daughter and scrutinized the faces of the three hovering young men before he asked them what brought them to Leeuwarden. Steward was immediately ready with a reply. "We're making plans for the Eleven-city skating competition and are looking for some help."

That brash statement got the attention of both Elske and Mr. Bert Scheepema. They promised that they would do whatever was in their power to help the Ter Loo skater when he reached Dokkum. Elske even came up with a practical suggestion. "We will give your champion a cup of hot coca so that he'll have the energy needed for the last leg of the long and grueling race."

As you know, Jay, your mother's maiden name was indeed Elske Scheepema, so this is the first time that your father met her. He was attracted by her beauty and vitality.

Piet took on the job of corresponding with the Scheepema family because he was the one who had taken the trouble to carefully record Elske's address. After returning from their trip to Leeuwarden, he wrote a long letter to both Elske and her dad in which he asked them to help Joost when he came to Dokkum.

Bert Scheepema had responded to Piet's letter with a long reply. He told "Piet and all" that he was an "Orthodox Protestant Christian" and was also a member in good standing in the Dokkum Calvinist church and that, as a young man, he had belonged to the Calvinist Youth Club.

"Now, however," he said, "I am disgusted with Calvinists such as C. Smeenk who have nothing good to say about the Dutch Nazi Party. With their dogmatic diatribes and the use of clumsy phrases, such as 'Revolutionary Unitary State,' they condemn the Nazi party instead of telling the world how they plan to address the real problems that face us. Everything they say reeks of negativity.

"I live in that real world and know from experience that we live in the middle of a hurricane. I used to own a successful bicycle shop in Dokkum. My business went bankrupt because no one has the money to buy a new bicycle. Every day now, I trudge from house to house with my repair kit and fix a few old bikes at people's homes. I make a few pennies in that way, but it is not enough to feed my family. As a citizen of this country and as a man who loves his family, I do not want to idle away my time in talk shops and that's why I joined the Nazi party; it is the organization through which everyone in this country can, as one powerful force and under the leadership of our hero Mussert, fix up this country. We, as Nazi party members, are the true nationalists who will be the real shining light on a hill. If you guys do not want to hide your light under a bushel, you need to join us."

Bert Scheepema also sent a couple of issues of the Dutch Nazi newspaper, *Volk en Vaderland*. On the last page of one of those issues, Piet found a little, penciled handwritten note stating, "Do not listen to my dad. He is becoming increasingly crazy and bitter; it all started when his shop and its contents were auctioned off and purchased for next to nothing by people who were supposed to have been his friends." The note was signed, "Elske."

The Eleven-city skating competition took place on December 16, 1933, and Joost was among the first skaters to pass through Ter Loo. At that early stage of the race, he was still full of energy and buoyed along by the hero's welcome that he received from locals who had gotten up early to cheer him on. During the rest of the grueling race, he continued to receive cheerful support from his team members but, as the day wore on, he fell increasingly far behind the top-ranked skaters. Shortly after completing the first half of the race, he developed serious blisters on both feet and his teammates had to renew the bandages several times at successive stops. Elske took care of the bandages when he came to Dokkum. It was after sunset when Joost, in a deeply depressed mood, finally crossed the finish line and discovered that he was four hours behind the two winners of the race.

But Joost's team welcomed him like a real hero. Hadn't he put their small town of Ter Loo on the map by being the first local skating champion to both compete in and finish the big race? Later, when their reluctant hero walked along the streets of Ter Loo, locals opened the windows and overwhelmed him with friendly greetings and invitations. Little girls from town filled all the buttonholes in his jacket with small cut flowers. It was as if the whole town had been drawn together by one man who had competed in the celebrated skating competition. For several days everyone forgot that he, just like his recently deceased father, was a committed communist.

The day of celebration in Ter Loo was a time of inspiration for Steward. He had brought together people who, for religious and societal reasons, normally avoided each other. In some ways, the 1930's Dutch Calvinist church community, to which our parents belonged, had some of the classical trademarks of a self-enclosed tribe which protected itself by means of a whole web of interlinking societal institutions such as labor organizations and parochial schools, as well as political organizations. Young Dutch Calvinists, like our parents, lived in separate communities where any disloyalty to party leaders was frowned on. They were forbidden to go to the worldly movie theatre and told not to read any newspaper or to listen to radio stations that were not approved of by their church-and-faith community.

As a young Canadian, I could never get a sense of how it was possible that this strange tribalism had shaped the political and social landscape in the Netherlands during the 1930's.

With the help of his skating team, my father felt that he had, at least in part, escaped from the narrow confines of his own tribe. Wasn't he the one who had gotten a person from the Baptist, Catholic, Calvinist and Communist tribes to work together on a combined project? Hadn't the town endorsed their work?

But that was not the way that my grandmother had viewed my father's actions. She felt that he was slipping into an unspiritual and worldly style of life. Her worries turned into a decisive action plan when she heard, from a good friend in Leeuwarden, that her two sons and Piet had participated in a Nazi march that had taken place on one of the main streets of that city. That friend had provided her with an issue of the *Fries Dageraad*, which included an article about the Nazi march and a photo in which Piet and Steward were clearly visible. That information convinced her that something had to be done. But what could she do? She knew that her younger son could be as stubborn as a bulldog if a scheme of his was being challenged.

It was Zak's fall into the canal that eventually convinced her that she must warn both of her sons that they were on the wrong spiritual path and needed to talk to Pastor Sven about the dangers of both Nazi and Communist ideologies. The idea of having them receive some mentoring from the pastor was especially attractive to Beppe because she hoped that her loquacious younger son might one day also become a pastor.

When I first saw Zak's summary of Beppe's demands, I tried to imagine what my father was thinking at the time. I was surprised that, according to Zak's notes, my dad had said nothing as he listened to his mother in that proverbial woodshed. Why had Steward mysteriously lost his voice when he was usually able to rush in and find something to say?

It took some time for me to realize that he said nothing to his mother on that day because he was fighting an internal conflict. He was unable to simultaneously say different and contradictory things that, to him, were equally important.

First, Steward had come under the personal influence of Bert Scheepema during the week immediately before Christmas. Steward, Piet, and Zak had gone to Dokkum for a long visit; it had lasted well into the evening. During that time, Bert had overwhelmed the young men with his passionate assertions that Holland had lost its way because its feuding political parties could not work together. Only the Dutch Nazi party, according to him, had the ability to unite the nation and rekindle its true Christian spirit.

Steward had been very receptive to Bert's arguments because of his own frustrations with a society in which good people were unable to earn enough money and feed their families. Wouldn't it be wonderful if a strong leader, along with a unified party, would simply tear down all the cultural walls that divide people? But how was he to explain to his mother that he had enjoyed his conversations with a Nazi?

Secondly, there was also the "Elske factor." Steward had hoped to get to know Elske better. But that plan went nowhere because the talkative Bert had invited the three young men into his home to recruit them for the Nazi party. It was only at the end of the visit that Steward was finally able to say a few awkward things to the young Elske.

By that time Piet had already presented himself to Elske as the secretary of the skating team in the two letters that he had sent to Elske before the visit. He had also received two friendly replies. He was attracted to the young woman but kept his emotions in check because he was sure that Elske, instead of liking him, would be drawn to his flashy and talkative friend, Steward.

Elske herself was repulsed by the wild ideas that her angry father was putting into words. However, she also felt that there was nothing that she could do or say to quell his ecstatic fervor. Piet noticed that Elske would shake her head when the angry tone in her father's voice became too unbearable for her. Throughout that long visit, she and Piet only spoke briefly to each other but, during that exchange, they agreed that they would try to get their parents to meet each other.

As it happened, the visit between the parents did take place, and Piet's own father was swept along by Bert's Nazi talk. Both couples were also aware that their respective children seemed to like each other. It was because of Bert's influence that Piet's dad temporarily joined the Nazi political party and voted for the Nazi representatives in the 1935 provincial elections.

But, in saying that, I am jumping two years ahead with my story. On that day, when Steward and Zak were confronted by Beppe's sharp rebuke, the dark Nazi clouds had not yet begun to cast their shadows over the daily life of the Ruintjes family. Steward certainly did not want to tell his mother that he had been attracted to Elske or assert that she was not a "Nazi girl." He also was not planning to be open about the fact that he was beginning to suspect that his best friend, Piet, liked that young woman, and that she also seemed to care for him. As he looked at his mother, Steward did not know where to begin. From Piet he knew that Elske was repelled by the Nazi movement; she believed it was a disease that was poisoning her father with a spirit of hatred.

The third cause of Steward's mysterious silence was his instinctive dislike for the young man, Klees Koorder, who lived in the city of Sebeek and had already emerged as the local leader of the regional Nazi youth movement. Klees had joined the Dutch Nazi party in 1933 and, as an articulate leader in the local Calvinist church, he was also able to convince five other young men from his church youth group to raise the Nazi flag and regularly march along the main street of their town. The tall Klees, with his commanding voice, almost always caused heads to turn in his direction when he spoke up. In comparison to Klees, who had all the physical traits of a natural leader, the short and shrill Steward felt that he was a natural underdog.

Steward's instinctive dislike for Klees was reciprocated and had family roots that reached back into the previous century. For many generations, the Koorder family had owned a small farm close to Ter Loo but, during the 1880's farm crisis, that property had slipped into bankruptcy, and Klees's grandfather had had to sell everything and leave the land. The Koorder family went through many difficult years, but they were eventually able to send their oldest son to the police academy and, in the early 1920's, that son, Gerbin, had joined the police force of Sebeek. With the stable income from his new job, Gerbin was able to leave the rural poverty of his youth behind him and create the stable urban home for his own son, Klees. Klees was obsessively proud of being a city boy and loved to mock people like Steward who came from rural Friesland, where the Koorder family had suffered decades of acute poverty and humiliation. Klees, along with his father, never forgot the fact that the 20-acre Koorder farm had been purchased by the Steward's grandfather and added to the Ruintjes estate during the previous century. Those acres were always referred to as the Koorder acres by the members of Steward's family.

As he was quietly facing his mother, Steward was thinking of Klees and his goose-stepping comrades. He disliked them, but his revulsion was mixed with feelings of both fear and jealousy. He so much wanted to be taller, to have a deeper voice and to leave the quiet rural world and live in the city. He was most envious of the fact that Klees had a group of young men around him. His own motley skater support team was only a momentary and transient success. But he also had no interest in being like Klees. From his perspective, the Koorders, as landless laborers, belonged to an inferior caste of society.

Chapter Six

The Anti-Nazi Pastor Sven
(Early January 1934)

AFTER BEPPE HAD CONFRONTED Steward and Zak about their association with the Nazis in Leeuwarden, she calmly dictated the terms that they would have to accept if they were to continue to have access to the family car. First, they had to break off all connections with the Nazi Party. Secondly, they could no longer have any contact whatsoever with the Nazi girl. Thirdly, they had to have a talk with pastor Sven because he would explain how their very souls could be poisoned by the Nazi ideology.

She had ended the mother-to-sons talk with a final word of warning: "Tomorrow I am going to see Pastor Sven and ask him if you have stopped by and visited with him yet."

Steward vented his anger when he and Zak were by themselves, and their mother was out of earshot. "We really were not Nazi marchers! We just happened to be there and only hung out with Bert and his gang for a few minutes. How could we help it that Piet and I showed up in a photo that was printed in the *Fries Dageraad*?"

As they walked down the narrow, canal-lined road that ran from their farm to the little town of Ter Loo, Zak did his best to keep up with his irate brother. Steward, in turn, almost stumbled on his own words as he said: "She never listens to me. But I do not intend to be smothered in the box that she wants me to live in."

Those harsh words first drifted across the quiet Frisian landscape and then, seconds later, they came back as an echo. When the two young men heard a faint echo of the word, "smothered," they both stopped for a second and looked at each other.

Zak used that time to pull out his small trusty notepad and write the following sentence. "I saw Douwe Kalma among the Nazi marchers in Leeuwarden this past November."

Steward read the short note and did not know what to say at first. He admired Kalma and, consequently, had read many of his nationalistic poems, novels and historical accounts. Steward and Piet had both dreamed of becoming active members of Kalma's ultra-nationalistic Youthful Frisian Society, but felt that the membership fees were too steep.

They were also avid readers of the rustic and romantic writings produced by the other authors affiliated with the Frisian movement. One of their favorite authors was Douwe Kiestra, and they had spent hours discussing his poems and short stories. They also desperately wanted to see his latest film, *Farm Agony*.

Steward, who was still angry, now directed his fury at his older brother. "You're lying! You could not have seen Kalma among those Leeuwarden marchers! He is a good Frisian man and would never change course and admire Germany. That's especially the case now that Hitler is in charge over there."

Steward's self-confidence, as later became obvious, was quite misplaced. Several of Steward's ultra-nationalistic Frisian heroes, such as Kalma and Vander Goot, would later follow a road that took them from their romantic Frisian ideology to the hyper nationalism of Hitler's Nazi party. Kalma had already started to go down that road in the early 1930's when he published the book, *Our [Frisian] Struggle* in which he tried to emulate Hitler's *Mein Kampf.*

During the World War II years, Kalma wrote numerous articles for outspoken pro-Nazi propaganda papers such as *Fryske Folk, Saxo-Frisia, Het Noordelander*, and *De Schouw*. For this Frisian nationalist, the call "Friesland above all else" had swiftly mutated into the ultra-German trumpet call of "*Deutschland Uber Alles*." During the war years, Kalma was awarded the Nazi *Harman Sylstra* prize for his contributions to the Nazi propaganda effort.

But that grim mutation of the Frisian Youth movement was still in the future in January 14, 1934 when Steward felt that he had been misunderstood by his mother. It was Zak who eventually broke through to him and convinced him to visit pastor Sven. He had not threatened his younger brother, but had simply said that if they didn't go together, he'd go by himself next morning.

The next morning Steward and Zak set out on their pilgrimage. When the parsonage came into view, they saw the pastor digging in his garden and turning over the soil. He greeted them cheerfully and told them that he had decided to dig up his garden while the heavy clay soil was still relatively dry. The brothers knew that pastor Sven was an avid gardener, and they made some small talk about when to start planting the seeds of cold-tolerating plants such as peas and spinach.

The casual conversation soon ended because Pastor Sven gently reminded the young men that he had already spoken to their mother about her worries. Then, in the same quiet voice, he said: "I don't have time to delve into those concerns today; I do, however, have time in my schedule next Monday morning at nine. Does that time work for you?"

They agreed on the time for the next meeting, and then he asked them to read a small article from a Dutch youth magazine.

He ended their brief outdoor conversation by telling them how to find the proposed reading material. "You can just open that back door of the house and you will find a small bag with the magazine in it. Oh, and feel free to bring your friends along next Monday."

On their way back to the Ruintjes farm, Steward did not say very much to Zak except to observe that he was quite relieved that the discussion with Pastor Sven had been very friendly. "He certainly does not seem to be mad at us and I'm OK with the idea of listening to him again next Monday. After that we will have done what our mother has told us to do and we can again have access to the car. I'll tell you one thing, there is no way that I am going to read that stupid article!"

Steward and Zak had no idea about what to expect from the proposed discussions, but the pastor had, as he told them much later, been mentally preparing for such a conversation for well over two years. He had just graduated from the Dutch Calvinist seminary in Kampen and had had numerous conversations with fellow students who had come from Calvinist churches in the adjacent German regions of Bentheim and Ostfriesland. Those German pastors saw how Hitler was swiftly capturing the hearts and minds of the young people in their churches; Hitler had taken control of all the ecclesiastical youth programs and channeled that religious energy into his nationwide Hitler Youth Movement. That organization was put under the direct control of an elite group of carefully selected Nazi acolytes. Church leaders who opposed the change were summarily fired or imprisoned.

Pastor Sven was acutely aware of what was happening in nearby Germany, and that was why he understood that some of the young adults in his own church denomination were attracted by the powerful energy coming from across their eastern border. He sometimes felt at loss when he tried to reach the youth in his church. Why, he would ask himself, were the children from seemingly stable Christian homes filled with such a sense of deep despair and anger? Why were so many of them ready to give expression to their anger by marching in step with Mussert and his minions? Why were they willing to help spread Hitler's message of hate in the Netherlands which, traditionally, was a peace-loving country?

After making the appointment with Steward and Zak, the pastor's eyes followed the two young men for several minutes as they disappeared down the road. He wondered if he should have had a longer conversation with them.

I should tell you, Jay, I was able to see all those musings and reflections of the pastor because they were carefully recorded in his personal diary which, after the war, was published by his wife.

After coming home, Zak carefully and repeatedly read the dark words of the article that he had received from Pastor Sven and then transcribed the following long quote in his journal:

> The Nazis pose a danger for Europe because of *their diabolical view of justice.* Their working assumption is that justice occurs when the *strongest* get their way because only those who are powerful have a right to exist. With this theory we come face to face with the devilish teachings of Nietzsche who did not beat around the bush when he wrote, "The weak and handicapped must perish. This is the most fundamental law of our philanthropy, and, for that reason, it is important that we help shove those who are weak over the edge."
>
> Nietzsche, with his vitriolic hate, saw himself as a true herald of the Antichrist and blasted the whole culture of Christianity. His sweeping condemnation [of all social services] affects the whole philanthropic infrastructure of our society. All our hospitals, orphanages, as well as our homes for the elderly and those with hearing disabilities must be burned to the ground. Nietzsche lampoons everything that elevates our societal welfare and wants to eliminate anything that, from a Christian perspective, is identified with what it really means be a human

being. Nietzsche wants nothing less than the total destruction of our present society. He doesn't care at all if large groups of people die. Happiness has nothing to do with contentment. Only power, strife and heroism can put us on the path to good fortune and only the strong are able to go down that path.

According to Hitler and his henchmen, only those who are the really strong have the right to exist. War is a natural phenomenon because it is the actual competitive setting in which the strongest demonstrate, by means of conquest, that the world belongs to them . . .

If Hitler once gets to power, there will be trouble—the spirit of war will again spontaneously erupt. Soon a door will be opened by someone, and a shadow will enter through the door. Will it be the heavily armed war god, Mars, and will he immediately take us to the darkest depths of Hell?

Or will the figure who enters the room be an angel who has a palm branch in his hand and is ready to lead us, at least for the time being, into an era of peace and prosperity? The author of Maeterlinck's dramatic story keeps the reader in deep suspense as the fearful plot unfolds.

The worldwide historical drama that is unfolding around us today would give us a heart attack if we did not know that there is a God who directs all things.

What he read made a deep impression on Zak, and before going to sleep, he added an urgent question to his trusty journal. "Why was I, as a weak person, born in an age in which there is really no room for the frail, helpless and ostracized?"

That evening he had trouble falling asleep. He kept dreaming that someone had thrown him into a canal and that he was sinking ever deeper into the icy water. His nightmare continued until Steward shook his flailing brother awake during the middle of the night.

He was still half asleep when, with a very unsteady hand, he wrote a little note to his sibling. "Thanks for waking me from a nightmare but there is something that we need to discuss tomorrow." After he put down the pencil he fell into a deep and dreamless sleep.

The note was still on his dressing table the next morning at 8 a.m. when Steward came whistling into the room and told Zak that he had done the chores for both and would have eaten all the breakfast made for the two of them if his mother had not stopped him. He then turned his eyes to the note.

"I'm not sure I want to hear about your nightmares," he said breezily, "because I don't want to pull my bed apart when I sleep." Then, a little more seriously, he added: "Tell me if there is something that I should know about, because, as always, I want to protect you from your enemies."

During two minutes of awkward silence, Zak's eyes drifted from his trusty notepad to the face of his brother and then back again. Finally, without mentioning any names, Zak wrote: "My dream was more than just a nightmare. I was pushed into a canal two days ago and I am sure it was done deliberately by the person who tripped me."

At first Steward was puzzled and asked Zak to explain himself. But when he realized that Zak had been pushed into the canal, he became very agitated. "Who did that to you?" he demanded. "Why didn't you tell me this earlier? Have you told the police? Have you told anyone in authority? Why would someone want to do something like that to you? Who else knows what took place?" Then, in a calmer, reflective tone, he added: "Was it perhaps an accident that someone bumped into you and caused you to lose your balance?"

Zak refused to answer any of those questions because he knew that his younger brother might, on impulse, attack the people who had injured him. During the previous decades Steward had, on several occasions, come home with severe injuries to his face and arms because he had fought with bullies who had, in one way or another, injured his frail and vulnerable older brother.

When he was unable to slow down the stream of questions, Zak raised his hand to call for a moment of silence. He sat down on the side of his bed, reached for his notepad, and wrote the following sentence: "I will not answer any of the questions about who attacked me until you have carefully read the article that Pastor Sven gave to us yesterday."

"Why not?" said Stewart, raising his voice. "I have the right to know who attacked you."

Zak was not intimidated by his brother's theatrics, but answered the logical "why" question. "The reason that I want you to read those articles, before I tell you more about what happened to me, is because there is a direct connection between what's written there and the motivations behind my being pushed into the canal."

Steward quickly perused the article that Zak had pointed out to him, and again told his brother to give him the name of the person who had hurt him. Zak, in turn, continued to be evasive as he penned the following note: "A group of people who believe that only the strongest have the right to live, pushed me into the canal. I do not know who it was who actually pushed me because, in the darkness, I could not see any faces clearly."

Steward did not believe that Zak, with his keen ears, had not recognized the voices of the troublemakers from Sebeek. He immediately suspected that it was some of his old rivals. "Was it Klees Koorder and his Nazi buddies who attacked you?"

From that point on Zak refused to answer any more questions. "I am not sure and so I can't say either 'yes' or 'no.'"

His brother angrily tossed each of those quiet missives into the garbage. Zak refused to divulge the full story of what had happened because he desperately hoped that he would be able to prevent open hostility from developing between his short-fused brother and Klees. There was also another factor that influenced his behavior. He had been deeply frightened by the attack and was unconsciously trying to suppress what had happened. He was, as a man of peace, unable to visualize the kind of person who would willfully attack an innocent person.

The next Monday, when the brothers sat across from Pastor Sven in his small office, the topic of war soon became the center of discussion because of a leading question asked by Sven. The brothers had wanted to forget about the events of the previous months and, for that reason, were very silent at first. They certainly did not want to talk about why they had followed behind the Nazi marchers in Leeuwarden and why they later accepted an invitation to go to the home of Elske and Bert. But Sven swiftly broke through the icy silence in the room with a surprising question that, at first, deepened the stillness in the room. "Do you think," the pastor asked, "we will soon see Mars, the god of war, coming into this small country, or will our next guest be an angel of peace who will take us out of our economic depression and into a time of prosperity?" Steward, who would normally have been eager to share his political views, remained stubbornly silent because he was still angry with both his brother and his mother for forcing him to go the pastor's study. The last thing he wanted to do was to talk about war and peace.

Zak eventually ended the long silence by writing a simple note and placing it on the table. "Mars is already in the room!" He had a frightened look on his face as he wrote those words with an unsteady hand.

The pastor looked at each of the brothers in turn before fixing his eyes on Zak and asking him to explain himself. Zak fearfully looked at the pencil that had stopped producing any more words.

There was another long tense silence before Steward eventually cleared his throat and told the pastor about the Nazi marchers in Sebeek who had shoved his brother into a canal. "I think I know the names of those guys who attacked him despite the fact Zak refuses to confirm my suspicions. Perhaps you can get it out of him. He obviously feels that those brutes represent the god of war. As for me, I don't care about the theology of what happened. My friends and I will track those monsters down and make them wish that they had not attacked Zak!"

Pastor Sven was quiet for a long time after Steward's angry outburst.

"Your statement, Steward, about the Nazi marchers," he finally said, "reminds me of the talk that I had with your mother a few days ago. She told me that she was convinced that a few weeks ago you had been swept along by some Nazi marchers while you were in Leeuwarden. She specifically wanted me to warn you about the dangers of Nazism."

In the awkward silence that again followed, Steward and Zak furtively looked at each other. The pastor finally took the conversation into a new direction by asking a very simple question. "Steward, who are the friends who are prepared to help you deal with Zak's attackers?"

At first Steward did not want to divulge any information about his friends, but soon a sense of pride got the better of him and he told the pastor how he and his friends had formed a support group for Joost during the time when he participated in the Eleven-city skating competition.

The pastor leaned back as he gently asked Steward one final question. "Do you think that your friends would be willing to help us continue this discussion about Nazi ideology?"

"I'm not sure how they would react to such an invitation," replied a dazed Steward.

Pastor Sven, looking at his watch, said that he would like to continue the discussion the following week. Zak nodded his head slightly. The pastor took this as an affirmative response to his proposal.

"Good!" He said, as he got up. "We'll meet in the council room of the church next Monday evening. There is nothing else going on, and I will see that there is some coffee for the group. I hope that your friends will also join us in our discussion."

That was the end of their first visit with Pastor Sven. Steward had dreamed of bringing his team closer together and that was what

happened during the Sven discussions that took place during the succeeding months. That closeness would eventually have a deep impact on
the lives of both of our parents. At first it drew them closer to their local
church and, eventually, it also pushed them away from that church. It
would, after the beginning of the war in 1940, also become the avenue
through which they became increasingly involved with illegal activities.
The fact that they were both members of an innocent-looking discussion
group did little, at first, to help me understand the mysterious distrust
that my father displayed towards your father after the war was over.

Chapter Seven

At a Cross-road in Life
(Late Jan. 1934)

"In the strife between Babylon and Jerusalem—between the anti-messianic and the messianic congregation—there is an iron law in play. We must, one way or another, respond to either the voice from heaven or the one from Hell."
—SCHILDER.

FROM LATER REFERENCES IN Zak's diary, I can tell you, Jay, that when he first came to Ter Loo, Pastor Sven never imagined that he would eventually get involved with a political resistance movement. Wasn't the spiritual welfare of the people of his church supposed to be his primary concern? But politics quickly bled into his church work. He saw that some people in his congregation were actively toying with the ideas that energized the Nazi movement and that troubled him because for him, the Nazis were agents of the Devil whom the followers of Christ must passionately resist. But how could he make the young men in his church see that the Christian faith and the Nazi faith were based on two utterly conflicting life commitments?

On Monday, January 21, 1934, the seven young men came to the church for the planned discussion. Steward and Zak had had no trouble convincing Piet to come along with them.

Steward had asked the other friends to come because he wanted to stay in touch with them. He had convinced Thijs Houtman to come by appealing to his Baptist missionary zeal. "Who knows, you may be able to help me bring Joost to Christ."

It also took little effort to convince the sociable Geert Grobbema to come to this gathering of young people. As a faithful member of the Catholic Church, that young man had never been inside a Calvinist church, but this baker's son was used to the Calvinist environment of Sebeek.

It took more than just talk to convince Joost Boosterman, the young Communist, to go through the door of a staunchly conservative church. Steward promised his boisterous friend that the Bible group was going to be an action group that would "do things." He did not say what they would "do," and certainly kept quiet about the promises that he had made when he convinced Hobbe Tuirman, the resident scholar, to join the group. Had he spoken to him about direct action, he would have been carefully instructed to not trust Joost because of the Communist's willingness to be allies with hostile capitalists as only a short-term strategy for gaining control of the group. Steward had often heard him express an utterly skeptical view of the Communists: "Now, when they are being beaten up by the Nazis in Spain, they are temporarily in favor of 'United Front' but, once they are in control, they will again follow their own drummer in Moscow."

Pastor Sven, as he had done with Steward and Zak during the previous week, asked a rhetorical question. "Do you believe that anyone who joins the Nazi movement is making a pact with the Devil?"

"Throughout all of Germany," he continued, "young men are joining the Hitler youth movement. Are all those young people becoming pawns of the Devil when they assist the Nazis by wearing party uniforms and marching through the German towns?"

Each of the young men in the room was absorbed with his own thoughts. Zak nursed his fear of the young Nazis who had attacked him. Thijs was troubled by the idea that he would lack the courage to talk openly about his religious faith to outspoken Hitler admirers such as Kees. Piet thought of Elske's misguided and angry father and, consequently, the question made him gloomy. Hobbe was worried that he had entered the camp of religious zealots because for him, the Nazis were only regular nationalists who were a little too passionate. Steward was troubled by the question because he was drawn to the energy of the movement, but also repelled by it because of what had happened to his brother.

Joost only clenched his fists when he thought of the Nazi movement. He was still furious with himself for not being able to help his comrades when the Nazi hoodlums had used pitched battles on the German streets to defeat them. Hitler, the new autocratic Reich Chancellor, had forced all German communists, who were not placed in prison, to go into hiding in order to escape the reach of his grasp.

It was Geert, the baker's son, who broke the uncomfortable silence with a quick-witted observation. "I do not want to be critical of anyone who is having some fun. I don't even care if those guys get a thrill out of marching down our streets. Just let them enjoy themselves as they see fit." Then, as he looked at the solemn faces around him, he ended with: "We should think of doing something that we enjoy doing because we can't just sit around here and do nothing while we endlessly wait around for our first steady job."

Geert's observation was both a light-hearted joke as well as a deep cry from the heart. All seven young men in that room had had plenty of free time to come to this impromptu gathering because they were either unemployed or under-employed.

After a few moments of sullen silence, everyone looked up in unison when Joost, with his deep booming voice, said, "yes, let's find something to do that's fun. I don't know about you guys, but I know what I enjoy doing."

That statement was greeted by many quizzical looks; Steward, however, answered the unspoken question with a wry rejoinder: "Joost likes finding things in the dark waters of the canals." While enunciating the word "canal," Steward let out a quick burst of nervous laughter.

Everyone in the group pretended that they knew all about Joost's secret passion even though they could not imagine that anyone could enjoy the work of endlessly going up and down canals to pull out mountains of filth. Zak was also puzzled by his brother's sudden laughter and, like Pastor Sven, had noticed that a quick grin had crossed Steward's face when he glanced at Joost. They both had their own dark suspicions about the details of a shared secret that united the two men.

And those worries were well founded because Steward, contrary to the promises that he had made to Zak, had gone directly to Joost and had explained to him how his brother had been pushed into the high banked Hendrikskade canal by Klees and his friends. After hearing the story, Joost had calmly told Steward not to worry. "I will teach that Nazi hoodlum a lesson he won't easily forget. In the future he will no longer think that it's fun to push someone into a canal on a cold winter day."

Joost was true to his word. Klees, earlier that same week, had been in a dreamy mood on his way back to his home in Sebeek. That Sunday he had gone to church with his girlfriend Kimke, and after the service, Kimke's dad had invited Klees to join the family for their Sunday dinner. Later, on his bike ride home, the young lover did not notice a dangerous shadow hidden in the murky darkness on the side of the road because he was still preoccupied with the memory of Kimke's sweet, soft kisses.

The shadow, of course, had been Joost. He had hidden himself behind a tree along the bank of the canal and waited until the Klees was directly beside him on his bicycle. The sun was swiftly setting on the western horizon. That was the moment when he reached out with his canal dredging tool and quietly hooked it to the back of the bike. He first caused Klees to swerve in the direction of the nearest canal and then gave the bicycle a powerful shove that sent Klees straight into the dirty water and oozing mud of that canal.

Then Joost slipped away into the gathering darkness. Even from distance he could still hear the loud curses that Klees was hurling into the misty air on that quiet Sunday evening.

After Klees had clambered up the bank, he abandoned his bicycle in the canal and set out for home. He did not accept any offers of a ride from car drivers because he was so repelled by the putrid smell that radiated from his filthy clothing. When he finally got home, he was shivering in his wet clothing and worried. Had an enemy been lurking in the darkness? In his imagination he repeatedly saw a dark claw reaching out from that tree and pushing him into the canal.

His father heard him come in and looked at his son in disbelief. "What happened to you?"

"I was pushed into the canal when I was on my way back from Kimke's home," Klees reluctantly confessed.

Mr. Koorder was not convinced by his son's story, and told him to change, wash up and get a good night's sleep so that he would no longer be afraid of phantom ghosts. "We will pull the bike out of the canal tomorrow and I will probably find out that you have again failed to keep the headlight in good repair. It is utterly dark out there, so without proper lights, anyone can bike off the road." He ended his brusque lecture with a universal parental complaint: "You never take care of your things!"

The next day Klees and his father found the place where the mishap had taken place. Mr. Koorder, as a father, had mocked his son's story about being pushed into the canal, but as a Sebeek policeman, he instinctively looked for evidence of a possible crime or prank. Were there any telltale footprints in the soft soil around the tree behind which someone might have been lurking?

After they had pulled the dripping bicycle from the canal, the policeman looked down to the foot of the same tree against which they temporarily leaned the bike. At first he thought that he had seen a fresh footprint but the water from the dripping bicycle immediately erased the evidence that might have been there. In his uncertainty he said nothing to his son about his suspicions.

Later that Monday, as he was temporarily off duty, Mr. Koorder happened to meet Pastor Sven in the bicycle store, and they had a casual conversation with each other. "It seems," Sven said, "that spring is early this year because the ice is almost completely out of the canals already." Then, looking closely at the policeman, he continued: "It seems that some people are already falling into the cold water of our many canals."

Mr. Koorder was not ready for that leading question. "Who has fallen into the canal?" he asked. "My son didn't fall into a canal but biked into one last night. He only has himself to blame because he never keeps his bike lights in good repair." There was a moment of awkward silence and then both men, at the same moment, remembered that they each had their own urgent appointment for which they were almost too late.

Pastor Sven wanted to get away from Klees's father because of a dark suspicion that was forming in his mind. The pastor knew that his own face might betray the frustrated emotions that he was feeling. He instinctively felt that Mr. Koorder, as a seasoned police officer, would quickly become suspicious if someone expressed a too keen interest in the mishap of Klees.

He also did not want to talk about Zak being pushed into the canal by Klees and his Nazi buddies because Zak and Steward had given that information to him in confidence. He also had no interest in unwittingly triggering a legal proceeding in which the words of the son of a police officer would be set against those of the good natured, frail and speech-impaired Zak.

The surge of frustrated emotions that he had felt earlier that day, when he had been in the bicycle store, were still in the back of Sven's mind as he looked at the seven young men sitting across from him in the church's council room. It all seemed so hopeless. He was, as some-times happened with him, overcome by a dark depressing mood when he thought about the power that the National Socialist movement was exerting from its base in nearby Germany. Anger had pushed Zak into the canal, and now, if he was not mistaken, that same spirit of anger had pushed Klees into another canal. In this very room, those volatile feelings now came out in the form of brutal laughter. They talked about want-ing to have some fun but were, one for one, all seething with frustration because they were walking in a desert of despair; their hopes of having even a sliver of a good life were quickly vanishing.

"Chose this day whom you will serve!" Those were the words that the Old Testament prophet had placed in front of the Israelites who had wanted to live in a "both-and" world. They wanted to *both* serve the God of Israel *and* the Baal of the adjacent nations. Sven had, through the years, often preached on that text. "Is it not clear," he would state as dramatically as possible, "that we must *only* serve our living God?"

When faced with a supernatural tour de force, the people of Israel had indeed exclaimed, "the Lord—he is God!" Before the miracle had taken place, the people had been mute; they had been silent witnesses to the spiritual battle that had been playing out before their eyes.

Sven was also silent for some time as he looked at the seven faces of the young men; he knew that they were being drawn by the magnetic power of the National Socialist myth made increasingly potent by an enflamed spirit of anger, resentment, fear, and overbearing pride. As he looked at the young eyes in front of him, he was aware that he did not have answers to any of their practical questions. He was not an Elijah who could, with God's help perform a dramatic miracle that would place a clear line in the sand and mark the difference between godly and ungodly ways of living and worshipping.

In an effort at redirecting the focus of the meeting, Sven got up and started pouring coffee into the cups that his wife had placed on the table earlier in the day. Then, in a jovial tone, he asked the group Elijah's ques-tion to the Israelites in a very indirect way. "What is one thing that we might be able to do to show that we are Christians and that demonstrates that our teachings differ from those of the Nazi movement?"

No one spoke for a long time, and even the spoons that had been used to stir the cubes of sugar in the coffee stopped moving. In that still-ness there was only one vague sound; it was as if a mouse was scratching on the back side of one of one of the panels in the room. Before long everyone in the room became aware that the curious sound was being made by Zak. He was sitting in the corner of the room and had a pencil firmly in his hand as he slowly put his thoughts into words.

Zak, after he had finished writing his note, handed it to Sven who, in turn, read it out loud. "I am afraid of Nazi anger. Help me to face my fears."

The pastor then asked the group, by a show of hands, if they would like to help Zak face his fears. Some slowly put up their hands and, before long, almost all the others also followed their lead. Steward eventually also joined the others in the show of hands. He was at the point of saying something and then only shrugged his shoulders. Joost had shaken his head ever so slightly and only half raised his hand. In the end all the hands were up.

Sven, because he didn't know where to take the discussion, took the ever-reliable call-another-meeting approach. "Great," he said, "We will again meet here at the same time in two weeks, Monday, February 4. In the next two weeks I want you to read Bible passages that deal with fear. You can find them yourselves. There are lots of situations where people in the Bible had to overcome their fears. You could look up the stories of Gideon, David, Jonathan, Daniel and his friends, or the account of Peter who denied Christ three times because he was afraid. You may finish your coffee and stay as long as you wish but, for now, the meeting is over".

There was a sudden hush in the room as everyone looked around. Joost broke the silence by getting up and putting on his coat. He noisily pushed the small sheet of paper with quotes from the Schilder book into his pocket and set out for home. The rest quickly finished their coffee and soon followed his lead. They all left with the uncomfortable feeling that they had joined a group therapy session in which participants were asked to meditate on their fears. How could one talk about something as abstract as feelings? Wasn't it a sign of weakness to even talk about such emotions? Weren't feelings like dangerous runaway horses that could pull one's life into utterly unexpected and dangerously new directions? Shouldn't emotions, for that reason, be suppressed?

Chapter Eight

Fear and Anger in Troubled Times
(February 1934)

"King Nebuchadnezzar made an image of gold, sixty cubits high and six cubits wide, and set it up on the plain of Dura in the province of Babylon. . . . Whoever does not fall and worship the image will immediately be thrown into a blazing furnace."

—THE BIBLE

ALL THE YOUNG MEN who had come to the earlier gathering, came back to the council room for the second meeting. They were all very subdued and talked amongst each other in hushed tones as they came in and found a seat. Even the talkative Steward had very little to say to the group. It was as if Zak's quiet question about fear had made them all very cautious.

Sven started the discussion by reading the Bible story taken from the book of Daniel; it was about the young Jewish men, Shadrach, Meshach, and Abednego. Those friends of Daniel had disobeyed King Nebuchadnezzar when they had refused to bow down to the king's ninety-foot golden idol that had been constructed on the Plain of Dura. The king, in anger, not only told his soldiers to burn those men alive, but also demanded that the furnace, in which those Jews would be incinerated, was to be made seven times hotter. Sven stopped his reading at the point where the three prisoners were to be thrown into the furnace that had been turned into an unapproachable inferno.

"Why," Sven asked, "was the king so viciously angry with these young Jewish men? He could have crushed them as easily as three little flies! And, secondly, how is it humanly possible that the three friends remained so utterly fearless?" Sven, who was usually calm and even tempered, became increasingly emotional and was almost breathless as he continued. "Why were the members of the pagan clergy, the astrologers, also so utterly furious with these young men? Why all this hatred? In their demented anger they were happy to burn those young Jewish men alive. Why was that?" For a moment he lowered the intensity in his voice. "The Bible is quite clear about Nebuchadnezzar's fears and uncertainties. Those three young Jewish men, with their faith in the God of heaven and earth, had placed a ninety-foot question mark in the king's mind. Perhaps he, Nebuchadnezzar, was not a god at all.

"The king, in a moment of fearful uncertainty, might also have remembered his earlier nightmare about the unstable gold-headed statue that had been obliterated by a huge rock. Hadn't he been told that he was the head of that monstrosity that would be demolished?"

Sven's voice once again became increasingly intense as he continued. "It was the hidden terrors in Nebuchadnezzar's heart that turned his anger into a hellish cauldron of hatred. Because of that fury, the three innocent young Jewish men were swiftly thrown into the seven-times-as-hot furnace."

Then the pastor stopped talking for well over a minute. The dramatic pause drew each of the young men from his own preoccupation.

Until that moment their minds had begun to drift in different directions. Steward, with a slight sneer on his face, gave the impression that he had heard this sermon before. Thijs, with an almost beatific face, had absorbed the Bible story and pictured himself on the Plain of Dura. Geert marveled at Sven's passionate telling of the story because, for him, religion called for serenity and not passion. Hobbe was his calm self and quietly took notes in which he summarized the main points that had been made. Your father Piet had also been paying attention but had a lost and somewhat worried look on his face. He could not figure out where Sven was taking them. Only Zak was utterly absorbing every word of the pastor and was busy with his pencil; he took down as much as he could with his awkward hand and finger movements.

After he had regained everyone's attention, Sven looked into the eyes of those around the table and, in a quiet voice, said: "None of you probably want to hear about Nebuchadnezzar. Wasn't it over 2600 years ago that he ruled? Why do we, in the Netherlands, have to worry about something that happened that long ago? What does all the anger and fear of that time have to do with us today? Haven't we, with our modern scientific world, banished all the ghosts and fears of the past from our lives? What is there to be afraid of?

"Or are there are still fears. The last time, Zak mentioned that he was afraid of the Nazis that walk on our streets. What are the rest of you afraid of today?"

Piet eventually broke the long silence. "I am afraid of a life which goes nowhere because I can't even find a place where I can put my feet on the ground. It seems as if everything that I touch turns into dust before I am even able to get a good hold of it."

All the other young men in the room nodded in silent agreement and sympathy.

Steward, with an impish grin, tried to break the mood of depression. "I am not afraid," he said in a loud voice. While enunciating the Dutch word for "afraid" (*bang*), he brought his right hand down onto the table with what looked like a viciously angry blow. Everyone laughed at his antics as well as at their own dark fears. They also looked, with some concern, at his hand which he quickly slid off the table and placed on his knees. Steward pretended that he had not hurt himself, but everyone could see the concern written on Zak's face as he studied the pained expression on his brother's face.

They were all still laughing when the door of the room opened, and Sven's wife stepped in. "I hope you didn't break the table," she said, "I need it to set your cups of coffee on it." As the coffee was poured and the cookie tray was respectfully passed around, Zak continued to examine Steward's face and to again steal furtive glances at his brother's bruised hand.

After the short coffee break, Sven picked up the thread of the earlier conversation. "Fear and anger can easily be a vicious good cop/bad cop team and, as such, it can easily take control of our lives. That is what happened to King Nebuchadnezzar. The hellishly hot furnace that he built was fueled by a deadly and volatile blend of both fear and anger; that explosive concoction turned king Nebuchadnezzar into a death machine.

"Isn't Nebuchadnezzar's deadly anger much like the toxic poison in the air around us today? Isn't it present in the Nazi party which wants to get into power in this country?

"I want you to listen to a selection from an article in a recent issue of your Calvinist Youth bi-weekly where Hitler is compared to the god-king Nebuchadnezzar."

> And the all-powerful Hitler made a golden statue that was as high as . . . No, it was not just 90 feet high and not just 9 feet wide—like the image of King Nebuchadnezzar in the valley of Dura. It was much higher and much wider because it was the image of the almighty [German] state.
>
> Hitler called together all his faithful servants. In fact, he reached out to the whole nation so that they could come to and bow down to the image that he had erected. . . And all the people did gather together and listen to the blaring sound of the National Socialistic trumpets, and everyone fell down and paid homage to the image of the powerful, all-knowing State.

After he finished reading the above section, Sven stopped momentarily before proceeding to the part of the article which lauded the small band of German clerics who stood up to Hitler in the early 1930's.

> Well, did everyone bow down? No, not really. In fact, one or two thousand pastors openly placed their trust in God and used that faith as a life anchor. The German Reformed pastors are few, but they didn't capitulate to Hitler when he tried to use his dictatorial governmental power to take control of their church-es. . . . Those Calvinists defended the ideal of a free church that is not beholden to the state.
>
> . . . It is less well known that some of the Roman Catholic clergy also openly opposed the anti-Christian theories and ac-tions of the National Socialists. By means of a series of sermons, Cardinal Faulhaber has also openly confronted religious Nazis who belong to the so-called "North German" faith movement. That false faith, as promoted by Hitler and Rosenberg, is a re-vival of ancient Germanic paganism . . . Cardinal Faulhaber also did not kneel . . . when commanded to do so by the sound of the National Socialist trumpets.

Geert had been listening intensely as Sven read the passage about Cardinal Faulhaber. He was surprised to learn about Catholic resistance because he was keenly aware of the compromising Concordat that the Pope had signed with Hitler. Sven first looked at Geert, but then looked at each one in the group in turn, saying in a terse voice: "No Christian is exempt from the challenge. We are all standing on the Plain of Dura. There is no place to hide in our modern world, and that's why everyone can see when we are standing up and also when we are bowing down to false gods. For all of us there is the problem of fear. We are all afraid of the worldly powers that are looming on the horizon; we are simply terrified by both Hitler and Stalin, and, in fear, our knees become weak."

Then he continued to read another excerpt from the same short article:

> Will Nebuchadnezzar-Hitler, in his grim and fierce anger, call those Protestant and Catholic believers into his presence and punish them severely? Or will he, like his colleague Mussolini, put water into his National Socialist wine? The answer from those churchmen will most certainly be the same as the answer that the three young Jewish men in Babylon gave to King Nebuchadnezzar: "Be that as it may, Our God, whom we serve has the power to save us. But even if he does not actually save us, you should know, O Dictator, that we will not worship your gods nor the golden image that you have erected."—Kroniek

As pastor Sven read that last passage, the dark and ominous tone left his voice because the word "fear" was less clearly etched in his mind. "Shadrach, Meshach and Abednego knew, from their friend Daniel, about Nebuchadnezzar's earlier nightmare of the golden headed image with clay feet and about the miraculous rock which, after rolling down the mountain, had pulverized that ugly monstrosity. That rock, in turn, grew into a mountain that filled the earth. They knew, as they stood before the raging furnace, that Nebuchadnezzar's ugly statue was standing in the shadow of their God who was as majestic, as a vast mountain. In faith they saw that majesty and not the overheated furnace."

Sven, after talking about the courage of Daniel's three friends, began to read from the book of Daniel. "The king's command was so urgent and the furnace so hot that the flames of the fire killed those soldiers; they had been among the strongest fighters in his army." The pastor then stopped reading for a long time as he looked at all the different expressions on the faces of the young men facing him.

"The strongest among you have the most to fear from this Hitler-Nebuchadnezzar monster because you are the ones who will be doing the dirty work for him. You will be treated just like the powerful soldiers who had to throw the three young Jewish men into that Babylonian cauldron.

Those strongmen were burnt to death by the white-hot anger and fear that caused them to come too close to the fire when they carried out the king's ghoulish death sentences. Hitler, in the same way, also wants supermen to work for him. He will command such guys to walk into fires for him. There is no room, in his kingdom, for the weak, the frail and those with imperfect genetic material."

During the moment of silence, pastor Sven's eyes rested on Zak who, in turn, shifted uneasily in his chair because he was embarrassed for having admitted that he had been scared. During that silent intermezzo, it appeared as if Sven was going to continue talking, but, instead, he abruptly asked if there were any questions. Everyone remained silent, so he welcomed everyone to come back in fourteen days.

Steward and Zak were the last to leave because it always took the awkward Zak a long time to put on his coat and to painstakingly fasten all his buttons. As the two brothers were finally prepared to go, Pastor Sven approached them and, looking at Steward, asked: "May I ask you do me a small favor?"

Steward and Zak both looked at each other in puzzlement and then, inquisitively, at Pastor Sven. Steward had no idea of what was on the pastor's mind. "No problem," he said with some hesitation. "What's up?"

Pastor Sven eyed Steward closely. "I want you to help me find the person who pushed Klees into a canal north of Sebeek."

There was a long silence in the room as Steward's face became increasingly red. Zak thought that his brother would express his feelings of anger and, instinctively, stepped away from him. Pastor Sven did not flinch as he continued to calmly let his eyes rest on the young man whom he would, in later years, tease for being as impetuous as King Jehu. Steward controlled his frustration as he half-heartedly said that he would try to be helpful. There was also some puzzlement in his voice as he half looked in the direction of the pastor to ask him whatever made him think that he could help him find the person who might have done something to Klees."

Sven then told the brothers about the conversation that he had had with Klees' father, and that he felt that he needed some help to find out what had happened. "I am, of course, deeply upset with the Nazi movement and I'm also troubled by what Klees may have done to your brother. But we will not douse the Nazi fire by throwing adherents of the movement into canals. As Christians, we should not respond to these troublemakers by imitating their actions.

Steward first looked at the floor, and then he abruptly started for the door. He waved to Zak and, in a muted Sunday voice, thanked the pastor for the discussion and then swiftly stepped outside. He had no desire to spend more time with a man who seemed to have the skills of an inquisitor.

What neither Steward nor Pastor Sven knew, at that time, was that Klees had also gotten into trouble with his father. I was able to reconstruct that part of the story from the post WWII Dutch court records. After the Netherlands was liberated from German occupation, Klees, like many Dutch Nazis, was imprisoned for many years. He had been sentenced by the judicial branch of the newly formed Dutch government. The transcripts of those proceedings have provided me with a compelling insight into the life of this young Nazi.

Mr. Koorder had, at first, laughed off his son's assertion that someone had pushed him into the canal, but with time, he became increasingly obsessed with the worry that there might have been some foul play in the picture. As a policeman, he could be tough with anyone who disobeyed the law, but that severity did not extend to his domestic life. He was a proud father who routinely overlooked the shortcomings of his tall, broad-shouldered son. He let everyone know why he was sending Klees to the elite High School or *gymnasium*. "There he can get the kind of quality education that I was not able to receive because my dad was too poor, and I had to start working at the age of fourteen." He was glad that Klees was much more politically active than he himself had ever been. He was often frustrated that he had had no time for politics, and was often completely tongue-tied when faced with a discussion involving political theories. He would, consequently, beam when he heard his son effortlessly use arcane political terms. He was especially proud of the young man's proficiency in the German language.

As a staunch Calvinist party man, Mr. Koorder had been only slightly disturbed when Klees began to openly mock the ideas and political platform of his party. "Isn't it good" the proud father would tell himself, that a young man can think for himself and ask tough questions?" Sometimes he would attempt to challenge his son's cynicism but, as a rule, he quietly listened to him. During the 1920's, Koorder had always strongly supported the Calvinist leader, Colijn, but in recent months, he often heard himself say that perhaps Colijn was all wrong about tenaciously holding onto the gold standard, that that policy might indeed be destroying the Dutch economy. He also agreed with his son that preachers like pastor Sven should stick to their church business and not meddle with the secular world of politics.

Mr. Koorder did, however, become obsessively anxious when he discovered that his son had started a subscription to the Dutch Nazi newspaper, *Volk en Vaderland*. He became almost desperate when the young man, in 1933, joined the Dutch Nazi party, regularly attended all party meetings, and actively participated in the numerous military rallies and protests. Even then, Mr. Koorder kept his worries to himself. Wasn't his son, after all, a good kid who would naturally mature and abandon ill-advised youthful infatuations?

As the weeks and months passed, he repeatedly mentioned to his wife that perhaps he should, after all, take things in hand and have a serious conversation with their son about his Nazi activities. He, as a Sebeek policeman, was a government employee and, as such, was not allowed to be a member of the Nazi party. His son was not affected by that rule, but it did not look good that someone from his own family belonged to a forbidden organization. He was especially worried about the social fallout that could result from his son's activities. Klees and his friends made their Nazi sympathies crystal clear to all the citizens of Sebeek as they regularly marched around town in their party uniforms.

Mr. Koorder had repeatedly postponed the time for the heart-to-heart talk with his son. It was his son's canal mishap that finally convinced him that he would have to act by having a frank conversation with Klees. The footprint by the tree convinced him that his son had already created enemies who wanted to hurt him. Several times, during the previous month, he had been approached by people on the street who had asked him if he knew about his son's Nazi activities. As a responsible parent who also had a very public job, he could not allow his son to continue being a member of the Dutch Nazi party.

The cordial father-son conversation that eventually took place produced an outcome with which Mr. Koorder was happy. Klees had respectfully listened as his father voiced the worries that were on his mind. He had ended with: "I am proud of you, my son, but your involvement with the Nazi party is not good for us as a family. It could hurt your future career as well as make my job more difficult!" There was a pained twang in his voice when he uttered the word "hurt."

He immediately regained his normally calm demeanor as he ended with an open question. "What do you think, son. Do you understand my concerns?"

Klees, who had been quietly nodding his head, said that he fully understood what his father was telling him and would do everything necessary to protect the family and his father's career. He told him that he and his friends would stop their regular marches through Sebeek and that they would stop wearing their Nazi uniforms. Mr. Koorder had also planned to bring up the topic of his son's subscription to the Nazi newspaper. His son, without even being asked, told his father that he would terminate his subscription to the *Volk and Vaderland*. Also, without being explicitly asked to do so, he told his father that he would write the people at the Nazi headquarters and ask them to remove his name from the party's membership roster.

Mr. Klooster was ecstatic with his son's apparent willingness to cut ties with the Nazis. What Klees did not tell his father was that Mussert, the Dutch Nazi leader, not only knew all about the government law making it illegal for civil employees to belong to the party, but had also found a simple subterfuge. People who could not legally remain a member of his Nazi party, could ask to have their names added to a hidden membership list. Klees asked the party to put his name on that secret list in 1934 during the same week he told his father that he would put a stop to his Nazi membership. He saw nothing wrong with this decision. Wasn't he both saving the face of the family and protecting his father's career as a policeman of Sebeek? Wasn't he, as the Bible taught him, obeying his father and mother?

As a nominally dutiful son, Klees also told his Nazi comrades that he was no longer allowed to march around town with them and that he would also not be able to attend the bi-weekly party meetings because he was no longer a member of the organization. "My father wants me to withdraw from all party activities." As he shared this news, he looked around to the other young men in the group and said, in a sad tone, "Your parents are probably also worried about your Nazi activities." Almost all those who were present nodded their heads.

It was then that he said, "I know what we should do! We can still meet every other week, not as a political party, but as a book club. We can, for example, discuss writings by the authors of the Young Frisian Movement. We can also still march together, but we will do it as a local exercise club. It will help us stay both mentally and physically fit and we never have to talk about our Nazi connections!"

What Klees presented to his fellow party members was not the result of a sudden inspiration but part of the general strategy that the Dutch

Nazis often used to circumvent restrictions that were being placed on their organization.

The Young Frisian Book club was a runaway success from the very beginning. The first meeting, on March 22, 1934, was a public event to which everyone in Sebeek and the surrounding area was invited. It was well publicized, and several people who attended the event became regular club members.

Klees was especially proud of himself for the fact that he had been able to convince Jan Melle van der Goot to be the keynote speaker and discussion leader. Van der Goot was still working on his book *Renewal of our Civilization*, and had the ability to speak with deep passion about power that he saw hidden in the Frisian Nazi ideology.

Piet, Zak, and Steward had heard about the upcoming meeting that was, they were told, sponsored by a society that had the name "Our Frisian Nation." They expected to learn more about the novels that Van der Goot was working on and had looked forward to a relaxing evening. They did not know that the innocent sounding sponsoring society was a local Nazi party that had taken on a different name.

When they entered the crowded meeting room, Zak was the first to notice that Klees was the tall man standing by the podium and preparing to introduce Van der Goot. Zak, with an instinctive feeling of panic, scanned the room for an inconspicuous place to sit. He found three available seats in the very back of the auditorium and dove toward them. His brother and Piet joined him more slowly because neither of them was, at that time, aware that Klees was in the room.

Soon Zak took out his trusty pencil and paper, and as quickly as his clumsy fingers could work, made a detailed summary of the lecture which, it turned out, was organized around four rhetorical questions. Zak became increasingly upset as Van Der Goot peppered the audience with his bombastic challenges. At some later date, Zak placed red check marks adjacent to each of speaker's talking points.

Now, years later, as I look at Zak's small red checkmarks, it seems as if a slow metamorphosis has taken place during the intervening years because each of Zak's tiny marks have turned into huge grotesque red meat hooks on which the ugliest parts of the Nazi body politic had been strung up in the same way that a butcher hangs a carcass from the ceiling before cutting it up. The meat hooks are still there, but the putrid carcasses have turned into the dust of history.

The first questioning hook that Van der Goot placed in the air in front of his audience was designed to mobilize the minds behind the pinched, unhappy, and hungry faces that, each day, looked at hands that were not working. "Don't we," he asked his listeners, "have the right to be happy and courageous as we live in this world?" After he roared with the two words, "joy" and "courage," his audience burst out with thundering applause. He didn't say it, but everyone in the audience knew that Hitler had institutionalized those concepts in his department of leisure affairs; it was known as the Strength through Joy Department and, through it, the dictator had made the grandiose promise that every worker could soon take a real vacation.

The second hook that he dangled in the air was designed to appeal to the regional and ethnic pride of his listeners. "Should Frisians, with their energy, honesty, down-to-earth nature, and pure Germanic blood, not lay claim to the truth that they belong to a superior ethnic group?" The rustic myth behind that fearful hook had already been sharpened by a whole generation of writers who belonged to the Young Frisian movement.

The third hook that he placed in the air also reflected his deep and hate-filled racism. "Shouldn't we protect the purity of our Frisian blood by making sure that we do not sin against nature by allowing ourselves to be tainted by the blood of people who are inferior?" Like others in the Dutch Nazi movement, his deep and poisonous racism was the bedrock of his anti-Semitism.

Steward, Zak and Piet began to feel very uncomfortable with the speaker when he hung the third hook in the room. It was the fourth question that finally caused Zak to abruptly get up and leave. Steward and Piet took one look at Zak's troubled face and followed him out of the room. Van Der Goot had been lampooning the religious and cultural organizations of society by saying that they were not rooted in the soil of reality. "As honest and earth-bound Frisians, who have their feet solidly on the natural soil, isn't it absurd that we still listen to the hypocrisy and lies of the church? Doesn't all that heaven talk pull us away from who we really are—people of flesh and blood?"

Once they were outside, Steward asked the three questions that were on each of their minds. "Was Van der Goot really suggesting that we go back to a form of ancient paganism?" As they walked a little further down the street, they began to ask themselves why they had stayed so long. Hadn't they become increasingly uncomfortable with the talk. Instantly Zak got out his little pad and wrote: "Klees?" Steward picked up the question immediately. "What was Klees doing there? Why did he introduce the speaker? Why were all his Nazi friends greeting us at the door with the program and why had seats been reserved for each of those friends in the front row?"

These questions troubled the young men as they bicycled against a strong and cold westerly wind. It wasn't until a few weeks later that they would discover that the local chapter of the Nazi party had indeed been behind the book discussion meeting. For the next several years it continued to masquerade as a book discussion group and as such, was the medium used by the local Nazi leaders to battle for the minds of the young people.

When Piet, Zak and Steward fled from the book club meeting, they symbolically distanced themselves from the local Nazi party. It still took six more years before those sharp differences resulted in open conflicts.

Chapter Nine

Who Is our Leader?
(Summer 1934)

"[Hitler's high priest Rosenberg] . . . wants to turn all Christian churches into places of pagan Nazi worship . . . [and get rid of the] Jewish Christ who has, [according to his Nazi ideology,] been poisoning the pure blood of the German race during the past centuries."

—Kroniek

As you know, Jay, the ultimate trajectory of Hitler's future empire was already clearly visible in 1934, but all too often, eyes don't see the clear images that are placed before them, and human ears block out the loud sounds that the person does not want to hear.

The people of the Netherlands, like most people in the rest of the world during that time, lived in a state of deep denial and closed their eyes to the fact that Hitler was turning Germany into a vast military fortress. Most Dutchmen felt that if a new world war should break out, they would be safely protected by the historic neutrality of their nation.

When Zak, Steward, and Piet, on March 25, 1934, came to their bi-weekly Ter Loo meeting, they were warmly greeted by the pastor. They were surprised when he told them that he had also attended the so-called book club discussion during the previous week. "I already knew that Jan Melle Van der Goot was an outspoken Fascist," he said with a sigh. "But, during that meeting, I was still taken aback by the depth of his commitment to the racist paganism promoted by Rosenberg and Hitler."

Sven tried, in different ways, to illustrate that it was the "spirit of the Antichrist" that gave energy to the Nazi movement. Hitler, he argued, had made a Faustian bargain with the Devil when he appointed Rosenberg as the spiritual leader of Germany. At one point, he took the group page by page through the four long 1934 articles that explored Rosenberg's dangerous racist theology. Despite all that effort, he often felt that he was getting nowhere. The young men didn't comprehend what he tried to say because they didn't see the connection between politics and the theological concepts that he was using.

One Monday in April 1934, as the young men were leaving and silently drifting into a moonlit night that was filled with the rich sounds and smells of an early spring, he watched them for a long time before they disappeared in the distance. While standing there, he again heard his own voice as he gave expression to the eternal first question that is asked in the Calvinist Heidelberg Catechism of 1562: "What is your only hope in life and in death?"

He still remembered how the young men had, in unison, answered "My only hope in life and death as well in body and in my soul is that I am not my own, but belong to my faithful Savior, Jesus Christ." Most of them had memorized that faith statement from their church. Then he repeated the same question and applied it to Rosenberg. "What does Rosenberg, in effect say about where he finds his only hope in life and in death?" After they had stumbled around for a time, he took them to a quote from the article which they had studied. "Rosenberg's only hope in life and in death is a life of passionate service to the racially purified German state that is under the leadership of Hitler."

While staring into the darkness of the night, he could still hear the slight echo of his voice as he loudly proclaimed: "The Zoroastrian leader, Nietzsche doesn't care a whit for the people of God and their sacrificial love. Such men act like Hophni and Phinehas, the sons of Eli, who stole the gift offerings that people brought to the temple. Instead of being leaders, such men are common thieves who stuff their own bellies with the best meat that they steal from their followers. They are scoundrels who spawn orphans which end up having apocalyptic names such as 'Ichabod' or 'Hopeless.' That was the name of Eli's newborn orphan grandson."

As he continued to stand in the darkness, he remembered that he still had to tuck his own young son into bed. But it seemed as if he was unable to move. He remained rooted to the spot where he was standing.

That was when he felt a light touch on his shoulder from the hand of his wife, Aukje, and he silently drank up the tender tone of her alto voice. "You've got to come inside," she said. "It's too cold to stand out here much longer. You don't have to worry about those guys. They'll be OK."

Emerging from his dark reverie, he turned around and tightly hugged his wife. He then kissed her and, in mock seriousness, whispered in her right ear: "You turn all mountains into mole hills! Shame on you! I want to climb mountains!"

She laughed gaily as they walked, hand in hand, back into the nearby parsonage. He went to his little son's bedroom and quietly tucked him in and listened to his even breathing. He then tiptoed out of the room again. He was supposed to have read the Bible story and say the evening prayers, but that would have to wait because he wasn't about to awaken the young guy from a gloriously deep sleep.

When he came back into the living, room his wife gave him a letter from his close friend Gert Schrovenwever, a Calvinist pastor in the nearby German town of Velsen. He opened the letter and they both took a deep breath before he started to read it out loud. There was nothing about Nazi persecution in the letter, but their friend Gert did tell them that he was going to be a German delegate at the May 10, 1934 Zwolle Calvinist youth conference and that he had also been selected to be one of the speakers. He did not say what the topic of his talk was going to be.

"You should go to that conference," said Aukje with her hand still on his shoulder, "and catch up with Gert. And you should take the young men in your group along with you. Isn't there some money in the church budget to help defray their costs? It would be a great outing for them."

"This letter settles it," he said. "Come hell or high water, I will find the money so that those guys can go to Zwolle." He again hugged his wife for her suggestion. They both knew that the annual conference was the highlight of their Calvinist church's youth program.

Pastor Sven and the young men from Ter Loo arrived at Zwolle on the first train that had come from Leeuwarden on May 10, 1934.

Religious freedom in the age of Hitler was the theme of the youth conference. For the 4500 young Calvinist attendees it was a genuinely exciting outing. The day turned out to be bright and sunny. For the Ter Loo group, it was a time during which they could momentarily escape from the economic depression that was tearing away at their lives.

Some of the speakers addressed their audiences in one of the local churches, but the main part of the conference took place in the civic center known as the *Buitensocieteit*. That's where the young men from Ter Loo went to listen to their first speech. They were all amazed by the sounds of the thousands of attendees as well as by the size of the full auditorium. The only seats that they could find were near the front.

There was a buoyant exuberance in the air as the Minister of Internal Affairs, Mr. De Wilde, stepped in front the podium and calmly began to address the topic of freedom. "A man of principle is a free man." The young men listened respectfully to the seasoned politician. They had expected it to be a day of Christian renewal and what they heard were words of assurance from a man who was not only a government cabinet member, but who also belonged to their Calvinist church and political party. He assured his listeners that Colijn, their party and national leader, based his policies on an immovable value system. "He will not be swept away by pragmatic considerations; his moral compass is firmly in place."

The young listeners in the audience were also told that a document explaining the political platform of their Calvinist party was already at the press and would soon be available. The book would have the title *At Peace in the Middle of the Storm*. There was loud applause when the seasoned politician ended his speech with a challenge for his young listeners. "To have that kind of peace you must stay true to your Calvinist value system and not succumb to the fascist ideals that are based on pure power politics."

In his notebook Zak gave a brief summary of De Wilde's speech and observed that some of the listeners, instead of clapping, kept their arms firmly crossed. They did not support a party that was supposed to lead the country but seemed incapable of helping people during an increasingly difficult time in their life. Several of those listeners raised their hands but the chair only recognized them by announcing that during the next hour, De Wilde would be in the foyer of this building and would answer any specific questions they might want to ask him.

It was Joost who took the chairman up on the offer and went to the foyer. He was somewhat awestruck when De Wilde showed up and told his listeners that he was ready for their questions. "You Calvinists are clear thinkers and will ask hard questions. Go for it."

Joost later told his friends what happened next. As a Communist, he had felt a bit uncomfortable about masquerading as a Calvinist, so he was thinking of quietly leaving when, from behind him, he heard someone challenging the elderly statesman with a stream of audacious questions. "Why can't your party get this country back on track? You are, with your trade policy and your fanatical attachment to the gold standard, destroy-ing industry. You try to tell us that we, as Calvinists, can be at peace in these troubled times. Are you guys drugged? This is no time to be asleep because the world is being ripped apart around us! Tell me why I am wrong with my worries! You claim, with your *Peace in the Middle of a Storm*, to be following the leadership of William of Orange who also used that motto. But that great man, the father of our fatherland, was a genuine leader who knew how to get things done. He may have been at peace during a time of war, but he didn't hide himself behind a smokescreen of words as the country was burning to the ground!"

Many of the young men in that foyer were stunned by the youth-ful challenger's brazen questions. But no one stopped him, and all eyes turned expectantly to the senior statesman who would know what to say. But De Wilde was also caught off guard by the young man who was just getting started and threw all caution out of the window as he continued. "You address us as 'Calvinists' but I want to be known as a 'Christian.' With your talk about being at peace in the middle of the storm, you high-handedly think of yourself as Christ who was not troubled by the storm in the Sea of Galilee. Christ was a man of power. Are you Calvinist lead-ers really men of power like Christ, or is the Calvinist party more like a man who is asleep at the wheel? Could it be that Calvinists have become like the prophet Jonah? He was also asleep in the middle of a storm be-cause he was a coward and hypocrite. He ran away from doing what he was supposed to do."

The words "coward" and "hypocrite" were still hovering in the air when those who were in the foyer became restless and started to quietly move towards the exits. De Wilde also seemed to finally come out of a kind of coma and, with his walking stick swaying, briskly left the foyer area and went outside. That was the point when Joost finally felt free to look back at the audacious questioner who had been standing directly behind him. He was stunned when he realized that Klees, standing next to two of his Nazi buddies, was the young man who had thrown those explosive questions at the stately De Wilde, and now he was basking in the appreciative grins of his friends. In their self-absorption the three Nazis from Sebeek hadn't even recognized Joost who, in turn, swiftly left the foyer and joined up with the Ter Loo group again.

The second convention speech that made a deep impression on Zak was the one made by Sven's friend and classmate, Gert Schrovenwever, who had just arrived by the morning train from the Germany. Sven and Gert had both graduated from the Calvinist seminary in the Dutch town of Kampen and each, on opposite sides of the Dutch/German border, had already served as pastors in small rural churches for almost three years.

When Schrovenwever stepped up to the podium he did not, like De Wilde, radiate an air of power and authority. The pastor was not a seasoned politician and did not try to rally his listeners to the flag of a Dutch Calvinist political party. His presentation was much more intimate and personal.

As the tall, gangly young man with his long nose and wavy hair, stood up to speak, everyone had to listen carefully to hear him as he spoke about difficulties that his small German Calvinist church in Velsen had been facing during the preceding years. "The youth organization in our Church can no longer meet freely. We have, in fact, quietly disbanded it and burned all records associated with it. If we had not taken those precautionary steps, it would have been absorbed into the national Hitler Youth program. The approximately thirty young people, who continue meet, avoid the Nazi government interference by having their bible studies in private homes."

When Schrovenwever first came to the podium it was difficult to hear him, but he became increasingly more audible as his speech began to unfold. There was fierce intensity in his voice that not only buoyed the volume of his presentation, but also caused all the young men in his audience to listen to his every word. There wasn't a rustle in his audience as he described the deep challenges that he and his German church were facing. Many young knuckles in the audience tightened as the pastor began to move toward the climactic ending. "We know from our history that when our soldiers are in the middle of an intense battle, they always pull together and, in unison, raise the battle cry, '*Rally around the Prince.*'"

The pastor proclaimed those last four words like a trumpet blast. The large assembly was utterly silent as the words "Prince" or "leader" resonated through the large auditorium.

After a dramatic pause, the pastor asked the question that was on everyone's mind. "But who, for a Christ follower like me, is my true Prince?" He stated the question in German, but everyone understood exactly what he was saying. He again paused for a moment before ending his address with a prayer-like meditation that everyone had to strain to hear even though there was absolute silence in the large auditorium. "I will only give my true allegiance to Christ who is my Prince and my Salvation."

In his notebook Zak added many red checkmarks to his summary of that the young pastor's speech, and noted that it had made a profound impression on those attending the conference. The morning session had ended with a rousing singing of Luther's song "A Mighty Fortress is our God." In his journal Zak copied down what he felt were the most moving sentences from that song.

> "And though this world, with devils filled. . .
> We will not fear, for God has willed.
> His truth to triumph through us.
> Let goods and kindred go,
> This mortal life also;
> The body they may kill
> God's truth abideth still.
> His kingdom is forever."

Chapter Ten

Steward and Piet Start to Drift Apart
(1935–1940)

As I STUDIED THE entries in Zak's pre-war journal, it became increasingly clear to me that the friendship between Piet and Steward was gradually being undermined by persistent tensions. What caused the disagreements between them? Was the rift the natural result of the fact that they, as young men in their twenties, were no longer teenagers? Did the women in their lives cause the friendship to become less important in their lives? By 1940, Piet was already married to Elske, and Steward was engaged to Marijke, whom he married in 1941.

I could never determine precisely what the problem was. What I did see in Zak's journals, is that with each passing year, their arguments became increasingly fierce. Their disagreements were partly rooted in character differences. Piet, as an instinctive pacifist, always wanted to ponder issues before taking action, while Steward was a risk-taker and a compulsive activist.

The temperamental differences between the old friends would, with increasing frequency, come into bold relief in the church youth group settings when political topics were discussed. The small Calvinist church of Ter Loo did not have its own youth program because Piet, Zak, and Steward were the only teenagers in that church during the 1930's. The three of them consequently joined a church youth group in the adjacent town of Terperdam; that group went by the name, the Mustard Seed Youth Society.

One day, during open discussion time in that youth group, Steward launched into a long jeremiad about how dreadful their Calvinist (ARP) party actually was. "Colijn, our leader, wants us all to take a sleeping pill and blissfully forget about the troubled seas around us. It doesn't help us if we tell ourselves that we can be at ease in the middle of the economic depression that is wrecking our land. Our Calvinist party has become a do-nothing club where endless talking is viewed as doing something. We need to get rid of Colijn and get a leader who does something."

Piet was usually a peace maker, but this time he was provoked by his friend's abrasiveness. "Do you, like Klees, want to abandon our party and give your allegiance to the Nazi party of Mussert?"

At the mention of the name of his archrival, Steward immediately redirected his attack. "We simply can't allow Nazis like Klees to be the chair of our regional Calvinist youth organization. He has to go!"

Steward then pulled a recent issue of Schilder's paper, *De Reformatie* out of his pocket. "Schilder says the same thing that I'm saying," he said as he unfolded it.

His hands trembled as he read a selection from one of Schilder's articles: "The Dutch Nazi Movement talks, acts and teaches in a manner that is in direct conflict with what Christianity stands for."

Zak, in his notebook, included a quote from Proverbs which indicated that he sided with his brother in this ballooning dispute. "Like a muddied spring or a polluted well are the righteous who give way to the wicked."

Piet did not agree or disagree with his friend, but said he would bring it up as a topic for discussion at the next Mustard Seed meeting."

From Zak's journal I could tell that Piet was true to his word and the "Klees problem" was discussed at length by the youth group at their regular meeting during the last week of January 1935. Eventually a petition, asking that Klees be removed from his leadership position, was sent to the church's regional assembly. That august body set up a committee that was instructed to meet with Klees and his father. Pastor Sven, who had asked to be on the committee, was not appointed because it was felt that the "Klees problem" should be quietly resolved and that there should not be any "open confrontations."

By the end of March 1935, pastor Bolstra reported to the Mustard Seed club that their committee had had a "calm and spiritual" discussion with Klees and his father and that their group no longer needed to be troubled by the leadership that Klees was providing to the Calvinist youth movement in the area. "He is no longer a member of the Nazi Party and is deeply committed to the spiritual welfare of the young people in our area."

The elderly pastor Bolstra looked directly at Steward when he ended his comments with the pointed observation: "Now we need to put this behind us and we must make sure that personal feelings do not get in the way as we joyfully move forward into the future. Sinful feelings that we have can wreck many good things in the Kingdom of God."

Zak, in his summary of this March 1935 youth meeting, made a little side note. "Steward was not very happy when Pastor Bolstra was speaking. I had to tug at his sleeve to prevent him from bursting out with what was on his mind. I left the meeting abruptly and he quickly followed me and spoke to no one."

As they fought against the strong westerly wind on that cold day, Zak could barely keep up with his younger brother who was again pressing all his pent-up emotions into the pedals of his bicycle. When they got home, Steward announced with a clenched fist, "We have to do something about Klees!"

The first thing that they did was to pay a visit to Pastor Sven to see how he felt about the benign way that the regional church committee was permitting a Nazi to be the regional leader of their Christian youth group.

Sven listened to them thoughtfully and shared their concerns about Klees' Nazi sympathies, but he also felt that they had done all they could do to remove him from his position as regional youth leader. "I will write up my concerns for the national synod of our church; it is due to meet this coming summer. I hope that, at the national level, we can get some clarity when we, as a church, affirm that membership in the Dutch Nazi party is not an option for those who are professing Christians. Such members should, most certainly, not be youth leaders in our churches!"

As pastor Sven spoke about the path of church politics that he was planning to follow, Steward only stared at the ground. He was sure that all formal statements that might come from the august and elevated heights of the national council of their Calvinist church were, by definition, impotent; they would not in any way change the way that actual people lived their lives.

Sven was not able to penetrate the passive-aggressive barrier that Steward had erected around himself until he said, as if in an afterthought, "As you know, we are entering an election season. Why don't you reassemble your team and, as a group, promote one or two of the non-Nazi parties and, at the same time, do everything to challenge the regional activities of the Nazi propaganda machine?"

The idea of doing something active to resist the Dutch Nazi movement quickly became a new obsession for Steward, but his friend Piet repeatedly asked him to cool down. He did, however, grudgingly agree to help him rebuild their team.

Steward's old team became alive again for a period of two months before the 1935 Dutch provincial election. They tried, in several small ways, to undermine the political campaign of the Dutch Nazi party in Ter Loo and the surrounding region. Piet and Hobbe were the brains of the group, and they deliberately went to all Nazi public meetings in the area and openly challenged the speakers. They prepared for those debates by reading the Nazi program brochures as well as reading the writings of Nazi critics such as Smeek, Schilder, Janse, and Kohnstamm.

Geert and Thijs were the members of the team who did the work of reaching out to people personally. They first compiled a list of the names of people who had come to the Nazi meetings and then they visited all those people and, with their personal charm, attempted to convince them to vote for the candidates of the party that they had voted for in the previous election, and not vote for any Nazi party candidates.

Joost and Steward viewed themselves as the "direct action team." They openly confronted the Nazi squads in a variety of ways. From spies within the Nazi party, they found out when and where publicity teams planned to paste their garish posters on walls, doors, and gates. Before the glue had even dried, Joost or Steward would quietly peel the offensive material off the surfaces to which it had been glued. Zak felt that, at times, the "direct action team" went too far. He suspected, for example, that on more than one occasion his brother may have punctured the tires of cars that were used to bring speakers to the Nazi rallies.

Zak functioned as the eyes and ears of the group. Because he was so silent, people paid no attention to him, and they often spoke freely in his presence and, in the process, provided him with valuable information that the whole group could use.

In early May 1935, Steward's team celebrated their successful political activism when, after the election, it became clear that the Nazis had performed poorly in all of Friesland and that it had received almost no votes from either Ter Loo or the surrounding towns. Nationally, the party had gained almost 8% of the popular vote but, in Friesland, the vote was only 3.2%. Near Ter Loo only 0.2% of the population had voted for the Nazi party.

At that celebratory party, Steward had a little too much alcohol when he announced to the whole group: "We placed some gashes on the head of the Nazi party in this area and we also lobbed off some toes of its operational feet. Next time we need to chop off its head and get rid of it!"

He waited for applause from his friends, but Hobbe, with a solemn face, put a severe damper on the party spirit. "The Dutch Nazi Party." he said, "is only a small twig of a vast tree that has not only firmly established its roots in Germany, Italy, and Japan, but its rootlets also draw moisture from the soil here in Friesland." As he spoke, he stamped on the ground. "I can't even imagine how many lumberjacks we will need if we really want to cut down that tree."

"Well at least we made some noise," Stewart shot back, "and we scared a few black crows out of that tree. And we should continue to make noise."

Joost raised his glass. "Three cheers for us noise makers!"

Everyone laughed at the image of scaring off flocks of the black birds that sometimes sheltered in the branches of the largest trees in the area. For the whole group, the laughter felt good. The result of this campaign against the Nazis was that Steward's team, despite some differences, again became somewhat more cohesive.

From the early summer of 1935 until August 1936, there were very few red check marks in Zak's notebook. It was a period of calm before the approaching storm of 1940. The rural economy had improved slightly after Colijn had finally abandoned the gold standard, and international trade had again begun to improve.

In August 1936, Zak's journals include an excerpt from the resolution of the national Calvinist church council to which Sven had sent the "Klees question." At its September 1936 meeting in Amsterdam, that august council had come down hard on church members who had joined the Dutch Nazi party. "The synod unambiguously affirms that there is no room for members of the Dutch Calvinist Church in organizations that promote Biblical falsehoods such as the 'leadership principle,' or the 'nationalistic totalitarian power state' . . ." Because of that decision the council instructed all members of the clergy to tell church members, who belonged to the Nazi party, that they must end their party affiliation or face the consequences. Those who refused to abandon the "unchristian doctrine" of the Nazi party would be barred from the church sacraments and, eventually, could even be expelled from the church.

Early in October 1936, Pastor Sven came back from Amsterdam and made a report to the Mustard Seed youth club about their denomination's decision regarding Nazi party membership. After the presentation, Steward declared: "It's time for a toast! We need to celebrate the fact that our church leaders, like the Dutch Catholic Bishops earlier this year, do have some guts. Now we can take care of Klees and kick him out of our youth organization!"

There was a moment of stunned silence as all the solemn young men of the group tried to think of what to say. Such activism made them uncomfortable, and they all looked expectantly at Piet, who, as chair of the club, was expected to lead the group to some form of action. Piet did not respond to the group, but turned to Pastor Bolstra, who was sitting next to him. "What do you think we should do, Pastor?" he asked.

The stately pastor, after clearing his throat, slowly rose to his feet and launched into a long homily in which he warned the young people to be *careful, compassionate,* and *cooperative.* "We must be *careful* not to judge anyone and to love all those who may temporarily have a blind spot when it comes to the issue of Nazi party membership." Zak, in his notes, observed that the good pastor said many other things before coming to his concluding statement: "As far as Klees is concerned, I strongly urge you to continue to be *compassionate.* Do not do anything reckless. Let the proper authorities do what must be done. It is his local church counsel that needs to take steps if action is called for. It is your job to *cooperate* with all people who are in *authority.*"

Pastor Sven finally broke the silence in the room when his chair scraped on the floor as he rose to talk. He carefully avoided looking in the direction of Pastor Bolstra. "We live in dangerous times," he said, "and, as on that night when the disciples were gathered around Jesus in the Garden of Gethsemane, it is our job as believers to be both watchful and prayerful. Jesus was alert when he sent Judas away before retreating to that garden. As believers we need to keep our eyes open so that we can spot the wolves in sheep skin that try to creep into our churches. You, as a group, can also be watchful by reading Schilder's booklet *Geen Duimbreed,* in which he explains why followers of Christ must not be Nazi party members." Pastor Sven left the meeting after he had thanked the group for their attentiveness.

Pastor Bolstra, with some reluctance, soon followed his colleague. He cleared his throat several times as he was leaving, and everyone knew that he wanted to add something to the discussion, but Piet, as chair, did not ask him to speak, and everyone else carefully avoided his eyes.

The Mustard Seed youth club meeting concluded soon after the two pastors had left the room. A motion was made and seconded and it was decided to indeed discuss the Schilder booklet. Steward, during the next 12 months, faithfully attended what he called Piet's "talk shop." He repeatedly voiced the same complaint. "We just sit there and talk, talk, and talk, but we never do anything." But, in spite of his negative attitude, he never missed any of the meetings.

He even attended the fall 1937 meetings when it was decided to discuss E.J. Roskam's booklet *Calvinism, the Nazis, and the Calvinist Church of the Netherlands*. Pastor Bolstra had provided the group members with copies of that booklet and told them that Roskam, as a Christian Nazi member, represented the opinion that had been opposed by Schilder. "We need to have an open mind and understand the opposing views— when it comes to the question of believers belonging to Nazi parties."

In part it was because of their temperamental differences that Steward and Piet slowly drifted away from each other between 1936 and 1940. The fact that instinctive differences did not lead to ruptures during these years was because both Zak and Elske again and again acted as peace advocates.

Chapter Eleven

Elske Comes to Ter Loo
(1936)

AT THIS POINT, JAY, I am going to focus on your mother's role in this story. She came to Ter Loo in 1936 and added color to the life of that little hamlet. Even as I write the word, "Elske," I have the feeling that I am desecrating a territory that is almost holy ground for you. I always envied the intimate bond of love that existed between you and your mom. During our long-ago years of friendship, I was always drawn to your house after school because I knew she would shower you with her exuberant love after you came home from school. What I was also keenly aware of, is that I could always count on being able to catch some drops from that shower of grace.

It was trouble at home that brought Elske to Ter Loo. From Zak's notes I could tell that the gentle romance between Piet and Elske, that had started to blossom in 1933, was like a quiet flame that burned steadily as the months and years passed. The two young people rarely had a chance to spend much time with each other because of the distance between Ter Loo and Dokkum, but they were in regular contact with each other by means of letters.

On October 16, 1936, the ties between the two young people underwent dramatic change because of what had happened in Elske's home. Her father, Bert Scheepema, never deviated from his adherence to the Dutch Nazi movement. He had thrown the church letter that asked him to meet with two members of the church council into the garbage. In that letter the council members explicitly told him that they felt duty-bound to adhere to the recently established denominational policy which forbade church members from joining the Nazi party.

The day after receiving that letter, Bert stopped going to the church of which he had been an active member for over twenty years. The church council had consequently decided to take the initiative and send representatives to the Scheepema home. The two delegates, Pastor De Koning and Jan Broersman, visited with Bert and his family on October 15, 1936.

As Zak later heard from Elske herself, things did not go well during that visit. The following extract, which explains the drama that took place in the home of Elske's family, has been taken from Zak's journal:

> At first my (Elske's) dad said nothing after Pastor De Koning had carefully explained why the teachings of their church were in direct conflict with the teachings advocated the Dutch Nazi movement. The pastor had, as part of his explanation, read from the resolution that had been passed by the national church council. My mom and I were both more and more anxious because we noticed my dad's face was becoming increasingly red as the pastor was talking, but we felt that we were powerless. The pastor ended his short presentation by looking directly at my father and saying to him: "All we ask of you, brother Scheepema, is that you promise to drop your Nazi membership. Your word, here and now, is enough for us."
>
> When the pastor had finished delivering the message that he had been instructed to bring, Mr. Broersma, the other church delegate, added only one sentence to the conversation: "Yes, that is all that we ask."
>
> It was the quiet raspy voice of the reticent and diminutive Jan Broersma that, for a moment, seemed to trouble my father. Mr. Broersma was, to us always simply known as "Jan." He was, like my dad, a small business operator. He was the owner and manager of a tiny corner grocery store two blocks from our home. From early in the morning until late in the evening, he would work tirelessly to keep his store spotlessly clean and in good order. Despite always being very busy, he'd invariably take the time to greet his customers with a warm smile and kindly ask them about their personal joys and struggles.
>
> Those who knew Jan, could see from the increasingly thick rings around his eyes, that he was having a very hard time making ends meet because fewer and fewer people could afford to purchase more than just the basic necessities. And, sometimes, they went hungry because there was no money for food. When

that happened, Jan would, as often as not, look the customer in the eye and whisper: "It's okay, I'll write it down."

He would, indeed, keep a record of all the unpaid grocery bills but never, in any proactive way, attempt to collect payment from customers. My dad, before his bike shop went bankrupt, was always ready to drop by and pick up something at the Broersma Grocer. It gave him a chance to break away from his own shop and talk with someone who was both a good listener and who had his own opinions. But, after our fall into poverty, Dad went to that store less and less frequently. I would often be the one sent to the store with inadequate payment for the groceries on my list. After loading the saddle bags of my bicycle with more things than I had paid for, Jan would wave me away and say: "Don't worry, girl. We'll figure it out later." My mother kept a careful record of our outstanding debt with the store, but as the years passed, she was increasingly unable to settle up with Jan.

I was never introduced to the secrets of our family finances, but from angry exchanges between our parents, I knew that our family received help from the relief fund of our church. Mom quietly accepted that help and used that money to pay for what the family owed Jan. Dad was too proud to even acknowledge that we were receiving help from the church.

The pastor, during his short talk, said one sentence that caused my father to completely lose control of himself. The sentence went something like this: "Anyone who listened to the bad news propagated by the Nazi party, automatically denied the truth of the Good News about Jesus Christ."

My father, who had spent so many hours talking with Jan, now abruptly turned into a savage beast as he attacked both him and the pastor. It was the word "bad" that seemed to have lit the fuse that caused the explosion. He accused the startled delegates of being hypocrites who threw mud at all those who were not afraid of looking at the facts. I can't get my dad's red face out of my mind as he screamed at the top of his voice: "You consider yourself ever so holy Look at what's happening in Spain where Germany and Italy are the only countries that have the guts to stop the godless communists from vaporizing everything that is holy in that troubled country!"

After listening for more than five minutes to the brutal words coming from my dad, I left the room and went outside to go for a walk. Even from outside our house, I could hear my father's hysterically angry voice.

Later, I heard from my mom that the church delegates did not stay very long after I had left the house. At one point the pastor had raised his hand to stop the headlong rush of my raving father. When Dad momentarily stopped talking, the pastor quietly repeated what he had said earlier. He told my dad, first of all, that he would have to refrain from taking the sacraments next Sunday if he did not promise to drop his Nazi membership. Secondly, if he insisted on remaining loyal to that Nazi party, then the church would have no choice but to terminate his church membership. Mom and I both assumed that that would also put a stop to the financial help from the church.

When I came back to the house my mother was crying in the living room, and my father had left on his bicycle. Between tears, my mom told me that the moment that the delegates delivered their ultimatum, my father had jumped up from his seat and yelled, "Get out! Get out!" at the two men. As they got up to leave and attempted to open our ill-fitting door, he almost threw their coats and hats at them. My dad then grabbed the door and kicked it so hard that he injured his large toe and put a major dent in the poor old door. All those sounds had deeply frightened my mother because she was sure that my dad had hit one of the men.

It is only because Zak had, in detail, spelled out what had happened in the Scheepema home, that I was able to reconstruct the chain of events that brought your mother to Ter Loo on Oct. 16, 1936. It turned out that Elske, after her father's outburst, had decided to leave her home in Dokkum and to make her way to Ter Loo. She had not been able to sleep during the evening after her father's insane outburst. As she was fitfully tossing and turning in her bed, she ceaselessly replayed all the events of the day in her mind. She thought about all the Nazi events that she had attended with her father. She had wanted to support him as he was going through a difficult time in his life. She again saw herself handing out all those issues of *Volk en Vaderland* and remembered how she had, out of loyalty to her dad, gone with him to the Nazi convention day at Lunteren in 1935. She had, in her mind, wanted to protect him but, in fact, she had been an enabler. She, along with her mother, had permitted her father to spend more and more time promoting the Nazi cause.

As time passed, it dawned on her with the clarity of a night-time revelation, that she and her mother should have done what their church, in its clumsy way, had tried to do with the visit of the pastor and Jan. She and her mom were the ones who should, long ago, have spoken openly to the man they still loved in spite of his infatuation with the twisted Nazi movement. They were the ones who had noticed the changes in his personality as he drifted ever more deeply into a crazy Nazi land, but they had done nothing to stop his slide into that swamp of anger. They had remained passive onlookers as the man that they loved had drifted away from them.

She had, in fact, not been a totally innocent bystander because, in her zeal to protect her father, she had gone to almost all the regional Nazi meetings during the past two years. She listened in as the fascist faithful gathered and were given carefully detailed scripts about how to speak and act if local leaders of the Calvinist or Catholic Church took their denominational mandates seriously and demanded that church members end their Nazi party affiliation. Her dad's angry outbursts and his insistence that his church membership had nothing to do with his political activity, was part of a script that she already knew by heart. She began to cry with increasing anguish when she imagined that the angry lines which she clearly saw in her father's face, were now starting to show up in her own face. Was she starting to change from being only a Nazi's daughter into a "Nazi girl?"

As she lay in bed, she again clutched the latest letter that she had received from her beloved Piet. She had, in the previous month, written him a letter that caused her days of deep agony. She had asked him why he had stopped visiting her. Was he no longer accompanying Steward and Zak on their monthly trips to the doctor in Leeuwarden? Was that why the three of them no longer stopped in Dokkum to pick her up and, as in the previous months, take her for short drives into the countryside?

She had received a reply that was, by now, all crumpled up and sweaty in her hand. Piet had written her and told her that Steward and Zak's mom had told them not to associate with her because of her connection to the Dutch Nazi party. There was nothing that Piet or Steward could do to convince the matriarch that that Elske from Dokkum was not really a Nazi girl. It frightened her that Piet had even placed that word in the letter. She knew that he was only repeating something that he had heard from his friend's mother, but the phrase haunted her. Was she turning into a party loyalist simply because she had helped her father?

Then she began to think of her father's struggle to find regular work and the grinding poverty that had taken so much joy out of the home life of her family. Her few dresses consisted of drab hand-me-downs that she had altered so as to make them at least somewhat fashionable. Her schooling had ended abruptly during the previous May. She had had the top grades in her class, but there was no time for schooling after she had finished eighth grade. Her family wanted her to find some work so that she could help put bread on the family table. In her old shoes, she had knocked on endless numbers of doors during the past summer and asked people if they would hire her to do some housework for them. The answers were always the same: "Dear girl, we would love to have some help, but there is simply no money for anything more than immediate needs." There would always be the sad shake of the head as the door was carefully closed again. Not one person even asked her for the letter of introduction that had cost her hours to formulate.

She had just heard the two doleful clangs from the city clock of Dokkum, when she sat up bolt upright in bed as a new thought raced into her mind. Her brain, like a broken record, told her that people with angry faces as well as those with kind, polite faces had avoided all small talk and had, instead, slammed the doors of their homes shut when she came by and asked for work.

Could it be that everyone thinks of me as a Nazi girl? Is that phrase branded on my forehead, and they see a bad person when they look at me? But Piet knows better, doesn't he? He knows that I am not like my dad. I certainly don't want to destroy our whole democratic system and replace it with a dictatorship!

Elske's eyes were wide open as she stared at the full moon shining through her bedroom window. She shivered as her mind started to chase itself in increasingly small circles while trying, again and again, to create a coherent picture out of the randomly dispersed puzzle pieces of her life. For a time, it seemed that she had become a frantic hamster running ever faster on an exercise wheel that had been maliciously lubricated.

A nearby church bell had just finished chiming the third hour in the morning when Elske came up with a plan. She decided that she would have to personally go to Zak and Steward's mother and apologize to her and ask her forgiveness for indeed being that Nazi girl that had drawn them and their friend Piet into the Nazi march in Leeuwarden. All she wanted to do was to tell her she was sorry for what she had done and that she had not had any bad intentions. Now she wanted to do everything in her power to mend her ways.

After making that resolution, she fell into a deep, dreamless sleep and woke up slightly before six in the morning. The house was quiet. Everyone was still asleep. She swiftly got dressed and, without waking anyone up, slipped from the house and, on her bicycle, started down the road that would eventually take her to Ter Loo. The small note that she left for her family only told them that she was taking a bike ride.

Mile after mile, she rehearsed the words that she planned to say to Steward and Zak's mother. Perhaps she had followed in the footsteps of her father and become a prodigal daughter of the church, but she was determined to change her ways. She wanted to free herself from the noxious fumes of anger and hatred that had seeped from the fascist cauldrons and into her parental home.

It was almost two in the afternoon when Elske, drenched from a drizzling rain, biked into Ter Loo, and asked for directions to the Ruintjes farm. When she rang the doorbell, Zak opened the door. At first, he just stared at her, but he quickly recovered himself and, with hand signals, invited her to step in and wait for a minute in the foyer. He then went into the kitchen and, using his trusty notepad, told his mother about their unexpected guest.

When Elske heard Mrs. Ruintjes coming down the hall, she felt like a schoolgirl standing in front of the class while unprepared to recite the memory work of the week. Throughout the long bicycle ride, she had rehearsed various versions of her misery-filled speech.

Beppe Ruintjes took one look at the pale shivering Elske and, with the eagle eye of an attentive mother, noted the look of desperation in the young girl's face. In a quiet voice she welcomed her into her home. Then she took her by the hand and led her to a chair next to the warm stove in the living room.

Elske wanted to blurt out her confession before she sat down, but Zak's mother said in a soothing tone: "We can talk later. Now you need some heat, rest and warm clothing." She took Elske's dripping wet coat from her and draped it over a chair back near the stove. Then she excused herself. In a few minutes she was back with some dry clothing.

"It will take me a few minutes to make some tea. That will give you the time to wash up and step into something dry which, along with warm tea, will chase the chills out of your body.

At the word "warm," Elske burst into tears as she went to wash up and change her clothing. When she came back into the living room, Zak had gone to help his brother with the chores; he also wanted to escape from the emotional drama.

Beppe Ruintjes sipped her tea as Elske talked ceaselessly. "I am ever so sorry for leading Steward, Piet and Zak astray. I was at that Nazi march in Leeuwarden so that I could be close to my father who, each day, was slipping into moods of ever deeper despair. I so much wanted to help my dad, but it was no use."

It seemed as if Elske would burst into tears again as she reflected on the past, but she stopped herself and said that she was determined to make a new beginning. "The first thing I must do is follow Christ and take the step of leaving father and mother behind. I simply can't go home and again allow myself to stew in my father's angry juices. I want to stop being a Nazi girl!"

After that exclamation Elske again broke down in tears, and my grandmother, who was never at a loss for words, was speechless as she held the shivering young girl in a long, silent embrace.

She eventually took a step away from Elske and spoke in a very quiet and self-reflective voice. "You are not a Nazi girl and you have nothing to be ashamed of. I am the one who is ashamed because of putting that label on you without even knowing who you were. I have a handicapped son and have a deep, ugly hatred for the way that the Nazis worship the strong and healthy. But that is no excuse for putting labels on people whom I do not even know."

Elske's life changed in many ways after her impulsive decision to come to Ter Loo. She never went back to her parent's home in Dokkum. Beppe Ruintjes became her mentor in a variety of ways. It was she who loaned her money for some new clothing, and she also helped her find a job as a live-in house maid with the elderly Mrs. Hoikema in Ter Loo. She was also the one who, on the day that Elske arrived at her doorstep, had sent Steward to Sebeek with a telegram to be sent to her parents in Dokkum.

Mr. Scheepema had, for a long time, stared in stunned silence as he looked at the telegram that he and his wife had received late in the evening. The message from Elske consisted of two short sentences: "I'm in Ter Loo with a good family—the Ruintjes. Do not worry."

At suppertime, his wife furtively placed a hot plate of sauerkraut and mashed potatoes in front of him; instead of eating anything, he stared at his food for an hour. His wife was as silent as a shadow while she waited in the kitchen for him to finish his supper. Peering through the door, at one point, she could see him as he stared blankly at the day-old issue of the *Fries Dageraad* that their neighbor had graciously placed in their mail slot. Eventually he did take a few bites of his food but, even then, he had not noticed that his wife had enhanced the sober dish by adding some greens from the garden and a triple portion of tasty sausage slices.

His anger had been red hot on the previous day but, during the hours that had passed since the time of the visit from the church delegation, his hatred had become cold and hard. He took one more nibble from his plate before throwing the food into the garbage can.

For almost three years, after coming to Ter Loo, Elske was the nurse, companion, and housekeeper of the ailing Mrs. Hoikema. From the wide front windows of that little house, she would, every day at 7 p.m. look down the road to see if Piet was coming for his regular visit.

Piet and Elske got married in the summer of 1939. Piet had not wanted their courtship to last for three years, but Elske had continually put him off when he broached the topic of arranging a wedding day, repeatedly saying they were still far too young to be married and that they both needed more time to grow up.

She was, in fact, also suffering from the permanent break that had taken place between herself and her father. He had even refused to come to Ter Loo on June 20, 1939, when she and Piet were married by Pastor Sven in the local Calvinist church. By that time, Ter Loo had become her new hometown, and she had stopped missing her friends in Dokkum. From Zak's notes I could tell that, as a happy young bride, she had also recovered some of her native buoyancy and boundless energy.

She really needed that optimism because, during the first year of their marriage, Piet was again and again mobilized by the ill-equipped Dutch army which was desperately trying to prepare itself for a German attack. When the invasion took place, in the first week of May 1940, the massive Nazi war machine swept over the Netherlands like an unstoppable tsunami. Piet was stationed in the Eastern part of the Netherlands and became a POW for a short time.

PART THREE

Metastasized Fear: Harold and Jay's Parents during World War II

Chapter Twelve

Adrift in a Fluid Moral Landscape
(Summer 1940)

AFTER THE GERMAN INVASION of the Netherlands in May 1940, many Dutch people, in a kind of catatonic daze, drifted along helplessly for months as they repeatedly asked the same questions. Why had Hitler overpowered the Dutch armed forces so quickly? And why had the members of Dutch government and their queen gone to London so swiftly? Shouldn't they have remained at their post and, as dutiful soldiers, defended their country?

Our parents also lived in a zone of disbelief during that first war year. They could not understand how it was possible that their country was now occupied by a foreign power. How had this disaster happened? For well over a century, their nation had stayed out of all the military conflicts that had ravaged Europe. It had even remained neutral during The Great War; that conflict had pulverized the old world when both Steward and Zak were still very young children.

But, starting in May 1940, German soldiers were marching down quiet Dutch streets and the new regional ruler, *Reichskommissar* Seyss-Inquart, was sending out increasingly invasive commands from the old seat of government in The Hague. What must be done in this shockingly new environment? Should all those German instructions, sent from Hitler's headquarters in Berlin, be meekly obeyed? Should everyone—policemen, civil servants, farmers, professionals, and regular workers—simply accept the reality that a new captain was now in charge of the ship of state? Should true Dutch patriots, instead of obeying those commands, do everything in their power to resist the new rulers?

That was the urgent question that Steward and his friends discussed when they got together in the hay mow of the Ruintjes farm on Sept 3, 1940. This was the first time, since the occupation, that the friends had taken the time to discuss the new environment in which the German occupation had placed them. Zak later placed a lot of red stars beside his record of this meeting.

Steward and his brother had absorbed their mother's fear that Zak, as a handicapped person, would not be safe during the coming season of Nazi rule.

Piet was still in shock from being part of an army that had just been pulverized by the Germans, and he was worried about his young wife, Elske. Joost, even though he had distanced himself from the communist ideology of his deceased father, was still devastated by the fact that communist USSR had allied itself with Nazi Germany the previous September. Thijs Houtman was worried that he and his father would no longer get jobs as painters because they had decided not to accept any contracts that involved assisting the Germans. That was what they told a Nazi recruiter who wanted them to accept a painting job at the new and expanded airport in Leeuwarden. That airport, they knew, would be used to attack England, and that was the very country that was sheltering the Dutch queen.

Everyone processed their fears in different ways. Hobbe Tuinman, the group's intellectual, took his cue from the Calvinist leader, Colijn. "I just finished reading his book *On the Frontier of Two Worlds*," he told Steward one day, "and I fully agree what that great man is telling us. Our country has reached a historical tipping point, and that's why we must accept the new rulers that have been placed over us. There is no road that will take us back to our democratic institutions and to the rule of our queen."

Hobbe had also wanted the Ter Loo group to go to the mass rally that Colijn and the Calvinist party was planning to hold in Leewarden on August 27, 1940. Over 13,000 people from throughout the province would come to that event and listen to Colijn in a large convention center of that city.

Steward had been uncharacteristically quiet when Hobbe came to him with his travel plans. He knew that his mother would not want him to attend any public gathering in Leeuwarden. He still remembered the edgy tone in her voice during the previous July when they were walking along a street in Sebeek and she spotted a Dutch Nazi vendor hawking the Nazi party newspaper, *Volk en Vaderland*. The salesman was walking towards them on the sidewalk, and even from the distance of a city block, they could hear him make his sales pitch: "Come one and come all and read the truth about our people and our fatherland and about our new leader." Beppe's response to the loud voice of the young man was to walk more quickly and to escape from him by going over to the other side of the street. She grimly stared at the ground as they passed the hated Nazi newspaper salesman.

It was only as they were driving back to the farm that she gave voice to her frustrations. She was sure that the elimination of handicapped people like Zak would be the first order of business for the German occupiers; they wanted to get rid of weaklings so that they could build a society with strong and heroic young men and women.

"As I think about the future, Steward, I can see the writing on the wall. There will be nothing that will keep these Dutch Nazis from shedding the blood of their own countrymen when the Germans have them fully trained."

That fierce protectiveness had caused her to take some radical steps to protect her son First of all, she made it appear as if he had died. An official death certificate was created for Idske. All family members, after the summer of 1940, always addressed him as Zak. Most people never saw him because he rarely went anywhere during daytime.

Secondly, in order to protect his secret life, they built a hiding place for him behind the barn. It was, in fact, a small tool shed which had been covered up with straw and a thick layer of dried manure. For those coming to the property it looked like an ordinary farm dung heap. Zak himself converted the interior of the building into two comfortable little rooms to which he could safely retreat if strangers came to the farm. Steward assured him that the Germans would always carefully avoid such an unpleasant-looking hiding place. "They will not want to get manure on their shiny boots."

Steward was conflicted as he listened to Hobbe describing the upcoming rally in Leeuwarden. He had, earlier during that summer, fully shared his mother's concern for Zak's safety in a Nazi occupied Netherlands and had helped her take the needed safety measures. He also knew what she would say about the public rally. "There is no reason to stick your head above the ground and let the Nazis just cut it off."

But the grim image of severed heads seemed out of place in August 1940 when the Germans still acted like good cops. Like most of his countrymen, Steward felt a deep sense of relief that his worst fears about the invading Nazis seemed to have been misplaced. But he was still uneasy about going to a public event which would indeed be infiltrated by Nazi traitors like Klees, who would be systematically compiling lists of attendees. Spies like him were like vultures as they hovered around at public gatherings and church services; they would test the air to determine if anyone present was "unfriendly" to the Germans.

In his uncertainty, Steward dodged Hobbe's question. "I need some time to think about whether or not I want to go to that rally. Why don't you guys just go without me?"

Later, he indirectly broached the topic with his mother. "The guys want to go to Leeuwarden and listen to Colijn, but I'll have to finish cutting that tall grass in the far end of the orchard."

His mother did not miss the question that was imbedded in this bland announcement because she knew that Steward actually wanted be part of something that could turn out to be an exciting outing. Her response to him was surprisingly indirect. "There should be no problem if you want to go along with them," she said, "but I would run the idea by Pastor Sven. He has a good head on his shoulders."

Steward tried to ignore his mother's suggestion, but his silent brother Zak, who now lived in an isolated no-man's-land and who had heard the exchange, again persuaded him to visit the pastor and at least hear what he had to say. The intimate bond between the two brothers had deepened during that first summer of German occupation as they both tried to recover from the shock of adjusting to the new masters of their country. The brothers again decided that they would once more catch Sven while he was out in his garden during the early morning.

The next day Steward and Zak got out of bed early and, shortly before seven in the morning, were already nearing the pastor's home. Steward, who was almost never tongue tied, felt strangely awkward as he attempted to explain his sense of confusion about going to the upcoming Calvinist political meeting in Leeuwarden. He started to talk about the rally but stopped in mid-sentence when he saw that the pastor already knew all about it. The same thing happened when he tried to talk about his mother's fears for Zak's safety. He finally blurted out his deep confusion. "I see no reason for not going, but I also see no reason for going.

Why should I spend money for the sole purpose of listening to Colijn's pessimistic understanding of what is happening in our land?"

Pastor Sven listened to Steward in silence. He let out a long sigh before he said anything. "As you can imagine," he finally said, "I am as frustrated as you guys. It's not your question that troubles me, but the problem that it touches on. Colijn, the captain of our Calvinist political party, is ever so eager to sail ahead with his ship of state and he wants to get his whole crew and all his passengers to stay on board with him. But there is a problem that Colijn and almost all the other members of the Calvinist party do not want to think about. Their political ship is no longer free to move; it is trapped in a solid block of black ice that has been formed by the Nazi winter."

Steward and Zak, who were very practical minded farmer's sons, gave each other quizzical looks because they had no idea what Sven was talking about. But there was no time to articulate their sense of confusion because Sven was running away with his own apocalyptic train of thought. "I like to think of the German invasion as the beginning of a Nazi winter because, since this May, many of the natural life colors in our society are slowly being erased from around us. We are entering a long winter in which everything is either as dark as the blackness of dirt, or as bland as the whiteness of snow. During winter, most of the color of life is drained out of the landscape, and that is what is happening to the human world in which we now live. That's why each one of us is caught in the inescapable tension of either being drawn in or repelled by the icy rules of our new masters. Do we continue to hope for a future in which there will again be a summer, or do we need to abandon such thoughts and brace ourselves for an eternal Nazi winter?"

There was a strange harshness in Sven's voice, as he repeatedly uttered the words "Nazi winter" and "color-bleached world." But then he stopped talking for a full minute as he again studied the questioning looks on the faces of his young visitors. "I'm not sure about the value of going to Leeuwarden. Can a big Calvinist political rally help me better understand how I should, as a Christian, live in this Nazi winter?

"No Christian can ignore the clarion call that we heard from Schilder. He told us that we need to get out of our cellars of fear and, as believers, put on the full spiritual body armor that the Apostle Paul spoke about to the Ephesians. Does that mean that Christians need to go to mass rallies? Or does it mean that we continue to calmly speak the truth and, like Schilder, find ourselves being thrown into prison?"

Sven momentarily stopped talking, and his voice was much quieter when he continued. "We have now entered into a time when the days are evil, and I, for one, need to pay attention and make sure that my feet are firmly standing on this soil that is located here in our little town of Ter Loo."

It was because of this conversation with Sven that Steward did not join Piet and Hobbe when they went to the mass rally at Leeuwarden in late August. Thousands of people from all over Friesland and adjacent provinces did go to hear Colijn talk about his hope for the future.

Hobbe and Piet tried to bring the excitement of that mass rally to their Ter Loo friends when they came home and joined the small group gathering in the Ruintjers farm on Sept. 3, 1940. Those who came that day, including Joost, Geert and Thijs, were looking for news about the world outside their small town.

Hobbe, who was usually very cool and collected at the group meetings, became very emotional on that balmy September evening. At the Leeuwarden rally he had been deeply moved by Colijn's words. As the different members of the group were looking for a place to sit down in the barn, Hobbe turned to Piet. "I think," he said, "that, with Colijn, we will get through this occupation and make our way to the new world that awaits us."

Steward overheard part of what Hobbe had said and asked him if he would mind repeating it for the benefit of the whole group. Hobbe, instead of repeating himself, elaborated on what he was trying to say. "Colijn is a Christian realist. He knows that we are under German occupation and that we can't change that. Our Humpy Dumpty democracy has fallen off the wall, and we will never be able to put those thousands of pieces back together again. There's nothing that we can do other than accept the changes that Hitler, as God's appointed ruler, is bringing to our land."

Hobbe stopped himself for a moment as he caught his breath. No one stepped in to pick up the thread of the conversation, so he continued his headlong race along memory lane. He could still hear the 13,000 fellow Christians cheer as they drank up the words of their leader who, for so many years, had been at the helm of their Christian political party. "I can tell you that Colijn was not a pessimist. He used powerful words as he encouraged us to stay loyal to God, to His Word, to our Christian political party and to our country. He said it would be a tall order to remain faithful but, by the Grace of God, it is not beyond our reach!"

There was a long period of silence as the young men reflected on Hobbe's words. They all desperately hoped that Colijn was correct, and that Dutch religious and social freedoms would be protected in Hitler's new Europe-wide Nazi regime. The Germans had, after all, explicitly promised that they would "guarantee the spiritual freedoms of the Dutch people."

As he was talking, Hobbe held an old issue of *The Standard* that he had brought along. That newspaper had been launched by Abraham Kuyper during the previous century and had, for generations, functioned as a beacon of truth in the homes of many Dutch Calvinists. Colijn, as Kuyper's successor, was a member of the paper's board of directors as well as a regular contributor.

When Hobbe had finished speaking, he carefully folded up the issue that had been in his hand and placed it on his lap. He and Piet were sitting on turned-over milk pails and were, therefore, much closer to the ground than the five others who were seated on the edge of a hay wagon that had been pulled into the barn.

The moment of silence that had followed after Hobbe's little talk was completely shattered when Joost burst in with the word, "bullshit!" Everyone turned to look in his direction, but he disregarded them because he continued to repeatedly blast out the same unpleasant word.

As his words echoed through the rafters of the barn, he jumped off the wagon and grabbed the carefully folded up issue of *The Standard* from Hobbe's lap. Everyone was silent as they saw the tall Joost stride toward the large sliding door. They could still see him as he walked to the manure pile and tossed the offending paper on it. Joost then went a step further. With his boots he pressed the newspaper into a mound of especially mushy dung.

"I just had to make sure that that newspaper found an appropriate home," said Joost as he returned to the others. "I was getting uncomfortable with the smell of defeatism that came with having that issue of *The Standard* so close to my nose."

Hobbe was, at first, too stunned to speak. In his home, all the daily issues of *The Standard* were always carefully folded up and placed under the coffee table after having been thoroughly read. They stayed there until Hobbe's dad found the time to clip out the articles that he wanted to save and file in the shoe boxes found in the small home library. In this way, Hobbe's father had ready access to many of the Calvinist leader's statements and ideas.

Hobbe jumped to his feet and waved the copy of Colijn's booklet that he had been holding. His voice was strangely hoarse as he glared at Joost. "How dare you talk about our newspaper and about Colijn, our leader, in that way?"

As an instinctive dramatist, who loved being provocative, Joost had no interest in getting into a physical fight. He attempted instead to make a joke of the situation. "Don't worry. I didn't stamp Colijn into the manure pile. It is only a copy of a newspaper that provoked me to action."

He let out a loud belly laugh that, he hoped, would drain some of the tension from the situation. Hobbe first looked at the others to see how they felt about what Joost had just done, and then, sensing that they were only puzzled by Joost's performance, he moodily sat down and un-clenched his tight fists.

Many hopes and fears were freely shared during the discussion that lasted deep into the evening of that day. Joost was the first one of the young men to touch one of the many hot rails now running through the new world that they had just entered. "I will tell you why I find the cur-rent issues of *The Standard* so offensive. Everything that the Germans publish, and whatever they allow others to write down is not just rubbish but propaganda, and, as such, it is toxic. As a heretic communist I know all about such tainted garbage. My poor deceased father used to read the Dutch communist newspaper—*The People's Rag*—from cover to cover and endlessly echo its vitriolic passions. I still remember him coming into my bedroom after I had gone to sleep and waking me up so he could read long swaths from that dreadful paper. One evening, after the reading was finished, he fumed for at least one additional hour about the horrors that the Nazis had committed in Guernica, Spain.

"My poor dad would have turned in his grave if he found out that Stalin and Hitler are now walking arm-in-arm as their respective armies are in the process of conquering the whole world and dividing the spoils among themselves. *The People's Rag,* my father's beacon of light, is now sending out utterly new light signals. Truth now means that, instead of hostility towards Hitler, there must be peace, love and friendship be-tween all Communists and all Nazis. All democratic countries have now become enemies of both the Communists and the Nazis."

Joost looked at Hobbe as he ended his emotional outburst. "I don't know the details but, for me, it is an obvious fact that the Calvinists' *Stan-dard,* like the communist newspaper, has become putty in the hands of the Nazis, and it is being used by them to infuse their poison into the heads and hearts of your Calvinist readers."

As Joost was talking, he was not only standing, but also wildly flaying his hands in the air. While his deep and dramatic voice echoed through the barn rafters, it almost seemed as if he had metamorphosed into a mad prophet. His voice abruptly faltered when he heard himself audaciously talk about "obvious facts." His powerful body momentarily lost its inner strength and, after sinking down into the hay on the barn floor, he pulled himself into an almost fetal sitting position. With his arms around his knees, he raised the somber question that was also on the minds of the others: "What must we do to find the truth now that there are lies, lies, and more lies everywhere?"

As the young men looked at each other, they heard one lone cow lowing in the distance. From the nearby canal came the sounds of loudly croaking frogs and, in the gathering darkness, they could still hear some of the restless and omnipresent flies that continued to swarm around their heads.

Piet was the first one to speak up after Joost's outburst. As a peace-maker, he was troubled by the tension that still existed between Joost and Hobbe. He had also been pained by Joost's disrespect for Colijn, whom he, like most members of the Dutch Calvinist party, deeply admired.

But there was no hint of anger or pain in his voice as he looked at Joost and spoke in a meditative voice. "I can still feel the red-hot surge of anger that overtook me when I was pinned down at the Grebbelinie by an advancing battalion of German soldiers. We could see their faces coming at us and all we wanted to do was blow them up. They had no right to smash into our country. But then the battle ended, and I was taken prisoner. The German soldier in charge of me carried my personal belongings because my shoulder was bleeding. Shortly after the end of hostilities, Hitler allowed all of us captured Dutch soldiers to go back to our homes and jobs. We should give the Germans a chance to demon-strate their goodwill in this new world about which Colijn has spoken and written."

There was a respectful silence as Piet was speaking because he was the only one in the group who had been in combat. Hobbe had done some guard duty along the Atlantic coast north of Leeuwarden but, when the war broke out, his part of the army made no contact with the Ger-mans. The northern divisions of the German 18th army, in their race to capture the strategically critical *Afsluitdijk,* had bypassed the area where

Hobbe had been stationed. When the Germans had defeated the Dutch, Hobbe had thrown his gun into a canal, and after changing into civilian clothing, went home.

Steward and the other young men had also not served in the army; they had been exempted from service for a variety of reasons.

Piet was encouraged by the respect that he received for having served in the Dutch army; it had, at least temporarily, slowed down the swift attack of the Germans. But he also knew that some of his friends had been offended by the phrase "German goodwill." In the corner of his eye, Piet saw Joost beginning to stand up to say something to the whole group and in response, started to talk faster and faster.

Only Zak noticed that Piet's hands were trembling slightly as he said, in a low voice, "Do you think I love the Germans? As we were defending our line, a shell screamed past me and tore through the wall of the adjacent bunker where Clarence, from our Mustard Seed club, had been fighting. After that shell exploded, I was given the job of collecting that poor man's body parts. We fought the good fight, but now it's time to put down our weapons and accept the reality that the German are in charge of our country."

There was a long silence in the barn as everyone was absorbed in their own world of thought. The clouds that had hidden the sun, had drifted away and allowed the last rays of the late summer sun to shine through the barn's western door. In the stillness, the eyes of those gathered in the hay mow were drawn to the vague light that hovered above them on the eastern barn wall.

At that moment that the shadow of a large hand was clearly visible. Joost had raised his strong hand into the beam of light streaming into the barn, and it was the shadow of his whole hand that was visible on the inside wall of the barn for a few seconds; then the thumb and three of the longer fingers disappeared into the shadow of a large fist. In the end, only the smallest finger was still visible. For a split second it looked as if a small obelisk, created by that small finger, had been carved into the wall of the barn. Then, as the sun went down completely, the shadow of the defiant finger also vanished from view.

At that point Joost muttered, almost to himself, "I don't care how much those Germans box me in. Even if I am still able to move only my little finger and use it to do something to cause them trouble, I will do just that."

When the shadow had vanished from the wall, Zak could see that Steward was deeply troubled by the fact that his friends were swiftly heading into different directions: one road was leading to compromise and accommodation, and the other taking them to the unimaginable dangers of resistance.

To hide his feeling of panic, Steward abruptly burst out with a forced boisterous laugh as he made a loud announcement to the whole group. "I like the idea of at least resisting the Germans in little ways with our smallest finger. That is why I have an announcement to make. Starting today our activism is going to be described as 'small-potatoes politics.'"

An awkward silence fell over the group after Steward stopped laughing at his own forced joke. He looked around anxiously. There was a tense nervousness in his voice as he faced his friends and blurted out the question on his mind. "Well? How do the rest of you feel about what Piet and Joost have just said? Shouldn't we be willing to at least take some small steps to quietly resist German domination of our country? Or are we going to play dead and not even lift one finger as they steal everything from us and then take each one of us to different prisons and execution blocks?"

Geert, who had been quiet until this point, entered the discussion. "Steward", he said, "you like to rush in because you see things in black and white. I like to walk slowly so that I can see where I am going. That is why I want to keep my ear to the ground and listen to different sounds of the conflict that is raging around us. What are people saying? How is the war progressing? What are Dutch Nazi traitors like Klees doing? What are they saying?"

The reference to "traitors" caused all divisions in the group to instantly evaporate. It was Piet who led the charge, and his voice was an octave higher as he began to recount a very personal and troubling story. "And do you know what Elske saw yesterday when she was in the public library of Ter Loo? Andy Uitvlucht, one of the Nazi friends of Klees, stormed through the library door and, without saying a word to anyone, grabbed the book, *All Quiet on the Western Front* from the shelf. Then, with all his might, he not only threw it at Mrs. Vellinga, the librarian, but also accosted her with a barrage of angry questions such as, 'How could you have allowed this damned book to remain in your library? Hitler has banned all such trash. Those kinds of defeatist books are for sheep; not for real men!'"

Soon Piet was almost as agitated as Joost had been earlier that evening. "Elske stayed out of the argument, but she saw that Andy was waving a sheet of paper in his hand as he began pulling more books off the shelf and viciously smashing them on the library floor. He spit out the word 'rubbish' as he kicked book after book across the floor."

"My wife was at the point of getting up and quietly leaving the library, when Andy angrily shoved some of the books into a garbage can and, with giant steps, strode out of the little library. As he was leaving, he slammed the door so hard that its glass shattered. Shards of glass ended up flying all over the library floor.

"When it was once again quiet in the library, Elske went to the librarian and asked her what had caused the uproar. The elderly Mrs. Vellinga was quietly wiping the tears from her eyes when she looked up and saw Elske. 'That man, and I don't know his name, showed me a list consisting of what he called "forbidden books." He said that the Germans are ordering us to get rid of all the books on that list. I don't even know where to begin. Where will this end? Can we no longer choose the books that we want to read?'

"Elske and the librarian cleaned up some of the mess and taped a piece of cardboard over the gaping hole in the library door. When my wife told me about that confrontation, I was, of course, very disturbed, but I also warned her that we must be very careful. We can't disobey the orders that we receive from the Germans. If we need to purge some books from our public, school, and university libraries that will simply have to be done."

Steward, as he stood up, began shifting his weight from one leg to the other. He wanted to say something, but knew that he would have to be careful because he was getting very agitated. He also noticed that Zak, through signals, was urging him to calm down and take the tightly folded sheet of paper that he was trying to give him.

Everyone thought it was just a personal note from the cautious older brother to the hot-tempered younger brother. They watched carefully as Steward noisily unfolded the sheet of paper and, as he did so, stopped shifting from one foot to another. He instead took a step closer to the group and, enunciating his words with gravity, announced, "This message is from our queen who recently spoke to our nation by means of the British radio. It is about the war that has overwhelmed us. She says, '. . . It is becoming increasingly clear that this war is fundamentally a struggle between good and evil. It is a battle in which God and our conscience is pitted against the dark powers in this world that oppose us and seek the rule over this world. This war is a struggle which belongs to the realm of the spirit and, as such, is a struggle that is usually deeply embedded in the hearts of humans. But now this spiritual conflict has burst out into the open in the form of this vast worldwide war . . . I urge you to continue to believe in the final victory of our cause . . . which is linked to our most holy possession—our faith heritage.'"

Steward then carefully folded up the sheet of paper again and, for the benefit of the others, repeated the queen's words again. "As our beloved queen has said to us, our conflict with the Nazis is as clear as the difference between *black* and *white*." While reading from the queen's speech he had picked up a stick from the barn floor and now, as he repeated the words "black" and "white," he slapped the stick against the barn wall as he uttered the word "black" and again as he said the word "white."

As echoes from the sound of cracking wood faded into the background, Steward, in a much lower voice, repeated his words of warning. "We must either continue to resist the Germans or capitulate to them." And in a deeply troubled tone, he added, "There is no middle ground."

It remained silent in the Ruintjes barn for a long time because no one knew how to cross the no man's land that was now beginning to open up between the words of Piet and those of Steward. That was why everyone was relieved when Hobbe somewhat defused the situation when he said: "We can both obey the Germans and still resist them if we create an underground library from which people can secretly obtain the books that are on the forbidden list." Then he added, with a grim smile, "This might be the beginning of our 'small potatoes politics.'"

Hobbe's statement did not bring an end to the divisions that were evident during the September 1940 meeting; it did, however, set in motion the first direct action of the Ter Loo underground group.

When Piet told Elske what he and his friends had talked about, she eagerly went back to the town library the next day. She first helped Mrs. Vellinga clean up the remaining shards of glass in the library and then, with Zak's help, repaired the broken window. After taking care of the immediate damage, she helped the distraught librarian develop a plan for dealing with the book censorship problem, announcing, "Zak is willing to safely hide the books that are on the Nazi's forbidden books list."

That was the very humble start of the Ter Loo resistance movement. Its first action, the creation of a resistance library, which, in the beginning, was nothing more than a small bookcase placed against the wall in Zak's hiding place. It held the banned books from the Ter Loo library. Eventually, however, Zak's secret library not only included banned books by earlier authors such as Daphne Du Maurier, Johan Huizinga, Arthur Koestler, R.C. Hutchinson, and Theun Vries, but was also expanded to include underground publications by authors such as J.A.H.S Bruins Slot (*The Crowned Robber*) and Jan Koopmans (*Almost too Late*).

Chapter Thirteen

Nazi Cockroaches in Ter Loo
(Fall 1940)

"I declare that I am of Aryan descent and that all my parents and grandparents are from purely Aryan stock."

—ARYAN DECLARATION

WHILE ENJOYING HER MORNING cup of coffee, Mrs. Vellinga again thought about the Dutch language *Radio-Oranje* report from England which she had listened to the day before. The sound of music coming from the BBC was only background noise as she placed her coffee cup back on the saucer and began to think about the plants in her garden that she would soon have to either dig up or transplant into an indoor container.

She was shaken out of her reverie when she heard the roar of a motorcycle coming down her narrow street. The loud chopping sounds ricocheted off the row houses that hugged each other as tightly as the books on her library shelves. The street itself was so narrow that cyclists coming from the opposite direction had to stop and lift their bicycles onto the narrow sidewalk to make room for the heavy motorcycle and sidecar.

When she heard the loud noises, Mrs. Vellinga instinctively started to move towards the table under which she planned to hide from a possible stray English bomb that had missed its target. The Battle of Britain had been going on for weeks, and everyone's nerves were still on edge as planes crossed overhead, and like others in her town, she was fully aware that death, in the form of a crashing fighter plane, could come at any moment.

The motorcycle came to a screeching halt in front of her house. After the riders had dismounted, Mrs. Vellinga automatically thought that the men were two German soldiers coming for her. With that in mind, she realized that she needed to immediately turn off her radio and switch the station from its BBC setting. Earlier in the summer, the Germans had ordered the Dutch people to never listen to British radio stations.

She barely had time to turn off the radio before there was a loud banging on her door. She did not have a chance to open it because it was ruthlessly shoved open by two intruders. She stared in disbelief when she saw that the two young men who faced her were not actually German soldiers. From their uniforms she could see that they were Dutch Nazis. The shorter man, Andy, was the library intruder. She had heard about the taller man, Klees, but had not yet met him. Andy had an angry scowl on his face, but Klees' dark red puffy face exuded only flashes of anger as he glared at Mrs. Vellinga and noisily cleared his throat. He then barked out a series of brutal questions.

"Why is your radio turned to the BBC station? Didn't you know that it is illegal to listen to British propaganda?"

Mrs. Vellinga had no time to answer the first question because Klees was already racing along with his second challenge. "Oh yes, I also need to know if you have already signed the Aryan Declaration that all government employees need to sign. The police department has no record of having received a signed copy of that declaration from you."

Then, looking around the small living room, he barked out his last demand. "Have you gotten rid of those poisonous books that Andy found in your library last week?"

In a quivering voice Mrs. Vellinga did answer that question. "Yes. They are all gone."

Klees stamped on the ground as he screamed at her. "Answer our question clearly and audibly!"

He was not satisfied with a somewhat louder affirmation from Mrs. Vellinga. "You say you took care of those books? If so, where did you put them? We want to make a fire and burn all outrageous books that are written by filthy Jews and other decadent writers.

Mrs. Vellinga finally found her voice as she looked at the young men. "All the books on your list have already been disposed of in the town incinerator. You can check yourselves and see that they are no longer on the library shelves."

The answer took both Klees and Andy by surprise because they had planned to take the banned books to the town square and ceremoniously burn them. Their dismay was not evident in what Klees then said to the distraught librarian. "Vellinga, you had better be careful with what you do or say. We must leave now, but we will be back. We are not going to forget either the radio or the Aryan Declaration which you still have to sign. Here is a copy. And, concerning those filthy books, we are going to have to talk to some other people to see whether you are telling us the truth."

The two Nazis strode through the open door that was letting damp and chilly air into the whole house, and Klees jumped on the still idling motorcycle. Andy, before stepping into the sidecar, picked up a golf ball size rock from the street and, as they were leaving, he threw it at the large plate glass window of Mrs. Vellinga's house.

There was shock on the ten anxious faces that were vaguely visible through the windows and lace curtains of the adjacent homes. Those neighbors clearly saw what happened next. The rock first put a hole and many cracks into the glass of the large window. Then, because there was a sudden gust of wind, the large pane of glass collapsed and sent a spray of shards into the house and onto the sidewalk.

Mrs. Vellinga stepped gingerly from her home and was in a daze as she looked around and started to slowly sweep some of the glass fragments into small piles. Soon several of her neighbors emerged from their homes and helped with the cleanup operation. As they worked, they all agreed that it was unfortunate that the window had been broken, but no one asked the librarian why those young men had come to her house. Neither did any of those reluctant helpers offer to clean up the broken glass that had fallen inside her house.

My grandmother, or Beppe, as I will call her from this point on, was not afraid to ask direct questions, but also knew when to be cautious. In the bakery, later that same day, she overheard the Luringa sisters whispering to each other about what had happened on their street earlier that day. She could not help overhearing Liz, with her sharp edgy voice say, "I clearly saw that Uitvlught boy throw the stone that shattered the window. I also saw the smirk on the face of that tall guy, Klees. Why they did that, I do not know." Then she repeated the same words again. It was almost as if someone was repeatedly hitting the replay button of her voice. "He threw a stone, and I don't know why, why, why."

Beppe overheard those audible whispers coming from behind the counter and realized that the Uitvlugt boy they were talking about was same Andy who had, earlier in the week, caused havoc in the town library. She also realized that the other criminal was Klees Koorder who, years earlier, had helped shove her beloved son Zak into a canal. She said nothing about her worries to anyone in the bakery. Instead, without a word, she took the loaf of bread she had ordered and left the bakery.

She started in the direction of Mrs. Vellinga's house but first biked around for a few minutes before finding the narrow alley that was adjacent to the librarian's home. After leaning her bicycle against a wall, she walked around to the front of the narrow house. She knocked on the door and looked at the gaping hole which had previously been a window.

Before long, she heard a high-strung voice call out from inside the house: "I don't need anything."

Beppe knew that she sometimes had a sharp edge to her voice but this time she mustered up the same gentle voice with which she had, five years earlier, greeted the distraught and drenched Elske. "I have nothing to sell. I am Elske's friend, and I just want to talk to you!"

On hearing who was at the door, the librarian opened it and let Beppe into her small and almost empty living room. An ornately designed bookcase only partly hid a large dark water stain on the east wall. The ugly blemish in the wallpaper had the shape of a dark and angry hand and it almost seemed to be reaching up and plucking the flowers from the age-compromised wall covering.

After Beppe stepped through the doorway, Mrs. Vellinga guided her to the kitchen. Beppe remained quiet until they were both seated around a small table. It was then that Beppe asked the question that no one else in the small town had dared to ask the frightened librarian. "What brought those men to your house and why did they accost you and break your window?"

In a tremulous voice, the librarian summarized the events of the morning. She ended by saying that she thought that the stone might have been accidentally kicked up by the motorcycle as it raced off. "Since it was an accident, I haven't felt the need to make a report to the police. "But," she added in almost inaudible whisper, "what worries me much more is that question about the Aryan Declaration."

Beppe's response to Mrs. Vellinga was very simple. "You are not safe here in your own house. You must leave this place and, at least temporarily, stay with us!"

Beppe, like most of the farmers from the region, knew all about Mrs. Vellinga's family lineage. The librarian's father, Herman Ambtsmann, had been the regional milk inspector in the late 1890's. The small town of Ter Loo had always been a somewhat awkward fit for Mr. and Mrs. Ambtsmann; they were both Jews and had grown up in Amsterdam.

Beppe also knew that their daughter, Betsie, had married David Vellinga. He, like her own parents, had also come from the Jewish community in Amsterdam. He had worked as an apprentice with the senior inspector for several years before becoming fully certified. David had been given his father-in-law's job when the elderly Ambtsmann died during the influenza epidemic of 1919. David himself was only 47 when, because of a mysterious car accident, he passed away during the sixth depression year. There was always talk of foul play, but nothing was ever proven.

The inspector's main job was to make sure that the health and safety rules were enforced in the many small milk processing factories that dotted the dairy farm part of Friesland during those years. Sometimes when an infection crept into a production facility, the inspector would have to visit the individual farms and attempt to find the source of the contamination. When they heard that the inspector was making the rounds, farmers could sometimes become very agitated. They would, when that happened, often greet each other by saying: "Has the Jew been to *your* place yet?" Such brusque queries would not necessarily reflect anti-Semitic feelings, but they did portray the reality that Jews, even the ones who had mostly been accepted in their midst, were still viewed as strangers from whom the locals tended to keep their distance.

Despite their Jewish ancestry, David and Betsie Vellinga were regular members of the Frisian community in which they lived. They had both been baptized and were confirmed members of the Catholic Church. Through his work, David had always worked closely with a wide variety of people in the area. It would have been natural for them to have many friends. David had had a graceful and outgoing personality. But, throughout their years in Ter Loo, there was always that mysterious distance between the Vellingas and the rest of the townsfolk.

After the death of her husband, Betsie had been appointed as the town librarian. That part-time job augmented by only a small measure, the meager pension that she received from her deceased husband's former place of employment. The job also gave her a chance to meet the townspeople.

It is hard to understand why the Vellingas, as Jews, always remained strangers in the tightly structured world of rural Friesland. Korrie, their daughter, became a certified nurse and accepted a position in the Jewish mental hospital, *Het Apeldoornse Bosch* in the Dutch town of Apeldoorn. She always felt more comfortable in the Jewish culture of that hospital than she had ever felt in her own hometown.

Beppe had no way of knowing that Korrie had already voiced her worries about the rising anti-Semitism when she had visited her mother the previous week. "The Germans are after us, Mom, in the same way that they have been after the Jews in Germany for almost ten years now. We, as Jews, are not even allowed, by the Germans, to seek safety in underground bomb shelters when sirens go off in town and a bomb attack is imminent."

Mrs. Vellinga had already been deeply shaken by her daughter's words, but now, with shards of glass around her, she had the feeling that her mind had become a broken record that endlessly beat the words ever more deeply into her brain. As the outside noises poured into her home, through the open window, she desperately wanted to crawl into some quiet space so that her heart would stop pounding and she could think clearly again.

A few days earlier, after Andy had come into her library, she had allowed Elske to see some of the emotional strain under which she was living. She had been overwhelmed by her kind words and had, as a consequence, momentarily let down her guard and given a helping hand as Elske and Zak whisked the banned books out of her library. Now she clearly saw that she should never have supported their plan to build an illicit library.

There was a long silence after Beppe told Betsie that she was welcome to stay with her on the farm. The librarian finally shook her head and whispered: "I can't do that."

When she saw the agony on the face of the troubled librarian, Beppe was quiet for a long time. She sank into her chair again and, looking at the librarian, said in a gentle voice: "Do you mind if I call you by your first name, 'Betsie'? You can call me 'Katje.'" As if in an afterthought, she added: "We are, after all, just two old people who are utterly confused by what is happening around us, and we need each other's support."

A large tear ran down Mrs. Vellinga's cheek when she heard Beppe use her personal name. There was a quiver in her voice when she silently nodded her head and said: "By all means, *Mevrouw* . . . I mean, Katje." In a hushed tone, she added: "No one has called me by that name since David died over five years ago."

"Betsie, you may feel that I am intruding in your life, but I came to your house today because of what your uncle, Professor Luimskuyl, told me. During the last twenty years he has been my rock of support. He has been an advocate for me and for my physically impaired son. It is because of him that we were able to safely walk through so many dark nights of deep despair. People from this town would sometimes stop me in the street and bluntly tell me, as they looked at my little Idske, 'Wouldn't it be better if he just died?'"

"Our last appointment with your uncle was six weeks ago, and he was ruthlessly blunt about what he saw as the writing on the wall. 'The Nazis' he told me, 'are quite clear about the fact that they are prepared to dispose of anybody whom they view as human trash. Jews like me as well as handicapped people like your son are the first candidates for their obscene purification program. If we do nothing to protect ourselves, then we will be flushed down the toilet in the twinkling of an eye.'"

The two women were silent when they reflected on the dreadful thought that the neurologist had put into words. Beppe looked the librarian in the eyes as she said: "The reason that I came here today is because your kind uncle asked me if I would be willing to regularly check up on you. He called you 'my sweet niece Betsie.' He also told me that he had helped your daughter, Korrie, get her job as a nurse at the Jewish mental hospital in Apeldoorn. I should have come earlier but, when I heard what happened to you, I came as fast as I could. Please allow me to help you in the same way that your uncle has helped us so many times during the past twenty years."

After Beppe had stopped talking, Mrs. Vellinga shook her head. "Even though I am afraid all the time," she said, "I am still determined to stay here because this is my home."

Then her voice faltered as she picked up a copy of the Aryan Declaration that her tormentors had thrown on the table. "Katje," she said in a quavering voice, "this really does scare me because it will not only make me a target of Nazi hate, but it will also cost me my job."

Beppe no longer argued with the demoralized librarian.

"We're going to get your window fixed," she said softly.

After leaving Mrs. Vellinga's home, Beppe went to the paint store and instructed the store manager, Mr. Koen, to have his handyman repair the window in the house on Boelelaan 223. "If it is at all possible, I want you to have it done today. You can send me a copy of the bill."

Mr. Koen knew that Beppe was one of his good customers and assured her that the repairs would be made before the sun had set. The work was duly done, and Beppe was later troubled by the hefty bill that had been sent to the librarian but which she took care of.

After leaving the paint store, Beppe went to the home of Pastor Sven and told him about what had happened to Mrs. Vellinga. The earnest young man listened to her silently until she had finished with her story.

He then told her what Klees had done. "That Koorder boy is nothing but trouble. Lennie, our milk delivery man, just told me that yesterday he saw those same guys speeding away from Uleske. While bringing milk to the front steps of the Medemblik home, he noticed that someone had painted the words: 'Go home, Jews' on that Jewish doctor's front door. The paint wasn't dry yet, so Lennie was sure that it was either Klees or Andy who had vandalized that home."

Beppe was about to leave, but the pastor urged her to stay for a few minutes and talk about what could be done. "Because," he said, "we can't just sit on our hands and do nothing about such acts of violence.

"But where do we start when even our policemen are paralyzed? Earlier today I briefly spoke with our new town constable, Hans Sybersma. I told him in no uncertain terms that they, as police, needed to put a stop to the violent actions of the Nazi boys. He vaguely nodded his head and, with a troubled expression on his face, assured me that he was deeply sorry for what had happened. He told me that his hands are tied because he had to report to German supervisors who, for their part, actively encourage young Dutch criminals such as Klees who are stirring up all this trouble.

"Mrs. Ruintjes," the pastor continued, "yesterday was really a bad day for me because the fear that I felt in the policeman's office has also entered the council room of our church. During our monthly Council meeting last night, I proposed that our church should have a special collection to raise the funds needed to help Jews like Mrs. Vellinga who are affected by Nazi violence."

Sven stopped talking for a minute and slowly shook his head as he again reflected on what happened next. "Boy, did I meet some stiff head winds! I was told, in no uncertain terms, that my proposal would be voted down and, on top of that, it would not even be recorded in the minutes of the meeting. If I wanted money to assist our Jewish neighbors, it would have to come from the church building fund and there it must be recorded as a church window repair. One respected elder stood up and was almost screaming when he came to his concluding sentence: 'I don't ever want to be caught standing between the Jews and the Germans!'

"I'm not sure how we should act during these dark days. I also called Rev. Bolstra from our sister church in Terperdam, and tried to say that Klees had to be put under church discipline for being an active member of the Dutch Nazi movement again, and for terrorizing people in our communities. The pastor, when he heard me mention the name of Klees, would not even let me finish my sentence; there was a breathless panic in his voice as he hurriedly said that he was busy and had no time to talk. He then abruptly hung up the phone on me."

Beppe thanked the pastor for his willingness to listen to her and ended with the words: "Indeed, we can't just sit on our hands and do nothing!"

That evening during supper time, Beppe told Zak and Steward about her day and that she had dropped in on Mrs. Vellinga before coming home. "I found her huddled in the kitchen," she said. "At least her window has been repaired, and I could see that she was somewhat more relaxed when I told her that she is welcome to stay with us any time she feels unsafe in her home."

Later that evening, Steward vented the frustrations he had been feeling since sundown. "We've got to stop the terrorism of Klees and his buddies. We also can't allow ourselves to be humiliated in this way! Are we supposed to crawl into the mud as these blustering Dutch cockroaches parade around in their Nazi uniforms and terrorize the people in our town?"

A week later, on a Saturday evening, Steward was able to assemble a few of his friends who met together in the tiny hiding place that was beginning to function as Zak's regular home.

Steward had called the meeting because he wanted his friends to help him put a stop to the terror campaign of the Dutch Nazis in the region. With the use of a map, he demonstrated how those troublemakers worked and where they would probably strike next time.

Looking directly at his friends, Steward raised his voice an octave higher. "We must do something to stop that violence. We should beat them up or, maybe run them off the road the next time they terrorize somebody."

The meeting was cut very short because the moment that Steward raised the idea of using physical force to stop the criminality of Klees and his gang, there was a blank wall of silence.

Hobbe categorically refused to even entertain the idea of taking any direct action because from his perspective, that would be doing something terribly wrong. At one point he got to his feet and said: "God has placed the Germans in authority over us, and we have to submit to their commands."

The meeting ended in disarray because Steward was unable to budge his friends. The only thing that the group could agree on was that they would take out a subscription to the recently started Calvinist underground newspaper, *Vrij Nederland* which, they had been told, could be purchased from someone who went by the pen name, "Harry."

After the others left, Joost stayed behind because he wanted to have a private conversation with Steward and Zak. There was determination in his voice as well as a twinkle in his eyes as he told them about some information he had gleaned earlier in the day. He had been quietly drinking a beer in *De Water Bak* when he overheard the loud voice of Klees coming from the other side of the bar: "Tomorrow evening, just when it's getting dark, we're going to Klewerdam and find the bicycle cart owned by that old Jew who lives there. Once we find it, we'll just push it and all those filthy rags into a canal. A good Aryan should take over the route where that Jew has, for years, been getting rich because he is the only fabric collector in that area."

The plan that Joost outlined for the two brothers involved ambushing Klees and his friends as they made their way to Klewerdam. But the attack never happened because Zak refused to help and because of the dense fog that enveloped the landscape on the morning of the planned ambush.

As it happened, Klees and Andy did try to go to Klewerdam on that foggy morning, but in a curve in the road, they drove their motorcycle and side car into the canal on the north side of the road. They spent several hours extracting their disabled motorcycle from the canal and painfully pushing it back to Sebeek.

Lennie, in preparation for his pre-dawn milk deliveries, was heading towards Klewerdam when he saw a slow-moving object coming towards him. He stopped his horse and milk cart and through the dense fog, asked the shadowy figures moving towards him if they needed any help. He was greeted by a volley of abusive words.

Later, however, he was quietly chuckling to himself because he was sure that he had recognized the voices of Andy and Klees.

Chapter Fourteen

A New Life for Klees
(Fall 1940)

AFTER THE MISHAP THAT Klees had experienced near Klewerdam, he temporarily stopped terrorizing the Jewish residents who lived in and around Sebeek. The other Nazi party members from his gang followed the example of their leader and, for many months, stopped their campaign of intimidation. Many Jews hoped that the worst of their troubles might be over, but Korrie and her mother had no such illusions.

Everyone had their own explanation for the temporary lull in the terror campaign. Steward hoped that the Klees' new-found caution stemmed from an old fear. Perhaps he would conclude their motorcycle mishap was not really an accident. Hans Sybersma, the Ter Loo policeman, was convinced that the personal letter that he had, as a fellow policeman, sent to Klees' father had temporarily ended the random acts of local terrorism.

Mr. Koorder was relieved that his son had finally heeded his words of warning. It had not been easy for him to be stern with his son, but by the end of September, he had become convinced that he would again have to talk to him about his abhorrent behavior. As a Sebeek policeman, he sometimes overheard the angry things that people said about his son's crimes.

The carefully prepared father-and-son conversation did not go very well. Mr. Koorder started the discussion by profusely apologizing to his son for again asking him to break his ties to the Nazi party.

"Our church," he said "will soon discipline you for belonging to that political party. You must not honor the Nazi creed more than you honor

God." He left it at that and said nothing about the anti-Semitic crimes that Klees and his followers had been committing.

Klees, in response to his father's mild reprimand, exploded with rage. He hammered the coffee table with his fist. "Church discipline!" he roared. "What do you and the other damned members of the Calvinist church know about discipline? The Germans are the only ones around here who have the discipline needed to straighten up our ruined society! I do not want spineless church people playing around with my life. The state of my soul is an issue that only involves me and God. The church should stick to its own business of getting people to heaven. It can't tell me what my politics should be!"

At first Mr. Koorder absorbed the abuse that his son had hurled at him in silence. Then, after a hush of several minutes, he meekly suggested that since it was already late in the day, they should both get some rest.

Klees, instead of taking the olive branch that his father had extended, glared at him as he spit out the words, "I do not need rest. I want action."

With those words he abruptly got up and snatched his coat off the hanger. He then dashed from the house and slammed the door behind him.

His departure, it turned out, was permanent because he found his own apartment and refused, for years, to have any interaction with his family. His father did not see him again until after the war when he visited the prison camp where his son was then incarcerated.

The same unfettered anger that had destroyed the ties that Klees had with his parents, also caused the termination of his engagement to his fiancée Kimke Mollema. The background to that broken engagement became part of the public record in 1947 when Bram Mollema, Kimke's father, was called in to testify against Klees.

What follows are some excerpts from the post war criminal case brought against Klees:

> Klees came to our house unexpectedly on June 15th, 1940, and announced that he and Kimke were planning to go the annual Nazi mass rally; it was to take place in Lunteren on June 22. This, you must remember, was only about a month after those monstrous Germans had destroyed our cities, killed our soldiers, and invaded our country.
>
> (Bram Mollema was quiet for some time on the witness stand before he was able to control his emotions and continue). I looked at his black Nazi uniform and felt a shudder go up my spine; I did, however, control myself as I calmly asked him to leave our home. At the door I told him that only if he denounced his

loyalty to the Dutch Nazi party—which our church had already condemned—could his engagement to my daughter continue.

(The father had a pained and meditative tone as he continued.) "Sarah and I should have been a better mother and father for Kimke in the following months when she continued to live and work in Leeuwarden and was also still seeing Klees. There was only one reason why she went along with him to Lunteren in June. He threatened to beat her if she didn't go. It was also pure fear that caused her to pretend that she still planned to go ahead with their December wedding.

The turning point in their engagement happened in early September when there was a Nazi rally in Sebeek. Arnold Meyer, a rising star in the Dutch Nazi party, was scheduled to be the keynote speaker. When Kimke refused to go with Klees to that meeting, he hit her on the head so hard that she fell unconscious on the hard floor. What did he do next? The scoundrel, afraid that he had actually killed her, swiftly left her apartment.

She had to be hospitalized for a week because of a head trauma. During that time, she was unable to come in for work and, consequently, she also lost her waitressing job. While resting up in our home, she finally agreed with us that the planned marriage to Klees must not happen. She insisted, however, that we should not press charges against the young man. The best that we could do was to send her away to live with a distant relative in Zeeland. (She still lives there). We were all afraid of what Klees would do next."

Shortly after leaving home and destroying his relationship with his fiancée, Klees made the decision to offer his services to the Germans as a paid spy. Mr. Ulermann, for whom he had done translation work during the previous summer, became his handler.

As the commander of Sebeek, Ulermann kept detailed notes in which he recorded all his activities during the war years. Those records are carefully preserved in the Dutch war archives and were used, as evidence, in the court case against Klees. The court transcript included the following quote from the Ulermann logbooks:

> On Oct. 10, 1940, Klees K. came to me and asked if my soldiers could help protect him and his friends from attacks by hostile locals. I told him that that would be impossible. He and his comrades would have to take care of themselves if they stirred up local hostility.
>
> I also told him that we had checked up on the motorcycle accident that they had reported and there may have been some

foul play because there were several different kinds of fresh boot prints in the area around the scene of the accident. I told him that the best we could do was to treat it as an open investigation, but because we could not rely on local police, we would not actively pursue the case.

I could see that Klees was shocked by my refusal to really help him, and he obviously felt that we didn't value the work that the he and the other Dutch Nazi members had done for our cause. I assured him, however, that we valued them as committed soldiers who were fighting in the same war that we were engaged in; like us they had to count on getting some painful battle scars. I praised him for his zeal and tireless dedication in the war against the real enemies of society—the Jews.

From his face, I could see that I had pushed all the right buttons. A kind of youthful pride washed over the face of the young man, and I was able to capitalize on that emotion when I changed the focus of the conversation.

I told him that I wanted to enlist him, for the time being, in another and equally critical front in the war that was being waged against our Nazi movement.

He looked at me inquiringly when I told him that, as German commanders in the Netherlands, we were often confused by the religious language that many Dutch people used as they discussed political issues. To us it seemed that direct acts of rebellion were often imbedded in the religious words of both the clergy and the Dutch laity. I emphasized to him that I could use the help of someone who was able to translate that god talk into clear German political concepts. We needed to know exactly what political and military trouble that we could expect to face as we brought the ideals of our movement to the Dutch church as well as the whole web of Dutch religious organizations—such as Christian schools and Christian Labor Unions.

From the expression on the young man's face I could see that he was listening carefully to me. I pointed to the envelope on the table and told him that it contained one thousand guilders which he could put in his pocket if he agreed to be my religious affairs consultant. All he needed to do for me was to report to me once a week and provide me with a written record of his activities. That way, I told him, he would help me to firmly deal with any religious related challenges to our Nazi authority. I told him that if I was satisfied with his work then, at the end of each month, there would be another envelope waiting for him on my desk. If I was really happy with his performance, it would probably again contain 1000 guilders.

I could see that Klees' hands trembled slightly as he took the envelope with the money and placed it in the inside pocket of his jacket. Then he saluted me and, with his impressively powerful voice, said, "I am prepared to be your religious affairs consultant. Heil Hitler."

After that visit to Mr. Ulermann's office, Klees wandered aimlessly around town for several hours. Different people later reported seeing him going in and out of various stores during that same afternoon. The last store that he visited was the Berkelmann hardware store directly across from the train station.

As the young man emerged from that store, at closing time, he must have observed Korrie Vellinga as she was taking her bicycle out of the bike shelter adjacent to the train station. She had just come from Leeuwarden and still had to make the hour-long bike ride to Ter Loo. It was going to be a dark ride because the sun was already low on the horizon. She quickly got on her bike and didn't notice Klees on the side of the road when she passed him.

Klees, on the other hand, had seen Korrie as she passed him. Something about her dark maroon coat and black scarf must have caught his attention; those were also the colors in Kimke's favorite winter coat and scarf. As he saw the young woman on the bicycle disappear down the road, a wave of anger washed over him as he was again reminded that Kimke had permanently thrown him out of her life. Somebody, he felt, had to suffer for the pain that had been done to him by that woman.

He had no idea where his former girlfriend had gone, but he could clearly see where this young woman was going. He had been hurt, and now he had the right to inflict pain on someone within his reach. His dark thoughts turned into a deadly action plan the moment it occurred to him that the young woman who had just passed him was a young Jewess—none other than Korrie Vellinga. He had seen a picture of her on the mantelpiece in Mrs. Vellinga's house and had often heard from Kimke, who liked to play the piano, that Mrs. Vellinga's only daughter was a most accomplished pianist.

Within minutes, Klees had jumped on his bike and was following his prey. It was already six o'clock when he started to follow her. An hour later, when he knocked on the door of Vellinga's house, a quiet voice called from the inside: "You can open the door. It is not locked." Mrs. Vellinga thought that the person at the door was Zak; he had promised to come by at seven to deliver the latest issue of the illegal paper *Vrij Nederland*.

Klees pushed open the door, strode into the house, and with one swift blow to the head, knocked Mrs. Vellinga out. She had no memory of landing heavily on the hard linoleum floor. Later, however, she would vaguely remember that it had been the voice of Klees that had growled out the words: "I told you I'd come back."

Korrie was sitting in the kitchen when she heard that loud crash in the front room, immediately followed by that low, growly voice.

Before Korrie had time to react, a powerful man had grabbed her by the hair, dragged her to her bedroom, and forced her onto the bed and raped her.

There was rank insanity in his rasping voice. "Your rotten Jewish body will benefit from some good Aryan seed."

He probably would have killed Korrie if there had not been another knock on the door—a quiet one. Klees heard the knock and swiftly got up, pulled up his pants and dashed out of the back door. He hopped on his bicycle which he had left in the narrow alley adjacent to the house, and vanished into the darkness.

This time it was Zak who was knocking on the door. At first, he heard no response from inside the house. He waited for some time and was about to leave when, on impulse, he decided to knock one more time. The door swung open, and in the dim light, he could see that it was Korrie, and not Mrs. Vellinga who was standing in the light of the doorway.

Korrie grabbed him by the coat and pulled him into the house.

"Help me," she said, "My mother has just been attacked."

As she said those last words she started to fumble with the deadbolt of the door. Zak took one look around the room and saw Mrs. Vellinga lying on the floor with a pool of blood near her head. When she had fallen to the ground her head had struck a sharp corner of the small coal burning stove in the living room. The ugly head wound was still bleeding profusely when Zak came into the room.

Zak swiftly slid the deadbolt into place for Korrie and then rushed to the kitchen to securely lock the back door.

When he came back into the living room, Korrie was on her knees next to her mother whispering something to her. Mrs. Vellinga was still lying prostrate on the ground, but her eyes were open. She was trying to say something to Korrie.

Zak, who still did not know what had happened, returned to the kitchen and brought back a cold wet towel. Korrie did not even look up as she took it from him and gently placed it on the dark welt that was forming on her mother's forehead.

By 8 p.m. that evening, Zak and Korrie were able to lift the tired Mrs. Vellinga off the floor and put her into a chair near the stove. Zak scribbled a note stating that he would be back soon with some help, and left the house.

One hour later, Zak and Steward came back with the Ruintjes car as well as a note from Beppe insisting that the Korrie and her mom stay, at least for the night, at their farmhouse.

Chapter Fifteen

Two Pregnant Women
(Spring 1941)

"[It is an] inescapable fact that our [Dutch] resistance to the Jewish Holocaust was an epic disaster. We [the Dutch people] indirectly helped the Germans when we signed the Aryan declaration and then we were quiet spectators as the Germans terrorized the Jewish people."

—ANNE DE VRIES

AFTER ARRIVING AT THE Ruintjes' farm, Korrie never left the side of her sick mother who, even when she was awake, was only partly coherent. The day after the attack, the elderly woman finally opened her eyes widely and her mouth began to form a real smile when she saw her daughter sitting near her.

That expression of love was instantly replaced by a look of fear. Korrie could barely hear what her mother was whispering to herself. "Perhaps it was not all a dream. Something must have happened."

Then, looking more closely at Korrie, she asked: "Where are we? What happened to me? Wasn't Zak the person who knocked softly on the door and came in? What has happened to you? You look ill."

Korrie, who did not know where to begin, only brought up the attack. "Someone broke into our house, and he hit you on the head. Beppe

Ruintjes has offered us the safety of her home and we can stay here as long as necessary."

Beppe, to get some fresh clothing for her guests, had gone to the Vellinga's home earlier that morning. When she entered Korrie's bedroom, she immediately saw an opened pocket-knife on the floor adjacent to the bed. She picked it up and inspected it carefully. On the handle she noticed that someone had carved the name, "Klees." She closed the blade of the knife and slipped it into the handbag she was carrying and which she had planned to use for the clothing that she had come for.

Before leaving the Vellinga home, Bepe decided to look around the bedroom one more time. It was then that she, as tidy Dutch housewife, noticed that the lightly colored bed cover had not been properly tucked in. Then, looking more closely, she also saw that it had been soiled by what looked like an ugly, dark bloodstain.

She shivered as she thought about what had happened in this house the previous evening. Klees had obviously been back and had almost murdered Mrs. Vellinga and had, it appeared, also raped Korrie. But how was she to talk about those things to the mother and the daughter? Would they agree to bring charges against Klees?

With those thoughts in her mind, she left the house too quickly because she almost tripped and fell as she came down the two front steps.

The ever-practical Beppe, who was usually fearless when confronting a difficult problem, did not know what to say as she sat near the door to the room where a mother and a daughter were whispering to each other. How could she help these terrified people? What should she say? Should she speak now about what she had observed in their home, or should she allow some time to pass?

As she waited, she was pulled out of her reverie by Mrs. Vellinga's hoarse voice. "We want to thank you for your hospitality but, this afternoon, we will go back to our own home."

Zak, as he was coming into the room, heard his mother sigh deeply as she said: "That's impossible. You simply must, for your safety, stay here."

Both Korrie and her mother seemed to talk in unison as they protested. "We can't be a burden for you and your family any longer. We plan to go home as soon as possible."

Their voices trailed into the mist as they looked at the determined expression on Beppe's deeply lined face.

"Why are you so insistent that we stay with you?" Korrie asked in a resigned tone.

Beppe looked at her closely as she answered. "I am afraid that Klees will come back to your house and, if he finds you again, he will kill both you and your mother."

The deadly silence in the room lasted for more than a minute before she continued. "Tomorrow Steward and I will go to your house and bring back anything that you may need; while we are in town we will also go to the police and make a crime report."

When she heard the word "police," Korrie got up from her chair with a look of terror on her face. "Please, do not contact the police!" she pleaded.

Mrs. Vellinga, who was pulling herself into a sitting position in bed, also shook her head. Zak could barely overhear as she whispered: "We have absolutely no confidence in the police. They have done nothing in response to the earlier hate attacks that took place. What will they do if they hear that two more Jews have been injured? They will get rid of this report as they have done with all previous injury reports affecting Jews.

At that point, Elske came to help. She had heard about the arrival of the Vellingas and had prepared a dish of mashed potatoes-and-sauerkraut for the family supper. After placing the food in the kitchen, she was drawn to the murmur of voices coming from the bedroom. Zak's tall frame blocked the door to the bedroom, so she gently touched his shoulder before stepping past him. She entered the room in time to hear Mrs. Vellinga bitterly utter the words, "new cruelty."

Elske went to Korrie and, after quietly introducing herself, said: "I can't even imagine what you and your mother have been through, but I am only a few steps away from here and will help you in every way that is in my power."

Later, during that same day, Korrie asked Elske if she would join her as she went back to her mother's home to pick up some clothing for herself and her mother. "We will go very early in the morning, and if you are with me, I won't be frightened when I enter Mom's home." Elske was glad to go with her.

The next morning, as they approached Ter Loo, Korrie abruptly stopped her bike and got off. Elske also dismounted from her bike and looked closely at Korrie's pale face. "Is something wrong?" she asked. "Are you feeling ill? We can sit in the grass on the side of the road until you catch your breath."

Korrie shook her head. "I am OK. Let's get going." She got back on her bicycle but soon had to stop again because she seemed unable to keep her balance.

It was then that Elske noticed that there were tears streaming down Korrie's face. This time she threw her own bike onto the ground and, looking directly at Korrie, exclaimed: "Something is wrong! What is it?"

Korrie tried to wipe the tears away, but it was no use. The combined feelings of fear, anger and revulsion overwhelmed her and, as she looked at Elske's gentle face, she started to cry hysterically.

Elske put her arms around her and said: "It's OK. Did that intruder hurt you the other night? We do not have to go back to that house. I can go sometime later by myself."

During the next hour, as they were biking back to the Ruintjer farm, Korrie kept repeating the word "dirty" as she talked about what had happened less than two days earlier. "I feel so dirty and can't even find the words to talk to my mother about the horrors of that night."

No report of the heinous attack made by Klees ever went to the Ter Loo police station. Mrs. Vellinga did not dare to go home again and eventually accepted Beppe's invitation to stay in the guest bedroom of her farmhouse. Korrie, after using up all of the two weeks of vacation that she had accumulated, went back to her job as a nurse in the psychiatric hospital, *Het Apeldoornse Bosch*.

Her job became increasingly tense because the German authorities terrorized the Jewish family members of her patients by hemming them in through their increasingly vicious restrictions.

Week after week, as she plodded to her job, Korrie had the feeling that she was pushing her way through a thick, impenetrable fog. She kept going, but it was as if she could no longer see the ground in front of her. What would happen to her mother? And what would happen to the helpless patients in the hospital who were increasingly isolated because their family support network was being systematically destroyed by the vicious Nazis? What was happening to her? She felt that she was utterly alone in a cold, hostile world. She tried to tell herself that the angry voices that she heard during the night were only figments of her imagination. There were, after all, no real wolves in the vicinity of the forest, or *bos*, surrounding the *Apeldoornse Bosch*.

Then, on December 15, 1940, she woke up from a nightmare. She felt sure that she had really been bitten by a wolf. She imagined, when she was fully awake, that her stomach muscles were still crying out in agony. Her mind was racing as it dodged around the fact that was beginning to take shape in her brain. Could it be true that she was pregnant? Was the shock of the rape perhaps not the reason why she had again missed her period? Her training as nurse told her that all the troubles that her body had been giving her during the past two months could only be explained by the fact that a new life was growing within her.

She remained sleepless until the first light of the morning. She then packed a light overnight bag, called in sick, and took the earliest train to Leeuwarden and from there, the train to Sebeek. By noon of that same day, she knocked on the door of Elske's small house.

Piet was not at home. Elske opened the door and welcomed Korrie into her modest but well-organized home. The only sound that greeted her was the bubbling of a large pot of brown beans simmering on the stove. Elske could see that Korrie was quietly crying, so she put her arms around her and hugged her tightly. That simple motion was too much for Korrie; she burst out in tears and, for the next ten minutes, she shook uncontrollably as she wept.

Elske at first continued to hold her tightly and then quietly led her to a sofa and sat next to her. Korrie was inconsolable and, through her tears, kept saying the same words. At first Elske could not understand what she was saying, but she finally realized what was tormenting the troubled girl. She was telling her that she was pregnant with the child of a devil.

Elske hugged her even tighter and said, over and over: "It will be okay." But even as she said those words, she could not imagine what Korrie must be feeling.

The hours slipped away as Korrie repeatedly burst into tears. Eventually she became quiet, and slowly turning around, she looked closely into Elske's face as she said: "You told me to come to you if I am ever in trouble, and you said that you would do what you could to help me. Well, I am in trouble. Tell me what should I do? How am I to hide my shame for the next seven months when an abortion is not an option for me? When my boss finds out that I'm pregnant, he'll just fire me immediately. I will never get a job again after the baby is born. How can I, all by myself, ever take care of this devil's child?"

"Korrie," Elske said, "I don't have any answers to your questions; you are, however, not alone."

Korrie's worst fears turned into a deeply troubling reality during the next four weeks when, each day, she suffered from a debilitating case of morning sickness. She had gone back to work, but was often not able to complete her assigned duties. By the middle of January, she decided that something had to be done because she could no longer adequately do her job. She had not shared her secret with anyone at work, but often had the feeling she was being watched closely whenever she walked along the hospital corridors.

Elske never stopped thinking about the plight of her friend. Finally, in consultation with both Beppe and Mrs. Vellinga, she came up with a plan which they hoped would help Korrie. Elske found a discrete midwife in the adjacent town of Sauerdam. Beppe, through Dr. Luimskuyl, asked the manager of *Het Apeldoornse Bosch* for an eight month leave of absence for Korrie. She needed that time, that manager was told, to recover from residual effects of emotional stress she had suffered when attacked in her house. Beppe was prepared to use her home as a place where Korrie could quietly live during her months of pregnancy.

Elske had been too worried about Korrie during the month of December to notice that she herself had already missed her second period. She and Piet had not yet planned to start having a family, but their carefully crafted plans had fallen apart by the end of December. That was the month when her doctor told her that she was pregnant.

Early in the morning of January 9, 1941, Elske caught a morning train that took her to Apeldoorn. She had no trouble finding the private home where Korrie had rented a room. Mrs. Hoekema, the landlady, opened the door after Elske had knocked only once.

"Korrie," the elderly matron said, "has just left the house. She has gone to the small grocery store around the corner and next to the barber shop. She had weekend duty, and for that reason, has the day off". Elske could not help but notice that the landlady furtively looked up and down the street as she spoke.

Elske thanked the landlady and set out to find the small grocery store that had been pointed out to her. She soon found her friend and noticed that she was blankly staring at the largely empty shelves where the jams and other spreads had been displayed before the war. The two young women greeted each other with a simple nod of the head.

It was only when they were outside the store that Elske gave Korrie a quick hug and said: "We need to talk."

Korrie took a deep breath, quickly wiped away a tear and said, in a tremulous voice: "Not here and not at this moment. Let's go for a walk after I take these things to my room."

After putting away her groceries, Korrie took Elske to a quiet street with stately houses and very few people on the sidewalks. Only then did they settle down on a secluded bench. The first thing Korrie said was: "I'm still pregnant and have no idea what to do."

Elske then outlined the interim plan that she, along with Korrie's mom and Beppe, had developed. Korrie was silent for a long time and there was a bitter edge to her voice when she finally replied.

"And then what? I, a single Jewish girl, am going to be saddled with a Jewish baby in a world where the Germans and their Dutch lackeys want to kill all Jews. What kind of life is that?"

Elske took Korrie by the hand. "Now I come to something that I haven't told anyone yet, she said. "I discovered, since we had our last conversation, that I am also pregnant. That is the part that Piet knows. What he does not know is what I want to talk about with you. I want to make it appear, when your baby comes, that your baby is a twin of my baby. After the war, when this Nazi nightmare has ended, I will immediately give your child back to you."

Korrie sat very quietly beside Elske for a long time on that dark green park bench. Restless gusts of wind wrenched the last leaves from the branches to which they had tenaciously clung for the previous two winter months. Elske always remembered those leaves as she thought of what Korrie said next. "During the last few weeks, I have often wished that I would just die. Then my troubles would go away, and I could rest quietly under the leaves. But now you give me a glimmer of hope. Perhaps I will be able to continue with my life."

During the days after that conversation, Korrie's life underwent a fundamental change. From her employer she received the medical leave that her uncle had asked for on her behalf. She moved from the busy city life of Apeldoorn to the quiet Ruintjes farm. Instead of caring for many mentally ill patients she now spent many hours with her ailing mother who, it turned out, was sinking into an ever-deepening depression. Betsie could not stop herself from thinking of all the troubles that she and her daughter would have to face during the coming months.

Korrie, after attempting to be cheerful with her mother during the daytime hours, would quietly leave the farmhouse after sunset and take long walks down the quiet, dark country roads. She often walked for two or three hours but, even after coming back, she was often still unable to fall asleep until well after midnight.

When she heard about Korrie's restless nighttime walks, Elske tried to convince her friend to stop risking life and limb on those dark and slippery roads. "Korrie, it is simply too dangerous for you to aimlessly go up and down these small, narrow country roads during these dark evenings. You could easily slip into the canals; that is happening all over the country these days because of the German's strictly enforced lights-out ordinances."

"I know the dangers," Korrie said, "but I will go insane if I don't get out of this house during the evening hours. Have you seen what the Germans are telling us Jews to do now? In order to get our food ration cards we need to have an ID. To get that ID, my mom and I need to report that we are Jews! Next they will tell us to march in front of a firing squad "

"Well," Elske replied, "If you are told to march in front of a firing squad then they will have to shoot me too because my baby and I will be marching along with you. You and I are Siamese twins, and they can't cut us apart from each other."

She laughed and gently placed her arm on Korrie's shoulder and walked beside her from the living room to the back door. Together the two young women disappeared into the night.

Through the poorly sealed window, Zak could hear Korrie repeatedly urging Elske to go back indoors but Elske did not listen to her friend. "We are Siamese twins and I have to go where you go."

And that is exactly what she did. All through the winter, spring and early summer of 1941, as Hitler's vast army prepared for its attack on Stalin's Soviet empire, Elske and Korrie took their daily walks along the quiet Frisian roads.

Korrie's baby was born on July 1, 1941, and Elske and Piet's son, Sypke was born two weeks later. The two boys, as twins, were baptized in the Ter Loo Calvinist church on July 27, 1941.

Piet and Elske went to great lengths to shield you, Jay, from Hitler's long arms by treating you as their natural son. In the Dutch public civil registry, Elske and Piet are listed as your actual parents and July 15th is the date that is given as your official date of birth. That was the actual birthday of their natural son, Sypke. The plan, all along, was to give you back to Korrie after the end of the war.

Korrie, your natural mother, did not witness the baptism of her own son because it was not safe for her to be in the church. Nazi spies, known as "sermon tigers," regularly attended most church services and secretly sent church related reports to their German handlers.

Klees was the tiger on duty to report on the church service of the Calvinist church of Ter Loo on the day when the two boys were baptized. As a Nazi operator he probably paid no attention to the actual baptism ceremony because he wanted to report on the sermon of Pastor Sven who, he knew, had repeatedly warned his parishioners about the dangers of National Socialism. He also had a personal vendetta against the pastor. Sven had been behind the church's effort to get hard core young local Nazi party members like Klees removed from the regional Calvinist Youth organization.

The note that Klees sent to his German handler was very brief and to the point. "Pastor Sven told his church members that Hitler is the devil. I recommend that you have him arrested immediately because his words undoubtedly fuel an anti-German mindset among his parishioners."

Pastor Sven's sermon, which can be found in the Ulermann archive, was indeed quite critical of the new rulers of the Netherlands. The title of the sermon was a simple question. *To What Blood Voice are We Listening to Today?* The sermon ended as follows:

> Today, tomorrow and the day after that, you and I will have to again and again decide what blood voice we want to listen to. Will we listen to the quiet voice of the pure, sprinkled blood of our Savior—who laid down his life down for us? Will we hear the pure sound coming from the sprinkled blood of the God-man who was one hundred percent God and one hundred percent man—a Jewish man?
>
> Or will our ears be deaf to that sound because we are afraid. Will we, with Cain, try to tell God that we are not our brother's keeper? Will God be happy with that answer when we stand in front of his judgment seat and he asks us why we were silent when the windows of our Jewish neighbor's houses were shattered by Nazi hooligans during the middle of the night? Will God be happy with us when we do nothing more than close our blinds when the green police, with their roaring trucks, come into our neighborhoods at night to arrest our Jewish fellow citizens and take them to places unknown?
>
> I ask you, brothers, and sisters of the Lord Jesus Christ, where should we be as the people of Israel are again being forced to march into the Red Sea—the Sea of Blood? Will we be thundering towards them as horsemen along with Pharaoh and all his demonic chariots? Or will we, with the voice of the sprinkled

blood of Christ in our ears, walk alongside the Jews who are being driven into a modern Red Sea? Are we prepared, in faith, to
witness miracles as our Savior and champion again holds back
the ugly walls of blood that threaten to engulf the people of both
the first and the second covenant?

Today, tomorrow, and the day after that, we must continue
to listen, with faith-filled hearts, to the better voice. A cloud of
Jewish witnesses, listed in the book of Hebrews, will breathe out
an Amen from Heaven if they see that we are really listening to
the sound of the better word.

Two days after the sermon had been delivered, Pastor Sven was arrested and his office was thoroughly ransacked by the six members of the
Gestapo who had come to take him away on the orders of Ulermann. The
word *"Deutschfiendlich"* was written in massive letters on first page of the
above sermon.

Chapter Sixteen

Living with the Sword of Damocles
(Fall 1941)

"Only a small number of those of us [Dutchmen]who are non-Jews stepped up to the plate and demonstrated brotherly love to our Jewish countrymen during that year when a large majority of them were murdered (summer 1942 to summer 1943)."

—WYBENGA

YOU, JAY, WERE STILL a Jewish infant during the apocalyptic year when the Germans put the final pieces in place for the organized mass murder of all European Jews. Steward and his friends, like almost everyone at that time, were unable to get their minds around what was happening to the Jewish people in their midst.

"When Hitler defeated us last May, everyone in the whole country knew that our new Nazi overlords were hell bent on suppressing the Jewish population in Europe. Anti-Semitism is a cornerstone of their damned ideology. The Jewish people are, for those tyrants, the arch enemies of the German people."

Steward had started the September 20, 1941, meeting in his family's barn with the above words and then continued as follows: "For every Jewish man, woman and child in the Netherlands there is, now, a sharp knife hanging in the air above each of their heads, and the thread holding that deadly weapon in place is as thin as a cat's whisker."

There was a breathless edge of panic in his voice. The five other young men, who sat on milk cans in the dusty hay mow, could see that he had a hard time controlling his stutter when he continued: "What every Dutch person also knows, is that anyone who tries to help even one of their Jewish countrymen, will also have that deadly knife pointing at his or her head. They will, as Pastor Sven told us a few weeks ago, also be pushed into the blood-infested Red Sea. But shouldn't we take that risk? Can't we step out of our comfort zone and hide some of those persecuted Jews in our homes and barns?"

In the following silence, the young men thought about the young pastor who had been taken to the dreaded German prison in Leeuwarden. They knew, from underground sources, that Pastor Sven had already been interrogated and tortured for well over two weeks.

What they had not heard yet was that he would receive a long prison sentence for inciting insubordination when, in his sermon, he had compared Hitler to the pharaoh of Egypt. Sven's punishment had been put into effect immediately. He was first sent to the transitional prison camp of Westerbork and later he was taken to Dachau where the brutality, overwork, meager rations, and illness ultimately killed him a year after his arrest.

The uncomfortable silence ended when Hobbe noisily cleared his throat. He was like a teacher who wanted the whole class to pay attention before allowing his carefully chosen words to leave his mouth.

His voice, however, was also strained as he spoke. "I agree that there is a Sword of Damocles hanging over the head of every single Jew and over the heads of those who assist them. But that's where my agreement with Steward ends. I strongly believe that the rope holding that sword in place is, in our country, still very strong. It is not as fragile as a cat's whisker. We have a system of civil rights that has stood the test of time for four hundred years. Those powerful rights will protect each Dutch citizen, and that includes every Jew in this country. Our Jews are also protected by the fact that they have always been well integrated into our society. There is no ill will towards them."

Once he got started with his speech, Hobbe quickly warmed up to his own arguments. "Look what our doctors are doing. They voted with their feet and dropped their membership in their national doctor's organization when the Germans forced the Nazi doctor, Croin to be their new president. Our physicians and caregivers are standing together and will not allow themselves to be turned into Nazi tools. They felt that they could act in unison because they know that the civil rights of our country give them a firm foundation to stand on."

There was a slight clicking sound in his throat when he ended his soliloquy with the plaintive question: "Don't you agree?"

His last question hung in the air like a desperate plea for several minutes before Geert, the baker's son, started to violently shake his head. He had been quietly listening to Steward and Hobbe, and had, like most careful listeners, avoided the wide-ranging and speculative discussions. When provoked, however, he was not afraid to express his views.

"As I sit here today," he said, "I am terrified by the picture that both of you are drawing. "I'm not as sure as Hobbe that our doctors, by themselves, will be able to restrain the blood-soaked hands of the Nazis. This week the priest of our church read from a recent sermon that had been given by the Bishop of Munster. The bishop used the pulpit to tell Hitler to end his eugenics program. German doctors, who are part of that program, are being used as brooms that sweep up all so-called 'unproductive people,' including the handicapped and mentally disabled, and throw them onto the rubbish heap. There are consistent rumors that specially designed death trucks or death camps are being used to carry out those brutal murders.

"In summary," Geert added, "I am not as convinced as Hobbe that our Jews and our handicapped people are safe. I agree with Steward that the hair holding those swords in place is as thin as a cat's whisker."

Geert was almost speaking in a whisper when he continued: "I'm not sure about you guys, but I know that I am not brave enough to stand under Hitler's sword."

No one could think of a response to Geert's confession. Fear, like a red-hot coal, silently glowed in their midst for several minutes before each one of the young men in the hayloft got up and furtively exited the barn.

Steward was following the others, who had already left the barn, when he heard the angry voice of Piet behind him. "What were you trying to do with this meeting? You will not be helping the Jews if you bring more of them into this community. If you do that, then, before we know it, the Germans will be at our door. What will you saviors do when the Germans throw Korrie and her little boy into their paddy wagon? Do you have the weapons to stop them?"

Later, according to Zak, Piet came back to those same frustrations. "This is going to be a disaster. I should never have agreed with Elske to take in that little boy!"

In his diary entries for the year 1941 Zak repeatedly used the words "disaster" because he felt things were more and more out of control with each succeeding month.

From Zak's point of view, it was a "disaster" when Piet and Elske decided to move from the little house adjacent to the Ruintjes farm to an apartment in the nearby town of Sebeek. Piet felt that their September 1941 move was long overdue. He had, for months, been desperately looking for a job that would provide a steady income for his growing family.

For weeks he had been frantic with worries about his family finances and then he heard, from an acquaintance in the old Mustard Seed club, that a job as a math teacher had opened up in the Christian school in Sebeek. The vacancy had become available because the German authorities had forced that school's principal to summarily fire an experienced math teacher, Klaas Tammerman, because he was Jewish.

Although he had completed only two of the ten evening math education courses needed for certification as teacher, Piet decided to apply for the position regardless. He accepted the job when it was offered to him and, on the same day, rented a small apartment in Sebeek.

Steward was not very charitable when he heard about his friend's new job. "How could Piet have accepted that position when Tammerman was fired without any cause whatsoever? They could easily have kept him on the payroll; his colleagues could have filled in and taught a few extra lessons for as long as the Nazis control this land."

In his diary Zak repeatedly referred to Piet and Elske's relocation as a disaster. Because of that move, Elske ended her habit of making a daily visit to Beppe's kitchen and bringing some levity even during the darkest days. Zak also missed Piet's company because he sometimes was tired of the increasingly edgy and abrasive Steward.

Zak's feeling that he was living in the middle of an unmitigated disaster also had a very existential dimension. During the fall of 1941 the German intelligence agency had arrested well over fifty people who, like Zak, delivered the illegal newspaper, *Vrije Nederland* to subscribers. With Dutch spies, the Germans had been able to successfully penetrate that paper's distribution network. Zak knew that the Germans might, any day, be at the door of his home and send him off to the same concentration camps to which his peers had been sent.

All of Zak's fears took a grim form, later that month, when Steward heard the roar of motorcycles coming along the road leading to the Ruintjes farm. He quickly raised the alarm and Zak, Korrie and Mrs. Vellinga were able to safely make it to the hiding place which insiders called the 'manure palace.' After the unwelcome guests had arrived at the farm and dismounted from their motorcycles, the two SS officers stationed themselves on the driveway while a third person, a Dutch policeman, walked up to the house and rang the doorbell.

After answering the door, Beppe kept her face impassive as she calmly studied the faces of her three unwelcome guests. She did not recognize anyone and braced herself for trouble. She was especially worried because she had not received any tips from the underground stating that trouble might be on the way. She also knew that the Germans were still systematically searching for the distributors of illegal newspapers.

The Dutch policeman, who acted as the spokesman for the group, introduced himself as Sipke Dollema. He looked uneasy as he asked his first question. "Has any illegal butchering taken place on your property?"

Beppe knew that her sons had, without any permit, butchered two hogs during the previous week and salted away the meat. She also knew of people who had lost their lives because of violating the ordinance against illegal slaughtering. The Germans, to systematically sweep up the resources of the Dutch rural economy, were unrelenting in their demands that all meat processing must be rigorously recorded; no one was allowed to short-change the quotas that had to go to the German army. Beppe knew exactly what her unwelcome guests were after, but she first took a minute to closely study the name on the badge of the Dutch policeman. There was a ring of power in her voice as she addressed the man standing before her. "I am Mrs. Ruintjes and this is the Ruintjes farm. We never do anything illegal here. The answer to your question is no. We have not done any illegal butchering here on this farm. Everything that happens here is fully legal and above board!"

The policeman, who had been standing close to the open door, took a step backward as if he was instinctively moving away from a blast of heat pouring out of a red-hot oven. After several seconds of delay, Sipke asked: "Do you mind if we take a few minutes to look around?"

Beppe's answer was very terse: "Sure, look around, but don't step in the many cow pies near the back of the barn. It has rained a lot lately so they can act like grease and easily cause a person to slip."

The inspection of the property was perfunctory because neither the German soldiers nor the Dutch policeman wanted to get their boots dirty.

For everyone living at the Ruintjes farm, this visit left behind a very bitter aftertaste because of what happened when the three guests were in the process of getting back on their motorcycles. One of the SS officers, as he surveyed the whole farm operation, turned to his comrade, and offhandedly said, "Hans, can't you almost smell the Jews that are hiding here on this farm?"

The SS officer made the comment while he was still quite close to Beppe because she was standing behind the slightly ajar front door of her home. With her sharp ears, she picked up the gist of what the German had said and was duly alarmed by what she read into the words. She was sure that her farm must be on a German blacklist, and that it was no longer safe to have her Jewish guests stay with her.

But what was to be done? Where were Korrie and her mother to go? Who would take them in? That same evening, as they were having supper, Beppe broached the delicate topic with her guests. She first shared with them what she had heard, and then addressed the problem directly. "It is no longer safe for the two of you to be our guests, so we need to go about finding a new safehouse for you."

Mrs. Vellinga, after some time, looked at Beppe and said: "I knew this day would come. We are going back to our house tomorrow."

Beppe got up from her seat so fast that the table shook violently and the milk jug resting on it almost tipped over. "That's never going to happen," she said, "as long as I am able to stand up." She smiled wryly as she continued: "Well perhaps I won't be able to stand up much longer, but for now, we need to have other plans. I have a very elderly aunt, Mrs. Hesslinga, who lives in Suawoude and her health is failing. She needs someone to help around the house. I am going to travel there tomorrow and, Steward, I want you to get into contact with Harry and obtain falsified ID papers for both Korrie and Mrs. Vellinga; it's no longer safe for Jews to continue to use their former names. Tell Harry that Mrs. Vellinga and Korrie's new names will be Jantje and Emma Bierma."

Mrs. Vellinga was too moved to say anything, but Korrie, who had been quietly playing with her food, finally put down her fork and found the words that her mother was looking for. "Mrs. Ruintjes, my mother and I will be eternally grateful for the hospitality that you have shown to us during these past months. It will be wonderful if we can move safely to

Suawoude. I will, after arriving there, help my mother get settled in. Then I'll go back to my job at *Het Apeldoornse Bosch*."

When she returned to her hospital job Korrie discovered that her workload had almost doubled during the intervening months because of staff shortfalls that were caused by German raids on Jewish homes in Apeldoorn and the adjacent regions of Twenthe and the Achterhoek.

Harry, who had provided Korrie with her false ID, also asked her if she would be willing to carry some bundles for him from Apeldoorn to Leeuwarden whenever she made a visit to see her mother in Suawoude or went to Sebeek to spend time with her son.

Zak had his own worries about Korrie's new activism. He felt strongly that she should not have gone back to the dangers of working at a Jewish hospital, and she certainly should not have been recruited by the underground. From his point of view this had all the makings of a true disaster.

Zak also always used the word "disaster" whenever he wrote about Andy Uitvlugt who, starting in 1941, could often be seen on the streets of Ter Loo. After seeing him leaving town late one snowy day, Zak had quietly retraced the Nazi's footsteps back into town and was surprised that they took him to the door of the home on Boelelaan 223—the Vellinga home which had been vacant for over 8 months. He could see, as he was quickly walking past that address, that Andy had pasted a homemade sign on the front door of that home.

Zak peeled the notice off the door and carefully folded it up and placed it in the small satchel he was carrying. When he came home, he spread it out on the table and could clearly see what Andy had in mind with his public announcement: "This is no longer a Jewish property but is now owned by the Lippemann-Rosenthal Bank." Zak knew that the Germans were using that bank as a depository in which they stored all financial assets in the Netherlands that had been stolen from Jewish owners. This meant that the Germans felt that they now owned this house. But who would be the occupant? Would it be Andy or one of his Nazi friends? With that question in mind, Zak kept the house under observation during the evening hours of the following days. He spent four long evenings lurking in the dark shadows of the very narrow alley adjacent to the house before he saw a sign of life in the property.

What he observed was troubling news for the underground in the vicinity of Ter Loo. Early in November 1941, Andy had the lock of the front door of the house replaced and then, later during the same month, a very pregnant Santje Folkema moved into the house. Andy had helped her move in, and a day later, came with some very new furniture. The neighbors saw him, approximately once per week, bringing food supplies and staying for the evening.

For Zak the arrival of Santje in Ter Loo was a disaster because he felt sure that she was a Nazi agent. Joost put that sentiment into words when he came to the Ruintjes farm during the week of Christmas 1941. "Our residential Nazi scoundrel first gets his girl pregnant and then uses his weekly visits to Ter Loo as an opportunity to stir up trouble. Last week he brought long heavy screws in order to again attach the sign 'Forbidden for Jews' to that big beech tree in the park. We had taken all of his earlier signs down, but now, through his girl, he has threatened our police with retaliation if he finds that signs placed in the park and in front of the bar have been torn down again and they, as civil authorities, do nothing about it."

There was a sense of disgust as well as a tinge of fear in his voice when he continued. "Up until now, Ter Loo has flown under the radar because we had not really come to the attention of the German authorities; but now, with Andy's girlfriend in our midst, I'm afraid that things will change for the worse."

As that troubling word "change" bounced off the walls of the quiet dining room in the Ruintjes farmhouse, a brutally cold wind was sweeping across the frozen pasturelands of Friesland and pushing endless amounts of snow into the frozen canals.

The tireless 1942 winter wind not only tore through all the flimsy houses of Europe, but it also raced across the vast, open Russian steppe. There, with icy temperatures, it immobilized hands, toes and other extremities of Hitler's soldiers, and it also paralyzed many of the machines in his vast army and air force. Those winter winds and low temperatures eventually transformed Hitler's fast moving and triumphant army into a beached whale; it was, for months, locked in place by both weather conditions and coordinated Soviet counter attacks.

Chapter Seventeen

Korrie's One Hundred Jewish Children
(Jan. 1942)

"We must never forget about Jewish men, women and children who are being ripped out of their homes. We simply must step in and help them."
—Vrij Nederland.

The third year of German occupation of the Netherlands began in May 1942 and, for once, a small glimmer of light seemed to be making its way through the dark war clouds. The hard winter, which all the people of Europe had just endured, had finally come to an end, and the warm summer sun again turned the landscape green. It seemed that all the ghosts that had been peering around the corners during the previous month had lost their ability to frighten people. The stunningly beautiful summer sun brought new hope to many unhappy faces.

During that summer, many Europeans really believed that the German soldiers, like hordes of marauding locust, would quickly disappear over the horizon. They imagined that empty stomachs would soon be full again and that ill-clad bodies would again be properly dressed in the very near future. Wasn't the time at hand when the hated and omnipresent ration cards could be thrown into the fire? Hadn't Hitler really hit his head on a brick wall with his attack on the mighty USSR, and hadn't the tough Americans entered the war? Wouldn't Roosevelt and his great country be able to quickly finish off that nasty man with a mustache? Hadn't Stalin, Roosevelt and Churchill already agreed that they would soon open a second front in the war and attack the Nazi fortress from the side of the Atlantic Ocean? Wouldn't the omnipresent cloud of Jewish oppression soon be lifted? Wasn't it a good idea to just sit tight and quietly wait for the war clouds to drift away? Why should one step into harm's way by helping Jews escape from the German dragnet at a time when it seemed that the war was winding down?

The beguiling optimism of that summer was built on a very narrow sliver of reality; it was not based on factual knowledge. It was true that the German war dragon had been bloodied by having crashed to the ground in the cold Russian tundra during the previous winter. But the monster was not dead; it wasn't even dying.

During the spring of 1942, the powerful German war machine was not retreating, but arming itself for the next battle. Many Europeans couldn't imagine that the war would continue for three more years; they only saw the large soap bubbles of hope that lazily hung in the air during the first part of the summer of 1942.

With its 1941 sweep into Russia, Hitler's army had overextended itself and, in 1942, the crippled attack monster was forced to pour all its energy into holding the ground that it had gained during the previous year. Hitler's switch from an offensive to a defensive war strategy meant that almost all of Europe, as well as a large swath of Asia and Africa, was instantly transformed into a vast armed fortress. It became a seething encampment that bristled with weapons. The German high command said they were fighting a *total* war. It was, for them, a *total* exploitation of natural resources, a *total* transformation of all fortress-enclosed humans into *Reich* slaves and a *total* destruction of all enemies of the new Thousand Year Empire. But how were priorities to be set? How were all the enemies residing within fortress Europe going to be exterminated?

Hitler had the answer to that last question. The Jews were on the top of his list of domestic enemies. Those who had imbibed Hitler's *Mein Kampf* manifesto firmly believed that Jews would destroy the Third German Empire in the same way that they had, supposedly, destroyed the Kaiser's Second German Empire in 1918. According to Nazi ideology, this new German empire could only survive if it was freed of all traces of Jewish life.

The blueprint for the ideal of a *Judenrein* Germany had been drawn up at the Wannsee Conference; it took place during a time when the deadly winds of the 1942 winter still raced across Europe and Asia. In May 1942, the first death train left the Netherlands and, during the following 18 months, well over 90,000 Jewish Holocaust victims were taken by train out of Dutch territory and, along with millions of Jews from Europe, murdered in the various death camps.

From personal experience, Klees knew what was meant by that phrase *Judenrein*. During the summer of 1941 he had volunteered for service in the Waffen SS and had been accepted into its ranks. That same fall, he had undergone two months of rigorous training and then, as part of the *Legion Nederlande,* he had been shipped off to the Russian front. He and his Dutch comrades arrived on the front during the dead of the Russian winter and assisted the marauding German army as whole villages were torched and the populations massacred.

But, in early March, Klees had been forced to leave the battlefield because of an injury. A sliver of metal from an exploding shrapnel shell had entered his left eye and permanently blinded it. Because of that injury, he was honorably discharged from the German army and was, as a wounded vet, able to go back to his hometown of Sebeek.

On May 6, 1942, Mr. Ulermann looked up from his desk and carefully studied the face of the battle-hardened Klees. "Sit down, young man," he said. "What happened to your left eye? Your whole face also looks a little different. I heard from Otto Reich, your *Legion Nederlande* commander, that your performance on the *Volkhof Front* was stunning. You and your squadron not only endured the cold bravely, but during one of the fiercest blizzards, held off the attacks of the godless Russian Communists for three days as they tried to penetrate our defense lines. You and your small group of men held firm until the relief force of the main army came to the rescue."

Klees gave a small smile of pleasure and said: "Thank you very much, Mr. Commander. I was glad to do it for our leader who taught me to be a true storm trooper. I am not worried about my injuries. I'm still able to use a gun because it's only my left eyesight that I lost." There was little of the old bravado in his voice because he was self-consciously holding a cloth against his face; he used it to mop up the small stream of fluid that flowed down from a place near his injured eye and trickled into his mouth. In his mind he knew that that the salty water came from a torn tear duct, but every time he again tasted the salty fluid, he imagined that he was becoming soft. Was he crying like a baby just because he had lost an eye? He willfully pushed all such foolishness out of his mind as he used his good eye to looked straight at the commander.

Commander Ulermann gave the young man a friendly nod before outlining the new job that he hoped Klees would accept. "As you probably know, Klees, I contacted Otto immediately when I heard of your battle injury, and we spoke at length about your future. I asked him if I could have your help again here in Friesland. I need your expertise because we have fierce enemies in this immediate vicinity. Your experience in the East taught you how the Jewish weeds in the Russian gardens were dealt with. In the middle of the storms of war, you soldiers were able to swiftly destroy those weeds. I now need your help in pulling up the Jewish weeds that are still choking the life out the good plants in our Frisian gardens."

Klees blanched slightly as memories of the Russian killing fields danced before his eyes. In the village of Solov he had helped drive the Jewish villagers into their synagogue before burning the building to the ground. All Jewish men, women and children had perished in the flames. Some of the young men escaped the burning building by jumping out of a shattered window, but they were massacred by volley after volley of machine gun fire before they were even able to reach an adjacent apple grove. There were many nights when Klees would wake up because, in a dream, he again heard the blood-curling screams that came from the hellish inferno which his hands had helped to create.

Ulermann let out a short, bitter laugh when he saw that Klees had a distant glaze in his one eye. "Young man," he said, "I can see that your eyes were opened when you were in Russia. I went through the same process of learning about war when I was stationed in Istanbul during the time of the Great War. The Turkish government decided that the Armenians were enemies of their state. With my Sunday school brain, I was indignant that a civilized country with which we were allied, would condescend to the brutal and brazen murder of well over two million of its own citizens. Then I decided that there was nothing that I could do; I was only a guard at the German Embassy. As time passed, I clearly saw that the Turks, like any state, had the right exterminate their internal state enemies."

Ulermann looked at Klees closely as he warmed up to his topic. "That is what we must do, Klees. The Jews are enemies of the German empire, and as such, simply have to be dealt with in the same way that the Armenians were taken care of by the Turks."

When the commander saw the worried expression on Klees' face, he switched to a tone of voice that was almost as gentle as that of a father confessor: "Do not worry, Klees, you will not have to fight in bloody battles with our Jewish enemies. We will not massacre the European Jews in the streets in the way that the Turks polluted their cities with the blood of the Armenians. The organization that we have in place is actually very simple. Jews are being requested to relocate themselves quietly, and all you need to do is help in that process of peaceful emigration. Those who are unwilling to go or are moving too slowly, will need some encouragement and that is how you can help."

For almost a minute Klees was mute; he nodded his head vaguely as he stared at his hands. When he finally emerged from the trance, into which he had slipped, he realized that he might have overstayed his welcome and abruptly stood up. He looked at the commander as he saluted with all the energy that he could muster: "Heil Hitler. I will do whatever you tell me to do, commander. I am at your service. Just tell me what orders you have for me."

After being told that he would soon be given his new instructions, Klees left the office and stepped out into the brilliant sunlight. His blind eye gave him pain as he started walking down the street; it almost seemed to be telling him that more sunlight was needed in his tension-filled mind. With his good eye he carefully surveyed the street and checked to see if anyone had seen him leaving the commander's office.

But no one saw Klees there that day. There were also very few people who knew that Hitler's plan for the Jewish Holocaust was already being carried out.

Starting in July 1942, train after train left the Netherlands and took tens of thousands of Jews to the different death camps. There, they were brutally murdered. A vast majority of over 100,000 Jewish Holocaust victims from the Netherlands died during the apocalyptical third year of the war. It was a time when many Dutch citizens felt that all they had to do was to sit tight; they firmly believed that the end of hostilities was in sight.

Zak, however, remained as vigilant as ever during that balmy summer of 1942. He never left the farm except for the times when, under the cover of darkness, he made his *Vrij Nederland* deliveries. He moved like a silent shadow as he distributed the newspaper because he knew that

the Germans and their local Dutch henchmen were tireless in their effort to capture those involved with its production and distribution. In the
middle of March 1942, the Gestapo had already come to Koudum and
found the printing press that had for months been used to produce the
newspaper. Now they were on high alert and ready to pounce on anyone
involved with the distribution process.

Beppe also never stopped being careful during that warm summer.
Her vigilance took the form of staying in contact with her trusted friends.
That was why she regularly visited Elske's home whenever she was in Sebeek. She also knew that Korrie, now known as Emma Bierma, usually
spent the last weekend of each month with both her friend and with her
son, Jacob.

Beppe knocked with three soft taps on the back door of her friend's
home on Friday May 22, 1942. Elske opened the door and stepped aside
as Beppe quietly stepped into the small entryway. Together they went
into the kitchen where Korrie was already seated.

Beppe had not come to make pleasant teatime conversation; she
wanted to talk about the worries that had kept her awake for many nights.

"Those monsters! First, they put barbed wire around your people,
Korrie. Then they tighten the wire inch by inch each day. Even as they do
that, they are filled with glee when they see that the thousands of metal
teeth cut ever deeper into flesh and bone. And now they are branding
every one of your people with that deadly yellow star which has the word
"Jew" written on it. Yes, pastor Sven was correct last summer. We—all
non-Jewish Dutch people—must be prepared to walk in the Red Sea into
which the Germans are driving you and your people. Whether or not
that will reverse the disaster that is happening on this very day isn't even
relevant any longer. We need to be where you are and, together, we need
to trust in the horsemen and chariots of the Lord of Hosts."

In the moment of silence that followed Beppe's outburst, Elske unfolded a sheet of paper on which she had copied down the article, "A
Star goes up from Jacob." It was from the most recent issue of the illegal
newspaper *Vrij Nederland*; it had just come out, and Zak had surrepti-
tiously distributed it in Ter Loo and vicinity. After she had gotten the full
attention of her friends, she began to read from it in a soft, gentle voice.
For the listeners it was as if the spirit of the deceased pastor Sven had
entered the room.

Today [May 16,1942] we again must remind ourselves that our country has, through the centuries, always been known as a place where the people deeply love their freedom. In fact, all people of the world know that the Dutch are an especially hospitable people. All the persecuted and oppressed refugees from countries around the world have always been both welcomed here and treated with great tolerance by our citizens.

Now our country is ruled by a ruthless horde of villains who are discriminating against many of our good and outstanding countrymen by treating them as criminals or lepers.

Elske interrupted her reading for a moment to add: "by forcing all Jews to wear the yellow star with the word "Jew" inscribed on it.

Then she continued reading:

How do the Jews themselves react to this criminality? Many carry the yellow star as a badge of HONOR. But the big question is, how do we, who are their non-Jewish countrymen, react to this atrocity—which brings shame on all of us. We are all part of this outrageous scandal. It brings shame on our whole nation.

Our fathers fought for eighty years to gain their FREEDOM [from Spain]. And what they battled for was not just any freedom but a freedom that, once and for all, would make it impossible for anyone to hate, mock or physically suppress those who are of a different race or a different religion.

Now, with this Jewish star, we Dutchmen again have more proof in our hands that the Germans aren't even vaguely aware that we are a people who passionately love our freedom. They are clueless when it comes to understanding our core value system. They simply don't understand what freedom means because they themselves have the soul of slaves . . .

But they will not succeed [with their criminality]! We will not allow them to shame the Jews. If all Dutchmen, or at least a large majority of them, take the initiative and pin the Star of David on their clothing then the Germans will have failed to achieve their goal. Such a united response may endanger the Jews because the Germans will try to lash out at them in anger. But they won't have an easy time doing that [because they will be confronted with a united Dutch nation].

[The Germans will soon see that] we treat with respect anyone who is branded with the golden star that has the word "Jew" on it. FOR US THERE MAY AND WILL BE NO DISTINCTION BETWEEN THE DUTCH PEOPLE WHO DO AND THOSE WHO DO NOT WEAR THE STAR.

Beppe furtively looked out of the window, and Korrie got tears in her eyes as Elske, in a clear and crisp voice, placed a special emphasis on those last words which, in the article, had been capitalized. All three women wondered if anyone outside the little house had heard the words that were still ringing through the room.

Elske then continued reading the brief article:

> The Germans wanted to hurt the Jews but, through this action, the whole Dutch nation has been wounded in the worst and most vicious way possible; her sacred honor has been violated. Germany will, with time, really feel the dreadful consequences of this action.
>
> [How will Germany suffer from this action?] Different chapters in the history of Israel tell the same story. Hostile powers that were arrayed against the people of Israel were destroyed. [We need only think of] Balaam who, as a crony of the Moabite king, Balak, had been ordered to place a curse on the Israelites. Three times God turned those curses into blessings: a STAR will come out of Jacob and a scepter will rise out of Israel.

From memory, Elske and Korrie, in tandem, recited the rest of that verse from Numbers 24:17: "He will crush the foreheads of Moab and the skulls of all the people of Sheth."

After the reading had come to an end, Korrie put her arms on the table and placed her head, face down, on her arms. She was crying soundlessly for several minutes before she slowly lifted her head again and looked at Beppe and Elske with tear-stained eyes. "When I first found out that Jews would be ordered to wear the Star of David, I would look out of the window each day in the hope that streams and streams of non-Jewish citizens would be walking along the street wearing the same yellow star. Isn't Christ the star that came out of Jacob, and shouldn't all Christian believers hold that star in honor? Isn't Germany the modern Moab that Balaam made his prophesies about? Doesn't that make it even more important that everyone, and not just Jews, place that star of David on their clothing. But that is not what is happening. I do not understand how life can just go on during a time when tens, hundreds and thousands of my people are just being taken away and, I believe, murdered. I do not know why everyone is so afraid. Why are the Jews so docile? Why is our Jewish Council in Amsterdam helping our enemy arrest train loads full of Jewish people? Those trains that then take our people to places unknown."

"That, my sweet girl," said Beppe, who had been listening intently to Korrie, "is exactly the question that I have asked myself every day after having read the Koopman's brochure about the fact that so many non-Jews in this country thoughtlessly signed the Aryan Declaration in 1940. His words still scream in my ears. 'When we signed that declaration, we, in effect, sold our conscience down the river because we acted as if there is no distinction between good and evil.'"

There was a moment of silence before Elske added her thoughts to the increasingly gloomy discussion. "What I am really haunted by is Koopman's concluding observation. He said that if we sell our conscience because we want to protect our place in history then we are really doomed. It would be one thousand times better if we were to be erased from the pages of history than if we continue to be alive and no longer have a conscience."

"Elske," Korrie said, "I have never heard such despairing talk from you. Aren't you supposed to be the voice of optimism among us?"

Her eyes sparkled as she used the word "optimist" and that glimmer of sunlight persisted in her voice as she continued: "I do not want you to think that I was crying just now because I am so sad. I am indeed terribly depressed all the time because of what is happening to my fellow Jews. But the tears that you just witnessed were also tears of joy. I can't express to you how happy it makes me whenever I am welcomed into this home.

"I also read and reread Koopman's article, 'Almost too Late.' It was very personal for me. After Klees raped me, I felt that I had been poisoned and it was too late for me to live a normal healthy life. I really felt like a dirty person, and that is the way that the Germans make us feel every day. Whenever I interacted with other Jews, during my first months back in Apeldoorn, I kept thinking that it is too late for all of us. We are all doomed to be exterminated by the Germans and their henchmen."

As she continued, Korrie began to speak more and more rapidly. "That sense of despair lifted like a dark cloud during this past winter. When the winter winds came last November, I heard reports that the German army was getting smashed in Russia. That's when it occurred to me that there was also a second basic message in Koopman's little brochure. He had said it was 'almost' too late to stop the German plan to destroy the Jewish population in our country but not totally too late.

"That tiny word 'almost' was like a rubber ball that just kept bouncing around in my head. What can we still do? What plans, during this eleventh hour, can still be developed to help my fellow Jewish countrymen? Day after day, last winter, I saw that question etched on the faces of the dwindling numbers of mothers, fathers, brothers, and sisters who came to visit their loved ones at *Het Apeldoornse Bos*. 'Should we go into hiding?' 'What will then happen to our child, spouse or parent who is a patient here?'

"It was last February, during one of the coldest days of that freezing winter, that I made a decision that my mother still thinks is absolutely crazy. I was walking back after a late evening shift when I heard group German soldiers coming from the opposite direction on the street I was on. From their wild singing, I could tell that they were quite drunk. My heart stopped. It was long past curfew. I did have my nurse's curfew pass and my fake ID had passed inspection many times, so that was not my concern. But those drunk brutes were not going to care about being legal. They often rape at random. There was no traffic on the street; I was painfully visible during that moonlit night."

Neither Beppe nor Elske had heard this story before, and were in rapt attention as they were listening. None of them heard the first whimpers coming from the bedroom—where Jacob had been taking his morning nap. But Korrie did hear those sounds and said, almost to herself, "I should talk in a lower tone. Oh, where was I? I know. The soldiers were coming into my direction, and I felt trapped. That is when I saw the little cave that some children had dug out in a snowbank close to where I was walking. I tiptoed over there and saw that it was big enough to crawl into. That's what I did. I backed into it, and, with my gloves, I carefully erased the footsteps that I had made in the snow. I had also found a snowball and I used it to block the entryway. I lay there for several minutes and waited for the soldiers to pass me.

"As they came closer, I could more and more clearly hear the words that were tumbling out of their drunken mouths. They had obviously just come back from the Russian front because they were singing about their grim soldier's life in the frozen tundra. They sang in unison about going home and then individual singers would add the details about eastern front realities that they would not miss."

> 'We're going home!
>> No more machine guns carried with hands.
>>> that have no fingers.
> 'We're going home!
>> No more endless forced marches on feet
>>> that have no toes.
> 'We're going home!
>> No more sitting in tanks without tracks.
>>> in Russian snowbanks.

'We're going home!
    No more flying our Junkers with frozen fuel lines.
       in whiteout conditions.
'We're going home!
    No more following a leader who's lost no fingers,
       but has frozen his brains.'

"That last sentence was spoken by a high-pitched voice and the whole company abruptly stopped singing. Through a small crack in the snow, I could see one soldier punch another soldier on the shoulder and, at the same time, say, 'George, you can't joke about our leader in that way.' Another soldier then slugged him in the face—a lot harder. A third soldier was almost going to pistol whip him when a deep commanding voice brought an end to the violence. 'Come on, guys. Let George go. We're all a bit drunk, so we all need to sober up. And George, I'll talk to you tomorrow when you can think more clearly.' After that there was a deep silence that lasted for several minutes. Then all that I heard was a crunch, crunch as the whole group of soldiers silently drifted down the street."

Korrie was quiet for a moment before she continued. "I was deeply elated as I thought about what I had just witnessed. The German army is falling apart, and it is God who spoke to me in a mysterious way. That was exactly the way that he talked to Gideon and his servant Purah when he told them that the mighty Midianite army was about to be destroyed.

"After the soldiers had passed, I decided to just lay there for a few minutes longer because I wanted to make sure that they were really gone, and I also wanted to quietly think about what I had just witnessed. I have no memory of what happened next because I was so tired that I fell into a deep sleep in that bed of snow and only woke up an hour later. By then I was feeling very cold, but also surprisingly rested and energized.

"I got home safely that evening and tossed and turned in bed for hours as I thought about what had happened to me. I also thought about the night when Gideon spied on the Midianites who, as we know from the Bible, were spread out over the whole land like a swarm of locusts, and whose fast-moving camels were as numerous as the sand on the seashore. And then it came to me. God, through the miraculous dream of the pagan Midianite, told Gideon, the reluctant warrior, that he had to pull himself together and do something to help God make the victory happen. He had to go out and lead the attack on the Midianites.

"Before going to sleep I decided that God, through those German soldiers, was telling me to put all fear aside and do something to help my fellow Jews. God would be with me in the same way that he had been with Gideon. The next morning, in the clear light of day, I could not stop thinking about that small cave in the snow that had been my refuge during the previous evening. I knew that, like Gideon, I couldn't save all the Jews, but the message that I received in that cave was clear to me. God told me to do everything in my power to help some of my people find places of refuge.

"Since that cold day, I have not, even for one minute, forgotten my resolution. Each day I talk to Jewish moms and dads who still risk coming to our hospital, and I passionately urge them to find hiding places for themselves and for their children.

"It started with a grand dream. I wanted to be a little Moses and lead a remnant of the Jewish people to safety. I dreamed of taking hundreds of Jewish kids from cities like Amsterdam, Apeldoorn, and Amersfoort and helping them find safe homes in rural Friesland. The long winter and the increasingly fierce raids in Amsterdam and other cities have, of course, made those grand plans impossible. But I am still determined to do something, and what I have in my hand here is a proof of that conviction."

Korrie then took out a small note pad and showed it to Elske and Beppe. "This is all that I accomplished since last February. It contains the names and addresses of one hundred parents who want their children to be brought to safety. The list includes the names of some mentally handicapped children who are currently in our hospital, *Het Aperdoornse Bosch*, and the names of their healthy brothers and sisters."

The spark of enthusiasm in Korrie's voice vanished when she continued. "It is so hard to convince my fellow Jews to overcome their paralyzing fears. So many just show up when they are called up and, like sheep, allow themselves to be led into the trains which will take them to the German slaughterhouses. I wish that we Jews could copy what just happened in the two hospitals for epileptic patients in Haarlem—the *Meer en Bosch* for male patients and the *Bethesda Sarepta* for female patients. When the Germans tried to force those institutions to hire Nazi nurses, the chief hospital administrators simply refused to follow that order by shutting down both of those institutions and placing the patients in private homes."

As she continued with her story, Korrie was speaking in a low whisper: "That kind of action would be impossible for the Jewish hospital where I work because most of our patients have no homes to go back to.

What's even worse is that family members have almost stopped visiting these patients because of travel restrictions and fears of arrest."

Korrie stopped talking for a moment, and then continued. "When I feel myself falling into a mood of despair, I always go back to Koopmans' little word '*almost.*' It really is too late to do something big, but it is not too late to take small actions. And then I think of my little boy. In the same way that it is not too late to rescue him, so it is not too late to hide ten, twenty, thirty or even one hundred other children like him; they must not be handed over to Klees and other Nazi brutes."

Korrie then turned to Elske and gave her the notepad. "I no longer need this because I have memorized all the names and all the addresses. You should do the same thing because that is the only way that the information can be safely preserved. I could, as a Jew, be arrested any time and be shipped off. If they find those names and addresses on me, I would bring the lives of hundreds of people into danger. I strongly advise you to also memorize the names and addresses of anyone whom you are planning to help. Get rid of the paper copy of that list as soon as possible."

With those last words, Korrie quickly stood up, took her coat, and went to the door. "It's fifteen minutes before my train leaves for Leeuwarden, and it will take me ten minutes to walk to the station, so I have to go immediately. Give Jacob a kiss for me. I know you and your friends will come up with plans to rescue those one hundred Jewish children."

One minute later the door closed and Elske and Beppe saw her hastily walking down the street that would take her to the train station.

After Korrie's footsteps had faded into the distance, Beppe picked up the little note pad and, looking at Elske, said, "Well now it's time to stop talking and start doing something. Where do we start?"

Elske, who was as much an activist as Beppe, had an idea. "Well, since we are both going to be involved with this project and we live in different towns, why don't we make a second copy of the names and addresses. Each of us will need a copy of the names if we plan to memorize them."

Both women thought it was an excellent plan, and, in another small notebook, copied out all the names and addresses that Korrie had brought. After they were finished, Beppe took the duplicate list with her to her home.

Elske kept the original list of names and tucked it into her apron pocket. She had to take care of the boys because they were awake and wildly shaking their little beds which, in turn, groaned with increasing agony as the screams of glee from the boys filled the whole house. After she had taken them out of their little beds, they kept her busy for the rest of the afternoon and she didn't have any time to think about what she had heard from Korrie.

At four in the afternoon, the front door of the house flew open, and someone briskly stepped into the living room. Elske, who was in the kitchen at the time, heard the door and instantly remembered that she still had the secret list in her apron pocket. She held a protective hand over that pocket when she stepped into the living room to see who had come into the house.

"O Piet, it's you. You scared me because you didn't announce yourself with the usual 'Hello I'm home' when you came in and, besides, you're early. Usually, you stay late to correct papers and get ready for the next class." At that point Elske looked closely at Piet's face and said: "What's the matter? Is something wrong? Is there a problem at work?"

Piet nodded, and walking up to Elske, whispered in her ear, "We had trouble at our school at the end of the day. Shortly after the children had gone home, a group of German soldiers stormed into our classrooms and, with weapons aimed at us, forced all of us to hold up our hands and face a wall. When they had the whole building under their direct control, a team of two soldiers took each one of us individually to an exit door and ordered us to go home. Then they posted guards at all the exits and kept our principal and one teacher under arrest. I'm totally in the dark about what the Germans are unhappy about this time. I should know soon because the executive committee of the school board has already called an emergency meeting. I am going there to find out what's happening." The words were barely out of Piet's mouth when he rushed out of the house again.

During the next three hours, Elske had an increasingly strong sense of foreboding. Dark worries, like so many black flies, seemed to be coming at her from all sides. What could possibly be going on? Why were the Germans arresting Mr. Albersen, the principal, and why was the fourth-grade teacher, Mr. Boersma, in trouble? Why were those Germans interfering with their private school?

It was late in the evening when a deeply disturbed Piet returned home. At first, he just sat on the chair by the table and rested his head on his arms. Finally, he raised his head and furtively looked at the door leading to the boys' bedroom. "Are the boys asleep?" Elske nodded her head and then she listened carefully to her husband as he told her in a dead monotone about the school board meeting that he had just attended.

"Mr. Tuinstra, the chair of the School Board, opened the meeting with prayer and then, told us why the Germans had stormed into the school. Two of the children in Mr. Boersma's class were, the Germans told us, from Jewish homes, and that was a direct violation of the German ordinance dictating that all Jewish children were to be expelled from all schools. 'No Jewish children,' the ordinance states, 'must be allowed to pollute any Aryan school.' It was a long and painful meeting, but in the end, the board unanimously decided that they could not accept any more German interference in the school, and, as a consequence, they would immediately shut down the school. It was Tuinstra who came forward with the argument that convinced the board that they had no choice but to shut the school's doors. I can still see him standing there in his muddy farm boots as he, with his thick fingers, again and again tried to push back the few remaining strands of grey hair that he still has on his head. 'Last fall we caved in when we were told that no person of Jewish descent could stand in front of our classrooms—we felt that we had no choice but to fire an excellent math teacher. Now we are told that we can't even offer education to the children of believers who, in this case, also happen to be Jews. Tomorrow we will be told that we can't use the word "Jesus" in the school prayers because our Savior was, after all, a Jew. We can't go on like this. The school must shut its doors.'

"The board, after passing that motion, made a number of procedural decisions directly related to the closure. All regular teachers will receive their salaries for four more months. But that regulation, Elske, does not help me because I am a temporary hire. So I am without a job, and, as of this moment, we have absolutely no income. What are we to do? I am not going to be a farm helper again. That chapter in my life is over. But there is also no work for me here in Sebeek. What are we going to do?"

After hearing the news about the school closing and the fact that Piet was now without a job, Elske unconsciously looked at her old button box, the family piggy bank, and could not help but remember that now it only contained a total of 39 guilders. That money would immediately vanish when they paid their next month's rent. Elske tore her eyes away from her meager stash of cash and tried to sound upbeat as she looked Piet in the eyes: "Come on, my man, it is time to go to bed. Let tomorrow take care of tomorrow's worries."

The next day both Piet and Elske were very silent during breakfast time. After getting up from the table, Piet started to pace back and forth in their small living room. The boys, sensing the tension in the air, started screaming louder and louder and, before long, were hitting each other with the toy trucks that Piet had made for them. The atmosphere in the small house was soon so unpleasant that Elske was relieved when Piet, at about ten in the morning, gave her a quick hug and said: "I need to clear my head; I'm going for a long walk."

Piet's walk ended when he was drawn to a large billboard in the window of the unemployment office. It read, "Come and work in Germany and you will receive double wages during your first two months." He was still reading those words when the door of the office building was flung open and a young man called out to him: "Hello, Piet. Can I help you? Are you looking for work? I think I have just the right job for you."

Piet knew the young man very well. It was Gerbin Bakker; he had been the treasurer of their recently disbanded church youth organization. "Look at this job description, Piet. A German farmer in Bentheim is looking for a farm helper who is not afraid of work. The pay is almost twice what you could make here in Friesland, and you will immediately get a signing bonus of fifty guilders when you sign up to work in Germany."

Piet did not even want to stop and talk with Gerbin because he was repelled by the very idea of working in Germany. He knew that the *Arbeidseinsatz* program was simply Hitler's way of sweeping up people from the occupied countries and turning them into cogs in the vast German military-industrial machine. But, perhaps, it wouldn't hurt to just have a conversation with Gerbin. It was wrong, after all, to shun the greetings of a fellow Christian.

With those thoughts still in his mind, Piet took the sheet of paper that Gerbin had thrust into his hands. His eyes swept past the small print and settled on the two bright red sentences that reached out and touched him. "Earn 50 guilders a week and receive an extra bonus of fifty guilders for signing up. You can send home over 250 guilders after only working for a month."

Piet was still reading the brochure when Gerbin skillfully raced through the sales pitch in which he promoted Hitler's work program. "You can make good money if you sign up, and, if you aren't happy with the work, you can quit and go home after a month from the day that you sign up. All food and lodging is provided so you can send home all the money you make."

The persistent salesman was not troubled when Piet handed him the brochure back and told him that he would have to talk to his wife first. "Oh, take your time, Piet, but I have to tell you that the 50 guilders bonus is only good for the first fifty people who sign up this week. At this point we have 49 people who have already given us their John Henry, and you will be number 50. The minute you go away, there will immediately be someone who will sign up, and the program quota will have been filled. I should also tell you that two guys from our Mustard Seed club just signed up yesterday—so you'll be in good company if you also become part of the program."

Piet had looked at the sheet for well over ten minutes when Gerbin finally asked him: "Are you going to sign up or not. I've got to get back into the office because I just saw someone walk in there. I do have to tell you that I will not be able to hold this offer for you."

Piet, on impulse, capitulated to the pressures of the salesman and signed on the dotted line. It was only after the contract had been signed, that Gerbin mentioned that the German job, which he had agreed to accept, would start in four days.

When Piet came home later that day and told Elske what he had done, she was shocked and without a word, went into their bedroom and shut the door. Piet, at first, heard nothing and then he heard muffled cries coming through the door. He opened the door a crack and could see that she was using her pillow to hide her cries of anguish. He was rooted to the spot for several minutes before retreating to the living room. There, with his elbows on the table and his chin resting in his hands, he tried to think about how he could back out of the commitment he had made. Why had he been so impulsive? He should at least have spoken to Elske before signing those papers.

He sat there for a long time and had not heard Elske when she walked up to him and placed her hands on his shoulders. Her voice was distant and had an almost automatic quality when she said: "You shouldn't have done that, Piet. You may have had good intentions because you want to be a good provider, but there is nothing good in a decision that will take you to the land of our enemies."

She was almost going to cry again when she uttered the word "our enemies," but she stopped herself by saying, "There's no need to cry over spilled milk. Come on, let me help you collect the stuff you'll need if you must leave for work in Germany."

Piet would have liked to talk about the financial benefits of the German job, but was unable to find the appropriate words because he was not even sure what he had agreed to do. Before rushing off with the signed work agreement, Gerbin had taken a duplicate copy of the original contract and placed it in Piet's hands. Now, when he saw that work contract in front of him, Piet realized he had not even read the fine print. He picked it up and tried to quickly read it, but the German words all seemed to mesh into one confusing fabric. It took some time for his eyes to focus on what he was reading. When he finally understood everything in the document, he was shocked by what he had to look forward to. The promised fifty guilders bonus would not be paid out unless he remained employed in Germany for a full year. The contract also explicitly stated that he would have no alternative but to accept another placement if the job, that had been his first choice, had already been taken by someone else.

The nightmare that he envisioned became a reality in the following two weeks. Piet did go to the region of Bentheim to report for work, but when he arrived in the town of Emlichheim, he was told that the farmer already had all the help he needed. Along with the four other young men from Friesland who had shown up for that same job, he was immediately taken to Dusseldorf and given employment in an armament factory. The imaginary farmer's job in Bentheim had been a ruse used by recruiters like Gerbin. They wanted to convince young Frisian men to sign up for the work program and made it look beguilingly innocent by portraying it as something that only involved working for a farmer in the nearby area of Bentheim. Gerbin, from his vantage point, had every reason for playing along with the German work program because he received a ten-guilder payment for every young man, he was able to send to Germany.

In the days after her husband left for Germany, on May 25, 1942, Elske faced a dilemma. Should she renew the rental contract for the Sebeek house for another year, or should she go back to the little house adjacent to the Ruintjer farm. There hadn't been any time to discuss this question with Piet before he stepped on the train that took him to Germany. In the end it was Beppe who persuaded her to come back to the farm. "The boys can play outside and there's lots of food on the farm—especially if you help me expand our vegetable garden. Your hopefulness always pulls me out of my deepest dumps, and that is all the rent I will ever want from you."

Moving day was not a complicated affair. Steward went to Sebeek with two work horses and a farm wagon and stopped in front of Piet and Elske's little house. Elske and the two boys were already waiting for him, and they were soon on their way; Elske sat beside Steward on the seat in the front of wagon, and the boys were behind them in a little play pen. All the furniture and personal belongings easily fit on the wagon. During the trip, which took well over an hour, Steward was grimly quiet and only asked Elske a few cursory questions about her future. He never mentioned Piet's name. Elske, who was still in shock about her husband's abrupt departure to Germany, was also not prepared to share her worries.

Both Steward and Zak helped Elske move back into the little house and then went back to the barn to move some hay that had been brought into the barn the previous day. While sweating in the hot barn, Steward fumed about Piet and his impulsive decision to work in Germany. "I don't know why I remained friends with that guy all these years. He pretends to be a Dutch loyalist but is no better than the German scoundrels who tell us what to do every day. Now he's even gone over there to help those rotten criminals."

For most of the rest of the summer of 1942, it seemed that Steward had forgotten all about Piet. Like many of his countrymen during that summer, he wanted to get on with his life and not worry about the dark Nazi clouds that still hung in the sky. He spent time with his young wife—my mom—who, by June 1942, was already six months pregnant. Like so many other Dutchmen, he wanted to do nothing more than take in the warm air of those long, beautiful summer days. He and my mom often took long quiet bike rides into the countryside—even going as far as the coast of the Zuider Zee where they went swimming. At other times, on a whim, they purchased an ice cream cone; it was one of the few food items that was, during that beguiling summer of 1942, still available without the use of a war coupon.

But, when July was almost over, the illusionary magic of those warm summer days ended for Steward, his family, and friends. That was when three events happened that reminded them that they were still being tightly held by the iron fist of their savage German masters.

For Steward and his young wife, Marijke, the first wakeup call came on July 20. They had gone to Sebeek to make some purchases and were on their way home when two German soldiers swiftly approached them from a side road. The soldiers, with guns pointing at them, yelled: "Stop! Raise your hands and step forward in this direction!" The shocked couple immediately stopped, got off their bikes, laid them flat on the road and, with raised hands, walked towards those soldiers. While concentrating on the soldiers with the guns, they did not notice that two other Germans, who had been hiding behind a tree, went up to their bicycles, picked them up from the ground and swiftly cycled away.

After their partners had disappeared around a corner, the two remaining soldiers calmly lowered their guns and took their time inspecting Steward and Marijke's ID papers. The real shock came, when, after they were told that their papers were in order, and they were free to go, they discovered that their bicycles were gone. After a moment of silence Steward, intending to say something to their attackers, cleared his throat. Marijke didn't want any trouble, so she quickly took her husband by the arm. "We have to go home now," she said in an undertone. "Later, we can raise a complaint about this theft."

The long walk home took them well over three hours and, during all that time, Steward said nothing to his young wife about the vengeance plans that he was dreaming about.

There were many other Dutch people who shared Steward's deep anger with the pilfering habits of the occupiers. Throughout the whole country, German soldiers turned into common thieves when they ruthlessly made off with the bicycles of thousands of Dutch citizens. The mountains of stolen bikes were sent east and used to give mobility to Hitler's soldiers as they desperately tried to defeat Stalin's army. That massive theft of 1942 did not make Dutch people happy because their beloved *fiets* was, in most cases, the only means of transportation at their disposal.

The second wakeup call for Steward, as well for all the people of Ter Loo, was the arrest and disappearance of local watch repairman, Izaak Gerritsema. He was called "the birdman" by all his neighbors because of the many bird houses in his small yard. Izaak, like Korrie and her mother, was a Catholic Jew, but, unlike Korrie, he was firmly convinced that the Germans would not trouble themselves with Catholics like himself. Beppe had on more than one occasion urged him to go into hiding, and his answer was always the same. "Who will take care of my birds if I'm not here?" He would then add, with a hopeful note in his voice, "Reichskommissar Seyss Inquart will never touch the Catholic Jews because he's a Catholic himself. Our church has lately baptized many Jews who, in that way, know that they are protected from deportation by the Germans. They can't all be wrong!" The birdman would always end his soliloquy with a self-depreciating question: "Besides, why would Hitler worry about an old, retired watch repairman who is already almost in the grave?"

Izaak was unable to imagine the depth of Nazi anti-Semitism. It was an all-consuming fire of hate that would burn or maim anyone that stood in its way. In the summer of 1942, that fire reached the doorstep of the Archbishop of Utrecht (Jan de Jong). He had been specifically told by the Germans not to allow a letter, which questioned the German treatment of the Jews, to be made public in his archdiocese. The archbishop did not obey the order; he did allow the letter to be read in the churches under his authority.

Seyss-Inquart, in response to the archbishop's failure to follow a direct order, had all Dutch Catholic Jews arrested and sent to death camps. On that dark August day, when the order was carried out, Isaak disappeared from Ter Loo and was never heard of again. Throughout the Netherlands, that week, the weeping and gnashing of teeth increased because one more large group of Jews had been thrown into the murderous mouth of the Nazi Moloch. The fact that these Jewish victims were members of the Roman Catholic Church only added to the feelings of terror. Was there really no limit to the Nazi thirst for Jewish blood?

The disastrous outcome of the Dieppe raid on August 19, 1942, was the third wakeup call during that summer. Steward and his wife, Marijke had, for months, been listening breathlessly to the evening BBC news reports on their radio because they knew that the Allied attack on the Atlantic wall of Hitler's fortress was going to happen soon. They also believed that, once the attack happened, the Nazi edifice would collapse as quickly as a house of cards; it would never be able to withstand a massive Allied assault.

Reality was a cruel task master on that grim August day near Dieppe. The Germans swiftly repulsed the attack and the walls protecting the Nazis' European fortress were undamaged. After the battle had ended and the surviving attackers had retreated, there were many questions which continued to hover over that battlefield for months. Had the much heralded second front been an illusion? Would the Allies ever be able to smash their way into fortress Europe? Was Hitler's army so omnipotent that it could, on its own, keep Britain, the USA, and the USSR at bay?

Would this war go on forever? Would Nazi rule become the new normal with which all Europeans would have to live into perpetuity?

Everyone responded to the Dieppe debacle in their own way. For Beppe it was a call to action. The day after the attack Beppe took the well-trodden path to Elske's little house. On arriving there, she discovered that her friend, who had seen her coming, had already opened the door for her. Beppe greeted her with a gentle "Good morning" and, after giving each of the two little boys a small hug, she told Elske that she had no time for a cup of coffee.

She, instead, began to pour out the thoughts that had been troubling her for a long time: "I was thinking, Elske, that almost two months have passed since we received the names and addresses of over one hundred Jewish children for whom we need to find hiding places. Korrie gave us the list because she wanted us to help her with the dream of safely hiding those kids with host families in this area. We both know that, through Korrie, God was telling us go into the Red Sea and help rescue those little innocent ones. Now, Elske, I am beginning to think that we have been too cautious. Yes, since that day you or I have visited almost every house in Ter Loo in the hope that we could find hiding places for those kids, but the payback has been negligible. Only Feike and Sjoukje Cramer, as you know, are willing to take two kids into their home. The two Bentink boys will be brought to Sebeek tomorrow; Steward will bring them in his hay wagon and bring them here. But how do we go on from here? We need to find hiding places for twenty to forty kids every week instead of only two in a period of two months. The need is ever more urgent because every week more trains are leaving Amsterdam stations and taking Jews on the first stage of their trip to the death camps."

Beppe, because she was talking faster and faster, finally had to stop to take a deep breath. Elske took the moment of silence to walk up to her and gently lead her to a chair and, with a hand motion, invite her to sit down. Beppe accepted the invitation and, still shaking her head, sat down without protest. Elske then sat down close to her and, with a forced laugh, said: "I have also concluded that we must not be very persuasive people. We can't convince anyone to take a risk and open the doors of their homes and invite their Jewish countrymen in. What should we do now? Is it time to just give up? Are we going to continue and just waste our time by simply beating our head against the wall? Is there nothing that we can do to help the Jewish children that God has entrusted to us?"

She looked directly at Beppe and said: "Yesterday, as you know, I made a trip to Apeldoorn, and I had a chance to talk to Korrie. She was very emphatic about what we must do from now on. When we make our visits, we must come with an actual endangered child in tow. Our neighbors may not, in the abstract, want to have Jewish children in their home, but when we bring children to the door and confront them with the ugly reality that real flesh and blood children will face if they are not helped, then they may not be so ready to slam their doors in our faces."

Beppe, in an alarmed tone, asked: "How can we do that? We can't just march up and down the streets and country roads with Jewish kids! We will not only endanger ourselves, but also those very children that we want to help!"

Elske quietly raised her hand. "Korrie knows that we should not just walk into people's homes with Jewish kids in tow and that's why she has a plan that will help us with our mission. She has contacted an organization that is trying to find homes for the thousands of new refugees whose homes, in the coastal towns, are being systematically destroyed because of Hitler's massive Atlantic wall plan. The Relief Organization for Atlantic Wall Children (ROAWC) is looking for families willing to take in displaced children from coastal cities where thousands of homes have been turned into rubble. It is Korrie's plan that those Jewish kids can, so to speak, fly under the ROAWC flag. That organization is looking for homes for 3000 kids in Friesland."

"Elske," Beppe said, "are you telling me that I should get people to take in Jewish children through false pretenses? People who take such kids into their homes put their lives on the line, and I, for one, would never want to trick them into taking those kinds of risks."

Elske shook her head and smiled briefly as she said, half to herself, "I agree with you, Beppe. As ambassadors of the Jewish kids, we need to be utterly honest with the families that take them in. Korrie's idea is that we become regional ROAWC representatives and, as such, go around finding homes for refugee children. It makes no difference whether the child is homeless because of the Atlantic wall or because he or she is a Jew. Only after a family is willing to accept a child into their home will we have a conversation about which child most needs a home. That is when we ask them if, by any chance, they are willing to accept a child who happens to be Jewish. If their answer is a resolute no, then we will come up with another ROAWC child who is not Jewish."

After Elske had spoken, Beppe had only one additional question: "Was there anything else that Korrie mentioned to you? From the expression on your face, I can see that she told you something else that you are scared to talk about."

Elske took a deep breath before continuing in a lower voice. "There is, indeed, something that she mentioned to me, but I was afraid to overwhelm you with that information; I don't even know if you are still prepared to be a part of Korrie's general plan. What she told me is that, in fact, four children from Jewish families have already been taken by boat from Amsterdam to Lemmer. Currently they are in a safe house, but a regular home must be found for them immediately."

Beppe was all business when she said: "Let's find homes for those helpless kids; we simply must do something for them."

The next day Steward went with a hay wagon to Lemmer to pick up the four children who had been brought there by means of the ROAWC network. It took Beppe and Elske almost 14 days to find a home for all those kids but, by that time, five more Jewish children had been brought to the Ruintjes farm—after also making the trip by way of Lemmer.

Day after day, and from morning until the evening, Elske made the rounds to the different farm families. Beppe would sometimes come along, but usually she stayed home and took care of the many children at the farm. Elske, while visiting a potential host family, always took two Atlantic Wall child refugees along, and her message was always very simple. "These two children may already have a home but other children, just like these little ones, are being killed by the thousand simply because they are Jewish. Could you give a home to one or two of those young ones for a week, a month or even a year? What do you say? May I bring one or two of those kids to you tomorrow?"

Each morning, as she set out to find homes for Jewish fugitives, Elske had to forget the mournful words of rejection that she had received during the previous day.

"I have to think of my family."

"I am too nervous of a person. That's why I can't take in a Jewish fugitive, but I could easily take care of one or two Atlantic Wall refugees."

"We can't afford to feed one more child."

"The Jews have always been able to take care of themselves very well and they will be able to do so now as well."

"We already are helping some other people."

"We have no proof that the Germans are harming the Jews; they are only taking them to work camps in another occupied country. There, just like the rest of us, they will have to work."

Hour after hour Elske would try, in different ways, to answer the same questions. Then, late in the day, she would bike back to her little home and again take the two tired children out of their bicycle seats. Sometimes all that she received for her effort was a vague commitment from someone who said they might accept a Jewish child for a week or two. The next day she would again load her two toddlers on her bike and stop by the place where she had received a slightly encouraging answer. Usually when she arrived a second time, the indirect "no" became a very direct refusal to take in any children whatsoever.

Over time, Beppe and Elske discovered that even though it was excruciatingly difficult to find a home for the first Jewish child, it was slightly easier to find a home for each successive young refugee. By the end of September 1942, they were able to place over 20 children in the homes of families living in Ter Loo and in the surrounding farms and towns.

Once a home had been found for a child, Elske and Beppe stepped into the background. It was Zak who would stay in regular and discrete contact with that family. He was the one who, for example, went to the Douma farm and delivered the false ID papers which stated that Idske Douma was the name of the young boy in the family. Zak was the messenger who would bring supplies of milk and brown beans to supplement the food pantry of the Douma family, and, if necessary, also helped them build cleverly disguised hiding places for their young Jewish guests.

Chapter Eighteen

Korrie and the Hospital Holocaust
(Jan. 1943)

" During the evening of January 21–22 1943, all the patients of the Jewish mental hospital Het Apeldoornse Bosch—approximately 1200 patients—were stuffed into train freight cars and taken away... [to Auschwitz where they were killed. Some were burned alive.]"

—RANDWIJK

ALL THROUGH THE FALL of 1942, Korrie continued to work as a nurse at the Jewish mental hospital. During those grim months, she stayed in close contact with Fritz and Jannie, two members of the Apeldoorn underground. They worked closely with her as she tried to find safe shelters for her patients and their family members.

Late in the afternoon of Jan. 20, 1943, as Korrie was getting ready to leave for the hospital and report for duty, she was startled by a quiet knock on her door. She was not expecting anyone, and her first thought was that someone had found out about her Jewish identity and was coming to arrest her. She walked toward the back door which led to the fire escape, but she stopped when she heard the emergency password that she had given Fritz. She opened her door quickly while Fritz, for the second time, was saying the code words: "We are bringing you a rabbi for supper."

Jannie and Fritz stepped into Korrie's small apartment and carefully closed the door behind them. Korrie could see the troubled look on their faces as Jannie mouthed the words: "You need to get out of here in the next fifteen minutes. We can't talk here. Is there a safe place where we can go and talk openly? After getting out of here, we will explain to you what we know."

Korrie nodded her head and, leading the way, took her friends to a small building on a secluded side street. When they were safely inside that windowless building, and they had securely closed the door, Fritz asked, "What kind of place is this? Is it safe? Will we be interrupted? What is that smell?"

Korrie told her friends how she had gained access to the little shed. "This is a small storage building that a baker in town, Mr. Holtrop, rents to store supplies and equipment that he does not immediately need. I hope the smell of musty flour does not bother either of you. With the shortage of everything these days, this building has been empty for well over a year, but Holtrop keeps paying the rent for it because it is a good hiding place. Three months ago, he gave me a key to it. He looked me in the eye and said, 'Just in case you need to find a quick place in which to hide for a short time.' He and his wife are both very active in the underground and they have already helped me more than once by secretly bringing Jewish kids to Lemmer in their enclosed baker's van. What brings you here today?"

Frits spoke first, and Korrie heard the despair in his voice. "From reliable sources in the underground, Korrie, we have been informed that the Germans are preparing to imprison all the residents and staff of *Het Apeldoornse Bosch* hospital and ship everyone to the east. The plans will be acted on almost immediately. A locomotive with forty empty freight cars is waiting on a sidetrack on the east side Apeldoorn train station. It is only a matter of hours before the hospital patients and staff members will be pushed into those cold freight cars."

After a moment of shocked silence, Korrie fell on her knees and covered her face with her hands. "My God! My God!" she said. "Forgive me for not saving more children."

Jannie knelt beside Korrie and she hugged her. "You have already done a lot," she said. "Now is not the time for blaming yourself."

Korrie wiped her eyes and stood up before responding to her friend's mild injunction. "Jannie and Fritz," she said, "you are the best friends that I have in this world, and you are right. Now is not the time for self-criticism but for action. That is exactly what I have told all the Jewish parents who refuse to go into hiding themselves and will not allow their children to be hidden."

But now I have an action plan for which I will need all the help that both of you can give me. There are 25 children in the hospital whose parents have told me that if a German takeover of the hospital is imminent, then they want their children to be taken from the hospital immediately and hidden with safe families. For that to happen I need to have your help."

Fritz and Jannie were amazed as they listened to Korrie's plan for the rescue of the 25 children. "First of all, I must call Steward and give him the message, 'The yeast has risen.' He will know that he has to come to Apeldoorn immediately with the bread truck of a friend. Once here, he will use that truck to take twelve children from this little building and bring them to Friesland. Holtrop has also agreed that we could use his bread truck so that we can immediately take the other 13 children to Friesland. He told me that he is too old for such a trip himself and asked me to find a driver."

Korrie paused to catch her breath before continuing with her list of commands. "Fritz, you have to get the Holtrop truck ready for a trip to Friesland. Jannie, you must stay in this little building and make the children who come here comfortable and keep them as quiet as possible. I am going to the hospital to get the 25 children who we are going to take to Friesland discharged from the hospital. While there, I will also give Beppe a quick call and provide her with the one-sentence password that she will pass on to her son. Steward should be here before five in the afternoon, and as soon as it's dark, we can set out from this building with all 25 children."

Later that morning, when Korrie came to work, she was ushered into an all-hospital staff meeting room; an intense discussion was under way about the coming German takeover of the hospital and the feared deportations. The hospital CEO told all staff members that they were free to leave immediately and, in that way, try to escape from the inevitable German dragnet.

At first there was only silence in the room. Then, one by one, the maintenance staff members, doctors and nurses left the room and started to mill around in small groups as they asked themselves the same fateful question in different ways. Should they abandon their patients during this hour of need? Was there any way that they could help them any longer? Shouldn't they look out for their own safety? How much time did they have before all choices would be taken out of their hands?

Korrie approached a group of twelve nurses and told them of her plan to bring 25 children to safety in Friesland. "Are you prepared to help me? If so, I want each one of you to take two children by their hands and tell them that you are going for a walk into the woods. After having safely escaped from this building, I want you to take them to the Holten storage shed. I have arranged for transportation from there. When the kids are delivered, I strongly suggest that you, for your own safety, escape and hide. Don't allow yourself to be caught in the massive German dragnet that will undoubtedly be thrown around the hospital in the next 24 hours."

The nurses asked Korrie many questions, but their main concern was very practical. "What children will we take? How will parents respond to something that has all the appearance of kidnapping? How can we simply leave the others?"

Korrie pulled 25 permission slips from her pocket. "The parents of these 25 children have given me written permission in which they urge me to take their kids from the hospital if they are no longer protected here. I will give each of you two of these slips so that you know which children to take. Have your two children roll up their bed blanket because they will need that for the cold trip that they will have to endure. When you bring your two charges to the Holtrop hut, give the slips to the young woman, Jannie who is there waiting for the children. She will take over from there."

Each of the nurses went to work immediately. During the previous months they had known that Korrie had been working with parents in an attempt to hide Jewish children. Now they had been given something definite to do to help the children for whom they were responsible.

The first two children came to the hut at about two in the afternoon and allowed themselves to be quietly wrapped up in their blankets. Soon the little hut was filled with the sound of frightened children. They sat close to each other in order to stay warm. The older children, with fear on their faces, tried to comfort the younger ones by telling them that they were going to have a day of adventure.

When all 25 children had come to the little hut, the sun was already disappearing over the horizon, and that was also the time when the two enclosed bread vans arrived. Steward was in the driver's seat of the one of the trucks, and Elske was in the passenger seat. She had insisted that she needed to come along in order to take care of the children during the trip back. Fritz was the driver of the second truck and Jannie was his helper.

Within thirty minutes Korrie was able to get all the children into the two small, vans. The older children were seated along the perimeter and tightly held the younger children on their laps. Elske would later comment, "It seemed as if Korrie had magical power over the children because of the way they allowed themselves to be crammed into those small bread trucks."

Korrie herself did not go with the trucks because she felt that she needed to go back to her apartment to pick up the children's medicines that she had stockpiled there.

Steward had estimated that it would take four hours to get from Apeldoorn to Ter Loo because he planned to take the back roads where there was less chance of being stopped by the military police who would want to see their passports. They had all the paperwork needed for making two flour shipments to Friesland but nothing allowing them to bring 25 Jewish children into the province.

There is little in Zak's notebooks about that white-knuckle trip from Apeldoorn to Ter Loo. It seems that they were only about ten miles from Apeldoorn when one of the younger children in Steward and Elske's truck, Alex Vogelzang, began to cry, "I want my momma." Elske tried to comfort him but, with each passing mile, his gut-wrenching cries became louder and more shrill. "I want my momma. I want my momma."

Alex's cries rang through the quiet pastures of Overijssel and Friesland during the whole trip from Apeldoorn to Ter Loo. With each mile, Steward gripped the steering wheel of the truck tighter and tighter until he finally stopped the truck and, looking at Elske, said: "We are going to have to place him between us."

"But how can we do that? If we get stopped and they see a child with us, we'll be interrogated, and that will be the end of it for all of us."

"I know," Steward said, "but if we get stopped with a screaming child in the back there will also be trouble. If he is with me in the front and he continues to scream like this, they may want to wave us on as quickly as possible. I will just apologize for my loud son and ask the policeman if he will allow me to get him to his mom as quickly as possible. So, if we are about to be stopped for a pass control, you should sneak into the back with the children and I will do my best to look like a dad who is at his wits end. Hopefully the police will not look at our false papers too closely or look through the curtain and see what kind of load we are carrying."

And that is how they were able to safely pass through the two police inspections. Both of those times the constable in the guard house got a pained expression on his face when the van rolled to a stop and he heard the young Alex belt out his heart wrenching cry: "I want my momma." The guard quickly waved them on and then also allowed the other van to proceed with only a cursory look at the papers that Fritz presented to him.

By midnight, the two trucks arrived at the Ruintjes farm. Beppe had prepared places throughout the house where the 24 children could sleep. By two in the morning, they were all finally asleep.

Elske had taken the crying Alex into her home and held him tightly in her lap for a long time. As the hours passed, his shrill cries slowly mellowed into a mechanical and sleep-filled murmur: "I want my momma."

Elske was finally able to bring her two sleeping boys back to her home at two in the morning because Alex was asleep. During the rest of that night Elske drifted in and out of a fitful sleep. When she woke up at six in the morning, she saw her two boys quietly standing near her and looking at the strange boy who was sleeping next to her.

"You boys are hungry? Let's be quiet so this guy can continue to sleep." She then gave both a big hug and went into the kitchen to prepare their oatmeal breakfast.

She was still in the middle of the painfully slow process of getting the boys to eat the unsweetened gruel when she heard the front door of her house open and close. She thought nothing of it and assumed that it was either Beppe or Steward coming to ask her a question or bring her milk from the barn. When Piet unexpectedly strode into the small kitchen, she was temporarily voiceless.

After she had finally found her voice, she peppered him with a long string of anxious questions. "What happened? Are you back for good? How did you get here so early in the morning?"

Piet wearily raised his hand and explained what had happened. "I received a weekend pass that permits me to leave work for a total of four days. I took the first train with connections to Sebeek. I got in late last evening, but when I got off the train, the German soldier on duty would not let me go home. He told me that he had to check in with his boss to make sure that my four-day pass was valid. They put me in jail until five this morning; that's when they verified my pass and finally released me. It's taken me this long to walk from the station. Seeing you and the boys, however, makes it all worthwhile."

As Piet sat by the kitchen table, he said: "I sure hope we have some food in the house because I am literally starving. I've only had two slices of dry bread since yesterday morning."

Elske placed what remained of the oatmeal porridge before him. "I have two eggs that I'll prepare for you, she said. "There are also some brown beans that I put in water to soak yesterday and that need to be boiled and eaten. I will prepare that for a solid noon meal; it will put some weight into your stomach."

Piet had barely started with the eggs that Elske had prepared for him when he heard a hoarse voice from their bedroom calling out: "I want my momma"!

He first looked at the two boys and then, with a puzzled expression, turned to Elske.

"That's Alex," she said. "He is staying with us for a few days."

"Who is Alex? Who are his parents? Why is he staying with us?"

Elske first tried to dodge his questions but, within a few minutes she said, "He's a Jewish boy who's staying with us for perhaps a day or two."

The normally even-tempered Piet now burst out in anger. "How dare you bring more Jewish children into our home? I work long days so that you and the two boys are able to have something to eat and a roof over your head. Haven't we done enough for our Jewish countrymen by taking in one Jewish boy? Do you want all of us to be shipped off to the concentration camps in Germany? And that's what's going to happen. The Germans will not show any mercy. They want all of Europe to be freed of Jews—*Judenrein*. At work I frequently hear that word being used."

Piet's voice became increasingly loud and shrill; it was buoyed by a spirit of pure panic. "I insist that that boy is out of our house by the end of the day. We can't take any more risks."

At first Elske listened to her husband in silence. Then she escaped to their bedroom, put her face down on the bed and, with only a minimum of sound, began to cry uncontrollably. She did not want to wake up Alex and she also did not want to scare the two boys. The pressure of the previous evening and the lack of sleep had been too much for her.

Piet followed her to the unmade bed and tried to comfort her, but she pushed him away with harsh words. "You can't just come home and tell me what to do. Instead of listening to me explain things you just bark at me."

Piet left her alone and sat down in the living room. He was restlessly dozing in the chair when, thirty minutes later, Elske emerged from the bedroom. "Well," she said in a brisk tone without looking at him. "Do you want to know why that Jewish boy is in the bedroom?"

Piet, who was thoroughly exhausted, jerked up in the chair. "Yes," he said, rubbing his sleepy eyes, "you may as well tell me the whole dammed story."

Elske then told Piet the whole story of Korrie's involvement with the Jewish mental hospital in Apeldoorn and her decision to rescue 25 children. As his wife was talking, Piet again became increasingly nervous and agitated. In the end, when she told him that she and Steward had helped bring those children to the Ruintjer farm, he got to his feet and burst out in anger: "If Steward is crazy and wants to jump into a canal, that doesn't mean that you have to follow him. We can't take the kinds of risks that you are putting us in."

The home where Elske and the boys lived was one unit of a small duplex which was adjacent to the Ruintjes farm; it had been built for the farm hands and their families. Steward and his wife, Marijke, lived in one unit, and Elske and the boys lived in the other one. One could easily overhear sounds coming from the adjacent units because the wall between the two small homes was very thin.

Piet's voice, on that cold January day, went straight through that fragile wall. Steward, who had just awoken from a troubled dream, clearly heard someone very close by say the words "Steward is crazy." He sat up in his bed and began to listen more carefully and it was then that he recognized Piet's voice. He thought that he might still be dreaming, but then he heard Elske's voice. "You must not talk so loudly, Piet. These walls are not very thick."

Steward was still sleepy when he got out of bed and stumbled into the kitchen. He was quickly more alert, however, when he saw a shadow pass by in front of the kitchen window. He first thought it might be a German soldier but then, as he looked more closely at the dark figure, he could see that it was not an enemy soldier. It was, in fact, his neighbor and former friend, Piet who was walking down the driveway and then turning to go down their narrow country road.

Steward put on his own heavy black winter coat and, with the word "crazy" still ringing in his ears, stepped outside. His wife was one step behind him and, grabbing the sleeve of his coat, stopped him long enough so that she could whisper in his ears: "Don't get into an argument with Piet. He is a good man."

Steward pulled the coat out of her hands and ran down the road. Within minutes he had caught up to Piet.

At first Steward tried to be polite but there was a sharp edge in the tone of his voice when he stopped running and looked closely into the eyes of his former friend. "Hello Piet. It's good to see that you are back from Germany. Have you quit your job, or will you soon be leaving us again?"

Piet eyed Steward carefully as he cleared his throat. "I'm okay, but also deeply worried about everything. I don't want to go back to that job in Germany but will have to go anyway. I have no choice but to go back to that crazy job."

Steward had fallen in step with Piet as they started with their introductory pleasantries but, when he heard Piet use the word "crazy" for a second time, he abruptly stopped walking and stared directly at Piet, who, in turn, also stopped.

There was terseness in Steward's voice as he said: "So now you think your German job is crazy. You seem to be quite ready to use that word lately. Didn't you use that same word to describe me when you were talking to Elske a few minutes ago?"

Having lost all self-control Steward continued to attack his former friend. "So, you think I am crazy, do you, as I help with the effort to find homes for helpless and handicapped Jewish children whose very lives are in danger? You think that you are sane as you go to your safe job in Germany where you are making millions of bullets for the guns that will be used to shoot down the American and English planes that are coming here to free us from our occupiers. Well, I have news for you. You are the crazy one! It's insane to work for the Germans because as you well know, they will be damned to the lowest regions of Hell."

As the abusive words rained down on him, Piet said nothing. He resumed walking and stared down at the blanket of newly fallen snow.

Steward was slightly unnerved by Piet's apoplectic silence and by the fact that both Elske and his wife were standing in the doorways of their respective homes staring at the two of them. "Well, Piet, do you have nothing to say for yourself? Who is the crazy one here? Don't you see that you're making yourself into a candidate for Hell by working for the German foot soldiers of Satan?"

Emerging from his silence, Piet, in a very unnatural voice, repeated what he had said to Elske earlier that morning. "We live in dangerous times and Elske and I can't take any more risks. With that trip to

Apeldoorn, you risked not only your own life but also her life—and the life of our two boys. You shouldn't have forced Elske to do something like that."

There was cold anger in Steward's voice as he stopped walking. "Look at me, Piet. I no more convinced Elske to come with me than she convinced you to go to Germany and work in a munition factory. She feels polluted by every stinking German mark that you send her."

Piet, who was usually not easily provoked, was now also furious. "How dare you walk with your dirty muddy feet into the privacy of our family life? What do you know about Elske's feeling about my job? What do you know about the Germans? Have you faced them in battle? Do you know what they will do if you, by your lonely little self, try to stop them? They will smash you to pieces and all of us along with you—including the 25 Jewish children that you brought here from that hospital!"

There was a sharp ring of panic in Steward's voice as he, in a broken voice, uttered the words that were both written down and underlined in Zak's notebook. "Let those German Devils come and kill me. At least I'll know that I have not helped them bring more fire into their hellish furnaces."

The angry exchange ended with one last utterance from Steward: "I am at least risking only my body while you, with your job in Germany, are risking your very soul."

After Steward's last outburst there was restless silence in the white landscape adjacent to the Ruintjes farm. To all those who witnessed the angry exchange, it seemed as if the echoes from the word "soul" continued to reverberate from every surface for a long time.

It was Elske, still standing by the door of her home, whose crisp voice ended that uneasy silence. "Come back here, Piet. You are going to catch a death of a cold out there without your coat."

Steward had been ready to hurl more harsh words at Piet, but at the sound of Elske's voice, he turned around and trudged back to his own home.

Chapter Nineteen

Zak and Korrie

(1943)

KORRIE HAD DREAMT OF saving 100 Jewish children, and she lived to see many of those children taken down the road to safety. During the eventful month of January 1943, she helped save 25 children from a fiery death in Auschwitz; the other approximately 1200 patients and 50 staff members from *Het Apeldoornse Bosch* hospital perished in that deathcamp.

How those mentally handicapped people died is a tragedy that is not often spoken about because it is so horrific. When the train from Apeldoorn arrived at the death camp, the helpless prisoners were pulled from the box cars and thrown directly into the flames of the terrifying furnace where corpses from the gas ovens were being incinerated. Many of those helpless patients were still alive and shackled in their straitjackets when they landed in the middle of that unimaginable hell-on-earth.

Korrie often spoke to Zak about that terrible night when the patients were savagely loaded into those icy train cars. She also never stopped thinking about those twenty-five children who had escaped that fate and had been whisked away to Friesland.

And, for Korrie, thinking and helping were two words that were closely connected. After the two bread trucks with the children had left Apeldoorn, she went back to her apartment one more time and picked up the medicines that she had been able to gradually stockpile during the previous months. She knew that some of the young ones who had been rescued would need to have medicines to stabilize them.

It was completely black that night when she left her apartment for the last time. She placed all those medicines into the two saddle bags of her bicycle. She was determined to get those healing resources to the young patients whom she had sent to Friesland.

It took her several days to bike from Apeldoorn to Ter Loo because she only dared to travel during the darkest hours of the night and she often had to make long detours to avoid towns. She trusted no one. She hid herself in barns and in haystacks during the daylight hours.

On the evening of January 27, when she arrived at the Ruintjes farm, she asked about the children even before she had taken off her coat. Beppe, who could see that she was gravely ill from hunger and deprivation, took her by the hand and led her to a comfortable chair.

"Rest here," she said, "I'll get you something to eat."

Korrie let out a long sigh of relief, sank into the chair and immediately fell asleep. But, after five minutes, she woke up with a start, sat upright in the chair and, to no one in particular, announced: "I have to see them."

At first her eyes were unfocussed and there was an air of panic about her. Soon, after Beppe had brought her a glass of milk, two boiled eggs, and a plate with two slices of bread on it, she started to calm down. She nibbled at the food for a few minutes, but the horrors of the previous days again started to envelop her. She became acutely alert as she raised her voice to a hysterical pitch, and again asked: "Where are the children?"

Beppe hesitated momentarily before answering her question. "They have temporarily been taken to the homes of five farm families located on this side of Ter Loo; within a few days we will find homes for them with twenty-five different local families."

Korrie, in her panic, was disturbed by the hesitation in Beppe's voice. "What I hear you saying, Beppe, is that all those kids are still living in limbo! Can't real homes be found for them?"

After that outburst, a stunned silence filled the room. During the previous weeks and months Elske and Beppe had bicycled hundreds of miles to the most distant farmhouses as they searched for places where fathers and mothers would be willing to risk their personal safety in order to shelter just one more Jewish child.

The image of so many doors being shut in their faces flashed through Beppe's mind as she looked at Korrie and thought about the new challenges they would have to face. How would they ever find homes for these hunted children who were not only from Jewish families, but who were also mentally handicapped?

It was at this juncture that Elske stepped into the room. She walked with quiet grace to where Korrie was sitting. "Let's remember what Daniel's friends said," she whispered: "'Even if we are thrown into the blazing furnace, the God we serve is able to deliver us from it.'"

After that Korrie calmed down and finished eating the food that Beppe had placed on a small table near her. Soon she started to drift into sleep again in the chair. Before she was fully asleep, Elske and Beppe were able to take her to the upstairs guest bedroom where she fell into a long and troubled slumber.

That first day, in her terror-filled dreams, she again relived all the horrors of the previous days. In her imagination she again saw the ghoulish madness on the faces of the soldiers that tore apart the hospital in which she had been working. She again saw how they callously dumped the mentally ill patients into icy trucks. She again felt the blinding anguish that motivated so many of her fellow nurses to voluntarily go along with their doomed patients and, in that way, to their own death. Shouldn't she also have helped take care of those patients?

Throughout that first night, she again and again recycled through the different names of the patients who had been wrenched out of the Jewish mental hospital in which she had worked all those months. She blamed herself for not rescuing those who had been loaded into those boxcars on that fateful January day. She eventually fell into a deep sleep. Even then, her hands would have momentary spasms; it was as if she was still trying to grab a patient escaping from her grasp.

When she got up the next day, she was wide awake and breathed an air of nervous energy. She quickly and quietly ate the slice of rye bread with cheese that had been placed on the table for her. She was soon ready for action and said to no one in particular: "This morning I am going to visit with all of the rescued children because, as their nurse, I need to make sure that they are responding correctly to their medications."

No one said anything for well over a minute. Beppe didn't want to be the one to tell her that it was utterly unsafe for her, a known Jewess, to be out in the open and visiting the five farms where the children were being hidden. The silence only ended when Elske came into the kitchen with the two young boys—one in each arm.

She gave her own son to Beppe and, with the free arm, quickly hugged her friend. Then, after making a quick half turn, she said: "Korrie, your little Jacob is doing well. Do you want to hold him?" Without waiting for an answer, she placed the boy on her friend's lap.

Then, standing behind her friend, she gently wrapped her arms around her and began to quietly whisper in her right ear. "Last year you had the dream of saving 100 Jewish children and, during the past twelve months, you have acted like both a hero and a crazy woman. You brought dozens of children to relative safety here in Friesland. Now, to protect those same children, you need to go into complete hiding and give others a chance to pick up where you left off. I say that because we know, from reliable sources, that you are on the top of the Gestapo watch list."

There was a twinkle in Elske's eyes as she continued: "And, while you are in hiding, you can shower all your love on your own sweet son. His big smile will bring sunshine to your darkest days—as he has done for me during these past months."

Korrie's eyes shifted from her son to the kitchen window through which she could see the road along which she and Elske had walked so many times during that long-ago year when they were both pregnant. Soon, in her mind, she allowed that road to take her to all the places where her other children were staying. After a long silence, she let out a protracted breath of air which, for so many months, had been tightly compressed in her chest.

"OK, Elske, I will go into hiding, but first, today, I want to see those children one more time. I want to have a fresh picture of their faces in my mind."

Elske agreed with that plan, and, with Korrie, made a brief nighttime visit to each of the five farms where the children were temporarily housed. After seeing the children one more time, Korrie stayed very close to the Ruintjes farm during the weeks and months after January 1943.

Normally she stayed in Zak's hiding place, because it was not safe for her to be seen on the farm property. While in hiding that year, she and Zak became very good friends and eventually, with stops and starts, that friendship evolved into a deep romance.

Zak never had any doubts about his feelings for Korrie. From the very first day he met her, he had been drawn to her and had done everything in his power to help her. Zak's gentle love for Korrie slowly became more passionate when he saw the courage that she displayed with her underground work with Jewish refugee children.

Zak not only loved Korrie, but, as it turned out, she also loved him. They were married during a private and secret wedding ceremony in early May 1943, by a pastor who was known as Johnny. This man, whose actual name was Pastor Appinga, not only brought a sea change into the lives of Zak and Korrie, but also helped bring a fundamental political change to Ter Loo

During the summer of 1942, Johnny had been forced to go into hiding when he discovered that the Gestapo had come to his house to arrest him for his political activism. Through his counseling and sermons, he had repeatedly urged the parishioners of his church in Klemden to go into hiding rather than following the German mandates ordering them to work in Hitler's factories. Quotes from his sermons, such as the following one, can still be found in the Gestapo records: "Your sons must not be shipped off to the pagan culture of Germany where they will be forced to help make the weapons that will defend Hitler's deeply evil empire."

Johnny was able to escape from the grip of the Gestapo because he was visiting a parishioner when the Germans raided his home. Later on his way home, an alert neighbor stopped him on the road and told him about the raid. He never entered his home again, but instead, went into hiding and took on his new name.

In the underground, Johnny's main job was to be a regional agent of a national organization that hid those young people who had defied the order stating that they had to report for work in Germany. This secret Work Dodging Organization (WDO) was the brainchild of two people who used the names "Fred" and "Rita."

Johnny, as an agent of the WDO, travelled throughout Friesland and established the local cell groups that, in turn, coordinated the search for safehouses in Friesland for men hunted by the Germans. He used his skill as a pastor in this endeavor, and depended on local contact people from the underground to help him find a meeting room where he could secretly give a sermon to anyone who was willing to come and listen to him.

Johnny's Ter Loo sermon was delivered on April 11, 1943, in the barn of Eppie Tolsma. For years Eppie had been hostile to those working in the Dutch underground. In his deep, husky voice, he had repeatedly condemned the work of the fledgling movement. "All underground workers," he would say to anyone who was prepared to listen to him, "are nothing more than troublemakers who have torn Romans 13 out of their Bible. As believers we may not play around with the Bible and think that we do not have to obey those who are placed in authority over us. If we go down that road, we have thrown out the Word of God."

Eppie was known in the region as "the big guy" because he was a very tall and broad-shouldered man. This Goliath had, two years earlier, roared: "I will not endanger my life by standing between the Germans and the Jews." That was the time when Pastor Sven had asked the church counsel for funds to repair the smashed window in the home of Korrie's mom.

What changed everything for Eppie was a German mandate, early in 1943, which stated that all young men who had served in the Dutch army in 1940 must immediately report for work in Germany. Ab, Eppie's son, had not only been a captain in the Dutch army, but he had also sustained a permanent injury; half of his right hand had been blown away by a German shell.

Ab was, consequently, one of the tens of thousands of Dutch vets who was ordered to abandon all existing job and family commitments and immediately report for work in Germany.

For Eppie, as for many other Dutchmen, this new act of Nazi tyranny was the proverbial straw that broke the back of the camel. He felt that the Germans had no right to take away his son. He had for three years diligently complied with everything that the occupiers had asked of him. He allowed them to have control over all the milk that his dairy herd produced. Month after month, he had staunchly refused to give in to underground pressure asking him to falsify his herd numbers so that surplus milk could be diverted to some of the regional refugees who were unable to obtain the official coupons needed to make purchases of any kind. All those who came to him for help were piously told that he could not go against God's will. After his son was ordered to report for work in a German factory, Eppie abruptly stopped connecting the will of God to that of Hitler.

One evening, after making deliveries of the latest issue of the illegal newspaper, Zak was stopped by the sound of a loud voice coming from Eppie's farm. Even from the road he could clearly hear what Eppie was saying. "We must put a stop to these Nazi Devils! If things go on like this much longer, they will kill us all!"

Zak was secretly thrilled by what he had just heard from this leading member of his community. So, on instinct, he grabbed his trusty little note pad and wrote him the following message: "Help us stop the German Devils by allowing pastor Johnny to give a message of resistance in your barn." He signed the note with the words: "The Underground." He added a little postscript after his note: "Write your response on the back of this note and place it under this same door tomorrow evening before

12 p.m." He then placed his memo inside an issue of the illegal newspaper and shoved it under the front door of Eppie's house. He rang the doorbell three times before swiftly disappearing into the darkness.

The little nudge from that note had the desired effect. From that day on, Eppie worked closely with the representatives of the underground. He never tired telling all comers: "God told me, through Johnny, that I needed to do everything in my power to help push the Germans out of this country."

Beppe had been the first to approach Johnny and ask him to come and talk to the people of the Ter Loo region. Steward made the local arrangements for the meeting.

On the evening of April 10, Pastor Johnny quietly walked into the Ruintjes farmhouse and Beppe whisked him down into the farm's hiding place. There he met both Zak and Korrie for the first time, and Beppe told him that the two of them were both on the top of the Germans' wanted list. She also explained that Zak, because of a childhood illness, was unable to talk, but that he could communicate in writing. She then pointed to a cot in the corner and said: "that will be your bed for the night."

After Beppe had left the hiding place, Pastor Johnny said: "It looks as if I am in good company because the Gestapo is also trying to get me in their claws. Well, comrades, I hope you sleep well; I am a tired soldier, so I am going to bed early to get some rest."

Early the next morning, Beppe quietly tapped on the door of the hiding place and handed down a tray with breakfast for Johnny, Zak, and Korrie. It took only a few minutes before the three of them were sitting around a small table and ready to eat their breakfast.

At first, as they were eating, it was very quiet in the small hiding place, but that changed when the pastor, almost to himself, noted: "This is the first time that I have had my breakfast while sitting under a manure pile. But that is what this war is doing to us. It is causing us to do strange things. I am sure that both of you have seen many unusual things which, I hope, you will not tell me about in any detail. When I am captured, it's better if I know nothing about what you are really doing. What's not known can't be divulged."

Korrie, ignoring the last sentence, began to tell him about all the work that had gone into finding homes for the dozens of handicapped Jewish children that she had rescued from Apeldoorn. Once she began talking, it seemed as if the flood gates had been opened and she could no longer stop herself from vividly seeing the face of each and every child that she had been able to help escape from the doomed Jewish hospital—as well as the many faces of the nurses, doctors, patients and workers who had disappeared into the train boxcars that carried them to their death.

While Korrie was revisiting those dramatic events, Zak instinctively placed his arm around her shoulders. As a result, she gradually calmed down.

After hearing the dark hospital story, Pastor Johnny took a deep breath and closed his eyes for a few minutes. Then, opening them again, he said: "I can see that the two of you are comrades in this battle against the Germans and, at the same time, a brother and sister in the Lord. I am going to thank God for your work every day that I pray for Ter Loo."

To lighten the mood for a minute, he looked at the small decorations on the wall and admired the efficient layout of the hideout. "This is a beautiful spot," he said. "I wish I could bring my wife to a home like this because then I might be able to sometimes spend time with her. I haven't seen her at all during the last four months. We are constantly moving around because of the need to never stay in the same secret hiding place for any length of time."

"Oh how I wish that I really had a safe home again," said Korrie, struggling to keep her composure. "The hospital and the patients were home for me, but now all that has been destroyed. My parent's home in Ter Loo is also gone because my mother was sent to a German concentration camp after having been betrayed by one of her countrymen.

"My only earthly anchor in life," she continued, "is the Ruintjes family as well as this wonderful man Zak. If we did not live in such dreadful times, I would want him standing beside me as my husband."

Korrie's words awoke something in Zak that he had not allowed himself to even think about during the past months. He had suffered his whole life from low self-esteem. During the war years he stayed in hiding and, even when he left the farm, he was as secretive and fleeting as a shadow. It was a lonely and insular life, but he had, through the years, trained himself to suppress his emotions.

That did not mean, of course, that he had no feelings. The very opposite was the case when it came to how he felt about Korrie. During the previous two years, he had fallen ever more deeply in love with her. He not only admired her courage, dedication, and perseverance, but also the quiet and deep faith-based friendship that she had with Elske. That friendship also caused him, again and again, to squelch his feelings because he did not want to interfere with the special bond that united the two young women.

Johnny, while carefully studying Zak's face, asked him if Korrie also had a special place in his heart. "If the war vanished over the horizon today, would you want to marry Korrie?"

The question took him by surprise because, in his mind, the war had become an omnipresent reality that shaped every move he made. He couldn't imagine life without the war. It had even become a strange kind of comfort blanket because he secretly feared that Korrie would forever disappear from his life if the war no longer held her in the farm hideout. "Who," he would repeatedly ask himself, "would want to have anything to do with a handicapped person like me?"

"If both of you really love each other and want to be man and wife," said pastor Johnny, "I can marry you before God any time that you want me to and, after the Germans are gone, the two of you can get the proper paperwork from the re-established Dutch government.

"Never," he kept repeating that morning, "pour buckets of water on the flames of love just because it is a time of war. Far too much of the air that we breathe every day is filled with poisonous fumes of hate. This is exactly the time when we must consciously cherish every spark of life-sustaining love. That is how it is for me. I am utterly dependent on the support of my wife as I flee from place to place. I am as unmoored as a piece of driftwood that is pushed around by every eddy and current that comes along. But, even when I do not see her, the love that I feel for Trudy and the strength that I derive from her prayers, is a daily anchor for me."

Chapter Twenty

The Milk Strike and the Scabs
(April/May 1943)

IT WAS A DARK, rainy April evening when Pastor Johnny delivered his homily in which he encouraged his listeners to open their doors to the refugees who were attempting to escape from Nazis. His words fueled a new wave of illegal activity in the vicinity of Ter Loo and, as a consequence, also triggered a new surge of Nazi retaliatory violence.

How could a simple talk, by this modern-day Johnny Appleseed, both plant seeds of hope and fuel an ever-expanding fire of anger and hate? I do not have any answer to that question, Jay. Hope and anger, during the last two war years, were like two powerful bulls that locked horns and battled for their lives near a deep abyss.

The sun had already set on that dark evening when Johnny entered Eppie Tolsma's barn. Twelve men had come to listen to him. They had silently hidden themselves in the dark corners of the hay loft because they were fully aware that coming to such an illegal meeting could result in an immediate death sentence. The single kerosene lantern lit only the faces of Eppie Tolsma and Johnny. Everyone else was hidden in the darkness.

After the dark shadows had stopped flitting into the barn, Eppie briskly introduced the evening speaker to the invisible audience. "This man beside me is Johnny. He is a friend of mine who has something that he wants to share with every one of you tonight."

Johnny then stood up and, in a clear voice, began to talk to the dark shadows in the barn.

"I come to you, brothers and sisters in the Lord, not as a pastor, but as one of the thousands and thousands of refugees—Jews and Gentiles, Christians and non-Christians, old and young, men and women—whose homes, families, and livelihoods have been taken away from them by the German tyrants who are ruling our country. Those ruthless villains have taken everything from us. Even our identities have been eviscerated. With our false names and illegal identity cards we have become fugitives and vagabonds who ceaselessly drift from place to place. We are strangers in our own country.

"But today I also come to you, not as a stranger and also not as a beggar, but as a follower of our true leader—King Jesus—who will, ultimately, not only destroy the false leader Hitler but also all those who belong to his godless movement.

"As a Christ follower, I am bringing you a question that has tormented me every day for the last three years. Have I been a faithful follower of our Lord, or have I become faithless during these long war years? Did I give food to Jesus when he was hungry? Did I visit him when he was in prison? Did I invite him in when he came as a stranger to the door of my family home? Did I care for him when he was sick? Did I provide him with clothing when he came to me with just a few rags on his back?"

"I am terrified by that multiple-choice questionnaire found in the bible. Am I a 'yes' person who is taking care of the master's needs, or am I a 'no' person who is blind to Christ's needs and the needs of all his brothers and sisters? From the Bible we know that a 'yes' person inherits eternal life, and we also know that the person with a questionnaire that is bursting with 'no' answers will be condemned to eternal punishment in Hell.

"Now, brothers and sisters, as we enter the fourth year of this terrifying war, those hard questions are screaming out at us with increasing urgency. How have things gone during the past three years? Have we, as believers, been 'yes' people or have we, since the beginning of this war on May of 1940, been 'no' people? Did thousands and tens of thousands of us place a 'yes' on our doors when we saw the Hitler terrorists at work hunting and capturing our Jewish neighbors on the streets outside our homes? Or did those Jews find the word 'no' written on the doorposts of our houses and barns when the German dogs were closing in on them?

"I stand here in this barn, today, not as an accuser but as a sinner who, until May of 1942, had the word 'no' written with clear black letters on the doorpost of my house. No unclothed, hungry, thirsty, or sick Jew was, until that day, welcomed into my home with open arms, and I most certainly did not visit even one of them in the concentration camps to which they were being dragged."

"That began to change for my wife and me on a dark stormy May 1942 night when the wonderful Jewish family that lived next door to us was herded into a police paddy wagon at 11:45 in the evening. Through drawn curtains we saw a mother, a father, two young boys and a baby girl as they were being dragged into the darkness of a German-created hell.

"In the shadows of that evening our minds spun endlessly through the same set of disheartening questions. Why didn't we do more to help our Jewish neighbors? Why hadn't they come to us for help? Didn't they know that they could be arrested at any moment? How could this kind of thing be happening on our quiet street?

"But, in the light of the following morning, we knew what we had to do. We simply had to take the 'no' off the doorpost of our house and replace it with a huge 'yes.' That is exactly what we tried to do. Yes, we did visit our neighbors in prison before they were loaded on a train with destinations unknown. Yes, we began to find food, shelter, and safety for some of our neighbors' Jewish family members, friends, and acquaintances. And, yes, we put our own life in danger. And yes, we have become fugitives ourselves. We have become strangers in our own land; we are, however, no longer a stranger to King Jesus. We believe that he knows us and will recognize us when the time comes and he wants us, as forgiven sinners, to enter his eternal home.

"Now I, Johnny, have a simple question for each one of you. Who of you is prepared, this evening, to paint the word 'yes' on the doorpost of your house and barn and, in that way, invite members of the rising tide of fugitives into your homes? The flood of Jewish refugees has abated because the heathen Germans have, with ruthless efficiency, already dragged most them away to the hellish cauldrons located in Germany and Poland. But, as this seemingly endless war continues, the tide of displaced refugees is increasing in size every day. This rising flood not only includes the last remnant of our terrorized Jewish population, but also hundreds of thousands of young men who have gone into hiding because they do not want to be part of Hitler's army of industrial slaves.

"I urge you, brothers, and sisters, place a 'yes' on your houses and barns. Invite one, two or more lost, hopeless, confused, and despairing refugees into your homes and hearts. If you do that, you will not only repeatedly be bringing Christ to your hearth, but you may, like Abraham, be pleasantly surprised because you have brought an angel to the kitchen table of your family."

The listeners, who had initially hidden themselves in the shadows of the hay loft, came one by one closer and closer to the place where Johnny was standing. They could see the sweat pouring off his face as he made his closing argument and stared directly at each person who emerged from the darkness and became visible in the flickering light.

Johnny's voice was little more than a whisper when he made his last statement. All ears were straining to hear the last things that he said: "From experience I know that you will be terrified as you first become Christ's 'yes' man or 'yes' woman. In time you will be able to overcome much of that fear because you will be comforted by the sure confidence that your 'yes' has already been sanctified by the blood of Christ.

"The same thing is not true if the word 'no' remains on your door-post. That word can, if it stays there, be taken down by the Evil One and replaced, at any moment, with the Sign of the Beast."

After Johnny had finished speaking there was a long silence. Then Eppie, with straw-muffled strides, approached pastor and, with his left hand, picked up the lantern that had been standing on a milk can. He then placed his large right hand on the can and, in a quiet voice, stated: 'I want to start being a 'yes' man today."

In the flickering light it appeared as if he had placed his hand on a sacred altar. In a louder voice he reached out to all those in the barn as he said: "Anyone who is with me, place your hand on my hand."

Within minutes almost everyone in the barn stirred and came to the light of the lantern and, one by one, they placed a hand on top of Eppie's strong right hand.

Steward was, at first, too astounded to react to what he was witnessing. He had, on more than one occasion, been called an "anti-German hothead" by some of the very men whose hand now rested quietly on Eppie's muscular and hairy hand. Was he supposed to completely forget all those insults? In the end, he pulled himself together and dutifully also placed his hand on top of the hand pile.

When the last shadow had emerged from the dark corners of the barn, Eppie cleared his throat and declared: "Okay, guys. All men are on board. Let's get to work."

With those words, Eppie brought closure to the impromptu ceremony and at the same time made it appear as if this leap into the dark world of the underground was as simple as pushing, with a collective heave ho, a car out of a snowbank.

During the next moment, it seemed as if the magic of the evening had been whisked away by a powerful and invisible wind. No one said anything else to support Eppie's words. Within minutes everyone had reclaimed their respective hands, and, after putting on their rustic caps, quickly vanished into the shadows of the dark night.

Johnny also did not remain in that barn for very long. After shaking hands with Eppie, he walked in silence towards the exit and prepared himself for the walk back to the Ruintjes farm. Steward, who had been waiting next to that door, sidled up to him, and the two of them walked with haste and in silence down the narrow dark road that took them to their destination.

But that strange, invisible wind was, in fact, the harbinger of important changes in the mental climate in the region. It cut through some of the thickest cobwebs of despair and apathy into which most of the people of Ter Loo had become entangled. Month after month they had glumly greeted each other with the paralyzing words: "Just look down and keep on walking."

In 1943, however, just continuing to move forward was becoming increasingly difficult because Hitler's dreaded sword was beginning to draw blood from the most sacred areas of their lives; it was beginning to touch the family life of many people. The dictator was taking more and more sons and young fathers out of their homes and turning them into conscripted bondsmen in his munition factories.

What made Johnny's words effective was the way that he appealed to the faith of his listeners when he asked them to help rescue young Dutch men from Hitler's slave hunters. Before leaving Ter Loo, Johnny appointed Eppie, Elske, and Beppe to be the three leaders of the newly minted WDO chapter. Their job was to find people who were willing to hide the refugees. Once places had been found, the WDO headquarters would ship out the men who wanted to escape from the German work dragnet. By the end of the war, the Ter Loo chapter of the WDO had successfully hidden 237 men, women, and children.

This new refugee pipeline also made it easier to find homes for Jewish refugees. For weeks Beppe and Elske had despaired of ever finding homes for all the Jewish children in their care but, after Johnny's April sermon, it took only one week to find permanent homes for the last 18 children that Korrie had smuggled from Apeldoorn.

Johnny's visit also left a deep and loving imprint on the personal life of Zak and Korrie. Zak had hidden in the shadows of the barn throughout the whole of Johnny's sermon and stayed in his hiding spot long after everyone had gone home. After going back to his shelter, he scribbled an almost verbatim version of the homily in his little booklet.

Long after the preacher's departure from the region, Zak kept thinking about the question that the pastor had asked him with respect to his feelings for Korrie. He also could not get the message out of his mind. Was he not a "yes" person? Wasn't Korrie also a positive person? Shouldn't they simply say "yes" to the love that was in their hearts? Should they really go ahead and ask the pastor to sanction their marriage vows next time he came back into the region?

It took Zak only a week to overcome his fears. He proposed to Korrie with one simple sentence on a slip of paper. "Will you marry me?"

Korrie's response was equally simple. "Yes. Let's get Johnny to marry us next week when he will be in the area again."

A week later, on April 25, 1943, Johnny quietly performed the marriage ceremony in which Zak and Korrie became man and wife. On that day the newlyweds also formally adopted you, Jay, as their son. It was a very brief ceremony that was squeezed between hours of WDO business talk. Only Johnny Beppe, Steward, and Elske witnessed the quiet event. It had been performed in complete secrecy because neither the bride nor the groom could, even for a moment, risk coming out of the shadows

Johnny's talk in Ter Loo occurred approximately a week before the 1943 national strike broke out and shortly after the Germans ordered all former members of the Dutch armed forces to immediately report for work duty in Germany.

The work stoppage began on April 29 when a group of factory workers in the Eastern Netherlands went on strike in protest against the new mandate. During the next twenty-four hours the strike had spread like a wildfire to every region of the Netherlands.

When his cousin in Deventer told him about the strikes in Twenthe, Eppie felt that the time for action had come. He visited each of the 25 men who had come to his barn earlier in the month and gave them the same command: "Go to ten of your neighbors and tell them to not allow even a drop of the milk from their farm to reach the Germans. Everyone must dump all refinery destined milk into the canals. Let people know that there will be dire consequences for those who break the strike and allow their milk to reach the Germans."

There was little milk for Lennie, the milk hauler, to pick up on the first day of the strike: May 1, 1943. When he arrived at the refinery, at the end of that day, he had only the milk from the farms of Martin Donselaar, Len Ver Hoef, and Wim Melema. He quickly unloaded the 8 milk cans from those farms and left the processing plant. He did not want to talk to anyone about what he had witnessed that day. He also did not want to explain why his wagon was almost empty when he reached the end of his route, and he most certainly did not mention that there was a chalky white hue from the milk in the waters of many of the canals adjacent to the different dairy farms.

Martin Donselaar, who was a Nazi sympathizer, had not only been a strike breaker, but had also warned other farmers about the retaliatory methods that the Germans would use to crush their strike. "Mark my words," he told everyone, "They will come here with their guns, and they will use them to kill people."

It was late in the evening of that same day in May, when Steward arrived at Eppie's farm to talk about what was to be done with the three regional strike breakers. Eppie came to the door and let Steward into the darkened house and took him to the kitchen. Once they were inside, he could read Steward's anger from his demeanor. The short young man was only partially coherent as he hurled out his first words: "We can't let him get away with this. If we let one strike breaker make his milk deliveries today, then tomorrow there will be 60 more scabs who will act like him, and this milk strike will turn into a flaming disaster."

"Stop, stop, stop!" growled Eppie in his deep voice. "What areyou talking about?"

"You know what I'm talking about, Eppie. Everyone knows that Martin Donselaar was a strike breaker today and he is trying to intimidate other farmers. If we do nothing, he will influence all the other farmers on the road between Ter Loo and Sebeek and in that way, get them to again ship out their milk tomorrow. This must stop! Either we are all on strike or we are not on strike!"

Steward then almost spit at Eppie as he continued: "You are a convincing talker, but where is your action. What 'dire consequences' will Martin feel?"

"Ok, Steward, I hear what you're saying. I want to sleep on it tonight. I promise that I will talk to some of the other guys tomorrow, and then we can decide what we may want to do." And, with that, he brought the conversation to an end.

Steward, with a face that looked as if it had been chiseled from marble, clung to his chair for one more minute and then abruptly got up and wordlessly walked out of Eppie's kitchen and his house. He did not even look back as Eppie closed the door behind him. Once he was outside, he repeatedly muttered the words, "or else" and "or else what."

As he passed the small home where Joost was temporarily staying, he knocked three times and then, after waiting for a minute, knocked more loudly for the fourth time. He instinctively took a step backwards when the door opened and Joost's hulking torso almost filled the whole frame of the entryway. "What are you doing here so late, Steward? Is something wrong? You should not deprive me of my beauty sleep in this way! Well, come on in anyway."

After entering his friend's small home, Steward said: "Yes, Joost, something is wrong, and I want to talk with you about it." Steward told him about the three Ter Loo farmers who were not only strike breakers but were also causing their neighbors to waiver. "And, to top it all off, Eppie is unwilling to put pressure on those skunks." There was a slightly hysterical tone in his voice as he ended with: "Are we going to let those Dutch Nazis get away with that?"

Joost, with his deep voice, let out a little belly laugh as he listened to his overwrought friend. "Calm down, Steward. Eppie still wants to be friends with everyone. He simply needs more time to really understand what the krauts and their henchmen can do."

Steward was incredulous as he burst out with the question that had been torturing him: "Are you saying, Joost, that we should do nothing?"

"No, that is not what I meant at all," Joost said. "We need to help Eppie understand that we all have a sacred duty to see that the ultimatums that are made by us may not be ignored. That is why I have a very simple plan. On Sunday evening I will go to Martin's farm and dump his milk on the ground for him and throw his milk cans into the canal."

"I should help you", Steward said.

"No," Joost said. "You stay out of it for now because you not only have your own family to protect but you must also not expose the people who are in hiding at your place".

That same Saturday evening when Steward had gone to visit with Eppie as well as Joost, a meeting also took place in the office of the Commander of Sebeek. Mr. Ulermann had just received word from SS Major Johan Mechels, his superior, that martial law had been declared for all the Netherlands and that the strike must be forcibly crushed immediately. Klees, Andy, and three German soldiers were in the room when he gave out his orders. "My instructions to you are simple. Early Monday morning, when it is just getting light, go anywhere you think that strikes may be taking place. Ask no questions. You must instead shoot and kill any actual or potential troublemakers that you see, and then just leave."

Early Monday morning, May 3, Albert Baanstra arrived at the farm of Martin Donselaar to milk his cows. He had been a farm helper for Martin for over twenty years and was never late for his early morning chores. Stepping onto the property he smelled trouble because he was greeted with the odor of sour milk. Peering through the early morning fog, he quickly discovered that not only had the milk from the previous day been dumped on the ground behind the barn, but that the milk cans themselves had also been dumped into a nearby canal; three of them were still floating, half submerged, in the water.

As he stepped into the murky water of the canal, Baanstra was so intent on retrieving the precious milk cans, that he did not hear the five motorcycles that were coming along the road.

Klees was the first to spot the shadowy figure in the canal adjacent to the Donselaar property. "Damn it." he yelled at those with him, "Someone is throwing Martin's milk into the canal."

He stopped his motorcycle, took out his pistol and, with one shot, killed the hapless Albert Baanstra.

Chapter Twenty-One

The Wild Years

(1943–45)

"[From 1943 onwards, when the Allies] pushed Hitler and his henchmen into increasingly tight corners, the Nazis responded by treating the people in the territories under their control in ever more vicious, wild, and inhuman ways."

—RANDWIJK

DURING THE LAST TWO years of the war, as the Allied armed forces re-captured increasingly large swaths of Hitler's Thousand-Year Empire, the Nazi's terror campaign against the people still under Nazi control, also became more and more savage. Almost any infraction of Hitler's ordinances could result in a death sentence. During those last two war years, almost everyone in the underground movement was repeatedly forced to ask themselves the same grim question: Should they fight Nazi terror with underground terror?

When I first began to study Zak's diaries, I was struck by the fact that Steward, Thijs, Geert, Hobbe, Zak and Joost, as a group, had evolved into an effective underground cell that carried out some very impressive operations. During September 1943 they were able to attack the coupons office of Terperdam and not only steal a large stockpile of food coupons, but they were also able to avoid any bloodshed when they locked the employees in a safe. With that stolen loot, they were able to purchase food for the 135 people who were hiding in homes throughout the Ter Loo region during the following winter.

The Ter Loo group also succeeded in rescuing a total of seven airmen who had parachuted into the region after their planes had been shot down by the Germans. Five of those aviators were eventually smuggled back to Allied territories. The sixth pilot remained hidden in Ter Loo until May 1945, when the Canadian army liberated the territory. Tom, the seventh pilot, didn't live to see the end of the war because he was killed in the attack that came to be known as the Ter Loo massacre.

I could retell many large and small tales of heroism that Zak carefully documented in his densely written notes dealing with those dramatic war years. There was, for example, the time when someone from the underground in Sebeek overheard a message indicating that five soldiers were racing to the Broekeboer farm to make a night-time raid. It was Zak who picked up the phone on that dark moonless evening and received the coded message: "The tenth sheep is very sick." Within minutes he was racing across open fields and pole-vaulting over the wide canals. He reached the Broekeboer farm just in time to help Bob, a British aviator, escape from the swiftly approaching German soldiers.

Zak's journals also provide detailed reports of the many times when food items that local farmers illicitly contributed to the food pantries of the different churches in town, had to be brought to homes where refugees were being hidden. Those secret deliveries were usually made late in the evening and there was always a danger of being immediately arrested or shot for violating the curfew laws.

Much of the underground's communication work was also done during those dark and dangerous hours. That was the time when the falsified passes were distributed and the latest issues of illegal newspapers such as *Trouw*, *BBC Nieuws*, and *Vrij Nederland* were delivered to the secret subscribers.

After repeatedly reading Zak's journals covering the years 1943–45, I could see that he was not just telling a series of success stories. He was also documenting an ever-deepening rift in the Ter Loo cell group. It was a fissure that eventually resulted in the group's cataclysmic demise in the summer of 1944.

The source of the deep conflict was sometimes innocently referred to as the "Klees question." Should dangerous enemies like Klees be executed? Steward and Joost felt that this German henchman was a real and ever-present threat to everyone living in the vicinity of Ter Loo, and for that reason, he needed to be killed. Thijs, Geert and Hobbe, on the other hand, were strenuously opposed to the very idea of deliberately hunting down and taking the life of a fellow citizen—even if that person had become a merciless German collaborator. "As underground workers," Hobbe repeatedly said, during the cell meetings, "we do not have the right to take the law into our own hands."

The first time that the idea of executing Klees was openly discussed by the group happened after the Nazi controlled daily newspaper from the town of Sebeek (*Sebeekse Dagblad* of May 5, 1943) published an article about Baanstra's death. The following quote is from that article:

> Today we received word from Commander Ulermann that the brutal murder of Albert Baanstra was the work of terrorists who want to harm our great German Empire. They will stop at nothing as they try to frighten the farmers and force them to continue their treasonous milk strike. Murder is their weapon of choice. They killed Albert Baanstra simply because he worked for a loyal patriot, Martin Donselaar.
>
> Commander Ulermann has let us know that a full investigation of this murder will be carried out by a Gestapo investigation team from Groningen. Anyone who knows anything about this murder must immediately pass that information on to SS Storm trooper Klees Koorder; he is the local contact person for the investigation. All criminals linked to that murder will be found and punished to the full extent of the law.
>
> We also want to remind everyone that all those who engage in or are seen inciting any treasonous strike related activities will be treated as dangerous terrorists and will be immediately executed.

Albert Baanstra's May 3, 1943, murder, and the ensuing newspaper article, frightened many people in the Ter Loo region. Everyone was fearfully asking the same question: "Who was the killer? Who will die next? Will our town of Ter Loo experience a blood bath? Isn't that what recently happened in nearby Trimunt, when sixteen Dutchmen were gunned down in cold blood by the Germans?"

Martin Donselaar believed that someone from the underground had killed his farm hand. He knew that all his neighbors hated him for his loyalty to the Germans and for being a strike breaker. He also suspected that the bullet that had ended the life of the quiet and demur Albert had been meant for him.

Martin's sense of cold terror was not helped when he went to Sebeek and told Ulermann about the shooting on his farm. The commander maintained a stony silence as he studied the face of the Dutch farmer. Martin, standing in the German's immaculate office, became keenly aware of the dark dirt stains on both his overalls and on his wooden clogs. His discomfort was enhanced by the presence of Klees who, as usual, was impeccably dressed.

When Martin momentarily stopped talking, the commander raised his hand and spoke with Klees for a few minutes before giving his verdict. "Mr. Donselaar," the commander said, "we are sorry about what happened on your farm; it's a good reminder for all of us that this is war and we all have to be prepared to make sacrifices. Look at Mr. Koorder. He gave an eye for our cause. The enemies are all around us and that's why we must always be vigilant, and, to advance our holy mission, we must always be ready to make the ultimate sacrifice. You can help us by telling us immediately if rumors of hostility toward Hitler reach your ears. Heil Hitler!" And with those words, translated into Dutch by Klees, he dismissed the confused and deeply disturbed farmer.

After the farmer had left the commander's office, Klees followed him outside and told him that a special investigative team would come later that day and pick up Albert's body and investigate the crime scene. Martin did not want more Germans on his property because their presence would only make his countrymen hate him even more. His feelings of panic were not mollified by the parting words from the aloof Klees: "Next week Wednesday I will come by your farm and tell you what our investigations have uncovered."

Many locals were indeed wary of Martin; they were convinced that the volatile Nazi farmer had himself murdered his farmhand.

The neighbors' dark suspicions seemed confirmed when they found out that Albert's body, instead of receiving a proper burial, had been whisked away by a German army truck shortly after the murder and taken to some undisclosed location.

Zak was the only witness to the murder that had happened on that misty Monday morning. It happened after he had placed the latest issue of the new illegal newspaper *Trouw* under the door of a customer. The morning sun was beginning to light the night sky when Zak heard motorcycles in the distance and hid himself in a tall stand of bulrushes adjacent to the road along which he had been walking.

From that hiding place, Zak witnessed the unfolding drama. As the loud cavalcade passed him, he got a fleeting glimpse of Klees who was riding the lead motorcycle. He saw Klees slow down and stop in the middle of the road and noticed that he ordered others to halt as well. From approximately 200 feet, Zak saw that Klees was carrying something shiny in his right hand. On hearing the pistol shot, Zak felt sure that the bullet was meant for him. One minute later, however, the five ruthless intruders wheeled their powerful motorcycles around and went back in the direction of Sebeek. Zak stayed in his hiding place long after the loud sound of the motorcycles had vanished into the distance.

Only after everything was quiet again, did Zak cautiously emerge from the bulrushes and stealthily make his way home. Korrie hugged him long and hard after he had climbed down into their hiding place. "You look as if you've seen a ghost," she said.

Zak nodded his head and, on his trusty notepad, gave her a brief explanation of what he had seen. "I was sure that Klees had seen me and was aiming in my direction when he fired his gun."

Korrie hugged him again. "Shall I tell Steward about Klees?" she asked.

Zak shook his head as he penned a simple note: "Only trouble will come from doing that."

Later that same morning, Steward knocked three times on the door of their shelter before coming in. He had a completely dejected expression on his face and a dull tone in his voice as he spoke. "Have you heard the latest bad news yet? Early this morning Albert Baanstra was killed in cold blood. Some are going to blame the underground for this murder; the Germans were, of course, the real killers. They have been killing and maiming people throughout the province. They think that if enough blood flows in the street, then the milk strike will end."

Without even looking at either Korrie or Zak he continued with his monologue. "They will get people back to work and farmers will again deliver their milk. But these murders will not help them for very long because pure fear will eventually drive many more people into the opposition. Soon there will be thousands of Eppies in the underground because they are finally really terrified of our savage occupiers."

During his short monologue, Steward had been absorbed by his own thoughts and had not noticed his brother's ashen face. It was only when he stopped talking that he noticed the frightened expression on Zak's face. Then, looking from Zak to Korrie, he asked his brother: "What is wrong with you, Zak? You look as if you have just faced a firing squad. What's wrong?"

Korrie, stealing a glance at Zak, said: "He had a long night with his newspaper delivery route."

But Steward, staring steadily at Zak, was not satisfied. "Zak, what has frightened you? You have got to tell me because I am your brother. I will do everything to protect you."

Zak then looked at Korrie and nodded his head. Korrie, in turn, told Steward about Klees, the motorcycles and the shot that had not hit Zak.

Steward was quiet for a long time before he spoke, and when he did, there was a dead tone in his voice. "That Klees has done enough damage to last a lifetime. The shot that you heard, Zak, was the one that killed Albert. There is no limit to the number of innocent people who he has already murdered. We have no choice but to eliminate that Nazi monster before he destroys the lives of even more peace-loving people."

Zak, thinking that his brother might do something rash, took out his note pad and wrote: "We, as an underground cell, have to be unanimous in such a decision. Without unanimity such an action will completely tear us apart."

Steward was not happy with that simple reprimand from his gentle brother. "What do you think, Zak? Are you afraid that I am going out there today and put a bullet in the brains of that monster? I wish things were as simple as that. The other members of our cell will, of course, have to agree with such a plan!"

The other members of the Ter Loo underground cell group, however, staunchly refused to support any kind of execution plans. No one disagreed with Steward when he said: "Klees is our most dangerous enemy in the region, and we all risk our lives every day when we allow him to arrest or murder our people. He is responsible for the death of Pastor Sven and now he has the blood of Albert on his hands. There is no telling what he did when he fought with the German army on the eastern front."

But all through the summer of 1943, Hobbe, Thijs, and Geert firmly refused to even think about killing Klees. Only Joost supported Steward's execution plan.

Hobbe repeatedly swayed the majority in the group with his arguments. "We must not avenge ourselves on people because, as God has said in the Bible, 'Vengeance belongs to me'.

He would then, with great passion, say to his friends: "We as individuals have no authority to take the life of anyone. Only duly appointed government officials can pass a death sentence."

That same summer, thousands of young Dutch men left their homes and, instead of reporting for work in Germany, had help from the WDO when they hid themselves in places like Ter Loo. No one in the Ter Loo cell group even had the time to think of Klees because they were too busy helping find food and shelter for those displaced young men.

That fall, when the refugee flood began to abate, Joost and Steward again raised the Klees question. "I see him everywhere," Steward told his friends. "He is secretly studying the underground movement in all the towns around here. "If we do not eliminate him quickly then we're the ones who will be looking death in the face.

"He's much more dangerous than the Dutch collaborator, Vergonet ever was," he concluded with a tinge of panic in his voice.

It was quiet in the stuffy hiding place after Steward had uttered the name of the man whose pen name had been "Vergonet." Earlier that year, an adjacent underground cell group had executed that mole because his betrayal had caused the death of several of their comrades.

It was Hobbe who, as usual, first found his voice. This time he did not speak with his deep authoritative voice but was, instead, very tenuous: "If we follow Steward's advice, there will be a high cost. The Dutch Nazis will go out and randomly murder three of our countrymen for every comrade of theirs who is killed by us. The Germans are fully behind those retaliatory measures. Are we ready to accept that cost?"

At that time no one was sure that the Germans actively supported reprisal killings (through their covert *Action Silbertanne* program), but members of the underground had their suspicions. They knew that three innocent people were often murdered in cold blood in the days after they had themselves attacked a local Nazi.

Joost finally broke the awkward silence left in Hobbe's wake. "I will accept that cost," he said quietly. "Klees needs to be killed. If that means that I also lose my life, so be it."

Thijs, who was usually quiet in group discussions, stood up and started to talk with a nervous tremor in his voice. "I am in full a-agreement with Joost. I believe that God no longer wants Klees to live on this earth." He stopped for a minute as he tried to get his breath. "But we should not condemn him to death before we do two things. First, first we should pray for his soul. I can't bear the thought of sending him to

Hell without at least praying for his soul. Secondly, we need to get the go-ahead from the *veemgericht* before we carry out the execution plan."

At the end of this meeting, the outcome was again inconclusive. Only Joost and Steward wanted direct action. The rest of the men, as a group, decided that the reason for the proposed death sentence would be written down and submitted to the mysterious underground panel of three judges who would either veto or give a stamp of approval to the proposed execution plan.

Early in December Hobbe read the verdict that had come back from the judges. "Further research is needed before Klees can be sentenced to death.

In the silence that followed that reading, all eyes in the group turned to Steward. They expected to hear protest from him, but he remained as silent as the others. He also was not forthcoming when Hobbe asked: "Who is prepared to carry out the needed research?" No one volunteered to help with that thankless task. The plan to execute Klees was dropped from the group's agenda.

Both Zak and Joost knew that Steward's plan to kill Klees would not be easily derailed. Zak tried to follow the guidance of the group, but was repeatedly rebuffed by the angry and critical tone in his brother's voice. "We can't live in fear," he would rant. "The moment that we allow ourselves to become mice is the same instant when the cat will pounce on us. You may want to hide yourselves in a mouse hole, but I refuse to be terrified by Klees!"

Zak used his journal to process his brother's insults. "Today Steward pulled himself even more tightly into his own cocoon of anger. He called me a frightened mouse and lashed out at Elske for supposedly helping a Dutch traitor. I am not sure what will happen next. He is also becoming less and less careful when he talks to complete strangers."

Steward was angry with Elske because she had helped Andy Uitvlugcht's former girlfriend, Santje Folkema. She was the notorious Nazi collaborator who had come to Ter Loo two years earlier and still lived in the house that had been stolen from Korrie's mother.

Zak, who had been keeping an eye on this local German spy, knew much more of her story than Steward. Santje's son Ernst, whose father was Andy, was born on December 13, 1941. During the first months of 1942, Andy often visited his girlfriend and brought gifts of food and money but, by the end of that year, he stopped coming and no longer supported her in any way. For Santje and her son that neglect was almost fatal because they almost starved to death as they waited for help from the man in their life.

Neighbors looked the other way when they saw the frail young mother and the little boy begging on the street for food. They had no urge to help a Nazi girl who was now going through hard times. Day after day they said the same thing to each other: "Just let her stew in her own ugly juices."

One cold day in January 1944, as she was coming home after making food deliveries to a Jewish family hiding on a farm near Ter Loo, Elske heard the piercing cry of a small child. She usually avoided going along the Boelelaan Street, but on that day, she wanted to get home as quickly as possible, and she knew that going through Korrie's old street was the quickest way through town. As she was passing her friend's parental home, she studiously avoided looking at Santje, who had just stepped out of the house and was holding her hysterically crying son.

Just as she was approaching the house, Ernst stopped crying, and Elske, through the corner her eye, saw that he had also stopped breathing, and his frail body was turning violently red. Elske involuntarily slowed down and, for a second, looked in the direction of Santje and her little boy. It was at that very moment that Ernst's little body, instead of breathing regularly again, exploded into a fit of dry, rasping coughing.

Santje saw that Elske, with a deep expression of pity on her face, was looking in her direction. When she saw Elske's sympathetic face, the frail young woman broke out in hysterical cries as she, holding her son, stepped into the middle of the street. "Madam! Madam! Stop! Take this boy with you. He will die if he stays with me. My boyfriend used to come by with food, coupons, and some money but I haven't seen him all winter. He must have found another milk cow. I do not care what happens to me. It is my boy that I am worried about. I do not want him to die! I am the one that screwed up my life. This poor little guy is just an innocent victim."

Elske, seeing several windows of neighboring homes being carefully opened, answered in a very loud voice: "I can't help you. Please back off!"

Well, Jay, your loving mother could not get the starving and sickly face of little Ernst out of her mind. As she made her way back to the Ruintjes farm, she remembered the many times that she had heard townspeople, when speaking about Santje, using the phrase, "that Nazi girl." Then she thought about her own life. She knew full well that she had been on the path towards becoming a Nazi girl. It had been Beppe's gracious love that had caused her life to change so dramatically.

When she finally came back to the Ruintjes farm, to pick up the boys, the whole Santje story spilled out of her. "We can't allow little Ernst to just die. We must do something to help him and his mom. After all, Santje is no worse than I was on the day that I came to your door. Everyone also saw me as a compromised Nazi girl, during those years."

Beppe looked up from her sewing and nodded her head. "You're right," she said. "That poor girl needs some help. I think there is still some milk as well as some dried beans in the pantry."

That same evening Elske again went to that same Boelelaan home and quietly placed a bottle of milk and a small bag of dried beans on the front steps of the home where Santje lived. She had intended to knock softly on the door and then slip back into the darkness, but Santje had seen the shadow pass the window of her house and, when she heard the faint knock on the door, she instantly opened it. Elske, who was startled by the sudden burst of light, handed Santje the food with the simple statement: "Here is something for you and your boy." After handing over her gifts, she quickly vanished back into the darkness. After that day, Elske regularly left small packages of food, money and coupons on Santje's doorstep.

During all that time, Santje never saw Andy, and never received any news from him. Then, on May 5, 1944, he came to Ter Loo in the middle of the day. He placed his bicycle in the narrow alley adjacent to Santje's home and then took a bag filled with food from the back carrier of his bike and approached the door of his girlfriend's home.

He politely knocked and then, not hearing a response from inside, he tried the door handle to see if he could slip into the house. The door was not locked. He nudged it open and then quickly stepped into the entryway with the groceries. Once inside he asked: "Is anyone home?" After concluding that Santje was not in the house, he went to the kitchen and placed his gift of food on the table, being careful not to harm the fragile contents.

He had just set the food bag down when he heard the click of the front door being opened, and almost at that same instant, he heard the sound of Santje's abrasive voice cutting through the thin walls of the house as she was telling Ernst: "Don't put your fingers in the crack of the door like that if you don't want them to again become as black and blue as the water in the canal over there!"

Then, leaving Ernst in the living room, Santje strode into the kitchen. Her eyes were first drawn to the big bag of food on the table and then to Andy who started to walk towards her with an oversized smile and outstretched arms as he said: "That's all for you, honey."

Santje instinctively backed away from him and started screaming: "Get away from me! Get out of this house now and take that bloody bag of junk with you!"

She grabbed the handles of the food bag and whisked it to the front door and then tossed the bag and all its contents through the door and onto the Boelelaan street.

In an instant the bag burst open, and all the food exploded onto the cobblestones. The small round Gouda cheese, which had been strategically placed on the top of the bag, acted like a malevolent Johnny cake as it rolled down the street. The packages of coffee, sugar and brown beans burst open and spilled their precious contents into the many deep crevices in the street. The glass milk jar, with its life-giving fluid, smashed into thousands of shards that glittered in the bright afternoon sun. The milk, sugar, coffee, and mud first jelled in the small puddles and then quickly vanished into the cracks between the cobblestones. A kilo package of fresh ground beef sat, as a dead lump, in the middle of the chaotic mixture of food, paper, glass and splattered milk.

Santje then picked up little Ernst and darted out of the house as quickly as she could.

Andy raced after her and, after catching her by the arm, ruthlessly pulled her back into the house. She tried, but failed to wrench herself free from his iron grip. He also threatened her in a low voice. "It's okay, bitch. I wanted to come as a nice guy, but now I'll have to use force to convince you to be a little more open about town secrets you are keeping from me. If you don't tell us all the stuff you know, then tonight it will not end well with you."

Several neighbors who had witnessed the drama that had played itself out on the street in front of their homes, overheard Andy's dark threats. Within a short time, word had spread to many homes in Ter Loo that something ominous would soon happen in their little town, but no one knew exactly what to expect. Would Andy come back with a cohort of paramilitary Nazis and place the town in lock down before making house-to-house searches? Would the Germans come and make arrests? Would they randomly kill people? Would Santje succumb to the threats of her former boyfriend and divulge the town secrets that she had come to know?

In almost every home the fear produced by Andy's threat was linked to a distinctly different nightmare. Some families were afraid that a father, the sole bread winner, would be arrested and sent to work in Germany. In another home there was the fear that the two work dodgers would be discovered, and the whole family deported. And then there were the seven families, so well-known to Elske and Korrie, where Jewish children were living as siblings along with the other kids.

In that climate of fear and uncertainty the underground agents living in Sebeek were asked by their comrades from Ter Loo to carefully monitor Andy's movements, once he got back to their town. What would Andy, along with the other members of the Sebeek-based Dutch paramilitary police, try to do? Would they help carry out the threats Andy had made to Santje? Would they get the Sebeek commander's permission to take German soldiers with them in order to search every home in Ter Loo? Would they, instead of acting now, bide their time and strike later?

Those were the questions that troubled Steward as he waited for a phone call from a friend in Sebeek who also knew about Andy's threats. He instantly picked up the receiver when the phone rang at approximately seven that evening. The voice on the other end of the line said: "Two additional empty milk cans are being loaded on the wagon now. Use them to send your extra cream tomorrow."

The message was clear to Steward because he knew that the term "milk cans" referred to two paramilitary police, who, as the message stated, were already on their way to Ter Loo.

Steward first told Beppe and Zak that he was going out to visit some of their neighbors and tell them about the disturbing information he had just received. Zak also brought the same message to the seven people on his contact list.

Later that evening, when he came back to the farm, Zak discovered that Steward had given his message to the seven people on his contact list, but had then also left the farm without telling anyone where he was going. Later that same evening Zak also discovered that Steward had taken the family revolver with him when he left.

Zak was duly alarmed by the thought of what his rash brother might be planning to do. Did he think that he could single-handedly defend the whole town of Ter Loo against Andy and his cohorts? Was he arming himself so that he could kill someone? Had he also drawn his friend Joost into his plans?

With that last question in mind, Zak went to Joost's well-hidden little dwelling and knocked on the door. After Joost led him in, he saw Steward sitting in the corner of the room. That's when he knew that his worst fears might indeed become a reality. Steward and Joost were planning to go on the attack. But what was he to do? He knew that he would be unable to change his brother's mind if an action plan had already been agreed on.

Zak decided that all that he could do was to stay in the background and quietly see what Steward and Joost were planning to do. That was why he followed the plotters as they made their way to a small bridge approximately three kilometers east of Ter Loo. He lost sight of them when they hid themselves under the north side of the bridge. Zak then hid himself behind an adjacent tree. From that vantage point he could observe the bridge under which Steward and Joost were hiding.

Later, as the sun was beginning to set, Zak tensed up when he heard the familiar sound of motorcycles in the distance. The original plan of Joost and Steward had been very simple. They would first check to see if Klees was among the men approaching them. That murderer was easily identifiable because, unlike almost all other motorcyclists of the region, he never wore a helmet. Secondly, if there were only two motorcycles coming towards them, Steward would shoot and kill Klees and Joost would, at that same moment, shoot to injure the second motorcyclist. They had also decided that if there were more than two people approaching them, or if there was any other kind of uncertainty then they would immediately abandon their attack plan.

Their hastily developed plan was already in trouble because they had not wanted to have Zak in the area. It went totally off script, however, the instant the bullets began to fly. As the roaring motorcycles came down the narrow road, both Joost and Steward peeked out from under the bridge and clearly saw the faces of Andy and Klees. Joost steadied his aim by holding his pistol against the railing of the bridge before firing off two shots at the fast-approaching Andy. The first bullet hit Andy's shoulder, and because the second one shattered the young man's wrist, his motorcycle spun out of control. It flipped over and trapped the driver as it slid down the road for almost 50 feet. It came to rest on the edge of the canal that ran along the north side of the road.

Klees, with the instinct of a soldier, reacted instantly to the sound of Joost's gun; he ducked down and swerved back and forth as he raced over the bridge. Because of that quick reaction, none of the three bullets from Steward's pistol touched him.

It was all over. Klees soon shrunk into a speck on the horizon and was not seen again that evening. He took another road back to Sebeek. Andy, in the meantime, was trapped under his bike and was powerless as blood, hot oil and flammable gasoline began to seep into his clothing.

At first Steward and Joost only stared at each other in silence. Steward was the first to find his voice. "We have to make sure he's dead before we get out of here." He again raised his gun and aimed it in the direction of the injured Andy.

Joost stopped him. "Wait a minute, Steward," he said. "Don't shoot. That's Zak over there by that tree and he's waving his hands wildly in the air! What does he want?"

He leaped from his hiding place and ran towards Zak who, in the meantime, was using his hands to signal the words: "Don't shoot him."

Zak and Joost then went to Andy who, because he was still in shock, said nothing. He was also suffering from the intense pain caused by a broken leg and by the hot oil that was seeping through his clothing and burning his skin. He was still only partially conscious when, an hour later, the three of them had extracted him from his motorcycle. It was well past midnight when they were finally able to bring the seriously wounded man to a bed in the Ruintjes farmhouse.

They woke everyone up when they arrived. Korrie came out of her hiding place and put an improvised splint on the broken leg. She also bandaged the bullet injuries and found some salve and put it on the worst scrapes. Zak, after waiting around for a long time, finally went back to his small home. As he lay in bed, he could not sleep because he was terrified by what he felt was about to happen.

Joost, after going home for an hour, also came back to the Ruintjes farm and was let into Zak and Korrie's hiding place. In the darkness he first unburdened himself to Zak and, later, also to Korrie. "There is no way that Klees will take the attack on his life lying down. He will be back here within 24 hours and start hunting each one of us down. We have no options. By early tomorrow morning we will have to either be ready to fight or we'll have to get far away from here."

Tom, the downed pilot, had been sleeping in a corner cot, but Joost's loud voice woke him up. When he heard that Andy was in the farmhouse, Tom got up and left the hiding place. Korrie and Zak assumed that he was going to the outhouse, but that was not his destination. He went to the back door of the farmhouse and made his way to the one room where a small candle was still burning.

Andy, all bandaged up, had been placed in the bed in Steward's old room. The door of the room was open, and Tom saw that Beppe, who was staying with the patient, was fast asleep in her chair. The flickering light of the candle also reached the face of the fitfully sleeping Andy.

Tom slipped into the room, raised his gun and shot a bullet through Andy's temple.

The explosive sound of that gunshot rang through the farmhouse. Beppe woke up with a start and instinctively held up her hand to stop a bullet from hitting her. Then, seeing Tom in the room, she asked him: "What happened? I dreamt that someone was shooting at us."

When she looked more closely at Tom, she saw the gun in his hand. "What are you doing with that gun?" she asked. As she was struggling to get out of her chair, her eyes walked over to the prostrate Andy and she saw the dark blood spurting from his forehead and oozing into the bandages that covered his scraped cheeks.

There was a hushed and anxious tone to her voice as she looked at the young pilot. "What have you done, Tom? We cannot just kill our fellow citizens in cold blood! If we do that there is nothing that will separate us from those evil Nazis."

Tom nodded his head politely but did not apologize. "I have sworn to my superior, the King of England, that I will always seek to obey him. Killing this enemy of England is only an act of obedience. If he escapes from this farm, then I will be killed. If he is dead then I won't be betrayed and, hopefully, one day, will again be able to serve my king."

"This will not end well" Beppe muttered half to herself, and with those words, she pulled up the sheet on Andy's bed and covered the face of the dead man.

Tom then slipped back to the hiding place and told Zak, Korrie, and Joost about the execution. Joost, in turn, went to Steward's home and woke up the whole family with his booming voice. "Wake up," he said. "We're going to have to prepare for trouble."

Within an hour everyone was up and walking around in a daze. How could they prepare for an inevitable German raid? What should they do with Andy's body?

As the hours passed, everyone worked desperately to prepare for a possible German raid. They took Andy's body out of the house and placed it in a shallow grave that had been quickly dug on the far end of an apple grove south of the farm. They hastily covered the disturbed ground with dead branches and leaves as well as some old dried and rotten apples.

All potentially incriminating papers in the house were burned and plans were made to retreat into Zak's hiding place if a raid were about to happen.

Zak, as the farm guard, stationed himself in a carefully hidden blind that was located adjacent to the road leading to Sebeek. He kept his finger on the button that would ring a small alarm bell in Beppe's kitchen.

Steward, in a frenzy of activity and panic, barked out random orders and suggestions to anyone within reach. By the end of that morning, he had already gone to each of his friends and told them about the events of the previous evening. "You guys," he told Hobbe, Thijs and Geert, "should no longer stay in this area because it is becoming too dangerous. I am afraid that this death and the disappearance of the body will bring the Germans to each of our homes. Find a temporary hiding place and then do not come back to your home, but then also find somewhere where you can hide permanently. Klees will track us down if we stay here."

All the friends agreed to go to their temporary safety address during the following evening, but on the way out of town, they made the fateful decision to stop by the Ruintjes farm one more time to discuss how they would stay in touch with each other in the future.

Chapter Twenty-Two

The Ruintjes Disaster

KLEES, DURING THE DAY after he and Andy had been ambushed, was restlessly busy in Sebeek.

Not wanting to risk being attacked a second time, he planned his next moves carefully. First, he went to the commander and asked for permission to go back to Ter Loo, this time with ten members of the Dutch paramilitary police force. He was also determined to retaliate for the attack of the previous day.

It did not take long before he, along with ten armed countrymen, set off down the road that took them from Sebeek to Ter Loo.

Everyone in the group stopped their motorcycles when they arrived at the bridge where Klees and Andy had been ambushed the previous evening. They carefully inspected the skid marks on the road and then looked around the whole area where the attack had taken place. Klees took out his binoculars and scrutinized each one of the farms that he could see from the vantage point of the bridge; he started with the adjacent ones and then moved to the ones further in the distance.

The Ruintjes farm was barely visible to him, but as he studied it closely, he let out an exclamation. "Damn it, you guys, there's someone walking down the road close to that farm in the distance. If I am not mistaken, that's the Ruintjes farm. First, we'll stop that person and then we're going to go to that farm and turn over every stick and stone to see what we can find."

Soon after setting off, they approached the spot where Klees had spotted the lone pedestrian who, in the meantime, had hidden himself in the tall grasses. Klees stopped in the middle of the road and shouted: "Whoever you are, I order you to immediately show yourself if you do not want one of our bullets in your body."

It took only a minute for a head to furtively peer from around the bush and Klees let out a loud barking laugh. "Oh. Hello, Piet. I would not have used such strong language to get you to come out of hiding if I had known it was you who was walking down the road. What's going on? I thought you were working in Germany. Are you in the business of killing the friends of Germany now?"

"I don't know what you're talking about, Klees. I just came back from Germany; I was wounded when an allied bomb destroyed the factory where I was working. I was given a month's leave because of my injuries. I came to Sebeek last night and am almost home now." As he was talking, Piet started to reach into his pocket to retrieve the train ticket which would provide proof that he had indeed come to Sebeek the previous evening.

Before the hand could reach the pocket, two of the thugs grabbed Piet and slapped handcuffs on him. Still studying Piet's face, Klees said: "Sorry, old pal. We have to be careful with everyone these days. Don't take it personally. Come and sit behind me on my motorcycle. That way you don't have to walk the rest of the way home."

When Piet hesitated, the same man who had handcuffed him, forcibly placed him behind Klees. A few minutes later, this small invading force stopped close to the driveway leading to the Ruintjes property.

Klees then ordered most of his men to encircle the farm and be prepared for any type of hostile action. Then he and one soldier, with Piet in front of them, approached the front door of the farmhouse.

There was a deadly silence as the two soldiers and their hostage made their way up the driveway. Zak had already seen the invading army coming, and, from his roadside hiding-place, had warned his mother to be prepared for trouble. There was no one else in the house because Steward, his friends and Korrie had all hidden themselves in the secret family hiding place.

When Beppe heard the loud knocking on her door, she waited a minute before opening it. She tried to remain calm as she said: "Hello, Klees. I'm all alone. What can I do to help you?"

Klees, in full attack mode, had no time for civility. He ordered his soldiers to tie Beppe and Piet to a tree. Then he then ordered five of his men to help him search the house.

While Klees and his helpers were ransacking the house, the other men searched every square inch of the farm property and soon spotted blood on the grass near the house.

An intense search of the whole property was renewed, and they soon found Andy's body in the shallow grave near the back of the property. The body was exhumed and placed near the tree to which Beppe and Piet were tied.

When confronted with the body, Beppe said nothing other than: "Someone must have placed him there to implicate us in a crime. We are a clean-living family and none of us have ever committed any crimes. God is my judge."

Klees tortured her for a long time and ended by whipping her face with his belt and screaming at her with profanities and accusations. "I don't need any god to know who the criminals are here. It's as clear as that ugly nose on your face. You and your family killed my partner, and you will pay for it."

Finally, turning to his men, Klees said: "Burn this property down and don't allow anything to remain standing when the fire has burned itself out."

Twenty minutes later the whole property was engulfed in flames. Klees and his men were standing around watching the spectacle when Klees fell to the ground. A bullet had shattered his shoulder. Klees and his men placed themselves in a defensive position as they, in vain, looked for the attacker; the fire's cracking had muffled the sound of the gunfire.

Obbe, Klees' lieutenant, took out his binoculars and surveyed the canals, road, and fields that surrounded the burning Ruintjes property. As he was looking in the direction of Ter Loo, he saw a small army of approximately 100 people coming towards the burning farm. He looked at Klees and said: "What shall we do? We're under attack by over one hundred people. Should we stay here and defend ourselves or should we retreat?"

Klees, despite the agonizing pain ripping through his body, was still able to give orders. "It's time to go back to Sebeek, men. We have almost done the work that we set out to do. Collapse the buildings by throwing some hand grenades into them, because once they have been turned into a pile of rubble, the fire will more effectively turn everything into ashes.

Do not kill our hostages. Leave them tied to the trees so they can tell the townspeople not to try messing with us."

After tossing four hand grenades into the burning property, Klees and his men, not wanting to face the wrath of all the people of Ter Loo, made their way back to Sebeek as quickly as possible.

For the first two minutes after the Nazis had left, there was only the sound of burning and falling debris. Then, in the smoky darkness of the fire, the shadow of someone could be seen swiftly moving through the bulrushes adjacent to the road. It was Zak. He had seen everything that had happened on the grounds of his beloved family property. He was also the man who had wounded Klees with a shot from his ancient hunting rifle.

Arriving at the farm driveway, he took out his pocketknife and swiftly cut the ropes that bound Piet and Beppe to the old linden tree that stood close to the road. The three of them then quickly jumped into the adjacent canal to escape the hailstorm of embers that were setting their clothing and everything else on fire.

While catching their breath for a few seconds in that canal Piet, Beppe, and Zak got the first glimpse of the tragedy that was unfolding in front of their eyes. One of the grenades that had been lobbed at the Ruintjes' home had been thrown too hard and too high and missed hitting the building that it had been aimed at. Instead, when it finally landed and exploded on the east side of the burning fire, it had plowed into the farm manure pile. The resulting explosion not only sent thousands of pellet sized chunks of cow dung flying upwards, but it also shattered the roof of the hiding place where the others were taking shelter.

For the first few seconds, Zak and Beppe were frozen with terror. They knew exactly who had gone into the farm hiding place during the minutes before Klees and his gang had arrived at their farm. Now that safe place had become a smoldering death trap because of one exploding hand grenade.

In his diary Zak was never able to write about what happened next, but I was able to reconstruct most of the details from fragmentary records found in the Ter Loo library.

While Piet, Beppe, and Zak were in the process of climbing out of the canal, they saw a dark shadow racing towards them; it was coming from the spot where the hiding place had been. The person coming towards them, they soon realized, was a soot-covered Elske who had only minor injuries as she screamed at them: "Come and help me! Several people in there are trapped but still alive."

Soon the first wave of people from Ter Loo, who had seen the fire from the village, began to arrive with their pails and pitch forks. They first brought the fires closest to the hiding place under control and then started to do the grim work of bringing out the injured and dead.

They first brought you, Jay, out of the wrecked hideout. You suffered from smoke inhalation but, for the rest, had not been injured by the explosion.

Steward was the second person who was brought out. His leg had been shattered by a falling beam and his hearing was permanently injured by the exploding grenade, but other than that, he did not have any lifelong physical injuries. Emotionally, however, he suffered for the rest of his life from having escaped a death trap that killed the others. He had been on the ground near the bookcase and Joost was standing up near him when the explosion happened. The next thing he saw was Joost on the ground beside him with blood streaming from his head. He tried to get up but couldn't because of a searing pain that shot through his whole body. Before slipping into unconsciousness, he was able to peer through the smoke and debris and see that there were other bodies lying motionless on the ground.

Five of the people brought away from the smoldering wreckage on that sad day in 1944—Thijs, Geert, Hobbe, Korrie, and Tom—had all been very close to the spot where the grenade landed, and had been instantly killed by the explosion.

Sypke, the young son of Piet and Elske, had not been killed instantly by the bomb. Korrie had been holding his hand when the explosion occurred. During the rescue operation Piet had burned his feet badly when he pulled his bleeding son out of the wreckage. He didn't even feel the pain as he carried his fatally injured son away from the burning skeleton of the Ruintjes property and gently placed him on the ground and on top of his own jacket. During the next hour, he and Elske were powerless as their little boy's whole body was in agony; his compromised lungs desperately tried to bring oxygen to millions of swiftly dying cells. After an hour, that seemed to have a million minutes, life finally ebbed out of Sypke's young body.

Chapter Twenty-Three

Quiet Tears amid a Spiral of Silence
(after 1945)

IN THE LAST PART of this letter, Jay, I want to take you from the Ruintjes fire that killed your birth mother, to the 1957 confrontation between our fathers which, as we saw earlier, permanently changed the trajectory of both of our lives.

During the last two years of the war, from May 1943 until the liberation of Friesland in April 1945, things were very quiet on the land that belonged to the Ruintjes family. Many locals had come to the funeral services that had been arranged for the victims of the deadly attack, but after the short graveside ceremony, almost everyone quietly went back to their homes and, for the duration of the war, never openly spoke about the fire, scarred bodies and the marauding Nazi vandals who had been responsible for the deadly Ruintjes inferno.

In the privacy of their homes, locals did talk about that disaster because they were convinced that someone from their own town had helped the murderers; Who, they wanted to know, had betrayed Steward and his friends to Klees and his Nazi gang?

Many locals were convinced that Santje Folkema, Andy's former girlfriend, was the culprit. As a German stoolpigeon she had, people felt, betrayed the secrets of their town to the Germans for the duration of the war and that was why she was undoubtedly the guilty one. They were sure that, after her fight with Andy, she had probably contacted him and told him about the hiding place at the Ruijntjes farm. They were convinced that someone who was a traitor one time, would always be a turncoat.

Other people in town were equally sure that Piet was the culprit. Hadn't he arrived at the Ruintjes farm at the same time when Klees and his attackers had shown up? Hadn't he given his heart and soul to the Germans by voluntarily working for them for almost the entire war? Hadn't Elske, his wife, been a little too friendly to Santje Folkema who, as everyone knew, was a German traitor? Hadn't Riemke Popma, who had been with Klees on the day the attack happened, specifically stated that Piet had told them about the hiding place? Wasn't that also Steward's view of the attack? Hadn't several people heard him blame Piet for the catastrophe?

When the Canadian army finally reached Ter Loo, in the middle of April 1945, the time of German rule had come to an end and the Dutch national flag could again be freely flown. Now was also the time when one could again talk openly about the dark years of German oppression.

After the defeat of Germany, the process of bringing the Dutch collaborators to justice was set in motion. Within months after the war's end, a total of 200,000 Dutch citizens were, by hastily established tribunals, accused of aiding and abetting the enemy. In a very short time, they were imprisoned in overcrowded and filthy camps.

That vast army of captives included thousands of people who had never actively betrayed their country. Within six months after the end of the war, many of those wrongly accused prisoners could go home, without having received a sentence of any kind. In the end, approximately 70,000 of the original captives were successfully prosecuted and received some kind of sentence for their war crimes.

Klees belonged to the group of war prisoners who had to face the special tribunal for war crimes. A citizens' committee from Ter Loo was able to reconstruct a detailed record of all the crimes that he had committed before and during the war. In the end Klees received a fifteen-year prison sentence. It was only the testimony of his father that ultimately saved him from a death sentence.

That same Ter Loo committee was also behind the arrest of Piet. He was accused of helping Klees and his comrades when they destroyed the Ruintjes property and killed five innocent Dutch citizens. It took six months before the case against Piet came before the tribunal. He was found not guilty when the evidence against him was definitively refuted. That outcome was a bittersweet victory for Piet. He was glad to be a free man again, but by the time of his November 1945 release, he had already spent six months in the crowded, lice infested prison known as Kamp Sondel.

The pain of those months in prison was especially agonizing during the three months when he received no visits from either his wife Elske or from you, Jay. During those months the two of you couldn't come since you were locked away in the internment camp known as De Beetse. The Ter Loo committee had imprisoned your mom because they accepted the local rumor that she was guilty of treason for the simple reason that she was Piet's wife. What's more, they distrusted her because Bert Scheepema, her father, was also a notorious Dutch Nazi. She was also viewed with suspicion because she had both helped and befriended Andy's girlfriend, Santje Folkema.

Zak had been restlessly busy all that summer and fall of 1945. He worked long hours as he helped make the Ruintjes farm operational again. When not working, he went to see you, his stepson, when you were in prison with your mom, Elske. He contacted dozens of regional officials and asked them to help him get the two of you, along with your dad, released from prison. In the end his passionate and persistent actions resulted in the early release of your whole family.

Steward had not helped Zak in his effort to free your family. During the first two years after the Ruintjes disaster he had gone through a deep tunnel of depression. He had lost his best friends and never completely recovered from the injuries that he had received on that terrifying day. He and his small family spent the last months of the war living with an uncle in Suawoude, Friesland. When the war was over, he came back to Ter Loo and threw himself into the work that needed to be done to rebuild the Ruintjes farm.

He began to emerge from that dark tunnel in 1947 when he started thinking of leaving the Netherlands and emigrating to Canada. Two years later, after some very important decisions had been made, that dream finally became a reality.

Beppe was never against Steward taking his family to Canada, but worried that things would not go well with him in that far away country. Wasn't he too temperamental for such a big move? How would he, with his quixotic nature, ever learn to adjust to a new world? Because of those concerns, she strongly urged Zak to go along with his younger brother and, as always in the past, act as a moderating force in the life of her tempestuous younger son.

From the very beginning, Steward liked that idea, but Zak objected. He did not want to go far away and never again be able to see you, his stepson. It was Elske who eventually came up with an idea that seemed to be an ideal solution. She and Piet would also move to Canada and purchase a farm adjacent to the property that Steward and his wife were planning to buy.

That was the plan that guided the immigration of both of our families. For almost a decade the Runters and the Knuffels families were the owners of farms that were adjacent to each other on the same dusty road near the town of Taqua, Ontario. Those were, for the most part, happy years.

The peace of those years was possible because both of our parents made a conscious decision to never discuss the war years. Even in the privacy of our home, all war talk was off limits. As your mother told you, shortly before she passed away, she had repeatedly tried to tell you about your birth mother, Korrie, but Piet always put her off: "He's still too young to understand why we adopted him. We can, when he is older, tell him about the way that he came to us when he was a war baby. I also need some more time before I can even allow my mind to go back to those war years. I will, for example, never understand why we lost our son."

Zak, the perennial peace maker, certainly helped make those good years possible. He loved you as his son but quietly and gracefully allowed Elske and Piet to be your parents. In Elske's love he saw the love that Korrie would have given to you, and for him, that was deeply satisfying. As the years passed, he not only saw you grow up but was also a kind of godfather who quietly enveloped you with his love and loyalty.

Zak, through his letter writing, showed unfailing loyalty to all those who had entered his life. After coming to Canada, he would send a weekly letter to his mother in the Netherlands and tell her about life in the new country.

Each month, in that same methodical way, he would write a letter to Dr. Luimskuyl who had, for years, helped him overcome the complications resulting from the debilitating seizures that had injured him so much as a young boy.

The doctor always replied to Zak's letters because he not only derived a deep pleasure from hearing from the first patient that he had had as a young doctor, but he also enjoyed helping Zak deal with ongoing or new health challenges. For years the letters between the patient and the doctor went as quietly and steadily back and forth across the Atlantic Ocean as the pendulum of a grand old clock.

Then, in an early 1957, Dr. Luimskuyl wrote Zak about how he was preparing to make a trip to Canada to visit an ailing sister who lived in Toronto. In passing he also wrote: "Is it okay if I drop by and pay you and your family a visit?"

There was also a small postscript added to the letter: "Please let Piet and Elske know that I am coming because, if possible, I would also like to meet them as well as Korrie's boy."

Zak wrote back immediately and welcomed the doctor to Canada; he told him that he would love to visit with him. He also told Piet and Elske, as well as my mom and dad, about Dr. Luimskuyl's planned visit. For several months, however, it seemed as if the planned trip had been called off because Zak heard nothing back from the neurologist.

During that time, your parents, Jay, disagreed about how to intro-duce you to your distant uncle. Your mom wanted to finally tell you the whole story of your birth mother, Korrie and her family connection to the Jewish doctor. Your father must have slipped into a frozen silence because he refused to openly talk about your birth origin. At the same time, however, he certainly did not want to be inhospitable.

Early in May 1957, Zak received a telegram from the doctor stating that he was in Toronto and asking when he could come over for a visit. Zak telegraphed him back immediately and stated that any day would work for him and that he would be glad to drive to Toronto to pick him up.

On the drive from Toronto to Taqua, Dr. Luimskuyl was very talk-ative as he spoke about how he had survived the war years. "I had a pa-tient who owned a small farm on a dead end-road that was near the town of Suawoude. During the first year of the war, he helped me build a small shack in a secluded area of his property; it was far away from any roads. That's where I stayed for the duration of the war; I used a small stove to prepare meals that only consisted of brown beans. The farmer, Mr. Snoek, was my lifeline to the world."

After the short visit to Taqua, the doctor was very silent as Zak again drove him back to Toronto. They had just passed Hamilton when Zak, out of the corner of his eyes, noticed that the doctor was leaning forward in the seat of the car and had covered his face with his hands. Zak found an exit near Burlington, pulled off the highway and stopped the car in the parking lot of a small park. Only then was he able look more closely at the doctor and see that the ever-stately Dr. Luimskuyl was crying quietly and uncontrollably.

After Zak turned off the engine, the doctor wiped his tears away and sat still in the car for a long time before saying anything. Then, for two hours, he talked about some of his darkest war memories—including the brutal murder of his whole family by the Nazis. While talking, the doctor often had to cut himself off in the middle of what he was saying because he had to again wipe away new tears.

After listening to the doctor, Zak reached over and gave him a long, hard hug. He then restarted the car and took him the rest of the way to the Airport in Toronto.

Later that day, in the quiet of his home, Zak placed a long entry in his journal where he recorded some of the things that the doctor had told him on the way to the airport:

> You probably think that I am crying because I only saw Korrie's boy for a scant thirty minutes during breakfast this morning. It was indeed a very brief visit, and I knew that Piet wanted it that way. At first he had not wanted his family to visit with me at all. Eventually he did change his mind and said that he, Elske and Jay would have breakfast with me at a fast-food restaurant today. We went there before you picked me up to take me to the airport."
>
> While Jay sat across from me at the table this morning, it struck me immediately that he really looks so much like his mother, Korrie. He also looks exactly like my oldest son, Brams when he was that age. While sitting there, it seemed as if my mind was slowly being vacuumed into a black tunnel; I was unable to shake the dark memory of the way that my lovely cousin and my son died during the war. In that darkness, all that I wanted to do was to cry out as loudly as possible and allow my screams to both express my grief and to appeal for help in dealing with my broken heart.
>
> But, looking at Piet's face, I knew that he did not want to see my grief. He wanted me to have a short visit with Jay and then, after breakfast, leave the restaurant and silently take my tears back to the old country.
>
> As you know, that's exactly what I did. We were in and out of that restaurant within twenty minutes and, as I left, I didn't even have a chance to give Jay a hug. That's why, to him, I will never be anything more than a momentary shadow that has only once flitted past his line of vision.

As you must know, Zak, secretiveness is what is making me cry out with such anguish now. I can't stand being a shadow that people do not really see. Throughout the war I was forced to become a ghost that had to hide in the murky darkness to remain safe. I have repeatedly tried to step out of that cocoon of darkness during the postwar years, but it never happens; people want nothing to do with the memories etched on my face. The tone in Piet's voice this morning was simply a repetition of the same old song. How will the average Dutch person ever be able to see me as a Jewish human being? Will I always continue to be a shadow in the phantom army that was taken, in fully loaded trains, to the death camps?

I see you nodding your head because, of course, as a handicapped person, you are very familiar with the reality that people see you and see through you at the same time.

Now it feels good to be able to cry openly. During the past twenty years I almost never stopped secretly crying in my heart for my family, the Jewish people, and for our poor misguided nation. But I could never wail openly because I was repeatedly told we must do everything in a good and proper way. The expression of emotions is not an option.

Did you see that movie about the Amsterdam strike in which three members of the German Gestapo, along with their dogs, chased down that little girl in a red dress? Do you remember how she screamed with the full power of her lungs as the dogs were closing in on her? Can't you still hear her voice as it echoed along the streets of the Dapperbuurt area of Amsterdam? That's how every Jew, with the support of every living follower of Christ, should have screamed every time that Germans, with the help of Dutch policemen and government officials, took steps to arrest us and send us off to be murdered.

Oh Zak, how I now wish that I had screamed and cried openly when I saw the pain-filled faces of those Jewish families from Germany that came to the Netherlands in the 1930's.

I felt their anguish, but did not feel free to cry because I had been so well trained to be quiet and only act calmly. Without any fanfare I found homes and income sources for three Jewish families who came to Leeuwarden in 1937. Had I really allowed my tears to flow, at that time, I would have urged them to also flee to faraway places such as England or the Americas. But, because of my dry-eyed help, they stayed in Friesland and were all murdered during the war years.

I didn't scream and cry in disbelief when Colijn slammed the Dutch borders shut in 1938 and placed the helpless German

Jewish refugees in those specially erected concentration camps. That happened even before Hitler's armies had invaded our land. I also didn't raise my voice when representatives of Colijn's conservative Christian coalition party came to my door and asked me for money to help fund the cost of the Westenbork concentration camp which they built for Jewish refugees. What's even worse, Zak, is that I actually paid out a total of 2,000 guilders for the building of that hellish Jewish prison; that same camp later became a temporary stopping point for my family and tens of thousands of other Jews who were on their way to Hitler's death camps

Instead of using my money to help build prison walls, I should have used it to help refugees and, later, construct hundreds of wailing walls which we should have built throughout the Netherlands. There, I, along with Jews and Christians alike, could have come and cried for the harassed refugees who had come to our country because Hitler had taken all their freedoms away from them in Germany.

If we had, during that first occupation year, erected such wailing walls then, while the Germans played their good cop/bad cop games, we would have had places to go to where we could have poured out our tears. Had we done that early on, we might have shaken the average Dutch citizen out of his deeply lethargic belief that, with Hitler at the helm, things would turn out just fine.

But let's face the facts. Did anyone scream bloody murder when the Germans, already in the summer of 1940, told all Dutch citizens to not allow Jews into the public air raid shelters? Even as bombs were landing on my family in Leeuwarden, all that we could do was hide under a table. I, unfortunately, was also as silent as a grave. Hitler's terror was like dry rot that destroyed all our voice boxes. I was also as mute as a mushroom when my grandkids were yanked out of their so-called Aryan school.

My silence was, as I can now clearly see, a fatal disease that was poisoning my life. Without even a whisper of protest, I saw my fellow doctors sign that demonic Aryan declaration. Later, when my hospital fired me and the other Jewish doctors, I simply accepted my fate and quietly slipped into the shadows. I did not bellow like a bloodied bull that was being butchered. If I had opened my mouth during that last work day, the other doctors, with whom I had worked for years, would not have been able to so easily look the other way when they saw me, in my scrubs, leaving the hospital for the last time.

Why, I ask you Zak, didn't I cry and scream at the top of my voice when I had to put on that token of Jewish leprosy—that fateful "J"—whenever I went outside on the streets of Leeuwarden? If I had I clearly raised my voice, would my fellow Dutch citizens, who passed me on the sidewalk, have been able to look past or through me? Why was I not able to show them the flood of tears that was hiding behind my eyes every day during and after the war years?

Zak noted in his diary that as he listened to the doctor, he first only cried inwardly, but soon the tears were openly running down his own face. Dr. Luimskuyl took out his handkerchief and first dried his own tears and then passed it on to Zak.

He then pulled himself up straight in the car seat. "That felt good," he said. "I should do more of that. Perhaps I should even go to all the terrible places where, during the war, I should have been crying aloud. It's not too late to still mourn for the people that we lost during those years."

The idea that they should more often use their tears to wash away dark war memories eventually became, after that eventful trip to the airport, a kind of fixed idea in the minds of both Zak and the doctor. First it was just an abstract concept they discussed in their letters to each other, but before the end of 1957, Zak left Canada and went back to the old country.

Once back in the Netherlands, the idea was converted into an active plan. Zak and the neurologist would go each month to one or another dreadful war site and leave behind some tears of remembrance as they thought about the people, the hopes and the dreams that had been shattered on that spot.

Where they all went, Jay, I really do not know, except for the fact that they often climbed to the tops of shattered fragments of the fortresses along the Atlantic coast of the Netherlands. Hitler's Atlantic Wall not only caused so much Allied blood to flow but it also shielded the dictator's henchmen as they carried out their master's most ghoulish command: "Murder all the Jews of Europe!"

In my mind I have a picture of two old men, on the top of a dismal fortress, shedding their gentle tears and, in that way, attempting to turn an angry pile of rocks into a silent weeping wall.

Sources Used for the Historical Novel *Forgetfulness*

HOW THE FOLLOWING BOOKS, JOURNALS AND DATABASES HELPED SHAPE THE NOVEL

THE HISTORICAL NOVEL *FORGETFULNESS* is primarily based on my, Richard Reitsma's, personal memories which were shaped by Friesland, the Dutch province in which I was born, as well as by my years (and education) in Canada and the USA. From 1971 to 1982 I lived in Amsterdam and completed a PhD in history during a time when the younger generation in the Netherlands attempted to come to terms with the horrors associated with the Dutch chapter of the Jewish Holocaust. The murder of over 102,000 Dutch-Jewish men women and children had left deep scars in post WWII Dutch society. The wounds causing those scars had come, in part, from the personal, familial, religious, and societal fissures that had cut through Dutch communities during the war years. I witnessed how the Dutch youth, during the 1970's, tried to cope with the war pains of their parent's generation but, as a post WWII immigrant kid, I did not really understand what had happened in my birth country during the war years.

In the historic novel *Forgetfulness*, I express my feelings of loss and recovery through the words of the fictional (Dutch Canadian) Harold who mirrors some of the emotions felt by the Dutch generation born shortly after WWII.

Those feelings must, of course, be supported by understanding, and that is where historical resources come into play. The writings of Lipstadt, Wiesel, and Hamerow have shaped my understanding of the Jewish

Holocaust. The historian Happe, in granular detail, explained how the Holocaust in the Netherlands evolved. Gosler was, in many ways, one of the victims of the Holocaust. Wiebenga, Ypma, and many links in the Fries Verzetmuseum made it possible for me weave the story *Forgetfulness* into the actual history of Friesland during WWII. The content of the illegal newspapers *Vrij Nederland* and *Trouw,* along with the writings of Randwijk, gave me many points of reference so that I could experience the mood that existed among some people within the Dutch-Calvinist subculture during the war years. A careful reading of many 1930's articles in the monthly *Nederlandsche Bond* church youth journal, gave me a feeling for the religious and cultural thinking that helped shape the minds of Dutch Calvinists that were part of my parents' generation.

A major theme within the novel *Forgetfulness* is the religious, political, and societal split that bedeviled the Calvinist sector of Dutch society during the 1930's and 1940's. Bouman and Zuidema, with fierce language, capture some of the raw emotions in the feud that had played out within Dutch Calvinist communities. The Calvinist writers, Schilder, Buskes, and Janse consistently and openly witnessed to the evils of the Nazi ideology of Hitler. Other Calvinist writers such as Vaart Smit, Boissevain, Ekering, Hylkema, and Roskam adopted a completely opposing point of view. They felt that Hitler was a kind of savior who had been chosen by God to rescue Christian Europe, including the Netherlands, from goddess communists. Still other Calvinists followed the lead of the statesman Colijn and took a middle-of-the-road approach to the Nazi movement. Ridderbos and Hegeman have explained how those clashes of perspective in the Calvinist sector of Dutch society played out before and during WWII.

Bank and Feldman use an international frame of reference to explore the contradictory ways that European churches responded to the threat of Nazi totalitarianism.

ALPHABETICAL LIST OF THE SOURCES REFERENCED IN THE ABOVE BIBLIOGRAPHIC ESSAY

Bank, J., & Lieve G., and Brian D. (2016). *Churches and Religion in the Second World War*. London: Bloomsbury Academic.

Burke, K. (1939). "The Rhetoric of Hitler's 'Battle.'" Originally published in *Southern Review* (Summer 1939). 1–21.

Bouman, A. & Booy, T. (1951). *Gereformeerden Waarheen? Inleiding tot een Gesprek over de Koers van het Gereformeerde Leven*. Kampen: Kok.

Buskes, J. J. (1960). *Hoera Voor het Leven*. Amsterdam: De Brug.

———. (1937) *Het Nationaalsocialisme als Bedreiging van de Kerk: De Les van Duitschland!* Assen: Van Gorcum.

Colijn, H. (1940). *Op de Grens van Twee Werelden*. Amsterdam: De Standaard.

Feldman, M., & Turda, M. (2007). "Clerical Fascism in Interwar Europe: An Introduction." in *Politics, Religion & Ideology*, 8(2). 205–12.

Fries Verzetmuseum Leeuwarden *www.friesverzetmuseum.nl*.

Gosler, J. (2020). *Searching for Home: The Impact of WWII on a Hidden Child*. Amsterdam: Amsterdam.

Hamerow, T. S. (2008). *Why We Watched: Europe, America, and the Holocaust*. New York: W.W. Norton.

Happe, K., & Reurs, F. (2018). *Veel Valse Hoop: De Jodenvervolging in Nederland 1940–1945*. Amsterdam: Atlas Contact.

Hegeman, J. H. (2024). *Call of Conscience: Protestant Clergy and Jews in the Netherlands, 1935–1945*.[to be published in the summer of 2024].

Hylkema, C.B. (1937). *Het Nederlandsch Fascisme: Wat het is, Wat het Leert, Hoe het Geworden is*. Utrecht: Nederlandsche Nationaal Socialistische Uitgeverij.

———. (1934). *Het Nederlandsch Fascisme*. Haarlem: Literbo.

Hylkema, G. W., & Hylkema, C. B. (1944). *Ras en Toekomst*. Amsterdam: De Amsterdamsche Keurkamer.

Janse, A. (1933). *Nationaal-socialistische Fascisten Politiek: Gezien in den Levensgang van Mussolini en in de Propaganda Zijner Geestverwanten in Nederland*. Aalten: De Graafschap.

———. (1934). *De Nieuwe Geest van de Nationaal-Socialistische Beweging*. Aalten: De Graafschap

Jong, M. de. (2019). *The Church is the Means; the World is the End: the Development of Klaas Schilder's Thought on the Relationship between the Church and the World*. Ede: GVO.

Lipstadt, E. (2019). *Antisemitism: Here and Now*. New York: Shockken.

———. (1993). *Denying the Holocaust: The Growing Assault on Truth and Memory*. New York: Free Press.

Nederlandsche Bond van Jongelingsvereenigingen op Gereformeerden Grondslag. (1932—1940). *Gereformeerd Jongelingsblad: Orgaan van den Nederlandschen Bond van Jongelingsvereenigingen op Gereformeerde Grondslag*. Rotterdam: A. ter Weeme.

Overeem, E., & Ridderbos, J. (1995). *Een Kerk in Beroering: Gereformeerden tusser 1933 en 1945*. Kampen: Kok.

Randwijk, H. M. van. (1970). *Waarmee Ik Maar Zeggen Wil*. Den Haag: Bert Bakker.

Ridderbos, J., & Hovingh, G.C. (2015). *Predikanten in de Frontlinie: de Gevolgen van Deelname aan het Kerkelijk Verzet in Nederland Tijdens WO II*. Barneveld: Vuurbaak.

———. (1995). *Strijd op twee Fronten: Schilder en de Gereformeerde "Elite" in de Jaren 1933–1945 Tussen Aanpassing, Collaboratie en Verzet op Kerkelijk en Politiek Terrein*. Kampen: Kok.

Roskam, E. J. (1937). *Het Calvinisme, de N.S.B. en de Gereformeerde Kerken*. Utrecht: Nederlandsche Nationaal Socialistische Uitgeverij.

Schilder, K., & Knoop, H. (1945). *Bezet Bezit: Artikelen van de Hand van Prof. Dr. K. Schilder, Opgenomen in de Nummers van "De Reformatie" uit de Eerste Maanden Na de Bezetting van Nederland—Juni-Augustus 1940*. Goes: Oosterbaan & Le Cointre.

———. (1936). *"Geen Duimbreed"!: Een Synodaal Besluit Inzake 't Lidmaatschap van N.S.B. en C.D.U.* Kampen: Kok.

Tijssen, H. (2019). *NSB Predikant Ekering en Zijn Keuze voor het Nationaalsocialisme*. Soesterberg: Aspekt.

———. (2008). *Tussen Avondrood en Zonsondergang: Dr. W. Th. Boissevain (1880–945), Discipel van Hoedemaker op Eigen Wijs*. Kampen: Tijssen.

Vaart Smit, H. W. van der. (1935). *De Duitsche Kerkstrijd*. Amsterdam: Holland.

Verzetmuseum (Amsterdam) https//www.verzetmuseum.org

Wiesel, E., & Abrahamson, I. (1985). *Against Silence: The Voice and Vision of Elie Wiesel*. New York: Holocaust Library.

Wijbenga, P. (1970—1978). *Bezettingstijd in Friesland*. Drachten: Lavermans.

Ypma, Y. N. (1953). *Friesland Annis Domini 1940-'45. Bijdrage tot de Geschiedenis van het Georganiseerde Verzet in Friesland*. Samensteld in opdracht de Vereniging Friesland 1940-1945. Met tekeningen Van Dick Osinga. Dokkum: J. Kamminga.

Zuidema, S. U. (1951). *Gereformeerden Waarom?* Delft: Keulen.

www.ingramcontent.com/pod-product-compliance
Lightning Source LLC
Chambersburg PA
CBHW070221030726
47505CB00006B/1758